GRAVEYARD SHIFT

THE ADVENTURES OF CARSON DUDLEY

Book Three
PARTS

Chris Weedin

A Supernatural Adventure Comedy Novel
Inspired by
Horror Rules, the Simply Horrible Roleplaying Game

A Crucifiction Games Book

Crucifiction Games
NO PAIN, NO GAME

BAD SCIENCE

"Don't know about you," Carson sounded more than slightly sickened, "but I'm glad I didn't eat before we came."

"Sorry," Kiki looked pale. "I just saw the shape and I thought... I thought it was..." she struggled, words failing her. "I don't know!"

"I don't know either," Dex nudged the mass with his boot, "but I'd say it just cost us the element of surprise," he shot Carson an accusatory glance. "Trigger Happy."

"Hm. Yeah. Little freaked out there," Carson glanced around worriedly. "Do you think anyone heard that?"

"It's a shotgun, Dud. Everyone heard it. And stop shouting."

"Sorry! Still trying to decide whether or not to puke."

"You got a bigger choice to make than that," Dex alone seemed cool and unaffected. "Somebody's on the way; you can be sure of that. It's time to call the play: throw down or evac. What's it gonna be?" He hefted his second gun dangerously and racked the slide. "You know my vote."

Carson stared at the torso on the floor, tense. "Yeah. Okay. That's one for throw down. Kiki, how about you?"

But she wasn't listening. From his elbow, she gave a startled gasp. Her attention had been snared by a pile of mussed and yellowed papers on a side table. The top sheet, annotated in red, contained what looked like anatomical drawings sketched in a sharp, clinical hand. She gazed at them, her face a mix of horror and fascination. "No... it can't be!"

Then everyone's ears caught a sound that none of them wanted to hear:

"*Meeeeoow...*"

OTHER BOOKS BY CHRIS WEEDIN:

Graveyard Shift: The Adventures of Carson Dudley
Book 1 - *Midnight Snack*
Book 2 – *Another Rotten Night*

Horror Rules, the Simply Horrible Roleplaying Game
Horror Rules Rulebook
Horror Worlds
Ghostowns & Gunsmoke
Script Crypt Vol 1: Psychos and Sickos
Script Crypt Vol 2: Four Damned Scripts
Script Crypt Vol 3: The Better to Eat You With
Script Crypt Vol 4: Very Bad Places

THE REVIEWS ARE IN FOR GRAVEYARD SHIFT!

"This book is AWESOME!!!!!!"
--M. Schnellman

"You can't stop reading it."
--Indiependent Books

"4.4 out of 5 Stars!"
-- Amazon.com, average customer review

"Chock full of vampire goodness, vengeful nuns and corn dogs..."
-- A. DiGleria

"... a fast paced, action packed, hilariously dark trip down a satire filled back alley!"
-- J. Looney

"If you're looking for a good afternoon read that's long on fun... look no further!"
P. O'Neal

"A rip roaring tale! Can't wait for the next book."
--C. Miller

"Horror comedy at its best! Think of what would happen if the Crypt Keeper decided to get a Slurpee while wearing beachwear..."
--E. Gutzwiler

"A tongue-n-cheek... occasionally irreverent... explosive read."
-- Dr. R. Herron, Academy of Historical Arts and Sciences

To Lindsey

We are all made up of many parts.   Though they may be separated from us, they are never lost.

Miss you, Little Sis.

Acknowledgments

SPECIAL THANKS TO: The Premier Kickstarter Backers!
You guys made Las Calamas come alive. Many thanks and God bless for giving your enthusiasm, support and pure awesomeness. As citizens of this troubled, mysterious yet stalwart city, I hope you take countless hours of enjoyment from reading its stories and adventures. And I hope you survive. Definitely that. But whatever happens, you've done your *Parts*!

Parts Party (You get a PARTY!!)
Daryl "Scruffy" Wilks

Head, Shoulders, Knees and Toes (You get to DIE!!)
Jamie Looney

Pair of Legs (You get to LIVE!!)
Adam DiGleria, Peggy Schaffer

Right Arm (You get a HIGH FIVE!!)
Tony Chin, T.J. Tranchell, MaryJane Magnenat

Three Fingers (You still got two left. That's something.)
Andrea and Danny Oxman, Rob Steinberger, Kevin Vasquez, Joey Dragon, Joseph Nicholas Dragon

SPECIAL THANKS TO: James Dart
Winner of the *REAL* 24/7 slogan contest (via Kickstarter) with his winning entry: *"Fast service for those on the run!" (*Ross Kinkade would like you to know that YOU are the kind of person Seven Corporation is looking for. Applications available online.)

SPECIAL THANKS TO: Author T.J. Tranchell
For his sweet Graveyard Shift short story *Grandma Loved the Beach.* Check him out online at tjtranchell.com!

SPECIAL THANKS TO: The One TRUE Creator
Who makes all parts work as a whole. Without Him, there would be no book. Or me. Or us. Or anything. Whoop!

CAST OF CHARACTERS

Carson Dudley

Kiki Masterson

Dexter "Dex" Jackson

Sister Becky Bischoff

Professor Jamie Looney

Peggy Schaffer

Doctor Julius Deth

Adam DiGleria

CHAPTER ONE

The Curio Shop

"Well... here we go again."

"In your dreams."

"Visions."

"That's a matter of opinion."

Carson shifted nervously, moving his weight side to side, rocking forward and back on the balls of his feet. "Oh yeah? Well, here's another opinion - that you're taking *forever* to pick that lock. I thought you were some kind of über mondo master thief or something? When we did the Super Maxi-Pad, you made it look like cake and that was like a mega Terminator lock with the blinky red eye and everything and this is just some broke down old Curio Shop..."

"Nervous?" Kiki's cool blue eyes stabbed back at him from where she crouched before the faded wooden door. Carson couldn't be sure, but under the shadow of her red stocking cap he thought he detected the ghost of a frown.

"Yes. Yes, I am. And apparently I'm babbling. Am I babbling?"

"Yes. And it's 'reformed' über mondo master thief, thank you very much." Kiki was still on pause, staring back at him, hands motionless in their intimate embrace with the lock.

Carson felt a trickle of sweat down his back. He shifted again, glanced nervously up and down the quiet street, and then back at Kiki. Her flat, cool expression was colored green and orange by the happily glowing 24/7 sign a few blocks away. It was a happiness he didn't share. Apparently neither did Kiki. She didn't look happy at all. She also didn't look like someone who was going to finish picking a lock.

Carson swallowed, momentarily stalled. In truth, it was more than just nerves. He had felt strangely off center the last few days, a feeling which had intensified when tonight's spontaneous invasion had been sprung on him earlier that day. He couldn't put his finger on it, but he wasn't nervous so much as he was... distracted? Disoriented? He chased the thought around his head. It went nowhere.

Carson cleared his throat. Whatever it was, he was determined to push through it. "Right. 'Reformed.'"

"Would you like me to continue now?"

Carson opened his mouth, then shut it, wisely swallowing his reply. He settled for a nod.

Kiki turned back to the lock.

Carson only made it a few seconds. "It's just that..."

"Do you want me to do this thing or not?!" This time there was no doubt about her frown.

"Sorry!" He squirmed. "I'm just feeling kinda naked out here, you know?! I mean, the cops, Kinkade, a pizza guy... *somebody* or *anybody* could come by at any minute and then we're..."

A huge black hand the approximate size of a catcher's mitt clamped over Carson's mouth.

"Let the Big Man handle this," Dex sighed over Carson's feeble attempts to extricate himself. "Apparently, the brother doesn't quite grasp B&E etiquette. Y'see, Dud, the way this works is the more you shut up, the more you don't get caught. Got it?" He flashed a sympathetic look at Kiki. "You just can't be subtle with this guy."

After a moment, and with effort, Carson stilled himself. With a final stern stare, Dex withdrew his hand.

"Sorry, guys!" Carson hissed. "Sorry! I'm just a little jumpy... we didn't exactly plan this out y'know... and no Sister Becky... plus, I'm getting *major* PTSD from my Vision, and now I've gotta pee! In light of which, incidentally, the last thing I need is *you* grabbing me from the shadows!"

"First off, sucka, you always go *before* a job. Second, you shoulda let me pack a piece. Then I wouldn't be so cranky. And third..." Dex

2

folded giant arms and stared hard at him, "...now that you had your baby panic, do you want to get serious or do you want to get out?"

Kiki had stopped again. She was staring at him too.

Carson looked away. He shifted his feet and his eyes, wary, searched the shadows for threats. The store, the street, the alley... nothing. Everything quiet. He swallowed hard and squared his shoulders. For the first time in minutes, his feet stopped shuffling. He met the gaze of his friends.

"No. I don't want out. Not on your life." He took a deep breath, let it out. "Sorry I freaked. I'm just a little jittery. If it happens again, you have permission to club me. Or taze me. But please don't do both; I have sensitive skin."

Dex grinned, his teeth a pearly picket fence. "Fair enough." He removed one hand from his nightstick. The other, however, remained on his Taser. "Just remember; you said I could."

Silence fell. The distant sounds of the city murmured in the background. Kiki turned back to the lock.

"Of course," Carson mumbled, "Maybe I wouldn't be so jumpy if you guys hadn't rushed me into this. It's like some kinda stupid high school dare. 'C'mon, Billy, let's go break into the scary old freakish Curio Shop that we suspect is involved in various shenanigans of evil, possibly including vampires and the walking dead...'"

"Oh, for..." Dex snorted, throwing his hands in the air. "You %^&*#@! pantywaste! If we hadn't 'rushed you into it', you'd still be playing patty-cake with the Wonder Bread and makin' goo-goo eyes at this place! You been all moping and scheming and this'n and that'n for the last three months! 'We can't go yet; I ain't healed up,' 'We can't go yet; I gotta kiss up to Kinky in manager training,' 'We can't go yet; I gotta pee!"

"Well, I *do* gotta pee! And I'll thank you not to bring it up, because I only have one kidney now, and I can't play favorites!"

A faint *click* snapped the air. "Got it." Kiki had long ago abandoned the debate and turned back to the lock. She slipped her tools into an inner pocket on her canvas jacket. "If you two are done being quiet and sneaky, we're in."

Dex settled for rolling his eyes and muttered something unintelligible, but Carson was sure he heard the word "gun" and several others that would have made Sister Becky reach for her ruler. Dreadlocks shook in the darkness and a sigh drifted out of them. "Alright... how you wanna play this?"

3

Carson hefted his bat, fought off a fresh wave of nerves and cursed himself silently. He wasn't sure what was wrong, but he *was* sure they were going in. Now. "Like we usually do," he grunted. "By the seat of our pants, ready for anything and prepared to see things we can never unsee. And, um... remember, this is recon. Just... recon. We're only here to look around." Carson put his hand on the door handle, glancing down the street in both directions. "I just wish..."

"She ain't comin', Bro. If the Old Goat had wanted to be in this rodeo, she'd a been here by now. We go in, or we go home."

Carson nodded once, tersely, as invisible in the darkness as Dex's threatening frown. Something was off, and he knew it. It had been all night. But he also knew the big man was right. With effort, he shoved aside his gnawing, stubborn uneasiness.

It was now or never.

"Alright," Carson sucked a lungful of cool, crisp, night air full of the familiar city smells of the Belfry District mingled with the musty, mysterious odor of the Curio Shop. "Ready?"

Dex grunted. "Steady."

Kiki drifted to one side, aloof but alert.

"Go!"

The door swung open with a screech like a barn owl made of rusty hinges and warped wood. It was loud. Carson's short hairs snapped to attention, and his stomach flipped, his uneasiness exploding into a flash of panic. Driven by a sudden need to be anywhere other than in plain sight in front of the store he was breaking into, he lurched stiffly through the door. The Curio Shop swallowed him.

Something banged his leg; then something else banged his shoulder. He stopped with a gasp, panic seizing him. Sharp. Corners. Shelves, his mind told him. Then, something banged his back. Meaty. Big. Dex's fist, his mind told him.

"Move, sucka!" The big man hissed. "You need a %^&*#@! tour guide?! My %^&*#@! is hanging out with a bullseye on it that says, 'Hey, copper, come throw me in your mutha trucka jail!'"

Carson edged out of the way, too shaken to retort, nerves raw and eyes darting wildly. Dex cursed again and shoved past him roughly. "It's hard enough to hide *this*," he indicated his massive frame, "without *you* in the way!" He swaggered past into the darkness, producing a small Mag light and beaming it guardedly about.

Carson stood rooted. He was having trouble focusing, his mind a wash of images and memories as his Vision tangled with his vision in a disorienting whirl. His heart, for some inexplicable reason, hammered like a prison chain gang on a pile of rocks. He wasn't sure what he had expected, but it definitely wasn't this – an overpowering sense of the familiar mixed with an overwhelming rush of the unfamiliar. It was like déjà without the vu. Carson slapped his cheek, shook his head to clear it. He realized his hands were white-knuckled on his bat, and he forced them to relax.

Something brushed his shoulder, and he jumped again.

"Whoa, slugger," Kiki breathed. "It's just me." She paused, squinting at him in the darkness. "You okay?"

"Just... need a... minute. It's... sometimes... uh... I'm... this is... whoa..."

She drew a fraction closer. There was genuine concern in her eyes. "Carson?"

An involuntary shudder ran through him, and he almost dropped his bat. "I'm... yeah. It's all... sure. The... yeah."

"Enough yappin'!" Dex's voice rumbled through the store in what passed for his whisper. "If we're gonna recon, let's recon!" A thin beam of light danced low across the shelves. "Hmph," he grunted. "They got some cheap crap in here." He wandered idly, staring at the cluttered shelves with their collection of shrunken heads, weird statuettes, voodoo dolls, incense burners and other bric-a-brac.

Carson gave Kiki a gentle push forward. "I'm good," he whispered, trying to force himself to believe it. "Go." The room felt like it was spinning.

As usual, Kiki flinched slightly at his touch but held her ground. As she searched his eyes, her own narrowed. "You sure?"

"Of course!" Carson hissed. "Yeah! Yes... just go, would ya?" He pushed her again, and this time she gave way. Carson stumbled a few steps after her, realized he hadn't blinked in over a minute and did so furiously, squeezing his eyes repeatedly like a child trying to blink away a nightmare. His heart, however, stubbornly refused to slow down. He ignored it.

Kiki drifted away into the store, keeping one worried eye on Carson and the other on the room.

Dex, meanwhile, had apparently decided there was nothing either of urgency or alarm in the tiny shop. He had picked up a ghastly multi-armed statuette with the head of a hippopotamus and the body of a naked old man. "Think I'll bring this one back for the Old Goat," he mused. "Christmas is comin', and I been looking for the perfect gift..."

"Put that down!" Carson hissed, panic suddenly spiking through him. "Put it... there's a... I'm thinking it's... thing!"

Dex's frown was purposeful. "What's up with goofy?" He fired the question sideways at Kiki, like a parent discussing a child he didn't trust to give a coherent answer. "Makes about as much sense as Keith Richards."

Kiki shook her head, perplexed. "Nerves? I don't know, I've never seen him like..."

Carson lurched to Dex's side, snatched the statue and slammed it down. "No touching! Can't you... your mother...!" His voice trailed off as the thought unraveled, choked by another sudden surge of uneasiness and paranoia.

Then, suddenly, he felt it.

Eyes.

Someone was watching. No, not some*one*. Some*thing*. He whirled, his bat knocking the statue flying and clipping Dex's elbow just at the tip of the funny bone, drawing a profound curse.

"Watch it, fool!" The flashlight jerked angrily, then settled, by chance, on a portrait hanging on the wall nearby.

Carson froze.

Not *a* portrait, he realized as his heart finally stopped hammering – and instead stopped cold. *The* portrait.

The one from his Vision.

Sights, sounds, colors, emotions. Flooding around him, flowing, smothering. For a moment, Carson felt as if he were falling down, drawn inexorably floorward by a force stronger than gravity, pitching headfirst into a bottomless pit of oil paint and gold filigree frame.

He thrust out a hand to steady himself and scattered a cluster of kitsch, throwing up a cloud of dust and a tremendous clatter. The noise was alarming, but he was oblivious. His eyes locked on the brooding canvas before him. It bore the image of a robed and hooded figure surrounded by dark trees, knife raised to sacrifice a young woman in white who lay helpless on an altar. Carson's eyes locked on those under the hood - dark eyes, soulless and bleak and hungry. Although it was the first time he had *seen* it, not just in a dream, he knew every inch of it. The portrait had been lurking just at the edge of his consciousness for months now, one of the most primal and living images from his Vision, but one he had never really confronted. Until now. Now, it was right in his face. He gasped a breath, realizing he hadn't for some moments.

A hand fell on his shoulder. "Bro... you okay?" This time the gruffness was gone from Dex's voice, replaced by genuine concern. "You don't look so good..."

"Out!" Carson croaked. "This is... we gotta... out!" He caught at Dex's hand and yanked, taking a staggering step toward the door and trying to drag his friend along. He didn't know why, but he suddenly knew the source of his nagging disorientation and fear. It was the portrait. And it was bad.

"Fine... voodoo ain't my jam anyway." Dex lumbered after him, flicking a glance at Kiki. "We're out, Mama. Shake a leg." Kiki didn't need any urging. She hustled after them without a backward glance.

It was a short trip to the front door, but to Carson it felt like a marathon. He burst out into the night, sucking deep lungfuls of cool air, spun wildly for a moment, then turned quickly away from a pair of approaching headlights and ducked into the alley.

As soon as Carson was clear of the store, his head-spinning started to slow and his pulse eased. The dread grip of panic that had seized him faded, leaving only echoes. He hurried a few more steps into the welcoming darkness and obscurity of the alley, still breathing deeply in spite of the sudden stink. Even that, however, seemed to help. It was familiar. Normal. Earthly. He sucked it in gratefully through his nose.

A dozen feet into the alley, he slowed his pace, shuddered and ran a hand through his unruly brown hair. "Sorry... yeah... whoo!" Carson shook his head, turning to face his worried companions. "I uh... guess I sorta freaked."

"*Sorta* freaked? That's what happens on social media when you accidentally hit 'post'. You - you went straight up gaga." Kiki moved in, concerned. "Has that ever happened before?"

"I... I dunno," Carson wiped sweaty palms on his jeans, still struggling to control his breathing. "Maybe once, that time my brother dared me to grab the electric fence. But whatever it was, it's over now. Whew! Man. That was unexpected." Carson dropped into a squat, letting his head droop.

"In more ways than one. Which makes me wonder..."

"Wonder away. I'll do what I can to help figure this out, but I gotta say, my brain still feels like the monkey house when they roll out a new tire swing. What are you thinking?"

Silence.

"Don't keep me hanging, Sister. I've had enough drama for one night." Carson rubbed his face wearily.

A muffled scream tore loose from down the ally and metal *banged!* Carson shot to his feet. The space where Kiki had stood was empty. She was gone.

A gasp tore from him.

Dex snapped his head around. He'd been looking the other way, keeping a wary eye on the street. He swore mightily and lunged for the alley's bowels like a freight train in a blue polyester security shirt, slamming into Carson who stood like a dead stump, frozen in shock.

"*Move*, fool! They got our girl!"

Carson staggered, lurched and crashed down into a mess of pallets, then was up and running instantly, right on Dex's heels as the big man thundered headlong down the alley, roaring like an enraged bear. The beam of his mini-light swung crazily, skipping over graffiti scrawls and smokey red brick and, every blessed few seconds, the struggling, kicking form of Kiki as she was swept away down the alley.

What carried her, Carson couldn't tell. He cursed himself and forced his stiff legs to pump harder. Weeks of physical therapy had returned much of the youthful spring to his muscles, but for some reason, tonight they seemed stiff and awkward like he was trying to run in a nightmare. Struggling to find his stride, he kept his head down and his eyes focused on Dex's back.

It was only thanks to this that he saw what happened next. With the unexpectedness of a chicken through a stained glass window, something fleshy and misshapen flew out of the dark and smacked Dex right in the small of his back. It stuck tight, gave an angry hiss and scuttled up toward his head with alarming agility.

Carson gasped and put on a burst of speed, shifting his stiff legs into high gear and throwing caution to the wind. He closed the gap in seconds, just as the thing was reaching for Dex's dreadlocks. With a ragged shout and no thought, Carson swung.

"Booyah!!!"

His swing went high and clipped the guard neatly in the back of the head with a woody *tonk!* Dex grunted and veered sideways, taking out a stack of tomato crates and sending an explosion of wood and vegetable parts through the alley. When he came out of it, the thing on his back was gone.

Cursing furiously, Dex threw a stormy glance over his shoulder. "What are you trying ta...?!"

And then the creatures were everywhere.

Hissing, spitting blobs flung at them from the darkness in all directions, tearing clothing with needle claws and tangling their legs. Carson shouted and swung blindly, covering his head with one arm and pelting madly forward, praying he would somehow avoid meeting brick. He was sure he hit Dex at least once more, but his friend was too preoccupied to care. Several of the things had stuck to him, and he was yanking and tearing at them, bellowing in rage and blind anger. Seconds later, still at a full run, Dex smashed headlong into a boarded up door. Helpless before him, the barrier vaporized and Dex disappeared into the blackness of whatever lay beyond.

Carson swept past. He jerked around a corner, felt something trip at his feet, kicked it free and was rewarded with a vicious growl as *something* flew off into the darkness. Then, he was clear and racing on, though it was a few moments before he realized it and stopped slashing with his bat. He thought fleetingly about Dex, but worry for Kiki crowded it out. Dex could take care of himself. Kiki needed him.

Seconds later, Carson pounded around another corner and in the nick of time caught a glimpse of a crumpled figure directly in his path. With a yelp and a desperate leap, he vaulted the body and flew straight into a wall, rebounding smartly and jamming his foot through an old plastic bucket that took him down. He came up fast, bat ready, head fuzzy. As his senses returned, Carson realized the bucket was still stuck to his foot, and he kicked hard, sending it flying across the alley where it crashed through a window. Amid the tinkle of glass, his ringing ears caught an odd, thudding-shuffling sound, pounding off into the darkness down the alley – footsteps of some kind, he realized gradually.

Then, he turned his attention to the crumpled form that lay on the alley floor and all else was suddenly forgotten. From the shadows, his eyes picked out a faint splotch of red stocking cap.

"Kiki!" Carson leapt to the girl's side, frantic, scanning for injuries. "You okay, girl?!" He took her arm, gently but insistently, willing her to be alright. "You hurt?! Talk to me! Holy cow!!"

Kiki stirred. "Yeah... umm... I think..." her voice was unsteady, eyes glazed and hat askew. Even shaken and scared, she flinched instinctively at his touch. "I'm... I'm okay..." she pushed awkwardly at Carson's hands, and he released her, too grateful and relieved to be hurt.

He stepped back and let her scramble to her feet, scanning shadows cautiously. "What in the name of the chupacabra *was* that?!"

"Don't know," Kiki tugged her cap back into place mechanically and struggled to straighten her jacket which had been jerked almost over her head by the force of her assailant. "Whatever... grabbed me...

must've had second thoughts." She flashed something at him in the darkness. Carson caught a glint of light from a business-like little folding lock blade knife, it's blade smeared with red.

"Maybe he didn't have insurance," Carson showed a grim smile. Then it faded. "Wait a beep... did you say '*what*ever'?"

Kiki stared at him, blinked. "Whoever. I meant *who*ever."

"Yeah, but you said..."

The thudding of very large boots announced the arrival of Officer Dexter Jackson. He took in the scene at a glance and stood wheezing, struggling to draw breath. Blood showed prominently in several large scratches on his face and arms.

"Damn, girl... if you gonna... make Dex run... you can at least... make it worth his... while... and make sure there's... some head busting at the end of it..."

"At least that door will never bother anyone again." Carson brushed at a few bits of wood that clung to the guard's torn uniform.

"Weak %^&*#@! door like that deserved to be... busted down," Dex shook splinters out of his hair. "Fixed... my critter problem, though. Turns out... it was the back door for that... Chinese restaurant. By the time I... plowed through the... prep table and bounced off the walk-in freezer... whatever was on me shook free. You see any more?"

"No. Not right now at least. But I'm bound to the next time I try to sleep. Ay caramba, what do you...?"

Kiki screamed.

From low among the shadows, a hand had seized her leg. Carson, on pure instinct and adrenaline, jerked a swing with his bat, low and fast. With a meaty, bone-jarring *smack!* it hit.

To everyone's complete and utter amazement, the hand came loose.

As they watched, it sailed silently across the alley, struck the far wall, bounced limply and dropped behind a pile of soggy cardboard. For a moment, no one moved.

Then, a sharp hiss tore from the shadows where the hand had first appeared, and everyone moved. Dex swung his light towards the sound. White light slashed, looking for a target... and found it. A pair of animal eyes, eerie and luminescent, flashed back, caught in the beam like a tiger in a trap. Beneath those eyes, a hissing, spitting mouth full of needle teeth menaced them, while bunched behind the teeth was a wiry, whip-like body, hairless and fleshy and pale and smeared with red on one side. Several bits of stitching showed, poking out like loose threads on an old coat.

They stared.

"I... I really don't... um..." Carson, of all of them, was the only one to find his voice. "Is that a... a cat?"

The thing hissed and spit again, savagely, clawing the air and fixing them with a baleful gaze. It gathered its hind quarters and bunched its legs, preparing to spring.

Then... *boom!*

A thundering report burst the air, and the creature was hurled back into the shadows. Dex paused, staring down the sights of a compact 9mm automatic at the spot the thing had vacated, his brain still trying to catch up with the reflexes that had caused him to draw and shoot. Just for good measure, he fired twice more.

The echoes hadn't even started to fade when Carson jabbed an accusing finger at him. "I *knew* you'd bring a gun!! I *knew* it!"

"Yeah... but ain't you glad I did?"

CHAPTER TWO

Missing Pieces

"What I wanna know is... who the frack sews a *hand* onto a *cat*? Really. That's it. That's all I wanna know." Carson took a gulp of Mtn Dew, gazing out over the chatting crowd in the restaurant but not seeing them.

Kiki absently swirled the ice in her glass, eyes staring blankly off into space. She still looked wild and unsettled. In her memory, the cat-thing's hot, green, reflective discs stared back, burning into her brain. She stared too long, and a shudder ran through her. Quickly she blinked the image away, rubbing her eyes for good measure. "I'm not donating to the Humane Society anytime soon. That's for sure."

"You alright?" Carson gave her the same worried look he'd given her a hundred times in the last twenty-four hours. "I'm guessing last night wasn't in the top three of your 'Things I Wanna Do In An Alley'."

"Not even on the list."

"You sure you're not..."

"I'm alright," Kiki chopped him off a little abruptly. "We've been over this, alright? Just the cut, and that's all patched up. Otherwise, it didn't hurt me."

Carson nodded. "Uh-huh. That's good. So what bothers me is that you're still saying 'it'."

"I am? Oh. I mean... *he*. He didn't hurt me."

"That's not comforting me. Especially since you didn't get a look at it. Er... *him*. Crabapples... now you've got me doing it."

"We've been over that too," Kiki sighed, shrinking into her seat. "I'm sorry I didn't have time to check his driver's license, but I was a little preoccupied surviving. He was big and strong and grunted a lot; that's all I remember. It was like a speed date where you have to use a pocket knife to make it stop." She hesitated, fidgeting with the tablecloth. "Of course, when it... *he*... dropped me... I did look back for a second. Got a glimpse of..." Another hesitation. "I don't know. Part of a... a face..." Kiki broke off, rubbing her eyes again. "It was dark," she mumbled. "Really dark."

Sitting across from her in the booth, Sister Becky leaned in and patted her hands. Kiki tolerated the contact for a second before withdrawing them and stuffing them protectively in her jacket pockets.

"There, there, Ms. Masterson. This vile business is all behind you now. Best to leave it so. That is why they put the door on the outhouse, as the saying goes."

"That's a beautiful image, very comforting," Dex groaned, shifting slightly so that the chair on which he sat did the same. "And spoken like someone who didn't see that creepy little rat-ball. I don't get the heebies easy, Old Goat, and I ain't necessarily hatin' on cats, but I'll tell you one thing you can take to the bank: I'm gonna kick the next couple I see. Hard."

They put the conversation on hold as a waiter in a Santa hat freshened their drinks. Around them the noise and efficient hustle of restaurant life ebbed and flowed. The multicolored glow of Christmas lights danced off silverware and glasses and a nostalgic swing tune of holidays past pepped along over muted speakers. Carson swept the familiar surrounds of the Taj Palace, soaking in the sights and smells and sounds of what, for everyone else, was probably a festive holiday outing. It was hard to imagine that, less than a day ago, he and his friends had been witness to things so blatantly different. Horrifying things. Bizarre and gruesome things. But then, he was starting to get used to bizarre and gruesome.

Kiki shivered again, evidently still struggling with the outhouse door. "I don't want to kick anything. I just want it out of my head. Vampires, zombies... I get those. But these things – I don't even know what to call them!"

13

"I've been thinking about that," Carson tugged his chin beard thoughtfully.

"You would," Dex grunted.

"What do you think of 'handi-cats'?"

Dex grimaced. "Sounds like an 80's cartoon about special needs critters. Why name 'em at all?!"

"Well, it's like the good nun always says: LIPSTIC."

"LIPISC, Mr. Dudley."

"Yeah. LIPISC. Locate, Identify... yadda yadda. I'd say we're definitely on 'Identify', and since no one's ever seen anything like this before, we get to name them." He shot Sister Becky a questioning look. "At least I'm assuming no one's ever seen anything like this before."

"I have seen many creatures of the Darker Realms with severed human hands, Mr. Dudley. In every case, however, they were held in jowl or claw. I have yet to see one affixed to a living creature. Fully functional nonetheless. Of course," she sniffed and smoothed her smock. "Not having laid eyes on the creatures myself, I cannot say with absolute surety."

There was a sharp point on her comment and Carson felt it. "Oh. Yeah. Um... because we ditched you. Sorry. Bad call. I, uh... guess I gotta take the hit on that one." He shuffled his feet and picked at a jalapeño popper.

"Indeed you should, young man," Sister Becky was quick to follow up. "Otherwise a great deal of trouble might have been avoided. You would do well to mind your patience in future situations. It was foolish to go without me. If you wish to forge us into a team, as you stated after our last adventure, then you must treat us as such. We must be at our full strength when we sojourn against evil. Disaster awaits the unwary."

"I know, I know. I guess I just got a little antsy, that's all. But you know..." Carson felt a sudden pang of self-righteous peeve. "You could have showed up on time, too. I mean, *an hour* late?! It's not like we were waiting on you for a movie."

Sister Becky's eyes narrowed dangerously. She studied him. Carson stared back, not hostile but not flinching either.

Eventually, the nun gave a grudging nod. "I acknowledge your point, Mr. Dudley. It is well made. Tardiness is a shortcoming that I am loathe to confess, but in this case, I must cleave to it. I shall forgive your impatience if you shall forgive my impertinence."

Carson eased back in his seat, letting the sudden flush in his cheeks fade. He wasn't sure why, but he liked the fact that Sister Becky had backed down. Since his queer panic attack from last nigh,t he had been feeling the need to exert himself, to recover his sense of confidence. "Forgiven. No hard feelings."

"In the future then – you shall await my arrival before embarking on any incursions? We are agreed?"

"You bet. I swear by Scotty's missing finger."

Dex glanced over. "Scotty's what?"

"Missing finger. You know... James Doohan, the dude who played Scotty on TV Star Trek. TOS. He was missing a finger."

"No way – how come they never showed it?!"

"Oh, they did. Hid it pretty good for some reason, but if you watch close, you can see it. Or, *not* see it, I guess. He had it shot off in WWII or something."

Dex shook his head slowly. "Brother... you think you know someone."

"Well then," Sister Becky perked up. "As much as I would enjoy discussing the parts of handsome Scotsmen..."

Dex barked a laugh. "You did *not* just say that."

The nun eyed him quizzically. "Why I should not have I cannot fathom, but if it gave you mirth, then it is best left behind. At any rate," she flashed them a coy look. "Would you like to know the cause of my tardiness?"

Carson leaned in. There was something sparkling behind Sister Becky's green eyes. "As a matter of fact, lady... I think I would. What gives?"

Sister Becky's eyes sharpened and her hands clenched reflexively on her napkin. She had slipped into her game face. Carson felt a tiny thrill of excitement.

Several seconds passed. The nun said nothing, just stared intently.

"I knew it!" Dex thumped the table, making water glasses dance. "I knew when that zombie ninja kicked your old gray head a couple months back it did some brain damage! Somebody owes me five dollars!"

Sister Becky shot Dex the withering gaze she reserved especially for him. A passing waiter was momentarily caught by it and flinched involuntarily.

"It would take much more to addle these faculties; thank you kindly, Mr. Jackson. I was merely taking a moment to form the appropriate reply."

Dex grinned and stuffed four mozzarella sticks in his mouth. "I bet that reply is gonna be 'Durrrr... I done got kicked in the head by a ninja and went brain crazy.'" He crossed his eyes and let some of the mashed appetizer spill from his mouth.

Sister Becky's hands tightened even more, threatening to choke the life from her hapless napkin. "I am prompted at this point, Mr. Jackson, to quote Proverbs 18:6 - 'The lips of fools bring them strife, and their mouths invite a beating.'"

"'Invite a beating?!' Was that a threat, Attila?"

"That was wisdom, Mr. Jackson. From God. I strongly advise you heed it."

Dex snorted. "You telling me *God* said that? Nuts. You made it up."

"I assure you, Mr. Jackson, I am not in the habit of putting words in the mouth of the Almighty. However, as long as we are on the subject, allow me to quote also Proverbs 15:2 - 'The mouth of the fool gushes folly.' And to clarify any further misunderstandings, the 'fool' is you and the 'folly' is half-chewed mozzarella sticks. Be informed - you have soiled your uniform."

Dex glanced down at his shirt front, now decorated with a large glop of brown. "Aw, geez..." he reached for a napkin. "Probably made that one up too," he grumbled to himself. "I gotta get me a Bible..."

Sister Becky turned her gaze firmly to the others. "Now then, if I am at last free from interruption and harassment, permit me to answer your question, Mr. Dudley. The reason for my tardiness." She paused, her voice suddenly heady with emotion. "It was the Council. They have agreed to hear my petition."

"Whoa!" Carson thumped the table. "Ye cats and little fishes! They finally did it! *You* finally did it!!"

Sister Becky leaned back. A smug smile dimpled lean cheeks. "Yes. Quite, Mr. Dudley. Although, with the Good Lord's assistance to be sure. I would wager that it was easier for Him to part the Red Sea than pry open the dry brainpans of those wiry old dodgers. However, the deed is done. The Council will hear my petition. Things are far from settled, mind you. This is no final solution, merely one more wrinkle out of the sheet. They have merely agreed to grant me an audience."

"So," Kiki spread her hands on the table. "Just to be clear – you're asking for your old job back, right? This Council at St. Timothy's, the guys who run the whole show, you asked them to bring back the spiritual warfare branch and put you in charge? Straight up? No mincing words?"

"Straight up, Ms. Masterson, to coin your phrase. And the only things minced were personal agendas and contrary arguments."

"Sweet!" Carson gave her a knuckle bump which she returned with gusto. "That's my nun! Man, if this goes through... all the resources of the Church behind us?! Holy scripture! What do you think?! Are we gonna have an official Super God Smackin' Wonder Nun on our team soon, or what?!"

Sister Becky leaned back and smoothed her habit, swapping her smug look for one of patience and deliberation. "That, my exuberant young friend, remains to be seen. An audience is a far cry from re-establishment of The Order." There was a deep, passionate stirring in her green eyes. "But what a marvel it would be..."

"Give it time, Sister. I've got a good feeling about this. In the meantime, let's celebrate," Carson lifted his glass grandiosely. "To our booty kickin' nun and the unexpectedly positive influence of a zombie onslaught. It did some good."

He joined the others in a toast, but just before Kiki sipped from her water glass, he caught her softly muttered words: "Not for everyone."

As he swallowed, Carson felt a pang of guilt. He knew Kiki hadn't meant anything by her comment, but he was also keenly aware of how much time and energy she had spent nursing him back to health, and what a sacrifice it had been for her. It was a point well taken.

He watched her over the rim of his glass, letting the past few months roll through his thoughts. During his recovery, she had hardly left his side. They hadn't talked much, Carson mostly sleeping, but she had been there. Every day. Every minute. Then he'd returned home to Granny's basement, and school had started and work, and she had drifted back into her life and out of his. Odd. He scratched idly at his chin beard. He hadn't realized until now that something had been missing.

"What?" Kiki was eying him suspiciously.

"Hm? What 'what'?"

"You're staring."

"I am? Oh. I am. Yeah. Just thinking about... school, I guess. Your school. And you being there. Now that you're back to the brain stuffing, I hardly see you. But hey, it must feel good to be back on track."

Kiki grimaced. "I'm not exactly what you'd call 'back on track'.

I've had to settle for whatever classes I can scrounge."

"Yeah," Dex jumped in with sudden interest. "In fact, weren't you saying something about a criminal justice thingy?"

"Sort of. It's Forensics. Criminal Justice but also science, so it still works for my degree. Besides," she added grudgingly. "Given the course our lives have taken lately, I figured... it might come in handy."

"Hot tamales!" Carson thumped the table. "I know last night wasn't exactly a trip to Disneyland, but it's good to have you on board!"

"Don't read too much into it. I'm not changing my major to Monster Whacking."

Carson shrugged. "It's still a good sign. And yet another reason to celebrate which, need I remind anyone, is precisely why we're here. We're supposed to be whooping it up over my promotion and the official formation of the Monster Whackers. So enjoy the moment and some free food... on me." At the mention of "free", Carson noticed storm clouds gather over Kiki's brow. He hurried on. "So, speaking of reasons to celebrate, Dex - how are things looking on your police gig? We're already looking at a possible Super Nun, a Super CSI and a Super Night Manager... what are our chances of adding a Super Cop?"

Dex shrugged. "My Army record will help... 'cept for the discharge part... and word is there's a new round of hiring coming up after the holidays." Dex shoveled another fistful of mozzarella sticks into his mouth. "First, I gotta drop a few pounds and get back to my fightin' weight. The PT test - it's a hump." He fished in the basket again but found it empty then glanced around for a waiter. "You mind, Dud?" He shook the container meaningfully.

"Knock yourself out." Carson watched as his friend ordered another entire sampler platter but opted to withhold comment. When Dex packed it away like this, there was always stress behind it. There was no sense adding to it.

"Even with all that, it's a long shot," the guard rumbled on. "But probably my only one. Security jobs are still in the can. Can't figure that, what with all the monsters and bodies we personally been experiencing the past couple months. Maybe if more people hired security guards, there'd be fewer of 'em dyin'. Any word on getting me back on at the 24/7?"

Carson noticed his friend worrying the tiny butterfly necklace that had once belonged to his daughter. Another sure sign of stress. "Fret not, my large chum," he gave Dex a thumb's up. "I got your back. Brought the matter up with Kinkade just the other day. Surprisingly, he didn't laugh. I took it as a good sign."

"Yeah," Dex snorted. "Especially after what we did to the store."

"To be fair, it wasn't *all* us. The zombies helped."

"You tell Kinky that?"

"For some reason, I don't think it would help our case. But I've been hinting plenty about the merits of Gold Shield Security. That, along with reports of gunfire in the alley across the street last night - not that I'm endorsing you making them – should really help."

Dex snorted again. "The alley... oh brother. I'm thanking my lucky stars he only heard about it. If Kinky had seen how bad we botched that op, he wouldn't touch me with a ten foot paycheck."

"I'll admit, it blew chunks. It was like watching the *Green Lantern* movie in slow motion."

"You're beein' generous. We got spanked. I've seen dogs doing business that looked more elegant than us."

"On the plus side, you got to shoot a cat."

"Yeah... there was that."

"Look, I know a lot of it was my fault. I'm sorry I flipped out in there, I can own that. But there's more at work here than just nerves and bad planning. Whatever grabbed Kiki..."

"*Who*ever," Kiki murmured.

"Er, right, *who*ever... plus those freakshow handi-cats... it can't be coincidence. All that weirdliness right at the *exact* moment we took our first run at the Curio Shop?"

"I have been pondering the matter as well, Mr. Dudley," Sister Becky stroked her chin sagely. "I do not, as a matter of course, accept the notion of 'coincidence'." She leaned in, beckoning the others into a conspiratorial huddle. "I have long suspected that the Curio Shop was more than it seemed. I shared as much with you at the close of our most recent adventure with the Functional Corpses. It is time to air some of my deeper speculations and see what comes of it. 'Hang the knickers on the line; are they yours or are they mine', if you take my meaning."

"Oh, I take it alright – but now I can't get rid of it," Dex blinked furiously and put hands on his temples. "Never use 'mine' and 'knickers' in the same sentence again, Granny. Ever."

Sister Becky spared the distraction of a retort, eager to continue. "Mr. Dudley..." she fixed Carson with her gaze, sharp and calculating. "When it comes to our little shop, you have reported feeling strange sensations on numerous occasions: odd emotions, dread, compulsions. Is this not true?"

"Dang skippy. It's like starting puberty again every time I go near it."

"And last night, during your attempt to investigate - even though I succinctly and specifically warned you on multiple occasions that it was unwise to do so without having me present - you experienced even more powerful emotions and sensations. Correct?"

"This is what forgiving me sounds like?"

"Answer the question, dear."

"Correct."

"Have you any theories about what caused it?"

"None," Carson sighed. He had thought about it a great deal and was no closer to understanding his behavior. "It just *happened*. I couldn't think, couldn't focus, couldn't breathe. It was just... being in that place. It was overwhelming. Like getting punched in the face with weird." Carson could feel his face growing red. The more he talked about it, the angrier it made him. "Any ideas?"

Sister Becky tilted back, touching her cheek thoughtfully. "Perhaps. However, I will keep them to myself at this point since I see no sense in idle conjecture. Suffice it to say that I sense something sinister at the heart of the Curio Shop. Something malicious, to be sure, but also something... intentional."

"Whatever," Dex grumbled. "Right now, it ain't that little *&@^ %! shop I'm worried about. The way I see it, we got one thing for sure – an enemy. Whatever went Frankenstein on them handi-cats."

"You said 'handi-cats'." Carson winked. "See? It's catchy."

Dex swore softly at himself. "Sonofa..."

"And you said *what*ever," Kiki corrected nervously. "It's *who*ever."

Dex rolled his eyes. "Y'all let me know when you're done slapping the Big Man, and we can get on with this."

"Actually, I think you have a point. You both do." Carson squared his shoulders. It was time to put last night behind him. He had just been weak, that was all. He would see that it didn't happen again. Ever. "We've got a couple of conundrums, whether they're connected or not. First, the Curio Shop. I think I've got an angle on that one - the painting. The portrait of the cultist dude I saw in my Vision and then again in the Curio Shop. That's big. It's gotta be. I think... I feel like... the guy in the painting is somehow at the heart of all this." A chill washed over Carson as he remembered the cold, dead eyes in the painting. "There was no way he was just a dude in a picture. He's a person. Or was. That's what my gut says. If we can find out who he was, dig up his story, we'll be one step closer to figuring out what the hoo-ha-hey is going on here."

"And as for Dr. Frankenstein's cat," Kiki added reluctantly. "I may have an idea there. Provided we can get a sample."

"Shouldn't be a problem. I happen to know an alley with 'sample' splattered all over it. So, you gonna share your plan?"

"Soon."

"What's wrong - cat got your tongue?"

"Just for that..." she glared at him darkly. "You can gather your own darn sample."

CHAPTER THREE

Cat People

The door chime gave its broken, warped song, bouncing off the tidy rows of sundries, sweets and snacks. For the few late afternoon mini mart shoppers, it was a minor distraction, a subtle reminder that not everything in life worked like it should.

For Carson, it meant one thing: home.

He paused in the doorway, letting the final, off-tune, off-tempo notes settle into his soul. It had been broken as long as anyone could remember and defied every attempt to fix it. Carson had never tried. He'd loved it even when he was just a customer before Jack had hired him. For Carson, it had always been part of the 24/7 and always would be. He sighed happily and strolled inside, a bounce in his step.

It had not always been this pleasant to walk into the 24/7. Not by a long shot. For months after his friend and mentor Jack had sold the place, it had been downright kick-in-the-crotch unpleasant, mostly because of the change from laid-back-friendly-backwater-neighborhood atmosphere to corporate rules and guidelines. But some things – the simple things – never changed. Carson breathed deeply, sucking in a nose full of savory aromas: fried meat, fried cheese, fried veggies and whatever the fried filling was inside the Nitro-Dipped Baja Belly

Screamers that the Li'l Pepe Corporation had recently assaulted 24/7 customers with. As the last one burned its way through his nostrils, Carson could feel sweat start on his forehead and became slightly dizzy. He was still getting used to that one.

In fact, he pondered as he continued toward the counter, he had been getting used to a lot of things lately. New procedures. New responsibilities. New pressures. Carson's eyes picked out the stiff, brown shaft that was Ross Kinkade. New boss.

Kinkade stood behind the cash register with a fresh trainee, expounding the many remarkable labor saving functions and mind numbing buttons of the Omni-Biz 7520 Transaction Processing System. Most of the staff just called it "the Punisher". The trainee was discovering why. Nervous teenage eyes darted left and right as if looking for an escape route and there was sweat on his brow. Carson waved a greeting and Kinkade responded as he always did – with a flat expression and a short nod. Then, the droning lecture continued.

Carson grinned as he stowed his jacket in the employee locker. He felt bad for the kid, but everyone had to pay their dues. It wasn't so long ago that it had been him in the hot seat. Learning his way around the Punisher had almost killed him. Josh was the only one who'd really seemed to click with it. A sudden melancholy muted Carson's smile. But that was a lifetime ago. Back when Josh was alive.

Or at least *not* undead.

Carson's brow wrinkled. He struggled with the thought a moment, then let it go. The whole thing with Fujikacorp and the Warlord of Death still felt unreal. As he turned from the locker, his eyes chanced across the plaque hanging in the back of the store: *Josh Decker Memorial Restroom*.

There were plenty of reminders that it hadn't been.

"Miss ya, buddy," Carson muttered. He stood for a moment, suddenly moody. It had been almost this precise spot, he realized, where Josh had died. Saving Carson's life. And then later, that night in the Super Maxi-Pad, on the scaffold... he shuddered.

Then Josh's friendly, small town drawl floated through his thoughts: *"If you can't fix it, don't fret it. That's how we do things back home."*

The memory brought a smile and his melancholy faded. That was Josh. A part of him would always be a part of the 24/7.

Carson clocked in and idled by the front counter, waiting for Kinkade to complete his training. He lounged against the nacho cheese tub, his favorite spot, soaking up the comforting hum and warmth and the burbling *splurps* from whatever was happening inside. He had never looked in. Some things should remain a mystery.

The Punisher, he concluded, was one of them.

"That concludes Chapter One," Kinkade finished. "I believe you'll find the next forty-seven chapters equally fascinating. We'll continue tomorrow with the knowledge transfer. I recommend you read ahead and be prepared. *That's* the kind of person Seven Corporation is looking for." His expression was as flat and featureless as the African steppe. The trainee's was anything but.

Carson watched the shifting patterns of horror with a mixture of amusement and pity. He wondered if there would be a tomorrow. Staggering under the weight of the Omni-Biz manual, the trainee made his way out the front door and into the cool air of a Las Calamas Winter, his first steps toward a night of endless tedium and excruciating soul searching.

Kinkade turned to face Carson, eyes magnified by his old-fashioned Coke-bottle glasses. "Carson." The greeting was as bland and corporate as his suit and tie.

"Evening, Mr. Kinkade." Carson noted that his boss was already tapping and swiping on his tablet. It still looked new. He allowed himself a tiny, secret flush of self-satisfaction. "Looks like MOLD is in full swing. What are we looking at, negative achievements or productivity milestones?" The corporate buzzwords still felt strange coming out of Carson's mouth, but he had been using them as much a possible to get the hang of them.

"You've been observing. What do you think?"

"Right..." Carson replayed his mental tape. This was something else to get used to - Kinkade asking him what he thought. Up until he made night manager trainee, the most Kinkade ever did was make him feel like he'd ticked off the high school principal. "I wouldn't turn him loose on Two-Fer Taco Night, but he did okay. Showed some promise."

"More work on Function 7?"

"Definitely."

"Do you think he'll be back?"

Carson shrugged. "He wasn't running when he left... though that was probably due to the weight of the manual."

Kinkade nodded once, tapped once, and swiped twice. "Yes. Quite." There was a faint flicker in Kinkade's expression. This was new, too. Carson wasn't sure if it was just a trick of the light, but he had come to believe in recent weeks that it was something close to emotion. Perhaps even humor.

In truth, this new side of his boss was a little unnerving. Carson was still so accustomed to bracing for impact whenever they met that he was uncertain how to deal with him in casual conversation. He had recently decided that, if he and Kinkade were going to work together, he would either tolerate the genuine Carson or get rid of him. So, he had decided to be himself. For now, it seemed to be working.

"I suspect, however," Kinkade looked up from his tablet, "That he will never be as proficient with liquid cheese as Stanley. It has been difficult to replace him."

"Yes," Carson forced himself to agree. "No one understood cheese like Stanley." It had been a few months since his rival had quit, but the memory still brought a smile to Carson's face. He had walked out almost immediately after hearing he had been passed up for the night manager job.

"Agreed. With the letter of recommendation I wrote for him, though, he should be well equipped to obtain gainful employment. My only reservation is that he may seek it with Fujikacorp." Again, there was the barest hint of emotion – this time a faint distaste.

"The Super Maxi-Pad? I thought they were out of the running... you know, after the whole... er... bacterial infection or whatever. Bad tacos or something, right?"

Kinkade shook his head. "They may be down, but do not count them out. With Ichiro Fujika's death, another will take his place. This was only one battle. The war still rages."

Carson, who knew a great deal more than Kinkade about Fujika's death and the battle that led to it, felt suddenly very much like changing the subject. "That may be, Chief, but we'll be ready for 'em. Night Manager Carson Dudley is on the job!" Carson saluted then suddenly regretted it as Kinkade fixed him with a familiar blank stare.

"Chief?"

"Er... sorry, it just slipped out."

Kinkade's eyes shrugged. "It's not disagreeable." Kinkade turned away to a quick survey of the Freezie lids, leaving the matter closed and Carson suddenly dizzy. There were a few things, apparently, left to get used to.

"But it's Night Manager *Trainee*," Kinkade added absently. "Let's be clear."

Carson grinned. But not everything. "Right. Well, better earn my title. Hey, are these the new posters?!" Carson reached for a pile of rolled tubes on the counter.

"Yes. From the slogan contest."

"Slick! Been waiting on these babies." Carson unrolled one, taking in pops of color, a speeding consumer and the trendy new 24/7 logo. "'Fast service for those on the run,'" he read, nodding. "I like it. Big risk letting your public pick your slogan."

"We value our public."

"Oh, hey," Carson's brain nudged him. "Speaking of valuing our public... I was uh... I was wondering if you'd had a chance to think about the whole security guard thing. You know, getting Gold Shield back in the house... guess there was some noise last night, and you know..."

"You're referring to Officer Jackson?" Kinkade was staring at him again. The tablet was still.

"Um... I... well yes, actually, although..."

"Customer safety is important. You may proceed."

Carson dropped the poster. "Er... do you mean..."

"I want you to rehire him."

Inwardly, Carson cheered. There was a fist-pump in his tone. "Sure thing, Chief. I'm on it! Great call."

"I trust, however, that this time his service will be more *pro*ductive and less *de*structive." Kinkade fixed him with a stern glare.

"Oh. Um... yeah... well, I guess..."

The boss's mouth twitched into an unusual and uncomfortable position. It took Carson a moment to recognize it as a smile.

"Oh! That was a... that was a joke! Of course! Yeah. Well, sure. I mean I knew it was... I just didn't think you could..." he stopped himself. The moment had passed. Kinkade was back into his tablet.

Carson decided to press forward, confused but encouraged by this new personality quirk. He had another matter to attend to and this seemed as good a time as any. He cleared his throat. "Erm... also..."

"Yes?" Kinkade didn't look up.

"I wanted to... apologize again for being late last night." Best to start with humility.

"Apologize? For taking a friend to the hospital? Loyalty and compassion, Carson. Excellent traits. *That's* the kind of person Seven Corporation is looking for."

"Yeah. Right?! Uh-huh." Carson scratched his head awkwardly, feeling like he should just get on with it. "So, um... speaking of my friend... that same friend... the loyalty and compassion one... turns out she needs a favor that's related to that whole thing – in a way - and I sort of was wondering if I could leave early tonight, but I know I've already..."

"Certainly. Leave whenever you like."

Carson gulped, speechless.

"Once you arrange coverage, of course."

"Of course." Carson forced his mouth to close. The new Kinkade was definitely new. Way new.

A buzzing sounded from under the man's jacket, and he slid a hand in for a phone. It was not, Carson noted slowly recovering from his shock, the phone he wore on his belt that he used for business calls. This one was different. Small, black, nondescript. It rang seldom, but when it did...

Kinkade turned away, his voice dropping to an indistinct murmur.

...he did that. Carson feigned disinterest and turned back to the posters. He'd made enough inroads tonight. This little mystery could wait. He hummed to himself, trying not to listen. After a moment, Kinkade turned back.

"If that's all, Carson," he said in a tone that indicated that was all. "I'll be in my office." With that, he disappeared into the back, phone glued to his ear. The door closed with a private, definite, "do not disturb" sort of thud.

Carson stared after him for a moment, his hum slowly dying. Kinkade was getting more and more interesting by the day. With a shrug, he reached for the employee phone list. Ten minutes later, Kinkade walked straight out of the office and straight out the front door. He said nothing, and Carson didn't either. An unrocked boat was a safe boat. He busied himself finding someone to cover his shift.

Once it was arranged, he returned to the routine duties of the store and to plotting the evening ahead. Dex should be here soon and then, thanks to Kinkade's inexplicable compassion, they would be able to connect with Kiki and, hopefully, get a jump start on their current mystery. Mentally ticking off his to-do's, he reached for his phone. There was only one left on the list. Flipping through his contacts, he poked a pale, weaselly face glaring back at him with a snarky look.

The phone rang.

And rang.

And rang.

And rang.

Carson hung up, frowning. He dialed again. Still nothing. He checked the face to make sure it was the right one, then stabbed again. This time, he let it roll. Twelve rings. Fifteen. Twenty. Finally, with his thumb hovering over disconnect...

"...and you can take *that* to the Whiner Bank, Whiner man!! And make *sure* you get your change and make a deposit and start saving up for next time, 'cuz there WILL be a next time, oh yeah, OH YEAH!! You can count on *that!!!*"

The call ended.

Carson's frown deepened. He counted to ten, breathing slowly, then dialed again. Another fifteen rings. Twenty. Then again...

"...in your FACE, Lucy Loser! Yeah! How does *that* feel, newb?! Huh?! How DO IT FEEL?! You mess with the *Leet*, you gonna get *beat*! And then take it in the *seat*! You're like a little baby suckin' on his mama's *teat*! That's LEET, baby boy... L-three-three-T, you crossbred, mangy, loser, short bus, son of a...!!"

"Leet!!" Carson cut him off. "Dude! You're live on the air, man! Take a breath!"

There was a slightly disoriented silence on the other end, punctuated heavily by the sound of video game noises: explosions, clanking metal, louder explosions, and a grim, plodding, orchestral tune that hinted at rubble strewn battlefields, blasted, smoking ruins and unspeakable carnage of the giant mechanized robotic kind.

"Did I answer the phone?"

"Yeah. Sort of."

"Charity?"

"Wow. Your Ritalin prescription run out again, or is this another Yoo-Hoo bender?"

"What?! I can't... hang on..." The amazing chaos of noise on the other end softened slightly. "Okay, Charity. You got 12 seconds. Then, I gotta go conquer the 'verse. Go."

"Ah," Carson nodded to no one in particular. Suddenly everything clicked. "*Skull Crushing Warbots of Doom* is out; isn't it? Okay, look, I won't take much of your fragging time..."

"You got that right." There was a burst of gunfire, some explosions and a spurt of profanity. Leet chuckled, evilly, in the back of his throat.

"Hm. First, consider therapy. Second, I got a job for you. I need a little intel."

"Maybe next week. I'm busy gankin' newbs. Thanks, good-bye..."

"Hold up!" Carson stopped him before he could disconnect again. "I'm just looking for the goods on the Curio Shop next door. Business records, property taxes, owners, all public stuff. Easy. Plus, there's this painting. Real creepy, hooded guy about to put the knife to some blonde bimbo. I think it's..."

Leet cut him off with a mocking snort. "You want it in velvet or on the side of a van?! Find your own art."

"Alright," Carson muttered grudgingly. "Not exactly a solid lead. Let's just stick with the Curio Shop then. I'm thinking..."

"I'm thinking Google. Just type in 'G – O – whoops, gotta GO! Sorry, Charity, newbs to school! Yeeeehaw! EAT HOT CHAINGUN!" The line went dead.

Carson fumed, glaring at Leet's face in his phone. He dropped it in disgust and turned his angst to cleaning. Leet would be useless for at least a week. Intel would have to wait.

Carson was still cleaning thirty minutes later when the door chime sounded. Dex peeked in. He looked cautious without trying to look cautious.

"'Sup, Dud. We alone?"

"Boss man's gone. It's just you, me and the corn dogs."

"Good," Dex strolled in, a moist-looking plastic bag under his arm. "I can't stand that guy."

"He did leave a message for you," Carson stiffened and adopted his best Kinkade impression. "Welcome back to the 24/7 you big, black, beautiful hunk of man."

"I LOVE that guy!" Dex gave the air a knockout punch. "Mmmm! Uh-huh! %^&*#@! happy %^&*#@! day!"

Carson clapped him on one massive shoulder. "Gratz, Big Man. Couldn't have happened to a more profane guy. Of course, we'll have to repaint the walls now, but hey – it's a celebration."

"You don't know the half of it, Bro!" Dex was practically glowing. His face sagged with relief. "Lost my only other gig today. I was really startin' to sweat it, man. And that ain't figurative. You know how when I sweat, and it starts to..."

"Yeah. Gotcha. Mental picture. Painful *and* permanent."

Dex caught his friend in an impulsive bear hug. "Thanks, Bro! Thanks a %^&*#@! million!" He squeezed and pounded Carson's back, ignoring his gasping attempts to draw breath. "Man!" Dex released an explosive sigh and his friend at the same time. "I can't figure how you pulled it off! Coming back from the dead was one thing, but getting Kinky to put me back on the ground?! Abso-*freakin'*-lutely amazing!" Dex swore with gusto and satisfaction. "How'd you do it? Begging? Bribery?! Blackmail?!"

"Jus' a 'sec... breathing..." Carson sucked air, weaving slightly. "Nothing... special... just sort of... asked."

Dex snorted. "Yeah. Sure. It was begging, then."

"Negative. Like I... said... just asked." Carson eased himself back onto his favorite stool. "I put... the 'man' in... manager."

Dex punched the air again, cutting loose with a fresh string of profanity. "Whatever! It don't matter how you saved this big black booty, just that you did it!" His face sobered. "I owe you one."

"I'll say. So... how about a couple of Victory Freezies... on me."

"$%@^&* straight!"

Carson winced. "Okay, but here's the thing," he swung out of his seat and set about filling cups. "If we're gonna keep you around, we gotta start working on your people skills. For example, try not to refer to our employer as 'Kinky', 'Corporate Death Suit' or especially 'the Walking Turd' anymore. At least not to his face. And really, dude... we gotta do something about that mouth of yours."

"What's wrong with my mouth?"

"It's a sewer. And I don't mean that figuratively. I think I've *actually* seen poopies flying out of there."

"I'm an expressive guy."

"Expressive is this..." Carson held up one of the Freezie cups, indicating the slogan on its side: *Gimme a Freezie, Pleasie!* "It's clever, it's colorful, it rhymes, it doesn't make anyone want to pour hot wax in their ears to block out the sound. That's expressive. What you do is more like rubbing someone's face in the hind end of a cat."

Dex gave him a glare.

"Look, I just don't want you to get booted again which may very well happen if Kinkade gets the kind of complaints he got last time."

"Complaints?! What the %^&*#@! would anyone have to complain about me for?!"

"Right. Okay. This may take a little more work than I thought. Let's start with your potty mouth. Truth is swearing isn't clever. It's lazy. It says, 'hey everyone, instead of being creative or interesting, I'm just going to use words that I thought were funny when I was in third grade'."

Dex frowned and appeared as if he was preparing to share his true feelings.

"Try this," Carson headed him off. "When you feel the need to be expressive, just grab any random word and slap some pizzazz on it. It's not *what* you say; it's *how* you say it."

The frown grew angry.

"Personally, I like to use products from the store," Carson cast around, found the cookie shelf. "For example," he rose, worked his face into a grimace and punched out the words: "Ginger *Snaps!* Or even... *Fiiiii-ggggyyy Newtons!*" Carson quirked an eyebrow at him.

For a moment, Dex looked as if he might snap. Then, with massive force of will, he removed his hand from his pepper spray. "Ginger Snaps," he sighed. "Ginger Snaps," he repeated the phrase softly, as if trying it out. "You really think my job depends on this?"

"And the paint. Plus, children come in this store. If nothing else, think of them."

Dex heaved another huge sigh. "No promises. The Army taught me to swear just like they taught me to fight - I got both deep in my soul. And I ain't sayin' 'figgy'. Ginger Snaps..." he muttered. Then again, "Ginger Snaps." Another sigh. "Alright. Enough of that. All this practice not swearin' is wearing the Big Man out. Let's get this show on the road," Dex took a final pull on his Freezie, the straw rattling dregs. "Who we waitin' on, Attila?"

"Oh, she couldn't make it. Had to prep for that hearing."

Dex snorted. "All that guff about sticking together and *she* bails. Figures."

"Kiki is going to swing by, too, so we can go together. Shouldn't be long before her class starts. Which reminds me," Carson gave a nod toward the sagging plastic bag Dex had tucked under his arm. "I'm assuming that's..."

"Yeah. And by the way, yuck," Dex tossed the bag onto the counter where it landed with a wet thump. "Next time you want mutant cat splatter scraped from an alley, do it yourself."

"Deal. And thanks for tossing that right on the counter, too," Carson snatched up the bag and reached for disinfectant. "So, did you find, you know...?"

"Naw, just some goo is all. The body was gone. Long gone, I suspect. The hand too. I even called, 'here Kitty Kitty'," Dex put a palm on his pistol. "You know. Just to be sure."

"We'll take what we can get. Right now, Kiki's forensics prof is our best shot at digging up a lead."

"If you say so," Dex eyed the plastic bag dubiously. "Still not sure this is the brightest idea. I'm having a hard time thinking this dude is gonna toss a mess of cat juice under the scope and give it the science just 'cuz someone says 'please'."

"It's better than taking it to the police. Parsons already thinks we're a menace to society; he might just arrest us because he feels like it. The worst they can do at LC3 is flunk us. Er... well, Kiki." The thought made him uncomfortable. "But they won't. I mean, why would they? It's just college."

"College," Dex grumbled, crushing his Freezie cup. "Don't know why she bothers. Now that we got the Internet, I don't even know why we have schools anymore. Ain't nothin' there you can't learn on YouTube."

"You're a true Renaissance man," Carson took a huge pull on his own Freezie, clapped a hand to his head. "Ow. Cold. Ow. Ginger *Snaps!* See?! Hear what I did there?! Expressive."

The door chime warbled and a gaggle of twenty-somethings paraded in, cheerfully texting each other. Sliding in behind them, Kiki. She lurked near the counter until Carson had rung up the others, and they had left.

As soon as the door was shut, Carson beckoned her forward with his best game show host introduction. "Welcome back from commercial break, ladies and gentlemen! Let's meet our next contestant! She's twenty-two years old, a student at LC3, loves puppies and the color red. But is she ready for everyone's favorite game show... *What's in the Bag?!*" With an elaborate flourish, he revealed Dex's shopping bag.

Kiki wrinkled her nose and drew back slightly. "Ew. Is that...?"

"Well, not all of it. Apparently, it's just the juice, so I can't give you full points on that answer. But, you do qualify for a one-way trip to Las Calamas Community College and an exciting interview with your Forensic's professor! So just as soon as..." the door chime warbled again as Carson's sub arrived. "And there we are! Let me just grab a Sarge and we'll be on our way." Carson headed for the cooler. "Anyone thirsty? It's on me."

"No," Kiki snapped.

Carson glanced back. "You okay?" He snagged a burly can out of the cooler, decorated with camouflage and an in-your-face label that declared *Angry Sarge's Atomic Energy Face Punch.*

"Energy drinks keep me up; that's all," she looked at her boots.

"Plus, I think those caused blindness in lab rats. Can we go?"

Minutes later, they were packed into Dex's cramped white sub-compact and enduring the ride across town. They veered and swerved, tires chirping and gears grinding, as Dex manhandled the vehicle in his usual nonchalant and hair-raising style.

"So... ow!" Carson's head bumped against the ceiling as Dex took a speed bump at close to forty. "What's the plan, girl? We got us a baggie full of yuck and a prof with the tools. How do you plan to bring the two together? Provided we get there alive."

"I got it covered. Don't worry." Kiki's didn't spare him a glance. Her face was stuck in a notebook filled with neatly ordered class notes.

"Carson trusts Kiki. He's just a little nervous given his track record."

"No cops, I got it. I'll be discrete."

"Finally," Dex rumbled. "Something we all agree on."

They rode in silence for a short time until they hopped the curb while Dex was zooming through a close yellow light and almost clipped the manger scene in someone's front yard.

"Gee whiz, Dex," Carson rubbed his head where it had smacked the window. "Don't you know it's bad luck to drive a car over Baby Jesus this close to Christmas? Oh, hey... speaking of Christmas, how do you guys feel about a party? I was thinking Granny's place, gifts, nog, the works. I know y'all don't have any place in particular to go, so I thought we could whip up some genuine yule, Dudley Style. Whaddaya say?"

Dex met his eyes in the rearview mirror and held them. They were grim. Seconds ticked by.

"Um... shouldn't you be watching..."

A loud honk drew Dex's attention back to the road. He jerked the little car back into its lane and poked his fist out the window. Carson was fairly certain what gesture it was making.

"I can see you're already in the Christmas mood. Should I take that as a yes?"

From the front seat, silence.

"A maybe?"

More silence.

"C'mon, big man..."

"I'm busy."

"Busy? On *Christmas*?! Who's busy on Christmas?! You've only got one gig, and that's..."

The eyes were back on him, this time grim *and* dark. The car lurched dangerously. Carson felt his hands dig into what was left of the upholstery. "Or, maybe we could talk about it later." He turned to Kiki. "What about you, woman? How about a little 'ho ho ho'?"

"How about a little 'no no no'." Kiki's tone was cold. She was still locked into her notebook in spite of the buffeting.

"What?! You too?!" Carson's look changed to shock. "Come on, Kiki... this is *Christmas!*"

"I don't do Christmas." There was no budge in her voice.

"Man..." Carson's shoulders slumped then stiffened suddenly as Dex zipped through a crowded crosswalk, eliciting a chorus of terror and outrage from its hapless occupants. The guard did not deign to reply but merely repeated his previous gesture.

"Call me crazy," Carson sighed, "but I'm just not feelin' the Christmas spirit here." He slumped in his seat, stumped. His thoughts wandered back through a glorious vault of holiday memories: Granny's warm, fresh baked goodies, his favorite carols, the tree glowing with lights, the candlelight service at church and the glorious morning of Christmas itself. Presents. Stockings. Traditions. Little oranges.

He shook his head. What was wrong with them?

After a moment of pondering, he squared his mental shoulders. This battle was far from over - just the first clash in an epic yuletide engagement. The party would happen. He would save Christmas.

The car jerked again as Dex narrowly avoided a sidewalk Santa. Carson caught a glimpse of the man's face as they whipped past close enough to touch. It looked as if he'd seen the ghosts of Christmas Past, Present and Future all at once, and Carson could almost swear Dex had done it on purpose.

Of course, victory may be, he reflected, slightly harder than he thought.

A few minutes later, they were nosing into a side lot in the shadows of stately brick and ivy buildings. Kiki led the way toward the science wing, face still buried in notes in spite of their pace. Carson glanced into the long evening shadows, pulling his collar close against the sudden chill of an offshore breeze. He liked the school even though it made him feel small.

Then something moved.

"Hey, what...?!" Carson stopped suddenly, staring. Something in the shadows. Something furtive. Small... or maybe not? "You see that?" The others followed the line of his finger toward a dark smudge of bushes. Windows glowed eerily upon them from a monolithic building beyond. Leaves fluttered in the cold breeze. Otherwise, nothing else moved. "Um, never mind. Guess it was nothing. Sorry." Carson shrugged. "Ordinarily, I'd say 'probably just a cat,' but under the circumstances..."

"Yeah," Dex's hand drifted away from his concealed semi-automatic. "Under the circumstances, I'd be liable to shoot you."

They reached Kiki's class just as the bell rang. Hurrying inside, she left them in the hallway. Carson caught a glimpse of a crowded lecture hall, dark wood, a raised stage stocked with tools, vials and specimen samples. Students bustled about, chattering, finding their seats. The door closed with a stately thump.

"Wanna hold the bag?" Carson held it out to his friend. Dex stood unmoving, arms folded across his massive chest. Without a word, he turned away.

After an hour, the bell sounded again. Wading through the flood of students, Dex and Carson spotted Kiki's red stocking cap at the front of the class next to a well built man in a lab coat.

"There she is," Carson took a steadying breath. "That must be her prof. Well, let's go let the cat out of the bag." He shook his package. It sloshed.

There was no answer from Dex. He was staring back at the ebbing crowd of students, eyes strangely unfocused.

"Hey... Big Guy? Hellooooo..." Carson snapped fingers in Dex's face.

"Hunh? Oh, yeah. Cat. Bag. You got it," Dex took a step then hesitated. "Listen, uh... you go ahead. You and Kiki are better at this kinda thing anyway. We don't wanna smother the man." Dex drifted off. Carson watched him for a moment then headed toward the stage with a shrug.

When he arrived, Kiki was already in mid-lie. "So I know it's unusual and all, but we were hoping you could give us some information about the sample. Anything at all. Oh, here he is now! Professor Looney, this is Carson, the friend I was telling you about."

They shook hands. The man had a firm grip and a direct gaze that might have been intimidating if he weren't grinning through his bristly black beard. His air was relaxed and personable, and he seemed the kind of person who was in his element anywhere – more like a soldier, Carson thought, than a professor. Carson put his age at mid-40's, but judging from his biceps and exuberance, he'd see another 40 easy.

"Professor Looney! It's a pleasure."

"Please. Call me Jamie," Looney pushed a set of lab goggles back on his gleaming bald head. "Cat person, eh?"

"Um..." Carson glanced sidelong at Kiki. She made a discreet nod. "Yes!" he confirmed loudly. "Cat person! You bet. That's me! Love 'em! Cats, cats, cats, can't get enough!"

"You weren't kidding, Kiki," the Professor chuckled warmly. "Guess that explains your concern about Fluffy."

"Fluffy?"

"Yes. Or... isn't that..."

"...the name of..." Kiki prompted, jabbing Carson in the ribs.

"...my cat, of course!" Carson caught on. "And I am *so* worried about him - or her. Totally worried!"

"Frantic in fact," Kiki pressed on smoothly. "Hardly making sense at all. Anyway, as I was just telling you, Professor, Carson found this blood near the house, and we were wondering if you could tell us anything about it. Anything that could help put his mind to rest."

"Yeah!" Carson jumped in eagerly. "Like, is it cat or maybe something else? Weirdo chemicals maybe, evidence of genetic manipul... ow!" Another elbow cut him off.

"I know it's an odd request, but that's how cat people are," Kiki shot Carson a threatening glance. "There's something wrong with their brains."

Professor Looney smiled. "Sure. Glad to help. Believe it or not, I get asked for unusual favors like this from time to time."

"Oh yeah?" Carson handed over the plastic bag. "Like what?"

Looney glanced at the ceiling, searching his memory. "The sandwich is a good one. I once ran a saliva sample for a young housewife to determine whether a half-eaten sandwich had been devoured by the dog or the cat. Seemed one of them had to go."

"Cool. Which one did it?"

"The husband."

"Ouch. Science is a harsh mistress."

"Not as harsh as this guy's wife. Anyway," he shook the bag suggestively. "Let me take this into my mad scientist workshop and see what I can find out. Stick around. I'll be back in a bit." Professor Looney disappeared through a door behind the stage.

"Fluffy?" Carson asked dryly.

Kiki glared. "He bought it; didn't he?" She promptly stuck her nose back in her notes. "Now, if you don't mind... test coming."

Carson lounged against a formidable oak table, waiting. As he idled, he gradually became aware of the smell of formaldehyde and some other chemical that reminded him of cleaning the bathrooms at the 24/7. After a few minutes he felt himself growing light headed.

"Whoa," Carson blinked and rubbed his eyes vigorously. "Science smells bad. Hey, do you wanna...?"

"No," Kiki skewered him with a glance. "Maybe Dex does. Why don't you go find him?" It wasn't a suggestion.

"Um. Yeah. Right. You're probably wanting to... you know. Study. And whatnot. Right, off I go..." he dropped off the stage and headed into the lecture hall, eyes searching. He didn't get far. Carson stopped almost immediately, picking Dex easily out of the thinning crowd. The big man was talking to someone. A woman.

And not just any woman, Carson noted. This was a good looking one. A *very* good looking one. A tall, attractive, sophisticated very good looking one with dark skin and smoldering eyes. Smoky hair hung down below her waist, brushing against a patterned skirt, knee high leather boots and an elegant white blouse. The hair swished and rippled as she spoke, murmuring like a river.

"Well, well, well," Carson muttered to himself, stroking his chin beard. "Looks like you finally found a way in which school is superior to YouTube." He watched for a moment then returned to the stage.

"You're back." Kiki didn't sound welcoming.

"Yup, but don't blame me," Carson raised his hands defensively. "Dex is occupied. He's taken a sudden interest in the student body."

Kiki offered a noise between a grunt and a sigh but didn't look up. With nothing left to do, Carson's eyes roamed the stage and the room, settling finally on Kiki. They hovered. She was pale and skinny, but he couldn't decide whether she was any paler or skinnier than usual. He found himself studying her just as he had at dinner the night before: circles under her eyes, battered canvas backpack shored up with duct tape protecting her prized laptop - and Heaven only knew what other sorts of electronic wizardry. Ever since she had opened up to him that night in the Fish N' Ships months ago, Carson realized, he had started taking notice of her. He no longer saw her as just a tough, resourceful loner. That moment of weakness, of utter vulnerability that she had shown – it was hard to forget.

Then, there was the hospital. She'd stuck by his bed for weeks, and they'd had some good conversations when he wasn't napping or groggy from meds. They'd gotten to know each other in a different way, beyond just chit-chat, monster hunting and the weather. But once class had started again, she had faded away. Literally and figuratively.

Kiki glanced up, and Carson looked away quickly though he was unsure why. When he snuck a look back, she had returned to her notes. He sighed and for the time being gave up trying to figure her out. The girl had walls, and they weren't the kind you stormed. He turned idly and started flipping through a copy of an *Introduction to Forensic Sciences* text that was left on the table.

"Jinkies!" Carson's eyes stopped on a particularly gruesome closeup of an autopsy. "I've seen vampire victims and a zombie's insides - up close. But this stuff is..." he stopped, not needing to look up to feel the deadly burn of Kiki's gaze. "... something I'm going to keep to myself." He made the motion of locking his lips and throwing away the key. After that, he didn't say another word.

It was just over an hour when Professor Looney wandered slowly back into the lecture hall. The place was empty and quiet, and even Dex was gone, having disappeared some time ago while Carson's attention was elsewhere. Looney crossed the platform to them, his pace slow and measured, matching a look on his face that was somewhere between puzzled and concerned.

Carson had seen the same look many times on the face of his favorite Las Calamas Police Detective, Patch Parsons. It usually came just before Parsons accused him of committing a crime, and it always made him uneasy. He slapped on a disarming smile and braced himself. "Wow, time flies! Any news?"

The Professor was silent, hand on chin, eyes on floor. After a moment, he looked up, blinking as if unaware they were there. "Tell me again," he asked slowly, "how you came across this?"

"Yeah, so," Carson shuffled his feet. "Frizzy..."

"Fluffy," Kiki corrected.

"Yeah, him - or her - she got in a... this big... I think what..."

"She went missing," Kiki smoothed over Carson's babbling, shooting him a glare that warned him against speaking. "Carson found the blood and tissue near her food dish."

Carson bit his tongue and stood silently, pouring all of his energy into a plastic smile. Not for the first time, he felt relieved at Kiki's skill at sweet talk. Relieved and slightly concerned.

"Uh-huh. That's what I thought. You see, the strange thing is..." the Professor glanced back as a pretty young blonde in a lab coat approached. "Ah. Any change?"

The girl passed him a clipboard. "I ran them again, Professor, just like you asked. Sorry. Same as before."

"This is my lab assistant, Peggy," Looney told them absently as his eyes pored over scribbled notes and important scientific-looking annotations.

The girl smiled a dazzling white. "Hi. Peggy Schaffer," she stuck out her hand, and Carson took it. It was warm and strong. "New to class? I don't remember seeing you before."

"Oh, no," Carson dismissed her question with a wave. "I'm not here as a student. I'm just here to not talk. I mean, to let Kiki... er... because there was blood near my dish. My cat's dish, of course. By which I mean Frizzy..." he could feel Kiki's glare burning a hole in him. Time to bail. "I'm a cat person."

"Ah," Peggy nodded as if Carson's statement wasn't the strangest thing she'd ever heard. "I'm a cat person too. Don't know what I'd do if my Gracie ever went missing. You must be worried sick."

Carson kept his eyes carefully averted from Kiki. He could still feel the heat of her gaze. "Oh, I'm worried, alright."

"Well, don't fret too much," the assistant patted his hand. She had an infectious, upbeat way about her and seemed genuinely concerned. "The Prof knows his stuff. He's pretty good around animals too. Except for that monkey that got loose in the lab... but that little critter deserved it. Whack! Anyway, if anyone can find out what happened, it's him." Peggy smiled her dazzling whites and flipped a pony tail. "Nice to meet you, Carson. Hope you find your cat." She loaded various vials and beakers onto a tray and headed for the back room.

After another minute or so of study, the professor lifted his eyes from his notes. "Hm. Weird. Well, I'm sorry to say that there *is* evidence of feline tissue in this sample," he glanced back at the notes, frowning. Carson couldn't tell whether it was a disappointed frown or a suspicious frown. "However... I'm afraid it must have gotten contaminated. There are also trace elements of... well... human tissue. But they're not... they're..." The sentence derailed. Looney tried again. "In addition, I found... there seem to be..." his voice trailed off.

"Seem to be...?" Carson prodded.

"Seem to be... other things. Obviously contaminated, I'm afraid. And just plain weird," he added with a mutter. Looney handed the clipboard to Carson, his mind clearly elsewhere. Carson took it obediently, glancing at the scrawls as if they made sense.

"I see. Yeah. Obviously there's... what you said. Uh-huh." His head bobbed.

Kiki snatched the results and studied them, quick blue eyes flicking over the pages.

Looney ventured a distracted smile. "I'm very sorry I couldn't help any more. I would be willing to suggest that maybe your cat scratched someone who tried to pick her up, but..." again, the professor's face clouded. "But the sequences are wrong. All wrong. It's like... well, here, let me show you; there's a page in our textbook, actually..." he turned to the table but found it empty. "Hm. Peggy must have picked it up. Well, I'll show you tomorrow, Kiki. Not that it will explain..." he paused. The Patch Parsons look crept slowly over his face again. "You know, there are a few more tests I could run. Something a little more in-depth. If you don't mind. I could hold onto this sample for a bit and see what I can turn up. I wouldn't want you worrying about Flauncy."

"Floozie," Carson corrected.

"Fluffy!" Kiki kicked him wickedly.

"Ow! Right!" Carson rubbed his shin with his other foot. "You can, uh... just keep the bag. And who knows? Maybe Freezie will just show up tomorrow at my doorstep, meowing for her tuna. There's always hope."

Kiki rolled her eyes.

"There certainly is," the Professor smiled. "Oh, by the way, Kiki – your lab fee. Registration says they still don't have it."

"Sorry. They will this week," she shouldered her pack. "We've kept you long enough, Professor Looney. Thanks again for your help." She headed for the door, tugging Carson along by the sleeve.

As they stepped into the hallway, they met Dex. Both could tell instantly there was something wrong – he was practically floating.

"What a night!" Dex waved a slip of flowery stationary at them. "Got my job back and a sexy mama's phone number! Things are finally lookin' up for the Big Man!"

"That's great," Carson tapped him playfully on the arm. "Glad you didn't have to get distracted by all that investigating. Now, let's get you out of here before it all falls apart. I know how much you hate college."

"Hate it?! What you talkin' 'bout, fool?" Dex shot him a glare, offended. "College rocks!"

CHAPTER FOUR

Nothings and Somethings

Boom!

The thundering report kicked back off cinderblock walls.

Boom – boom – boom – boom – boom!

More shots chased the first in rapid succession, the *tink!* of shell casings hitting the ground barely audible. Safe behind his protective earmuffs, Carson whistled and shook his head. Seconds later a paper target was zipping toward them on the wire, showing a pattern of lethal devastation. The grouping was tight and professional, every hole in the black, guaranteeing that if it hadn't just been a paper target, it would never be a threat to anyone ever again. It wasn't one of Dex's best.

"Dude," Carson shook his head. "I was right. You *are* slipping. That's the third round tonight that you only doubled my score. You got a brain fungus or something?"

"I wish," Dex stared at the target, disappointment etched on his face.

From a nearby stall, another shooter studied Dex's work, eyes wide behind the yellow plastic of his safety glasses. He whistled his approval. "Nice paper!"

"Maybe for you," Dex rumbled absently. The man's face fell. Dex didn't seem to notice. He wadded the paper and tossed it with disgust into a garbage can. "Must be all this exercise," he said the word as if it hurt. "It's crampin' my style." He rolled his shoulder experimentally, squeezing tender muscles. "No sense wastin' anymore time tonight with the rest of the losers. Let's beat it." Dex lumbered from the shooting range into the hall.

Carson caught up his bag and trotted behind. "Still working out with Sister Becky, eh?" He made no effort to smother a grin. "I know the answer by the way. I just can't stop saying it."

Dex shot him a dark look. "I noticed." He sighed. "Problem is, she's the best trainer I ever had. Makes my PT Sgt look like Pee-Wee Herman." Dex rolled his other shoulder. Carson noted that this time he actually winced. "Course..." a self-satisfied smile spread over Dex's dark features. "It's workin'. Don't tell the Old Goat, but since she started giving me tips... BOOM!" He flexed a massive bicep by way of demonstration, making his t-shirt stretch like a leotard on a blue whale.

"I didn't know she was into fitness."

"Into fitness?!" Dex snorted. "You oughtta see her run laps. I thought 'Old Goat' was an insult, but the way she hoofs it... brother." He rubbed one giant thigh, voice growing grim. "One of these days, I'm gonna keep up, too. Then she'll see. 'Lift those knees, Mr. Jackson! Higher, Mr. Jackson!' I'll lift those knees alright, you bitter, salty, slave-driving..."

"Wait - did you just say 'keep up'?"

"Don't push it. I'm armed."

"Fair enough."

"And then there's her gym... if you can call it that. Not a piece of gear in the whole place was built in the last fifty years. Just four walls, free weights, couple of heavy bags and some ruts in the floor so you know where to run. Place still has recruiting posters up from WWII. But what she does with it, man, it's a miracle. It hurts like Hell, but it's a miracle."

"Speaking of Hell," Carson stopped. They had reached the end of the hall and now stared up a flight of stairs. A long, steep flight of stairs.

"Aw, *&@^%$!"

"Don't you mean, 'Aw, Ginger Snaps?'"

"I mean 'Aw *&@^%$!' We ain't in the store no more," Dex rubbed aching thighs, glaring at the steps with the same look Carson had seen him give a store full of zombies. Gritting his teeth, Dex lifted a leg and took the first step.

"Repeat after me," Carson prompted cheerfully. "I think I can... I think I can..."

"Repeat after me," Dex gritted. What came next, Carson didn't want to repeat.

They reached the top several painful minutes later and made their way through a crowded maze of camouflage pants, ammunition, holsters and other para-military paraphernalia.

Carson stopped at the door to call back over his shoulder. "See ya, Joe!" A taciturn man behind the counter with a buzz cut of sandy hair and an eye-patch glanced at him. He neither spoke nor gestured.

Carson led the way onto the street. A cool evening breeze was blowing in off the sea. The sun was low, dashing a wan purplish stain across the white-capped bay. "Nice guy, Joe. Too bad he was born without a personality." As they set off, Carson glanced back at the sign hanging over the store: *Jersey Joe's Guns and Stuff.* "I wonder what the stuff is?"

"As long as he's got the guns, who cares about the stuff? And you say that every time. It's makin' me mad."

"That's just because you're in excruciating pain. Lucky for you, I know just what you need - how about a smooth, comforting, icy blue Freezie, Super Jammin' Jumbo size? That'll cool your aches. We can celebrate your triumphant return to the 24/7. First night back!"

They arrived at Dex's compact, and he wrestled himself inside, alternating between cursing and groaning. The Gold Shield emblem on the door rocked as he settled in. "Fine," he gritted. "Just make it a small."

"A *small?!*" Carson slipped into the passenger seat and braced himself as usual as they nosed out into traffic. "I wasn't aware that you were aware food came in that size."

"Cop test. Coming soon. After the holidays. Gotta get ready." Dex massaged one calf, seemingly oblivious of the oncoming traffic.

"Mm-hm," Carson stared out the window, watching the city of Las Calamas flash by, the bright decorations and Christmas cheer of the Romero district a dazzle of streaky lights. The way Dex drove, it was best not to watch the road. "Sorry, chum, I'm not buying it. Shooting lousy, ordering smalls, acting responsibly... *voluntarily* spending time with Sister Becky?! And you've only said three swears the whole night. Either all those concussions are catching up to you, or you've been bit."

"Bit?! By what?"

"Oh, I don't know... maybe something about five foot ten with long brown hair and curves that would make Michelangelo reach for his chisel."

"I got no idea what you're talking about," Dex's gaze drifted from the road along with his attention.

"Um... pedestrian..."

"I see it," Dex jerked the wheel but didn't bother with the brakes, sweeping within inches of a bike taxi filled with holiday sightseers. They all seemed to have a sudden new zest for life. "Sorry."

"See? That's exactly what I mean."

"What?"

"You just said 'sorry'."

"Oh. Sorry."

Carson eyed his friend. "You *have* been bit."

Dex's eyes locked firmly on the road. He mumbled something unintelligible. They drove in silence for a moment. Then Dex cleared his throat. "Um... can I, uh... can I talk to you about something?"

"Dude. After all we've been through? Let 'er rip."

"Yeah, well... I ain't exactly..." Dex struggled for words. "I ain't exactly comfortable with all the... the gooey stuff."

"And by 'gooey' I assume you mean 'feelings'."

"See?!" Dex slammed the dash. "I can't even say the word! How am I supposed to..."

"Just like shooting, Bro. Take a breath, line up the sights, then pull the trigger. Same same."

Dex took the breath. "Eye on the target," he muttered. "Pull the trigger."

"Trust me, it's worth it. So lay it on me. What do you have that's broken?"

"Delilah."

Carson blinked. "Your 'Delilah' is broken?"

"No, dummy. That's the girl. From Kiki's class. Michelangelo's chisel and all that."

"Oh, right! The biting."

Dex nodded aggressively. "You got that right, man. I'm bit and bit bad. Ginger *Snaps!* Ain't felt like this since..." his voice trailed off again as his eyes looked into the past. Judging from the anguish on his face, what he was looking at wasn't pretty. Carson had seen the big security guard take the full onslaught of an enraged vampiress without flinching. This was something deeper. "Well, for a long time."

Carson sensed a stall. The vampiress had been tough, but he could tell that, for Dex, this would be even worse. He set his jaw. They'd made it through that ordeal together and they would do the same here. "This goes back to your ex," he prompted. "Doesn't it."

Dex's hands tightened on the wheel. A familiar shadow fell over his face, a veil of pain, sorrow, loss, guilt and a weight of other dark emotion so intense it seemed to live there.

Dex nodded, once. "Yeah." More silence. Carson waited. Traffic lights flashed by. Dex drew a deep breath. "But it's more than that. A whole lot more." Another stall.

Carson was silent for a moment. "Tia?"

Dex shot him a look. For a second, his brown eyes were so hollow and empty that Carson felt he could fall into them and be lost forever. Dex looked back to the road. Silence.

"I know she was your daughter. I see you with the necklace. And I know you lost her."

"Been keepin' it bunched up too long. Sometimes I feel like if I don't let it out, I'm gonna... I'm gonna..." Dex's voice trailed off.

"Punch a nun?"

Dex's lips quirked into a faint smile. "Yeah. Maybe that."

Carson smiled back. The tension seemed to ease a fraction. "Pull the trigger, dude."

Dex cleared his throat, but when he spoke his voice sounded thick. "Shari is my ex. Never told you about her, I guess. Or anybody else. She was... she wasn't so bad. We were in love, once. Mighta worked out too, but I guess... well, I guess I pretty much messed it up. All started when I got canned from the Army. Cuz of this," he hefted his weighty belly. "Maybe my attitude, too, I guess," he added grudgingly. "Kind of had a rough side. Fights and whatnot. Taking orders ain't really my thing. Anyhow, after they gave me the boot, I just kinda lost it. Nothing seemed to make sense anymore. Shari and I started fighting worse and worse; I couldn't hold down a job. Didn't even really try. I was in a haze, man. Couldn't pull out of it. I was drinkin' a little – hell, maybe a lot – scarfin' junk food, staying out all night. Really workin' myself into a hole. And little Tia, my Baby Butterfly..." Dex's eyes went hollow again and he looked away, ignorant of traffic, stop lights, everything. This time, Carson let it go.

"She was my everything, man," Dex wiped a hand across his eyes. "Only thing that kept me anchored. And I... I let her down." His hands squeezed the wheel again, knuckles showing white. "One night, I was having it out with Shari and I snapped. Just left all in a huff. I was bent. Head all full of fury. I banged out the back door, through the yard. Left the gate open. We lived in the 'burbs, then, outskirts of LC. Rough neighborhood."

"Chaney District?"

Dex nodded bitterly. "That's the one. Real sorry *&@^%$ place. Gang bangers, druggies... but even worse were them dogs. I shoulda known better." He stared out the window, eyes dark with self-loathing. "There was a pack that ran in our 'hood. Bad ones. Wild. Pit bulls and what not, mean as sin. Tia must've come out to check on me, lookin' to take care of Big Daddy, just like always. They figure... they think... cops said the dogs, they... they came in through the gate. Maybe she tried to run... don't know fer sure. She was a coupla blocks away when they... when we... found her." Dex's voice was as hollow as the haunted look in his eyes.

They drove in silence.

"She was five, Dud. I couldn't even keep her alive 'til she was six."

Carson said nothing. There was nothing he *could* say.

They pulled slowly up to a stop light. The red washed over Dex's face. He cleared his throat. "Anyway, that was it for me and Shari. There was no cure for us after Tia. She blamed me, I blamed me... and for once we agreed. I just started hatin' on everyone and everything. Mostly me."

"Dex..."

"Don't. Don't you tell me it wasn't my fault. Don't you *ever* tell me that! I know what I did, and I know what it cost. And I know who to blame."

Carson let it go.

Red traded for green and they lurched forward. "So. Now, I meet Delilah." Dreadlocks shook. "I looked at a few women over the years. But there wasn't room in me for anything but hate. Guess when you hate yourself, it's just easier to hate everything else, too." Dex shifted gears and settled moodily back into his seat. "Especially dogs," he muttered. "I *really* hate dogs. But Delilah... I didn't see this one coming."

Carson glanced at his hands. "We never do."

Dex didn't seem to hear him, lost in his own ponderings. He shook his head, concentrating, forehead creased. "Dud, there's somethin' different about this one. I ain't felt it before. Not even with Shari. I don't know, maybe it's all this stuff we been through lately. Starin' death in the face, gettin' tight with folks I can't push away - no matter how hard I try." Dex kept his eyes fixed firmly ahead. "Maybe it's havin' a real friend. I dunno... maybe I'm finally coming around to the gooey stuff. Or some $%@^&* like that."

"Time can change anything. Well... almost anything."

"Whatever it is – this thing with Delilah - I can't just sit on my thumbs and let it slip on by. I feel like this is my last chance, y'know? Like if I don't figure out how to stop hatin', I'll get stuck there until I just... I don't know... explode."

The car slowed and Dex nosed it into the curb. With a start, Carson realized they were in front of Granny's house. He was home.

"So there it is," Dex heaved a sigh as big as he was. "The whole sorry mess. Dexter Jackson 101. Real %^&*#@! train wreck, ain't it?"

"Yup. Sure is. Just like everyone else. It's a little problem we all have in common. It's called 'life'." Carson's crooked smile flashed in the dark. "Question is... what are you gonna *do* about it?"

"Yeah," Dex said softly. "That is the question."

The car idled gently along with their thoughts. Finally, Dex stirred.

"Look, uh... I'm gonna take a rain check on that Freezie. I need to drive a bit, clear my head. I wanna be ready for my shift. First night back and all that."

Carson clambered out. If there was something else to say, he couldn't think of it. He stood watching the taillights as the little car disappeared into the winter night.

After a moment, he turned up the walk, headed to the house and let himself in. He suddenly realized that he needed cookies, and he needed them badly. "I'm home, Granny!" he called. "And my tummy wants a... oh... hey." Carson stopped, his eyes settling on a familiar black robed figure seated at the small dining room table. Sister Becky inclined her head politely. Beside her, Granny pushed her seat back, the trademark crooked Dudley grin decorating her pleasant wrinkles. It was, however, a fraction of a second late in coming. It had replaced a much more grim and concerned expression.

Carson paused. "Am I... interrupting something?"

"Not at all, dear boy," Sister Becky answered smoothly. Almost, Carson thought, a bit *too* smoothly. "Roberta and I were just chatting about old times. Please, do join us." She indicated an empty chair. Carson sat obediently.

"You two catch up," Granny rose and bustled about gathering tea cups. "I've got some tidying up to do in the kitchen. Then, we'll see about that tummy of yours," she winked at her grandson, then disappeared through a swinging door. The clink and rattle of dishes drifted back faintly.

Carson narrowed his eyes. "Okay, so what..."

"Let it lie, Mr. Dudley," Sister Becky clipped him. "If you put your head in the oven before the pie is done, you'll come away with more heat than treat."

"But you two..."

"Let it lie." Her tone gave no other options. Carson nodded mutely. "Now then," Sister Becky smoothed her robes, changing both inflection and topic as if she had flipped a switch. "Since we have a private moment, please update me on the investigation. Did you meet with Ms. Masterson's professor?"

"We did. Not much there, except 'it's weird'."

"Do not despair, lad. It is early in the hunt yet. Prayer and patience pave the way."

"I have gone to church twice this month."

Sister Becky smiled and patted his hand. "I am sure the Lord is thankful for your company, Mr. Dudley."

Carson was surprised, as usual, at the supple strength of her hands. He thought back to Dex's talk of the gym and smiled. "Hey, speaking of the Man Upstairs, there is something you can help me with," he cast a cautious eye toward the kitchen then dug a wrinkled sheaf of papers from his back pocket. "It's my dream – Vision – whatever. I've been going over it again after the whole alley thing, and I wanted to run something by you."

"By all means, Mr. Dudley," there was a glint in her emerald eyes. "Of course," she checked herself. "I must be cautious. As you know, I have been in talks with the Council, and I must tread carefully. They have asked me to abstain from practicing the trade until they have made a thorough study of my request."

"Abstain? You mean you're not helping us anymore?!"

Sister Becky clucked dismissively. "Tut tut, my lad! No need to worry that particular bone. It is merely a temporary formality. I shall resume my duties in short order, and quite possibly with the full support of my Order. Until then, well, let us just consider this a spiritual consultation. Now then. Out with your question."

The news gave Carson a vague sense of unease, but he unfolded the papers obediently and spread them on the table. "Okay. A lot of this still doesn't make sense – okay, *most* of it still doesn't make sense – but this one part keeps jumping out at me. The part where I met Pete..." he skimmed the handwritten page with his finger. "Right. Here's the bit. He had me count the rooms I'd been through in the Curio Shop when I was following that Herron chick. He said it was important. There were seven of them. I think that means something. Like... I dunno... seven challenges... ordeals, maybe."

Sister Becky leaned back, steepling her fingers. "Plausible," she nodded. "Seven is frequently a significant number in Scripture."

"That clicks, then. Cool. So follow me," Carson was warming up. "Then, Pete built up to this whole 'need to know' thing and that it was right now that I needed to know it - like the whole world was depending on what he was about to tell me."

"Mm. Yes. And if I recall correctly, that something was oral hygiene."

"'No one gargles at midnight.' Yeah. Kinda threw me even for a Vision. I thought it was just dreamytime, subconscious nonsense at first. But then, when Dex and I were snooping around Fujikacorp..."

"You found yourself saying those exact words."

"Darn straight. And those words led us to discover Haruki Nubuyuki. Or his corpse anyway. That's what kicked off the whole deal, put us on the trail of the Shogun and helped us stop the Warlord of Death."

"Fateful words indeed."

"Even more than 'save the Cheerleader, save the world'. So, I figured if the gargling thing was a clue, then maybe so was the rest of the stuff Pete said right after. Check it out," Carson followed his finger down the page, reading out loud. "*...the first is done. History. The second is here; we covered that. Next, next comes... death. And death, and life, no interruptions. Then, a long journey to a very dark place. You'll have a choice ta make there about the light. That could end it all, right there. After that - the wild one. And the little one. She'll be in trouble, big. Tell Dex to be strong. And look outside. Now, just a couple more, yer close, soljer. Here's the next; there's five. Don't forget. Five. And last... the end. They'll all come back, I reckon, or purt near. And one o' the lights'll leave. For ever, this time. No foolin'. Has to be that way, wish it weren't, but there it is. But when it's over, it's over. If you want.*"

Carson pushed the paper away and sat back, tugging at his chin beard. "If we assume seven challenges... ordeals... whatever you wanna call them... one for each room anyway, then I think Pete's hints break up into seven parts too." His eyes were eager. "Seven ordeals. Seven warnings. Or maybe..."

"Clues?"

Carson's head bobbed. "Exactly! Pete laid it all out: *the first is done. History.* That's Vanessa, it's gotta be. Then, when he says *the second is here; we covered that,* I'm sure he means the gargling. Fujikacorp. The Warlord of Death. Slam dunk." Carson paused, realizing his heart was pounding.

Sister Becky's face was implacable, but her eyes were narrowed in a way that gave him confidence. "Go on, lad."

"If I'm right, we just stepped into our third ordeal the other night. This alley thing – the cats – whatever grabbed Kiki. We're ready for our next clue."

"Out with it then, Mr. Dudley! Let us not delay."

Carson turned back to his notes. "Let's see... *next comes death. And death, and life, no interruptions.*" He looked up, his face a study of concentration. Then it sagged. "I got nothin'."

Sister Becky frowned along with him. "Yes. Quite." She pursed her lips. "I must confess, the phrase is most enigmatic. However, it is hardly surprising. In my experience, the true meaning of Visions and revelations often remains unclear until the proper moment."

They were interrupted by Granny Dudley, who entered from the kitchen with a plate of fresh baked cookies. Carson swept his notes into his lap with a sigh. Whatever the meaning of the clue, it would have to wait. Their conversation turned to idle chatter.

"Have you invited Sister Becky to the party yet, Carson?" Granny asked.

"Now that you mention it, no," Carson brightened, glad for a distraction from this latest puzzle. "Big Christmas shindig brewing, Sister B. If *anyone* is down with the Season, I figure it'd be you. Right about now, I could use some Christmas cheer. Whaddaya say, can we count you in?"

"Ah," Sister Becky folded her hands inside her robes and her eyes wandered upward in a blissful stare. "A celebration of the birth of our Lord and Savior. Such a blessed, grace-filled, joyous event of eternal portent. Truly the pinnacle of the holy season."

"Great! Then you'll come?!"

"Absolutely not."

"Perfect! You can bring eggnog... wait... did you say '*no*'?!"

"I did indeed, Mr. Dudley. I am afraid the notion of a Christmas celebration is completely foreign to me. I have always spent the holiday in quiet contemplation, when I had a moment to observe it at all, of course."

"Oh, Rebecca," Granny scolded gently. "Surely for the sake of tradition, you could make an exception?"

"Unfortunately, my work in the Order gave me little time to develop such things. My traditions were more of survival and life or death combat against the forces of darkness."

Carson was crestfallen. This was strike three. "Yeah. Well. It's hard to compete with that."

"Indeed, Mr. Dudley," she beamed a pious smile as a look of wistful remembrance drifted across her wrinkles. "Now then, I must be off. Speaking of the Order, I must prepare another briefing for the Council at St. Timothy's. They have requested additional information."

"Another briefing?" Carson frowned. "That's, like, number four, isn't it?"

"Five, lad. The Council is nothing if not thorough."

"So is a colonoscopy."

"There are other similarities as well," Becky nodded vigorously.

Carson grimaced. "I've gotta get ready for work anyway," he rose with her. "Night Managers In Training are expected to be on time."

"Ah, yes. Your new position," Sister Becky fetched a shawl and fussed with draping it about her shoulders. "I trust you're finding it to your liking. Spending a great deal more time with Mr. Kinkade, I presume?"

"Yup."

"And how has he seemed lately?"

The question seemed odd the moment she asked it. Carson hesitated as he helped Granny collect the dishes. It was innocent enough, and yet... he glanced at the nun. She had paused in adjusting her shawl, regarding him with a disarming smile. She was casual. Too casual.

"Er... fine, I guess. Still a little stiff. Sometimes I have trouble telling between him and the cardboard cutouts. But other than that, he's not a bad boss. Actually, he's a lot better since we wrapped up that stuff with... with..." he shot a sidelong glance at Granny. "With our competition. "Nice, almost. Why do you ask?"

"Oh, no reason. Just making idle chatter, cows chewing cud and all that," Sister Becky brushed the question off and finished adjusting her shawl. "Off I go. Thank you for your hospitality, Roberta," Sister Becky embraced her friend, "and our earlier conversation. We must pick up the threads of it again when time permits."

A tiny cloud flitted across Granny's face. "Yes. I suppose we should."

As he descended to the basement, Carson couldn't help but feel that there was more *unsaid* in that brief good-bye than there was *said*. It also reminded him of the unknowns in his own life and made him even hungrier for answers.

Thus, it was during a lull at work a few hours later that he took a chance and called Leet again. It had been a few days since they'd talked, and Carson was hoping the novelty of *Skull Crushing Warbots of Doom* had worn off. The phone rang. And rang. And rang. Not a good sign. He hung up and tried again, determined not to let it go. This time, after almost twenty rings, there was a click. His hopes spiked.

"Hey, Leet...!"

A recorded voice cut him off. "If you waited this long you're either a telemarketer or Charity. Either way, kiss it. I've got newbs to school. It sounds like this..." a loud burst of electronic explosions punched Carson in the ear, mingled with Leet's hyena laugh.

He flung his phone, fuming. "Crabapples!" Carson surged off his stool and headed for the bread aisle, intent on some therapeutic restocking. Then, on impulse, he snagged his bat and headed for the back door instead. This kind of frustration would require more than restocking. It demanded something more violent. Shouldering his way outside into the alley, he grabbed his bag of therapy cans from behind a dumpster. Selecting a large chili can, he tossed it into the air and swung hard from the shoulders.

Smack!!

The tin missile rocketed across the alley, pinged off another dumpster and careened over the wall of the neighboring store.

Out of the park.

A second one followed it. Carson shook out his arms. He was madder than he thought. After a half dozen more, he was just starting to loosen up when a voice made him jump.

"Hello, Carson."

It was a whisper. Soft. Scarcely louder than the breeze. Carson's heart jumped, and he swept the alley, bat poised. After a moment, he caught sight of a shadowy figure, hovering against the bricks in the mouth of the adjoining alley. He forced himself to relax. But not too much.

"Well, well... if it isn't my friend the Ghost."

"It's good to see you." The whisper again.

"I'd say the same, but I've never actually *seen* you."

"I apologize. Occupational habit."

"That makes you a leper, a ninja or Batman."

"I've been called worse."

Carson couldn't be sure, but he thought he detected a hint of amusement. "Yeah? Well, judging by how you saved my bacon with Kinkade a couple months back, I'm leaning towards Batman. Cleaning up the alley... I still owe you for that one."

"There's nothing owed. The debt was mine... ours... to repay."

"I know, I know. Pete."

A moment of silence. Of memories.

Carson tilted his head, squinting against the glare from the street lamp, trying to make out something of the shadowy figure. He couldn't. The placement was perfect. Whoever the Ghost was, he knew what he was doing.

"Glad to see you on the mend."

And he seemed to be well informed. Carson's hand drifted unconsciously to the scar that was a tombstone for his recently departed kidney. "Gracias. I see you've been keeping up on current events."

"Another occupational habit. I understand there was a corporation involved."

"As a matter of fact, there was."

"They can be complicated."

"And dangerous."

"That depends on their agenda."

Carson couldn't be sure, but he sensed Ghost was staring over his shoulder at the 24/7. "That's an interesting thing to say..."

"How is Kiki?"

The question caught Carson by surprise, and he wondered for a moment if it had been intentional. He put himself on guard. "She's okay. Had a rough patch, but she's through it."

There was an implied nod. "She's tough. Resilient."

"Uh-huh," Carson stared at the shadow, calculating. It was time for a surprise of his own. "She can also hold a grudge. She hates your guts, you know. It almost killed our friendship when I told her you and I had met."

Silence reigned. Carson wasn't sure the shadow was even still there. He took a hesitant step forward, peering into the black, but a furtive move assured him the Ghost hadn't slipped away. Yet. As usual, the movement was defensive, backwards.

"I apologize," the whisper sounded genuinely contrite. "It's been a long time. I wasn't sure how she would react to hearing from me."

"I wouldn't expect an invite to Christmas dinner."

Silence again.

"She's really why you're here, isn't she?" Carson pushed. "Why you've been helping me?"

Still more silence. This time, it spoke volumes.

"Thought so. You should know, I hate to play hard ball, but I watch out for my friends. And Kiki's one of my best."

"Then, we're on the same team," the voice was a little louder this time, just above a whisper and with a clear note of conviction. "I assure you, Carson, my intentions are only the best. We... I... care a great deal about her. Her safety, her happiness - they're of my utmost concern."

"Then, I'd stay away from her."

"Yes," the whisper held a note of melancholy. "Perhaps you're right. Perhaps she is better off this way. With you to keep an eye on her. Can I count on you to do that, Carson?"

Carson scratched his beard, pondering. He didn't know why, but he felt suddenly sorry for the man behind the whisper. Maybe it was the hint of genuine regret he heard in it. Or maybe it was because he knew what it felt like to be pushed away by Kiki. He broke out his crooked smile, shrugged. "You bet. I'm doing it anyway. Might as well get some cred for it."

A breeze blew through the alley, stirring a few odd scraps of paper. One of his mashed tin cans rolled, clattering softly.

"Good," the voice was back to its usual whisper, sounding relieved. "She'll need it."

Something about the words made Carson's short hairs prickle. "Need it? Are you saying she's in some kind of trouble?"

"It's hard to say." There was a pause, as if the voice was weighing, considering. "Las Calamas isn't safe. There are forces at work."

"Well, that's about as creepy as after hours at the clown convention," Carson's short hairs were now standing at full attention. "Any chance you could elaborate on that?"

"It's more intuition at this point. I'm still working on the intelligence."

Parts

Carson's thoughts flashed back to another night, another alley –
outside the Curio Shop. The thing had grabbed Kiki, not him. Not
Dex. He shivered. Chalking it up to the breeze, he pulled up his collar.
"Intelligence. Fine. Just let me know when you get some, will ya? If
I'm going to keep an eye on her, the more I know the better." He was
struck by sudden inspiration. "Listen, speaking of intelligence... as long
as I'm doing you a solid, maybe you can help me out with a little
something-something?"

"Intelligence is my business," the voice had taken on a curious tone
- professional. "Or at least... was. What do you need?"

"There's a little building across the street out front. The Curio
Shop. I'm interested in it. Can't seem to dig up anything, though, like it
just sort of appeared. I'd like to know where it came from. Who owns
it. What kind of plumbing it has. Anything."

"I'll see what I can do."

"Cool." Carson hesitated, weighing. There was another matter,
but after hearing Leet's reaction, he wasn't sure it was worth asking.
Still... the worst the Ghost could say was "no". "One more thing.
There's a painting. Hooded guy with a honkin' knife, virgin on an altar,
big heavy gold frame, like something you'd see on a velvet painting
from the 70's. Got a real *Rosemary's Baby* kind of feel. I think it's
connected somehow. Can't say why. You know - intuition."

"Got it," was the only whispered response. There was a soft slap,
like the closing of a leather notebook. "That all?"

"Yes. Er, no... how about we shake on it?" Carson leaned his bat
against the dumpster. "It's my personal policy not to make back alley
deals with shady figures my friends hate without shaking on it first. So,
let's cement this deal like honest gents – I'll keep an eye on Kiki; you
dig me up some intel. Deal?"

The shadow hesitated. Another cold breeze blew through the alley,
stirring boxes and sending another shiver up Carson's spine. He waited,
hand out.

Finally, the figure stirred. "Alright."

From the deep dark cloaking the mouth of the alley, a shadow
drifted. It was a man, somewhat small, but whether naturally or
because he was hunched, Carson couldn't tell. The stark glare of the
street light revealed a round, worn face, dusted with gray stubble and
marked by years of concentration. And hard, hard living. That much
was equally obvious from the threadbare brown wool overcoat, shabby
fingerless gloves and patchy trousers. Carson was struck by the

similarity to his old friend. One of Pete's kind for sure.

And yet...

There was something more. Something in the soft gray eyes. The round wire frame glasses. The set of the chin. There was a hint of self-control there, of fallen nobility, of importance, of a past. Something in the man's carriage that said things had not always been this way. He took Carson's hand in a soft grip, reluctantly.

"There," Carson did his best to sound reassuring. "Now I feel all better. So, seeing that we're officially in cahoots, what do I call you?"

Gray eyes studied him a moment, peering out from under the shadows of an old-fashioned cap that had seen better days. "Ghost will do." The man hunched his overcoat up around his ears, adjusted his glasses nervously. "Give me a couple of days. I'll be in touch." With that, he faded back into the shadows and was gone.

Carson stared after him for a moment then turned back to the store, wondering whether he'd ever see the strange little man again.

He did. Sooner than he thought.

The following evening, Carson and Kinkade were reviewing the week's receipts in the back office when a rattle and a clunk sounded from the back alley. Kinkade spared a look from his tablet. The noise repeated. He flicked eyes toward Carson. "See to that, will you? We can't have our cans abused."

"Not on my watch," Carson rolled out of his chair and trotted obediently for the back door. He swung into the alley, intent on chasing off whatever prowling animal or vagrant he encountered. But the alley was empty. And intact.

"Hello, Carson," a familiar whisper snagged his attention, drifting across the darkened alley.

Carson stepped out, drawing the door quickly closed. "Sorry, thought I saw a Ghost. Then, I realized I did."

"I've got something for you on the Curio Shop."

Carson felt his pulse jump. "Whoa – I've been wasting Yoo Hoo."

"I beg your pardon?"

"Never mind. Inner monologue. What did you find?"

There was a dramatic pause. "Nothing."

Carson frowned. "Nothing?! But I thought you said..."

"I did."

A spark of realization fired in Carson's brain. "Oho... so you mean 'nothing' as in the *something* kind of nothing, not as in the *nothing* kind of nothing."

"Exactly. There is no information on the Curio Shop at all. Anywhere. No public records, no property taxes, no business license, no mortgage, no permits. Nothing."

"That is something."

"In my experience, when someone goes to those lengths to make sure a place doesn't exist, the reasons it does are unpleasant." There was a new tone to the whisper. Ghost was engaged. "Tell me... what is your interest in the Curio Shop?"

"I like shrunken heads," Carson brushed off the query then forged ahead to make sure Ghost knew the topic was off limits. He still wasn't sure how much he trusted the man. "I also like paintings. The velvety kind. How about that front?"

"Nothing."

"Is that the *something* kind or the actual *nothing* kind?"

"It's too early to tell." There was a slight, thoughtful pause. "But it's enough to keep me interested. This kind of nothing might turn into something. We'll do a little more digging."

"'We'?"

"My associates and I."

"Great. Let's just not let the circle get too big. Let me know what you find." Carson realized with relish that Sister Becky was right. Prayer and patience *did* pave the way. "So I was thinking, sometimes I used to hook Pete up with a snack when he helped out. Not that I'm saying you need it or anything, but I know the man used to love a good Snickers bar or maybe a microwave burrito in a cup of hot water from time to time. Though with his digestion, I'm telling you, that was *not* a good idea."

"No. Thank you." There was an expectant pause.

"I sense a 'but'."

"Kiki...?" Ghost's voice trailed off suggestively.

"You... want me to give her a cup of hot water with a burrito in it? Oh... right!" Carson smacked his forehead. "Kiki! Right! Keeping tabs. I'll, um... take her out to dinner! Soon. Check up on her. Stealth mode. She'll never suspect a thing."

"Good. That's safest. One more thing: we need a signal, should you wish to contact me. The nature of our arrangement could lead to some uncertainties. It's important to maintain lines of communication."

"Got just the thing," Carson fished Pete's red bandana out of a pocket. "How about if I hang this from the back door light?"

"That should do," Ghost's inflection indicated that he recognized the bandana and found it appropriate. "When we see it, we'll be here. Count on it."

Carson smiled. It was good to have allies.

Heading back into the store, he almost ran smack into Kinkade. The manager's face was buried in his tablet as usual. If his attention wasn't wholly consumed with the device, Carson would have suspected him of eavesdropping.

"Ah, Carson. Our cans?"

"Safe and unabused."

Kinkade paused in his tapping and swiping and looked up from the screen, eying Carson critically. "Are you alright, young man?"

"Um... yeah. Great. Ready to roll." Carson felt slightly uncomfortable under the scrutiny. He tried to edge past Kinkade but was stopped by a Freezie display featuring Santa sucking down the newest holiday flavor, Pumpkin Sp-ICE Winter Blast.

Kinkade's eyes loomed behind his boxy TV glasses. "Are you certain? You seem tired."

"Well..." Carson didn't want to contradict him, and since he wasn't sure where the line of questioning was going, he decided to go with it. "I guess. A little. Just a late... er... morning. But it's nothing a slam of Sarge can't cure. I'll just grab one." He attempted to slip past.

"Nonsense. I can't have my Night Manager In Training running at partial efficiency. It sets a bad example. You've been working hard, Carson, you deserve a break. Take the rest of the night off."

Carson stood staring. He'd seen Kinkade keep people late but never – *never* – send them home early. He kept staring for a moment until he realized Kinkade was waiting for an answer.

"Gee. Well..." In truth, his mind wasn't exactly on work, and it would be the perfect time to check in on Kiki. Ghost's strange warning was starting to make him worry a little. He checked his watch. If he hurried, he could still catch her at school. "I guess I could use a little R&R. That is, if you're sure you don't..."

"Things will be fine here, Carson. Go. Get some rest."

"Roger that," Carson headed for the door before Kinkade could change his mind. "Guess I'm just lucky I've got a boss who watches out for his staff."

"That's why our motto is so important," Kinkade indicated the bronze plaque by his office door. "*Eterno Vigilis,* Carson. That's what keeps us strong." Kinkade was starting at him, brown eyes intent.

Carson knew the translation well: *Always Watching.* Until now, he'd always been annoyed by it. For once, he could see the promise. With a wave, he was out into the night.

Carson's sneakers scuffed as he shuffle-danced toward the bus stop. He found the idea of seeing Kiki appealed to him more than he thought it would. He also found the idea that Kinkade had apparently been replaced by an alien bothered him less than he thought it would. Life was good. Ahead, the crosstown bus was just pulling in to the stop. Carson broke into a run, only too happy to give legs to his euphoria.

When he arrived outside the Forensics class, it was still in session, so he bided his time drumming trash can lids and peering occasionally through the door's tiny window. The lecture hall was nearly full, everyone scribbling determinedly to keep up with Professor Looney's animated lecture. Carson picked out Kiki sitting in the front row, looking at least twice as studious as the others. Her red stocking cap remained motionless, locked in place as she wrote, eyes flicking between notebook and projector screen. Carson grinned.

The bell sounded, and students were stirring and packing and milling for the exit, and he was pushing his way into the room. He made his way to the front, catching up to Kiki just as she was stuffing her notebook into her pack. He plopped down into the chair beside her. "I missed most of the lecture; is it okay if I borrow your grade?"

Kiki looked up surprised. "Carson?! What are you doing here? Professor Looney hasn't found anything yet, if that's what..."

"*Nnnnn!*" he made the buzzer sound. "Not even close. Just so happens, I was in the neighborhood. You know what a sucker I am for nineteenth century architecture, so I'm cruising the campus and next thing I'm thinking, 'Hey, Kiki goes to school here – I should stop in and say hi.' So... hi."

"Hi," she finished stuffing her pack. "Actually, it's good that you're here. There's no news on the alley thing, but I did stumble across a little something that may be of interest to Dex. Any chance you brought him along?"

"Nope. Solo mission. Although, maybe I should have, given his sudden interest in college. Or at least, one particular set of college legs."

"He'd be particularly interested in them tonight. Specifically, what's holding onto them."

"What do you..." Carson turned, following her line of sight. "Whoa. Is that...? Yikes!" His eyes picked out the tall, attractive legs and dusky skin of Dex's romantic interest. Only this time, she wasn't alone. She was ruffling the hair of a miniature version of herself, six years old at most, currently squeezing her legs with unbridled affection. "Hm. That's Delilah. And I'm guessing that's Delilah's daughter."

"That complicates things."

"Absolutely. People who cling to your legs always make things complicated."

"What about people who cling to the rest of you?"

"They make things sweaty. Why do you ask?"

"Things just got sweaty," Kiki jerked her chin.

Carson looked back and watched as a tall, lean man with gray sandpaper hair and a comfortable tweed three piece suit embraced Delilah. *"Aye caramba,"* he breathed. "Complicated *and* sweaty. Still... things could be worse."

Then, the man released her and stepped back.

"They're worse," Kiki stared, jaw dropping. "That's Patch Parsons."

Carson watched numbly as his nemesis, Detective Patch Parsons, Las Calamas Homicide, picked up Delilah's daughter and swung her fondly through the air. "Great horny toads. Detective Parsons - the boyfriend of Dex's would-be girlfriend!"

"Actually," Kiki studied the scene. "I think it may be worse than that."

"Worse?! How could it be..."

As the little girl giggled and squeaked, they heard one distinct word float down to them through the hall:

"Grandpap!"

"He's her dad."

"Oh my. Gin-ger *Snap*," Carson stared for a moment then turned away, hiding his face as Parsons glanced casually about the room. "This isn't going to go well."

"It's been months. Do you suppose he still remembers you two?"

Carson made a face. "Between Dex and me, I'm his favorite. And he told me never to talk to him again unless I had a dead body in my trunk."

"You don't own a car."

"He knows."

"Definitely not going to go well." They watched as Parsons and his family disappeared through the door.

"Wow. Heavy," Carson heaved a huge sigh. "Only cure for this is felafel. Whaddaya say – you, me, the Taj Palace? Let's drown Dex's sorrows over a bite to eat and figure out the best way for you to tell him. My treat." Kiki stiffened. Snatching up her pack, she made for the door.

Carson thought she might not have heard. He hurried after. "Er... so... is that a..."

"What is it with you and handouts?" She sounded angry.

"I prefer to think of it as friendship. Look, I just thought you might..."

"Might *what*?" She *was* angry.

"...be hungry. That's all."

"That's twice this week. Do you think I can't take care of myself?!" Kiki was walking faster now, and Carson had to hustle to keep up.

"No, it's not that. I just thought we could, y'know, catch up. I like to eat; you like to eat - or based on your reactions, maybe not - but it's just an innocent..."

"No," her answer was flat and unfriendly.

Carson felt the air from his happy balloon leaking out. "Um... okay. Cool. At least let me walk you home."

"No!" Kiki rounded on him, her face horrified. "I mean, I got... things... to do!" She turned away without meeting his eyes. "Gotta split. Later." With that, she ducked through the door and disappeared.

Carson stood on the threshold of the empty lecture hall, listening to the dying echoes of her footsteps and wondering what in the world he'd said. He was replaying the conversation for the third time when a soft noise behind him in the hall caught his ear. He whirled, suddenly jumpy though he couldn't say why.

The hall was empty. The dark eye of the window, tall and ornate and sightless, stared back. But it was empty, too.

There was nothing

At least... nothing he could see.

Carson had the very distinct and sudden impression that *something,* however, could see him. Something just outside the glass. He leaned forward, peering closely, feeling his heart start to pound.

The buzz of his cell phone startled him.

"What?!" he answered a little more tersely than he had intended.

"Aww, cheer up, Charity," a familiar voice chided him. "Whatever's buggin' widdle Carson can't be that bad."

"Leet?"

"The one and only. Thought I'd throw you a bone. Seem to recall you needed something awhile back. I'm fresh out of Yoo-Hoo and got me a monster thirst worked up. So, chop chop – why don't you head on over with a case? I'll dig up that dirt for ya, and then I can get back to gankin' Nancy-boys. What was it, now... a Cheerio Shop...?"

Carson realized, with a sudden wicked delight, that he was going to enjoy this. "Forget it."

He heard a chair squeak on the other end. "Come again?"

"I said, 'forget it'. I don't need you."

"Geez, Charity, don't get your panties in a twist," there was a slightly needy tone to Leet's voice. "I had my game on, okay? Now, I'm taking a break. For you, man. You need the Leet; you got the Leet."

"That's just it. I *don't* need the Leet. I already got my intel."

"You already got...?"

"Yup. I've got another source."

"Another...?"

"One that doesn't expect handouts and doesn't blow me off for video games."

"Doesn't...?"

Carson pictured Leet's pinched face puckering. It made him happy. "Anyway, thanks for the call, but I won't be needing your services at this time. Or maybe ever. On the bright side, it looks like you've got plenty of time for ganking. Me, I'm gonna go have myself a bottle of Yoo Hoo. Nighty night."

Leet finally found his voice. "Another source?!" he spluttered. "We'll see about that!! Who the...!!"

Carson hung up. It felt good. Really good. He smiled as he stepped out into the empty, echoey shadows of the hallway. At least the night wasn't a total loss.

CHAPTER FIVE

House Call

Cheese dripped. A huge, orange, goober of unwholesome, affront-to-nature, artificial cheese. The glob lengthened, stretched, fat at the bottom, skinny on top, gravity sucking at it with irresistible hunger. The chip from which it was suspended was held motionless, unheeded, frozen in Dex's giant brown fingers. Dex ignored it, dazed eyes fastened dumbly on Carson's face.

Carson stared at the gooey blob, mesmerized. "Aw, dude... c'mon... the cheese, you gotta... it's gonna... dude... three seconds... maybe less..."

Overcome by sheer physics, the cheese pendulum broke loose and splatted on the glass counter.

"Aw, man..."

Dex was way past caring. "Did you say... Parsons is her *dad?*" He sounded numb.

"I believe I said 'Daddy', but you get the idea," Carson wiped up the cheese mess with a wet rag.

Dex sat back, looking like he'd just discovered his nachos were made from raw raccoon. He slid the tray away. "I ain't hungry."

"Cheer up, Officer Jackson," Carson gave his friend a consoling pat on the shoulder. "Parsons may think you're a lunatic, gun-toting homicidal danger boy... but at least his daughter is single."

Dex groaned and smothered his face with his hands.

It was Gang Night at the 24/7, a quiet Wednesday evening. The lowering sun shot its wan, fading rays through the empty store, glinting off the tinsel of an artificial tree decorated with Freezie cups and plastic hot dogs. Dex's misery was all the more poignant against the cheerful holiday scene.

"Her dad," he groaned again. "Her..." he glanced sidelong at a husband and wife with their small daughter, all making careful selections from the warmer. Desperately, he wrestled with his tongue. "Her... her..." Carson tapped his finger suggestively on Dex's chip tray. "Her... um... nacho chippin' dad," he finished lamely. "Thanks, Dud."

"He's actually a guest lecturer," Kiki twiddled the remains of a corn dog stick, most of her attention focused on the text book in her lap. "Came in last night to tell us how forensics operates in the real life cop world. A favor for his daughter. They must be close."

"Owie," Carson made a face. "Close does not bode well. Since, you know, that's where *you* want to be."

"For what it's worth," Kiki offered, "I think he's a good cop. I know you all don't see eye to eye, but he's smart. By the book, very dedicated."

"Maybe we could keep it on the down-lo," Dex suggested weakly. "Maybe he won't notice?"

"Not a chance," Kiki flipped a page, openly dismissive. "Parsons is a very devoted daddy and an even more devoted grandaddy."

"Grand*pap* is, I believe, the term they prefer," Carson offered helpfully.

"His wife is deceased and those two girls are everything to him. Plus, he's a detective. That's what he does. He detects. Trust me; he'll notice."

Dex groaned.

"Stiff upper lip, Mr. Jackson," Sister Becky beamed a pious smile at him as she dabbed her mouth daintily with a paper napkin. "Love has scaled steeper cliffs than these. 'The courting is worth the climb', as they say."

"Love never tried to climb over Patch Parsons," Carson dropped a handful of potato balls into her tray. They were angry red and had bits of meat poking out of them. "Here... try these Rudolph's Rockets. New Christmas stuff. They're cousins of the Cayenne Pepper Bacon-Tater

Cheese Slams, only hotter. Careful – they make more than your nose red."

"How delightful! Thank you, dear."

"Speaking of gastric distress - how are things with the Council?"

The nun's beaming dimmed as the lines of her aged face drew into a frown. "Alas, Mr. Dudley – the Council has tabled my request."

"Yowza, slippery slope! I thought you were making progress?"

She shrugged. "I admit I am at a loss. They gave no reason. Nor, indeed, are they compelled to. Still, tabled does not mean dismissed. I choose to view this as a temporary setback. My only recourse is to wait."

"Or goose 'em."

"I beg your pardon, Mr. Jackson?"

Dex was slouched back, staring off into space with a distant expression. "Goose 'em. You know... give 'em a little push."

"I am afraid I do not follow."

Dex's mind was clearly elsewhere. He gathered his gear, brushing crumbs from his blue polyester shirt. "Tell 'em you want that hearing. Remind 'em of some of the good you've done – with heat, if you gotta. Bring up the old days, tell 'em how you put the smack down on some nasty business, saved lives and whatnot. You've done good. They oughtta know about it. You looked the Warlord of Death in the eye and then stopped him killin' the whole city. That's gotta be worth something," Dex pushed his chair back and rose, strapping on his heavy laden gear belt.

Sister Becky stared at him, momentarily speechless.

"What?" The big man caught her look. "I just wouldn't take..." he glanced at the little family, now choosing Freezies. "...nacho cheese dip from a bunch of old dudes, that's all. Not if I knew I was right."

"Mr. Jackson," Sister Becky struggled to find words. "Thank you."

"Yeah. Whatever," Dex mumbled. "Gotta get my patrol on." He lumbered for the door.

Carson watched him go. "Who was that?"

"If prayer can move mountains, Mr. Dudley - and I assure you it can - then we may yet have a chance with our Mr. Jackson."

"Yeah, now if only..." Carson froze.

Kinkade had just entered the store.

He looked up from his tablet and halted. Brown eyes surveyed the scene critically: the feast, the obvious fraternizing with customers, the glaring absence of any real work.

Carson drew a breath to explain.

"Ah," Kinkade interrupted. His eyes had focused on Sister Becky's tray. "Rudolph's Rockets. Good thinking. Be sure to record their responses." He gave a curt nod then turned on his heel and was swallowed by his office.

The door closed with a thump.

Kiki whistled. "Forget Dex. Who was *that*?!"

Carson scratched his chin beard thoughtfully. "I'm still trying to figure it. Maybe, he's been replaced by an evil clone. Biological construct. Doppelganger, maybe. What's your take, Sister B.?"

Sister Becky's eyes had not left the office door. There was a stirring in their green depths. "My take, Mr. Dudley," she mused softly. "Is that our Mr. Kinkade is a very complicated man." She snapped a look at the potato ball in her hand. "And that these 'Rudolph's Rockets' could use more bacon. Otherwise, quite palatable." She popped the last bite into her mouth then slid gracefully off her stool. "Now, it is time I took my leave. I have decided to take Mr. Jackson's advice," she froze suddenly as a flash of *what-am-I-thinking?!* crossed her face. "Lord in Heaven," she muttered. "I am." She crossed herself then squared her skirts. "Tonight shall be a night of preparation and prayer. 'The horse is made ready for the day of battle, but victory rests with the Lord.' Proverbs 21:31. This goosing shall be a battle indeed, and I intend to be ready for it."

Carson watched her go. "The world has turned upside down."

"Mm?" Kiki looked up from her textbook.

"Well... most of it. Test coming up?"

"Midterm. Big one. I thought I'd hang out here for a bit and study, if you don't mind. My place is... noisy. That is, if you don't think..." she tilted her head toward the manager's office.

"Kinkade?" Carson scoffed. "I'm starting to think I could set fire to the store, and he would say 'thank you' and give me the rest of the day off. I wouldn't worry about him. But if you want quiet, you should kick it in the stock room."

Kiki gathered up her books. "Thanks. I, um... I owe you one."

Carson felt a tiny surge of elation. With all the strike-outs and weird vibes from Kiki lately, it was good to have something go right for a change.

It was several hours later when Carson knocked softly on the stock room door. Kiki glanced up from her studies, realizing with a start how time had flown. "Come in," she yawned, stretching.

The door opened. Carson stood there, an odd, faraway look on his face. "I just had the weirdest experience. Can we talk?"

"Oh... so... did Kinkade...?" she started hastily gathering books and papers. "Do you need me to...?"

"Hm? Oh, no," Carson waved her off. "He's long gone. Left an hour ago." He was staring at the cans of nacho cheese stacked against the back wall.

Kiki could tell that he wasn't seeing them. "You okay?"

Carson looked at her for the first time, and something in his expression sent a chill down her spine. "I'm not sure." He blinked, glanced over his shoulder into the store then back. "I just sold cat food and razor blades to a guy in a doctor's coat."

Kiki let the news sink. Slowly, she closed her textbook. "On any other week, I would let that pass. But today... I need details."

Carson glanced over his shoulder again unconsciously, collecting his thoughts. Behind him, the front windows stared back like giant, vacant eyes. It was dark outside. Nightmare dark.

"So, this... guy... came in a few minutes ago. Real weirdo."

"Define 'weirdo'. Carefully."

"Scrawny, sickly, kinda green looking, hunched a lot. Wore a lab coat, a pair of those old-timey goggles - very steam punk – and this... 'cap' I guess. A white skull cap." Carson's eyes were distant again. A tiny shudder went through him. "And, uh, he bought some stuff. Weird stuff."

"Cat food and razor blades, for example. Anything else?"

Carson checked a receipt he was holding. "D batteries, plastic garbage bags, neoprene gloves," he glanced up then back at the receipt. "And a jar of mayo."

Kiki watched him. His eyes roved absently, and he kept making strange small gestures with his hands, as if he were trying to process things. "Okay. I agree. That is weird."

"He smelled like formaldehyde," Carson shook his head disagreeably. "I, uh... I didn't like him."

"Bad hoodoo?"

"Made my stomach churn."

"Did he say anything?"

"That's weird too. He didn't say Jack. Not a word. No small talk, no hello, no answer to any questions. Just paid for his stuff and split."

"Did you get a name? Credit card, maybe?"

"He paid cash." Carson shuffled his feet and glanced at the nearby shelves. He was still not meeting her gaze.

Kiki leaned back, aimed keen blue eyes at him, arms crossed. "There's something you're not telling me."

Carson swallowed. After a moment, he tried to speak, then stopped. He took a second, swallowed, tried again. "His hat moved."

"It... moved?"

Carson nodded, a haunted look in his eyes. He made a circling motion around the side of his head. "Just... a little. Kinda bumped under there. Like something was... it moved." He looked unsettled. "I think he's a bad guy."

"A bad guy? Why?"

"Because he *looks* like a bad guy!" Finally, Carson's emotions stirred. He waved his hands in frustration. "If it's one thing I've learned during our past couple of train wrecks, it's that if someone *looks* like a bad guy, they usually *are* a bad guy!"

"Carson... you can't just..."

"Yes! Yes, I can! Vanessa: bad guy... er, girl," he started ticking them off on his fingers. "Fujika: bad guy. Warlord of Death: *big* time bad guy. Patch Parsons: bad guy. And... you know what else?" he paused dramatically. "I think Mr. Cat Food and Razor Blades is connected with what happened in the alley." There was an edge to his voice now. It was the beginnings of resolve. And it made Kiki uncomfortable.

"Okay, set the parking brake for a sec," she got up, feeling the need to move. "Weird is one thing but leaping to the startling and more than a little disturbing conclusion that this guy *somehow* had *something* to do with those..." she groped for words. "Whatever-they-were's back in the alley... where's your logic?!"

"First, they were handi-cats. Second... my logic?! Here's my logic! We get attacked by Frankenstein's felines, and then a guy in a *doctor's coat* buys *cat food and razor blades right across the street from where it happened!* Bam! Not to mention all that other stuff! I mean, what *normal* person dresses like a mad scientist and takes out a shopping list like *that* in the middle of the night?!"

"What shopping list?" Dex's voice floated back from the front door, chasing the fading echoes of the door chime.

"Good! Someone who will listen to reason!" Carson turned and swung out into the store. Kiki followed him, though reluctantly.

"That's why you sign my checks, Whitey. Listenin' to reason and whoopin' Ginger Snaps. Now, who needs which?"

"A guy came in here a few minutes ago, a real weirdo."

"Yeah?" Dex rumbled, leafing through the gun magazines by the front counter. "What did he look like?"

"That."

Everything stopped.

The door chime gave its sickly warble again. There, framed in the doorway and bathed in the faint orange and yellow glow of the 24/7 sign overhead, stood a strange, sickly figure. Thick black goggles highlighted dark pools of shadows beneath cadaverous cheekbones. The mouth was a small, horizontal slash lined by pale thin lips, barely visible. On a large, odd-shaped head that could only be described as egg-like was clamped a white surgical skull-cap.

The figure hesitated. It may have been watching them, or maybe not. The goggles made it impossible to tell.

Kiki cleared her throat pointedly, and Carson and Dex shook themselves from their frozen stares, turning to hastily made up activities. The sallow figure stood a moment longer. Then, it drifted into the aisles.

A few moments later, it approached the counter. The store was deathly quiet. One by one, a small selection of items appeared on the counter, carefully placed by hands made invisible by black neoprene gloves. Carson took his place by the Punisher mechanically, his eyes glued to the stark whiteness of the skull cap. One by one, he rang up each item and bagged it.

Needles and thread.

A few jars of baby food.

A cat toy.

The register *dinged* a subtotal. The strange figure held out a neat, orderly stack of bills. Carson licked his lips. He broke his gaze from the cap and looked the stranger directly in the goggles.

"Sorry... out of change. We take credit." The goggles held his gaze for a moment. Their smooth, shiny, black surfaces reflected nothing like the inky, impenetrable depths of space. Carson swallowed. "Or checks."

A moment crawled by. Silently, purposefully, the money disappeared into the lab coat. Out came a checkbook as black as the gloves. Pen scratched across paper. Rip. The check lay still and dead on the counter between them. Eyes back on the skull cap, Carson passed the bag slowly across. Without a word, the figure drifted out the front door.

Several seconds passed.

"Okay," Kiki broke the silence. Her voice sounded dry and raspy. She cleared her throat. "I'll admit, he does give off a certain vibe."

Dex snorted. "If weird was sparks, it'd be the Fourth of July. Nice move with the check, Dud. At least now, we got a name."

Numbly, Carson picked up the paper and pointed his eyes at it. Silence. His fingers began to clench and unclench unconsciously.

"Dud?" Dex peered closely at him. Carson hadn't moved, eyes riveted. "We got a name, right?"

Carson cleared his throat. "Um, yeah. Yeah. We did. We got a name."

"This ain't twenty questions, fool! Out with it."

Carson cleared his throat again. He spoke the words slowly and clearly. "Doctor... Julius... Deth."

"What?!" Kiki snatched the check. "No way..."

Carson rubbed his face, as if trying to massage reason back into his brain. "Dr. Deth. His *name* is *Dr. Deth...*"

Dex frowned at nothing and everything. "So we're leanin' more toward whoopin' Ginger Snaps?"

"*His name is Doctor Deth!*" Carson's volume rose noticeably. "What more do you need?!"

Dex shrugged. "Works for me."

"Now, hold on..." Kiki raised her hands placatingly, but Carson was having nothing to do with it.

"No. No way! No holding on, no waiting, no sitting on our thumbs until the freaky monster whatevers come and tear us a new one, not *this* time! This dude is a bad guy; I can *feel* it! He was behind the alley attack, he made those handi-cats, it was him! The Curio Shop, it... it... I dunno... attracted him, maybe. You heard Sister Becky – this can't just all be coincidence! He sent his critters after us that night, and now he's coming back in here, just like Vanessa did, just like Fujika did, waving it right under my nose - *right under my nose*!! He might as well have a big old fat name tag: 'Hello, My Name is Dr. Deth – I am a Bad Guy!' Man!! His name is Dr. Deth!!!"

Kiki pursed her lips. She was carefully studying the check. "It may not actually be 'Deth'. Look at the signature. It's a little sketchy." She traced it with her finger. "This capital 'D', for example, could be a 'B'. And this letter... it *may* be a 't', but it also looks like..." she turned the check on its side, "...it could be... an 'l' and a 'c' just written close together..."

Carson snatched the check, eyes flicking fiercely over it. "'Dr. Belch'?! Seriously?!" He flung the paper onto the counter. "Wake up, woman! Can't you *feel* it?! Carson Dudley's Weird-o-Meter is doing a big fat party dance right here in the middle of the room and this time... this time, I am not ignoring it! Not this time. I've made that mistake before, and people got killed. Bad." His eyes flicked toward the back and Josh's sign. "Not this time!"

Kiki's brow puckered. She was running out of objections. "So... what are we going to do about it?"

Carson bounced on the balls of his feet, pacing. "I don't know." He stopped suddenly. "No. I do know. We'll track him down. We'll figure out where he's holed up and poke our noses right into his wicked little scheme. Whatever it is."

"Shouldn't be too hard," Dex shrugged. "His address is on the check." He tapped the header on the little paper.

Carson stared at it, then up, then back. He squinted, reading. "*Hot Tamales! His address is on the check!*" His arms shot under the counter and came up with his bat. "It's like he's daring us to follow him!"

"In my experience, that's called a trap," Kiki frowned, hugging herself nervously.

Carson vaulted the counter and trotted for the front door. "Quick stop by Granny's to pick up the King, then. If it is a trap, I definitely want a shotgun in my hand. After that, we head for Deth's place."

"Wait!" Kiki took a step, then stopped, looking like she was caught in an undertow and trying to figure out whether to swim harder or just ride it out. "What about the store?! You can't just..."

"Yes. I can." Carson caught the OPEN sign in the front window with the corner of his bat and flipped it. "We're closed."

"But Kinkade..."

"He can fire me."

"Yes. Yes he *can*!"

"Hold up, fool," Dex butted in, his face registering a sudden realization. "He can fire *me*, too! What about that?! Think about the Big Man!"

"Sorry, dude. This is bigger than you. Bigger than all of us. Tag out if you want to - you too, Kiki. I'm not gonna force you to come. But we decided a few months back that a pretty serious nasty was on the loose in Las Calamas and that we were gonna do something about it. We were gonna be monster-whackers. I say a dude who stitches body parts onto cats and tries to kidnap girls at least qualifies for a look-see. What do you say?"

Dex stared hard at him. He fingered his badge, glanced around the store, then at Kiki. Finally, he sighed. "What the hey. Already been fired from here once anyway. Let's roll."

"What about you, kid?" Carson fixed a steely gaze on Kiki. "You gonna ride this runaway train?"

Kiki echoed Dex's sigh, shoulders slumping. She could tell there was no point arguing. "Might as well. If I can't stop it, at least I can try to keep it on the tracks."

It was a cramped and tense half hour before they located the address. Kiki rode shotgun in Dex's car, hunched over her GPS, quietly guiding Dex through dark, empty streets. That left Carson, as usual, in the back. Dex yanked the wheel to bring them into their destination and sent Carson's face into the side window.

"Ow! Watch it dude – precious cargo."

Dex grunted. "There's a baby on board all right. You wanna keep whinin', maybe you should get your own ride. Now that you got that big ol' salary rollin' in."

"Can't; it's all gone. Plastic surgeons and chiropractors."

"Whatever," Dex flicked off the lights. "We're here." They stared down a darkened, barren street, listening to the hum and occasional rattle of the little four cylinder engine. The car sat against the curb in the outskirts of the Shelley District, bordering on the sprawling Las Calamas suburbs. While much of the district was made up of old commercial buildings, apartments and duplexes, they had wandered into a section of warehouses, storage units and empty lots. Some held the remains of rundown buildings, while a few were empty pavement or bare, sun browned grass. It was across just such a lot that their destination squatted, brooding in the darkness. The building was long, low and took up the better part of a block. A flat roof and several rows of tall, age-blurred windows made it look ugly and unfriendly like a grinning, flat-topped skull.

"Long way from the 24/7," Dex rumbled softly. "Heckuva trip to pick up cat food."

"I don't like this," Kiki wormed down into her seat. "Dex is right. Why go all the way to Belfry? It doesn't make sense."

"What kinda of place is this, you figure?" Dex mused. "Old warehouse, maybe? Loading dock on the backside, there. Plenty of room for... whatever."

"Plenty of privacy, too," Carson wriggled painfully, trying for a better look. "For whatever."

"Whatever it is, it looks like someone's home," Kiki pointed at a dim glow leaking from a small window down low on the building's side, almost at ground level. She frowned. "Basement?"

"Only one way to find out. And coincidentally, it'll restore circulation to my legs. Let's get out and take a look." Carson clutched awkwardly for his seat belt, and after a brief struggle, they were standing side by side in the empty street. A faded newspaper skidded past them, driven by a cool offshore breeze. The breeze brought something else as well.

Kiki sniffed. "Is that...?"

Carson nodded. "Formaldehyde."

Nearby a board clattered, followed instantly by the sound of rapid scuttling as some night creature darted off into deeper cover. Dex scowled and shot a glance at the shifting, murky shadows in the vacant lot that lay between them and the building ahead. "I hear a 'meow', I start shootin'." One of the Wonder Twins, his pair of beefy semi-automatic pistols, hung loose in his right hand. "I'm just sayin'."

"Any word from Sister Becky?" Kiki huddled close to the car, sweeping the street cautiously with her eyes. She looked cold.

Carson shot a glance at his cell phone. "Nope," his reply was terse. "Nada."

"She won't be happy if we go without her."

"Then she should learn to check her voice mail." Carson felt a twinge of guilt, remembering his promise to the nun after their last misadventure. Ruthlessly, he squashed it. "Whoever's missing a hand may prefer that we put a stop to this little freakshow. Let's move." Carson led the way down the street.

Moments later, they reached the shadows of the warehouse and found refuge between two large smudgy windows. Carson had the momentary, unsettling sensation that they were vacant staring eyes. He checked the safety on the King and yanked his thoughts back into line. The low basement window with the glowing light was right beside them. After a steadying breath, he bent low and angled his head to peak in. Grime and age obscured much, but he could just make out a small room, lit by a single bare bulb.

There was movement.

Carson's heart leaped. Someone was inside. He squinted, peering hard. Or some-*thing.*

"Whaddaya see?" Dex hissed. He watched the shadows about them warily.

"Can't tell," Carson whispered back. "Too much crud on the glass. But someone's cooking mad science down there, I can feel it!"

"Or meth."

Carson ignored him. "We need to find a way in. Let's move."

After a brief search, they located a small side door. Kiki made short work of its rusty lock, and Dex led the way inside. A small, dark room greeted them, furnished with an ancient rusty time clock and a broken table in one corner that lurked like a spider with missing legs.

"Clear," the big man murmured.

Kiki switched on a small mag-light and played the beam over bare floorboards and peeling paint. It settled on another door. They moved on. The place was covered with thick layers of dust and littered with debris, and they made their way as silently as they could, wincing at every creaky board and squeaky hinge. It wasn't long before they found stairs. They stood silently, staring down the long, narrow wedge. At the bottom was a door. A closed door.

"Hold up..." Dex cocked his head. "What is that? I can't place it."

The three intruders stood silently, listening hard.

"It's the sound of weird. And it's calling us," Carson slipped forward, taking the steps faster than he should. Reaching the door, he put his ear to it. "Still faint... whatever it is. Whoa..." he frowned, sniffing. "Unlike the smell. That's more than just formaldehyde. Maybe it *is* a meth lab."

Kiki shook her head. "No. Not meth. More like science."

"If that's science, it's bad science." Carson hefted the King warily. "Very bad science." Gently, he tried the door handle. It turned with a soft creak. "Knock knock..." he whispered softly and poked his head inside. "Clear," he muttered, then slipped through. It was another small room with four doors opening off the sides like valves of a heart. Faint light shone under one of them. Carson headed straight for it without hesitation.

They made their way through more dark rooms, skirting around cracked furniture and various cast-offs from the warehouse's heyday. Much of the clutter had been pushed to the sides, and the dust was disturbed by the passage of many feet.

"Definitely got that lived in feel," Dex observed. "Somebody's making this home stank home."

Kiki lifted a quick warning finger to her lips, and her light went out. "We're about to find out who," she breathed. She pointed down a short hallway to an open door through which substantial light was showing. The clink of glass and a strange buzzing sound reached their ears.

"Let's go see if the Doctor is in." Carson wormed past Kiki and worked his way to the door, peeked around, then waved them on. Dropping to a crouch, he slipped inside. Kiki and Dex followed.

They found themselves in a cluttered room choked with overturned chairs and dusty desks. Panels from several old cubicles gave good cover. On the far wall, three large, dirty interior windows gave view into another office area. The light was streaming from there. They hunched forward, crouching, and peeked cautiously through the windows.

"Sweet Aunt Fanny's Salsa!" Carson breathed.

They had found Dr. Julius Deth.

His unmistakable figure was hunched over a thick slab of a table, working with slow, deliberate movements. Something was laid out before him, something partially covered with a stained drop cloth and obscured by smudges in the windows. Surrounding him in the room, piled on various tables, was a collection of the most eclectic, thought-provoking and occasionally frightening scientific and quasi-scientific equipment imaginable. Everything from the antiquated to the ultra modern was represented, from the arcing and sparking of Tesla coils to gleaming, surgically tempered steel centrifuges.

Even more disturbing were the parts.

An assortment of tables held an assortment of containers: beakers, Petri dishes, vials and jars of various sizes and shapes, all of which contained an assortment of organic matter. A few were recognizable: eyes, skin, fingers, what appeared to be a dog's paw. Others were not.

It was a surreal, mind-numbing, hair-raising scene.

"Call him what you want," Carson was first to find his voice. "But I'm sticking with 'bad guy'."

"We got us some backstreet, chop-shop, mad science goin' on here, no doubt," Dex tilted his head, trying to see around a particularly nasty splat on the window. "Wait! Is that...?" He swore softly.

As they stared, a scrawny, hairless, four-legged creature strolled languorously across the doctor's work bench. From the thing's side, attached with bloody stitches, protruded a human hand. It was slowly, softly caressing the head of the cat to which it was attached.

Kiki choked back a dry heave. Carson's jaw dropped. Dex

checked the chamber of his automatic to verify that it was cocked and ready to shoot.

The handi-cat sidled up to Dr. Deth, its human hand reaching for a jar and offering it to him. Deth reached out with a small utensil, took a scoop of white and slowly, deliberately, maneuvered it to his mouth. The tool came out clean.

Carson made a face, eying the jar with distaste. "Well," he whispered. "That explains the mayo."

Suddenly, the cat thing stopped, the hand on its side tightening around the jar. It turned, green eyes flicking about the room, darting over the window that concealed them.

Deth stiffened, his head snapping up.

"Down!" Kiki hissed.

Carson obeyed but held off a fraction of a second longer than the others, just long enough to see Deth toss the dirty sheet over whatever was on the slab. Then, Carson sank out of sight, holding his breath. Beside him in the dark, he could see the whites showing around Kiki's eyes, practically feel her heart hammering.

A minute passed. Nothing.

Dex poked him and motioned upward. Carson risked another peek. The room was empty.

"Clear," he breathed. "They're gone." He sank back against the wall, cradling the King protectively. "Sassafras! I thought a room full of zombies and a mystery pit from Hell was the weirdest thing I'd ever seen. Now, I'll have to update my Facebook."

"Good," Kiki nodded vigorously. "I know a Starbucks with good WiFi. You can post from there." She pointed herself for the door and started crawling.

"Wait!" Carson snagged the back of her jacket. "Not yet!"

"Why not?!" she hissed.

"I... I... I don't know. To be honest, I never really thought this part of the plan through!"

Dex released the safety on his weapon. "I did."

Carson looked at him. "Hold up there, Trigger Happy. Let's load our brains before we shoot our guns." He pondered a moment, frowning in the dark. "We gotta find out what he's up to. I say we sneak in there and take a peek under that sheet. I don't know about you, but to me, it had a real *'I can stitch a hand onto a cat, wonder what I can do to people?'* kind of feel. If we hurry, we can get in and out before he comes back. Let's move!" He rose to a crouch and hurried back out into the hall.

"This is crazy!" Kiki was on his heels, her flashlight once more slicing a line through the dark. "What if he catches us?!"

"Then, it'll save time," Dex looked extra grim in the semi-dark.

Carson padded softly down the hall. He reached a door and checked it. Locked. He tried another, found only an empty storeroom. "Gotta be this one," he muttered, heading for the last one in the hall.

Kiki flashed him a helpless look. "Okay, it's bad... it's weird, sick and twisted, yes, I'll give you that. I just watched a surgically altered hairless cat feed a grown man mayonnaise, and I'm likely never to sleep again, but you have to face facts – we still don't have any evidence that he's doing anything bad to *people*!"

"Then let's find it," Carson twisted the handle and pushed.

As he had predicted, the door opened onto the doctor's work room. Electrical coils hummed, and the smell of chemicals slapped over the trio. They stood for a moment, eyes locked on the doctor's work table. The *something* lay still and unmoving beneath its stained sheet. From this new vantage point, up close and personal, it showed a definite, unmistakable, undeniable humanoid shape.

"Ten to one that's not a cat."

Dex grunted agreement and waved his pistol toward the far side of the room, indicating an alcove that had been previously outside their field of view. In the gloomy shadows, they could now see what appeared to be an examination table, complete with leather shackles for wrists and ankles. On a chair beside it, lay a pile of rumpled, discarded clothing.

"That doesn't prove anything. Completely." Kiki's tone betrayed her. Even she wasn't buying it.

"Maybe not. But I know what will. Dex... cover me," Carson took a step toward the shrouded form. He paused, glanced back. "Close." In moments, he was beside the table, knuckles tight on the King. He reached out his hand, shotgun at the ready...

"*Carson!!*" Kiki's shrill shriek tore the room. Carson's eyes darted like lightning, caught a glimpse of a humanoid shape to his right. He fired, point-blank and blind. A *boom!* and flash lit up the room. Glass exploded and crashed and a wash of fluid splashed onto the floor.

Scrambling backward, Carson stood tense, ready to fire again, Dex like a sudden mountain behind him. Nothing moved. As panic faded, their senses focused on Carson's target. It was not, in fact, a person, but had once been a large glass tank, filled with greenish liquid and lurking in the shadows at the edge of the room. Now, it was shattered and emptied; its contents spilled onto the floor. It was those contents that had caused Carson to fire and that now held their eyes transfixed.

Before them on the floor, lay a pulpy mass of flesh. It was a mix of pinks and veiny blues and, although completely indistinguishable from any orderly form of life, it was disturbingly close to the size and shape of a human torso.

"Don't know about you," Carson sounded more than slightly sickened. "But I'm glad I didn't eat before we came."

"Sorry," Kiki looked pale. "I just saw the shape, and I thought... I thought it was..." she struggled, words failing her. "I don't know!"

"I don't know either," Dex nudged the mass with his boot. "But I'd say it just cost us the element of surprise," he shot Carson an accusatory glance. "Trigger Happy."

"Hm. Yeah. Little freaked out there," Carson glanced around worriedly. "Do you think anyone heard that?"

"It's a shotgun, Dud. Everyone heard it. And stop shouting."

"Sorry! Still trying to decide whether or not to puke."

"You got a bigger choice to make than that," Dex alone seemed cool and unaffected. "Somebody's on the way; you can be sure of that. It's time to call the play: throw down or evac. What's it gonna be?" He hefted his second gun dangerously and racked the slide. "You know my vote."

Carson stared at the torso on the floor, tense. "Yeah. Okay. That's one for throw down. Kiki, how about you?"

But she wasn't listening. From his elbow, she gave a startled gasp. Her attention had been snared by a pile of mussed and yellowed papers on a side table. The top sheet, annotated in red, contained what looked like anatomical drawings sketched in a sharp, clinical hand. She gazed at them, her face a mix of horror and fascination. "No... it can't be!"

Then, everyone's ears caught a sound that none of them wanted to hear:

"*Meeeeoow...*"

They looked. Across the room, atop a large brass cylinder wrapped in copper tubes, crouched a handi-cat. It's human hand rested on a light switch.

Dex swore.

His gun jerked up, and a split-second before he fired, the lights went out.

Boom, boom, boom!

Parts

Muzzle flashes lit up the room, bullets tore through walls and slammed through brass. Steam erupted, engulfing everyone with a wave of heat and wet. Instantly, the air turned slick and muggy.

There was a squeal and a crash.

"Kiki!" Carson shouted into the sudden, ear-ringing darkness. "Sound off! Are you...?!"

"I'm okay," her voice came weakly from the floor. "Just fell over... something." She gasped. "My light! I dropped it!"

"Crudlickers! Where...?!" Carson dove to the floor, and together they scrabbled, clutching and groping blindly and bashing into wooden legs and rusted metal pipe. Around them, blue electricity sparked and arced from the Tesla coils, casting weird shadows.

"Make it snappy!" Dex hollered. "I like to see what I'm shooting at, but I ain't picky!"

"Very dark... workin' on it!"

Kiki squealed. "That's my...!"

"Sorry...! How about this...?!" There was a sharp slap. "Ow! Well, at least you found my *face*!"

"Look over *there*...!"

"Where?! I can't see you pointing! Dark, remember?!"

"By the thing... the tank... it may have rolled..."

"Great, yeah, I'll just crawl around in the broken glass with the mass of yuck flesh and try to find the... oh MAN! Oh, that's gross... I think I touched it!"

Then, came another sound. This one stopped them dead and made their blood run cold.

A low, deep, throaty *grrrrrrowlllll* that rattled Petri dishes and made the glass vials on the counter shake. Whatever it was, it was inside the room.

Carson could feel every single hair on the back of his neck stand up. "Dex... that doesn't sound like a cat! Tell me you got eyes!"

"I'm on it!" The guard stood in the center of the room, every sense on full alert, slowly turning, pistols up and ready. "C'mon, sucka..." he muttered. "Show your ugly face..."

"Got it!" With a triumphant shout Kiki surged to her feet. A beam of light snapped on and stabbed out into the jumping shadows. It lit full on a snarling, savage muzzle. Or rather, two of them. The thing stood mere feet from Dex, corded muscles, patchy skin and a pair of brutish heads they could see clearly stitched onto a single canine body. The breeds were different, but the teeth were not: long, bared and ready to bite.

"Ginger *freakin' SNAPS!!*" Dex's gun swung around.

It wasn't in time. Claws scrabbled as the thing lunged, savage barks tearing from both throats and blowing hot saliva into the air. Dex dove to the side, guns booming but shots going wide. Kiki dove the opposite way, her beam swinging and dancing like a lightsaber in a Jedi duel. She struggled to stay clear and still give light to Dex.

"Dammit, woman!" Dex bellowed over the sound of tearing cloth and growling. "Hold it still! Hold it STILL!"

"Where are you?!" Carson lunged forward, then back, banging into something hard and metallic, shotgun swinging wildly. "I can't see...!"

Dex's guns boomed again, and something hot whipped by Carson's face, slamming into a beaker that exploded and showered him with chemicals. Instantly, his eyes were burning, and he swiped them desperately with his sleeve, gasping in pain. Over the noise, came a thumping and thrashing, which sounded a lot like someone bashing an automatic pistol into a dog. Then, behind him, a door opened with a *bang!* and more savage barks tore the room.

"Heads up!!"

Carson wheeled and fired blindly. He heard glass explode, then pumped and fired again, this time rewarded by a meaty *smack!* and an animal grunt. Barking stopped abruptly.

Carson gave a whoop of triumph. "Gotcha! Unless that was you, Dex... sassafras! Dex, was that you?! Kiki, get your light over there!"

Kiki's flashlight, more controlled, swept the room from where she now crouched atop a table. Carson's eyes still burned, his vision only slowly returning. He wiped them fiercely and chambered another shell. "Dex!"

The white beam swung past a hulking shape, then back, finally illuminating the security guard. The front of his uniform was torn and smeared, his nostrils flaring with rage and his breathing heavy. There was red on him. "Thanks," he gritted. It didn't sound like he meant it.

"Sorry!" Kiki sounded the same. "But, I feel it's important to note that I was gonna vote evac!"

"Forget it. We're in it now. And I don't think we're done yet..." Something crashed and Kiki's light swung, disorienting them and once more upsetting the scene. More fierce barking erupted, and Dex fired twice, shooting blind.

The back of Carson's neck tingled. Some instinct made him whirl at that precise moment, gun ready. He was standing beside the dirty windows through which they had first observed the doctor's lab. Through their smeared surface and his blurry vision, he looked directly into the gaunt, lurking features of Dr. Deth, now standing in the precise spot from which they had spied out his lab. Gleaming black goggles were fixed directly on him with just a thin pane of glass between them. In a blink, Deth was gone.

In that instant, Carson knew - this was the man who had tried to take Kiki. A hot surge of rage swelled up inside him. "It's Deth! I got him!"

The King roared, blasting out a window, and Carson dove headfirst through the remnants, feeling shards cut him but ignoring them in his sudden red anger. Rolling awkwardly to his feet, he tore down the hallway, around a corner, through a large empty room, into another hallway, then skidded to a halt. No one.

He listened hard and was rewarded by the sound of a door softly closing. Behind him. He dove back into the last room, eyes roving, found a narrow door in the shadows and kicked, aiming just above the knob. His sneaker crunched wood and the door flung wide. Carson plunged through without a second's pause.

A light sprung on, dim and flickering yet dazzling in contrast to the pure dark. It swung crazy shadows about the room, and before his eyes could adjust, his nose gave him a boost of information: the sudden, sickening stench of excrement. His dazzled eyes caught the blur of cages, a whole wall of them, and a sudden chattering filled the air, followed by a rippling burst of rustling and flapping.

Wings.

Lots of wings.

Carson took a step back, processing, blinking furiously, one hand shielding his eyes from the assault of the bulb. As they adjusted to the light, he picked out the figure of Deth, standing still as stone beside a door across the room. Beside him was the wall of cages, inside of which a mass of dark shapes roiled and churned madly. One of Deth's hands rested on a large, rusty lever. Carson had no trouble guessing what it did.

The muzzle of the King came up.

"Freeze!"

The switch fell. A rush of screeching, flapping shapes burst from the cages, surging toward him in a black cloud, knocking the single bulb swinging.

Carson pulled the trigger.

Click.

Empty.

He threw his hands up with a wordless shout as the cloud slammed into him, pelting and pressing and tearing at his arms and head and face. He could see hot red eyes, black feathers, could feel the press of hairy bodies as the wave pressed him back, swirling and biting and clawing cuts in his flesh. Dimly he could see shapes in the cloud. Crow's wings. Rat's bodies. His skin crawled from head to toe.

Then his anger returned, and his bat was out, and he was swinging.

Great swipes tore through the mass, smashing bodies out of the swirl of black and cleaving wide arcs of clear space. Feathers exploded. Bones crunched. The black crowd broke. Charging forward, Carson dove headfirst through the flock, still swinging furiously. He caught a glimpse of the far door, just starting to swing closed behind Deth. Head down, he hurtled into it, banged through, whirled and hooked it with a shoe, kicking it shut with a slam that caught several of the flying creatures in the jam. The door required several more kicks before it stayed shut.

Breathing hard, Carson fell back, realizing with a jolt that he was once more in complete darkness. He raised his bat, wiping blood grimly from his face. Deth was close. He could feel it.

"Let's DO this, Chinchilla!"

Then, something slammed into him with the force of a freight train, and he was flying. Bouncing off a wall, Carson heard cracking and hoped distantly it wasn't his bones. Then, he was on the floor, and something was on top of him, cold hands with the sinewy strength of pythons clutching and grasping for his throat.

Instinctively, he brought up a knee into what he hoped was a groin, but the assault didn't slacken. He drove upward again, desperate, letting panic and rage flood through him. This time there was a grunt. Carson threw a punch and a "Booyah!", feeling his fist crunch into cheekbone, trying his best to put his shoulder behind it. Since their last encounter, Dex had taught him how to punch. And how to make it hurt. He drove another shot and his knuckles smashed into bone and something squishy, possibly an eye. Another grunt. Then a growl. Something hard and bony drove into his gut and knocked the wind out of him, and he felt himself lifted bodily by a terrific strength and smashed down onto the floor, driving out what was left of his air.

Thankfully, Dex had taught him how to fall, too. Carson had relaxed instinctively and thrown his arms wide just before he hit. It was clumsy, but he found himself still conscious. More importantly, it brought his outstretched arm in contact with his bat, which he only now registered had flown from his hand. Galvanized, he seized it and swung. Faithful hard wood thudded satisfyingly into something meaty. Trusting to luck and rage, Carson swung again, furiously, and struck home. He felt his opponent flinch back. With breathing room now, he rolled to his feet, took a two handed grip and lashed out with all the blind, desperate strength he could muster. Wood cracked on bone once – twice - then a crash sounded and something fell, and something broke, and something splashed across the floor.

One of the somethings must have been electric, as fat white sparks popped and sizzled suddenly in the dark, filling Carson's eyes with dancing blobs of light. He staggered back, shielding himself with his arm. Then, his foot kicked the familiar shape of the King, and as he stooped with relief to retrieve it, a *whoosh!* and a rush of fire flared into life. Blue-green flames sprang up in a sheet, igniting a pool of chemicals and chasing their streams across the floor in waist high walls. In seconds, the room was engulfed.

Choking and panicked, Carson back peddled, reversed as a sheet of flame erupted in front of him, then leapt over another patch and came up hard against the door. Now with a way out, he spun to check the room before he made his escape.

His eyes locked first on Dr. Deth.

The gaunt figure stood silently, impassively, arms limp and still at his sides, trapped in a corner by the fierce and sudden flames. Flat, greenish features betrayed no emotion. No panic. No desperation. Cast in harsh shadows from the glow of the fire, they merely stared, cold and impassive. Black tinted goggles reflected the dancing flames as they pressed closer, moving inexorably toward him. There would be no escape.

Carson held the soulless, eyeless gaze for a moment as the smoke swirled and the flames rushed and crackled hungrily. As he did so, he caught a subtle, almost imperceptible nudge of movement. As if massaged from beneath by a slow, rolling, unseen force, a small section toward the top center of Deth's cap *moved.* Carson's skin crawled. Then, a wave of black smoke and heat washed across him, and Carson whirled and drove through the door and was gone.

CHAPTER SIX

Victory

"I'm calling them 'crats'. As in crow-rats. What do you think?" Carson held the restaurant door for Kiki.

"I think you're nuts. For naming them. It was a little creepy before, but now your obsession is starting to worry me. And keep your voice down."

Carson rolled on, unfazed. "As for our little doggy friends, I'm going with 'two-jo'. You know, like 'Cujo' but..."

"Yeah, got it. Two heads. Still very worried."

"Shh... this is us!" Carson hustled Kiki through the doors and into the foyer, eyes glued to a large flatscreen looming at them from the bar area. Kiki stood behind him, shaking the clinging remnants of a cold rain off of her thin canvas jacket. A news report spilled out over the humming, early evening crowd.

"...few details on the fire which consumed an abandoned warehouse located in South Central Shelley District. Authorities have not yet released the cause of the blaze..."

"I'm guessing it started when a band of brave local citizens confronted a crazed mad scientist who never had a doggie or kitty as a kid and decided to make his own – then it all went terribly wrong. Just spitballing here," Carson winked.

Kiki silenced him with a fierce look, glancing around nervously. Carson just grinned his crooked grin.

"...although arson has not been ruled out. Fire officials have also been tight-lipped about any fatalities caused by the blaze..."

"Probably because they're good and truly freaked out at the shish kebab they found in there. I mean, how the heck do you explain barbecued crats?!"

This time, Kiki's eyes flared in open anger, and an exasperated gasp escaped her. She ducked her head and crossed to the opposite side of the foyer.

"What?!" Carson threw up his hands innocently. "No one's even listening!" Someone from the bar glanced back at Carson, who smiled and waved.

Kiki stood fuming and exasperated, trying to look inconspicuous behind a cardboard cutout of a Chinese man dressed as a cowboy. The cutout sported a large combed mustache that made him more than faintly reminiscent of Burt Reynolds. In his hands, he held chopsticks and a bottle of BBQ sauce.

"What's *wrong* with you?!" Kiki hissed. "You could go to jail! *We* could go to jail!"

"If I didn't know better, I'd say you were worried about me."

"I just don't have a lot of friends."

"Not buying it, little lady," Carson sauntered toward her, doing his best over-the-top John Wayne. "Sounds to me like it's more than that."

Kiki pointed blue eyes at her shoes then up into his face. There was something strange in them. Something new. "Maybe it is."

Carson's gut, for reasons he couldn't say, gave a hitch. John Wayne fell away. "Oh?"

Kiki was still holding his gaze. "I've always thought of you as a brother."

Carson's gut unhitched, and he felt it fall into his sneakers. It was not the answer he had expected. Or hoped for, he suddenly realized.

She could see it in his face. "What? What did I...?"

"Nothing. No. Brother. That's... great."

"Really, Carson... I... I didn't..."

"No, no... no big. I just... don't think of you as a sister."

And there it was.

It was a simple statement, but at the same time, it was deeply, unavoidably and irrevocably complicated. Carson had known subconsciously, for some time now, at some level, that this was true, but it hadn't quite hit him as it did now. And it hit him. He stood rooted to the moment and to the floor as the gravity of what he'd said sunk in. He only hoped that Kiki would miss it.

Or maybe he didn't.

A few seconds ticked past. Then, her cool blue eyes widened. It wasn't *what* he had said, but *how* he had said it. Her jaw opened a little, and her cheeks went faintly white. Carson stared back. Together, their stares gave birth to a painfully awkward silence.

"Uhhh..." Carson started. But that was as far as he got.

"Wazzup, monster-whackers?!" Dex burst through the door, shaking water from his dreadlocks like a malamute, with Sister Becky in tow shielding herself with an umbrella, and the moment was swept away in a flurry of greetings and back-slapping. Carson, for one, was more than thankful and gladly left the awkward moment to die on the floor. For her part, Kiki said nothing. Absolutely nothing.

Minutes later, they were seated and absorbing the restaurant's eclectic ambiance. An odd mix of Asian artifacts and Texas-style décor, it looked as if a Chinese museum had exploded inside the Alamo. Tall, exquisitely painted oriental urns capped with longhorns stood in the shadow of lariats hung from dragon-headed sconces. Pictures of cowboys graced the walls alongside Chinese calendars and Buddhas, while one corner was taken up entirely by a statue of a golden bull being ridden by a traditional Chinese peasant wearing a ten gallon hat and biting into a rack of ribs. It was the same man from the cardboard cutout in the foyer.

"Texas Chang's Golden Bull BBQ," Dex shook his head quizzically. "Still having trouble gettin' my brain around it. You seen this guy's commercials? Burt Reynolds 'Texas' Chang? Who names their kid 'Burt Reynolds Chang'?! I thought we had laws in this country to prevent child abuse." Dex shook his great head. "The brother can't put enough English together to order a pizza, neither."

"But his BBQ is the best."

"Can't argue that," Dex turned to the menu with a hungry look.

"So why the switch?" Kiki glanced around. "I thought the Taj Palace was our victory place."

Carson forced himself not to analyze her tone. He pushed the memories of their exchange in the foyer away. Far, far away. Then, he shrugged. "Just felt like it was time for something new. Last night's victory was a little more upscale, so I thought I'd find an eat-house to match. You know... something new."

Kiki glanced at her menu. "There's new and then there's fu-ribs. '100% tofu – straight from Granny Chang's secret recipe'. I'm not sure I'm ready for that."

"Hey, I could have picked that new Norwegian Mediterranean place – what's it called - Norwenean Fusion? They serve those yummy lutefisk gyros."

"I think I've had enough 'fusion' lately. This is good."

"Oh, it's better than good, Little Sister," Dex leaned across and stuck his nose in her menu. "Just stay away from them fu-ribs. *Ribs* without *meat*?! It ain't right. Let ol' Dex pick somethin' out for you. Like this here... 'the Texas Change-Sauce Massacre'. Mmm... now that's a big boy plate..."

After a whirl of conversation and ordering, they slipped into a recap of the previous night. The talk continued long after their food was delivered, and Carson found himself continually shushed by his comrades. Although he realized his voice was carrying and even drawing stares, he found himself beyond caring – he was on too much of a victory high. He smiled at an elderly couple in the next booth, who were staring slack-jawed at him as he wound up his description of Dr. Deth's final moments.

"So, anyhoo... that was that. I just dodged my way past the crats and a three-jo, hooked up with you guys back in the lab and... well, you know the rest. Sayonara Dr. Franken-Weirdo." Carson shoveled another spoonful of sweet n' sour baked beans into his mouth and chewed happily. The elderly couple rose and left, napkins still tucked.

Kiki watched them go. She sighed and shook her head. "Not that I'm encouraging it, but I thought it was 'two-jo?'"

"It is. This one had three heads. Two on the front, one on the back."

"The *back*?" Kiki raised an eyebrow, her analytical wheels already turning. "How did it...?"

"Don't know, don't wanna know. As long as I'm not coming out that end, I don't see the point in even thinking about it. And, by the way, you are the only person *in the world* who would ask that."

Dex dug at a piece of rib meat lodged in his teeth, working at it casually with a toothpick. His plate was long since empty. "What a sicko. I didn't mind puttin' holes in his pets, but I'm glad we got rid of the Doc before the freak show got outta control. He woulda done humans before long. Dude got what he deserved."

"I think he was already there," Carson mused. "Whoever - whatever - jumped me in the lab, it wasn't Deth. Unless, he's on the Ultimate Mad Scientist Crossfit plan. This thing was like a brick outhouse."

Kiki cleared her throat, a small, nervous sound. "Yeah. You may be right..." she glanced around, looking unsettled. "Those pages I found, just before everything went Island of Dr. Moreau... they were diagrams. Blueprints, sort of." She suppressed a shiver. "Only they weren't for a machine."

Dex leaned back in the booth, his frown deepening. "I take it back. Dude *didn't* get what he deserved." He ground the toothpick meaningfully between strong white teeth.

"Perhaps not," Sister Becky, who had been largely silent for most of the meal, finally spoke up. "But it is sufficiently comforting to know that he will not be fostering any further abominations. We have one Creator already who seems to have things well in hand."

"So... you're not mad we didn't invite you?" Carson had been holding off on his formal apology pending the outrage from Sister Becky that he was sure was coming.

"Not at all, dear boy," the nun reached across the table to pat his hand. "As you recall, I am still under... shall we say 'quarantine'... by the Council. It was actually a mercy that you were unable to contact me. Any involvement in such undertakings would only hinder my efforts at securing a formal hearing." She smoothed her skirts. "At any rate, I appreciate your thorough recounting of the affair. Most intriguing. Especially your description of the corrupted beasts and this laboratory. I have encountered on several occasions those who would pervert God's Creation to their own nefarious ends. Attempts at this manner of construct usually end in utter failure or some pathetic creature mewling for its own destruction. The stitched nightmares in this case, however, seem to be on the order of something entirely different. By your accounts, they seemed fully functional."

"'Functional'?!" Dex pointed to a long, closed gash on his forearm. "I'll say they're functional. You're talking almost a whole bottle of Super Glue for these scrapes. I almost had to go to needle and thread. One of 'em bit me on my..."

"Yes, yes, Mr. Jackson. Your colorful retelling graces us all with its wit and splendor. However, I am more interested in the equipment you have described than the anatomical position of your injuries. It seems, by many measures, to be quite antiquated for constructs of this sophistication."

"There were a few newer machines," Kiki offered. "I've seen some like them in Professor Looney's lab even. But yeah... now that you mention it, there was a lot more old school than new school."

Sister Becky pursed her lips. "Crude methods, by and large, to produce such a remarkable result. And this vat... this shapeless mass of flesh..." her pursed lips shaped into a definite frown. "This concerns me deeply." The old nun folded hands inside her sleeves, suddenly deep in thought.

"That's not all. It seemed to me like he was..." Kiki's voice trailed off. Concern flickered in her blue eyes. "Controlling them, I guess. He never said a word, but it was like he was telling them what to do. Somehow. Handing him tools, switching off the lights. I mean, how weird is that?"

"Most interesting, my dear," one grey eyebrow twitched up. "Most interesting indeed."

"Oh, brother," Dex muttered, rolling his eyes. "Here it comes..."

"This would seem to smack of the supernatural."

"BOOM! There we have it," Dex scoffed. "You can't just chalk it up to mad science; can you, Old Goat?! Gotta roll everything into some freaky-deaky, ghosts and goblins spookfest! Supernatural," he snorted. "You're just jealous 'cuz our bullets beat your blessings."

Sister Becky dismissed his attitude with a sniff. "Science vs. supernatural is indeed the debate here, Mr. Jackson. Since I have studied both in depth, I feel I am more than qualified to pass judgment. As I am certain Ms. Masterson will agree, the science of genetic recombination is magnificently complicated, not to mention the daunting task of reanimating tissue. I would postulate that what you witnessed in Mr. Deth's laboratory is simply beyond the scope of modern science. If that is the case – and I assure you it is - what possibility do we have but to turn to supernatural causes?" She looked to Kiki for confirmation.

Kiki looked uncomfortable. "Well," she cleared her throat. "I'm not so sure. I mean, they're different. On the one hand, you're talking about science and on the other hand, faith."

"Different?" Sister Becky smiled good naturedly. "Science and faith? Nonsense, child! They are one and the same. Science simply means 'knowledge', and our Lord strongly encourages the pursuit of that. Therefore, science and faith are not only entwined but intimately so."

Kiki frowned. "How can you say they're the same? What about the origins of life, the Big Bang theory, evolution?"

"What about them, dear?" Sister Becky's face was placid. "I did not say they were in agreement, merely based on a similar process. Everyone is entitled to their own beliefs, even Mr. Darwin."

"Uh... 'beliefs'? Science has proved..."

"Much. Yes. But it has left even greater amounts unproven. As an intelligent, educated young woman, you must certainly have studied the topics you just cited? What of their glaring discrepancies: inconsistencies in dating methods, the contradictions of entropy and the nagging little problem of irreducible complexity, to name but a few?"

"Granted, there are still some issues to work out. But I prefer to do that with things I can measure. Things I can see. And touch."

"Such as Mr. Darwin's missing links? Have *they* been measured, seen, touched? I need not remind you, my dear, that they are still *missing*. The evidence is simply not there. What is it, then, that holds you to these conclusions?"

"Well," Kiki hesitated. "I guess I just have faith."

"Precisely."

"Hm. That didn't turn out at all as I expected."

Sister Becky patted her hand kindly. "Not to worry, Ms. Masterson. Not all scientists subscribe to all theories."

"Not all atheists do either," Dex interjected. "The Big Bang," he snorted. "*Something* from *nothing*? Just a poof and a puff and a whoop there it is?! Easier for me to believe in some big dude with a white beard rolling snakes outta cosmic playdough than that fairy tale."

A mix of surprise and distaste struggled for control of Sister Becky's features. "I am impressed, Mr. Jackson. With the exception of you characterizing the Almighty as 'a Big Dude', I believe we are, for once, in agreement."

"%^&*#@! straight."

"And now, you have ruined it."

"Good. Every time you and I agree, Atilla, it makes my shorts itch," Dex gave a hearty scratch at his unmentionables.

"Thank you, Captain Crude," Carson rolled his eyes. "Look, at this point, the bottom line is: *who cares*?! We won! Natural, supernatural or *au-naturel*, we put it in the ground. If it's one thing Dr. Deth learned about science, it's never bring a two-headed dog to a gun fight. That's what I call survival of the fittest."

"Straight up, Brother," Dex nodded his agreement. "That's one big bang I can get behind - the kind that comes from a .45."

"Alright then," Carson lolled back in the booth. "Back to business. With Deth out of the way, we can focus on finding out what's *really* going on in Las Calamas. The way I see it, we're onto something. Something big. It's time we go at it hard. We've got two angles to work: the Curio Shop and this Herron chick – or possibly 'this Herron vampire chick'. Both very scary."

Kiki quirked an eyebrow. "Hadn't we pretty much tapped out our leads on those?"

"Yes. Yes, we had," Carson looked at her smugly, fingering Pete's red bandana. "That's why I got some new leads."

Kiki stared at him for a moment. Then, she shrugged. "Suits me. As long as your plan doesn't involve me going on a monster hunt during finals week. I need my study time."

Dex grunted in agreement. "Or me missin' work. Kinkade let us off easy after last night – though I'm still scratching my big shaggy black..."

"Head," Carson offered.

"... about why."

"Whoa," Kiki gawked. "So, you're saying you still *have* a job? You walked out last night and closed the store, a store that *never* closes! You abandoned your post!"

Carson made a dismissive wave. "It's no big. I gave Kinkade a ring earlier and told him I had to close early - personal thing. He said no prob, I could fill him in later."

"No prob?! Ross Kinkade?!" Kiki gaped. "Does this smell fishy to anyone but me?"

"Oh, it do, sister," Dex rumbled heartily. "But as a direct beneficiary of his brain damage, I am asking exactly *no* questions." He folded his great arms across his chest resolutely.

"Okay," Kiki narrowed her eyes at Carson. The wheels were turning. "How about this - don't you think it's a little curious that every time Kinkade looks the other way and gives you some leash, someone gets hurt? Or..." she lowered her voice, glancing around. "Worse?"

"Aw, c'mon," Carson stretched lazily. "You worry too much. It's just the ol' Dudley charm finally kicking in. Kinky's warmed up to me is all. It was just a matter of time."

"Sister B.?" Kiki glanced at the nun for support. "Anything?"

Sister Becky merely shrugged. Her eyes, though, were thoughtful.

"See? Nothing on the official nun-o-meter. And that's good enough for me. Now, let's roll. I got places to be," he rose to his feet and snatched up the check.

Kiki reached quickly for her wallet, but Carson headed her off. "And dinner is on me," he said nonchalantly and to no one in particular. "You guys rock." He watched her from the corner of his eye and saw her struggling. In the end, she said nothing, just pulled her hand back reluctantly. Carson breathed an inward sigh of relief and led the way to the front counter.

As he stood waiting for his turn, Sister Becky spoke up idly from his elbow. "Oh, Mr. Dudley... one last item before we put this matter entirely to rest. What of your Vision? You were developing a theory of sorts, as I recall. Does this latest incident measure up? Any connections?"

"Nope, not a bit," Carson signed his receipt, shrugging. "Guess it was nothing." As they turned to go, he paused, reaching into his back pocket. He drew out the rumpled, well read folds of paper that held the record of his Vision. For a moment, he studied them, felt their weight in his hand. The hours he had spent pondering those words... then, he shook himself. "Must have been gibberish after all," he crumpled the paper and tossed it into a garbage can. "So much for visions."

Sister Becky's gaze lingered on the can, but she said nothing.

Carson and Dex rode back to the 24/7 together and were soon deep into their shifts. Dex made frequent pop-ins to escape the cold drizzle that continued to fall, but although it dampened his uniform, it didn't seem to dampen his mood. He was just heading back outside from just such a visit, whistling an Elvis song, when Kinkade arrived. Night had fallen, and the rain had turned practically icy. The guard watched surreptitiously from the shelter of the gas pumps while Kinkade and Carson chatted. After a few minutes, Kinkade walked his severely tailored suit into his office, then back out, and with a final wave at Carson, left the store. Slipping into a shiny, new, black BMW, Kinkade drove away.

Dex made his way inside. Carson glanced up, leaning comfortably against the nacho warmer. "Dex! You look thirsty. Freezie?" Carson snagged a cup and started pouring himself a drink.

"Uh-uh," Dex shook his head. "I'm still fat."

"Calories don't count when you're celebrating. Perhaps, I can tempt you with one of these treats nature never intended: direct from Sweetie Pies, it's their brand new offering... Tweeners!" Carson snatched a brightly wrapped cellophane package from an end cap and tossed it to Dex. "As in 'in-betweeners'... it's a cross between a candy bar and a piece of chocolate cake."

Dex frowned at the moist, weighty package. "More like a cross between a heart attack and stage one diabetes. Pass." He tossed it back. "But I will take a dose of whatever crazy you just sold to Kinky," Dex shook his head admiringly. "You got a gift."

Carson popped a multi-colored spoon straw through the lid of his drink and took a long pull. "Yeah... ow... just a sec... Freezie burn... ow... there it is. Ahh... better. Kinkade's cool. We have an understanding."

"An understanding that you can walk off the job whenever you Freezie well feel like it, and he'll just say 'okay' like the world's best dressed dumb guy?"

"Nice. With the Freezie thing. It really makes you a lot less terrifying to the customers. And, yeah, something like that. Ow." Carson rubbed his forehead vigorously. "Still a little... ow."

"I gotta get a new boss. Rodney would be shooting pink slips out his..."

"Nose," Carson offered, still rubbing his forehead.

"...about now." Dex sighed and shook his head. "If I hadn't seen it, I wouldn't have believed it. Dude's glasses must be too tight."

"You wanna see another eye-popper, stick around," Carson's eyes twinkled mischievously. "I'm just getting started. Oh, and stick this on the front door, will ya? I got some things to do out back."

Dex glanced at the paper Carson had handed him. His brows furrowed. "What makes you think...?"

A soft tap sounded at the back door, cutting him off.

"Just call it intuition," Carson grinned, trotting for the back door. He swung out into the alley, jerking up the hood on his sweatshirt. The rain had mostly slackened, but a few fat wet drops insisted on trying to paint the bricks. Under their cover, a shadowy figure detached itself from the safety of a dumpster and stepped close to the pool of lamplight. Not too close but close enough.

"I saw your signal," came a whisper. "What's up?"

Carson reached up to retrieve Pete's bandana from where it hung beside the door. "Hey, Ghost. Thanks for dropping by. For starters, Kiki's doing good. I'd say she says 'hi', but I'm pretty sure if I even mention I've been talking to you, she'd kick me in the crotch and never speak to me again."

"That's fair. But she's well? You're keeping close?"

"Yeah," Carson felt a strange flutter when he thought about his last few meetings with Kiki. "Mostly. She's got a lot of pressure from school, I guess. Always got her face in a book. But that's our Kiki."

Ghost nodded, a faint stirring in the gray night.

"I wanted to thank you for the intel last time, too. It was... helpful."

Another faint nod. "I saw the news. The fire?"

"I can neither confirm nor deny that it was us. But it was us."

"'Us.' Kiki was there?"

Carson couldn't tell whether the tone had changed. It sounded neutral and controlled. Analytical. But the air felt different. "She's fine. Just fine," he assured the voice. As casually as possible, he checked his watch. "So, anything else for me? Specifically regarding a particular curio shop? Or a really unfortunate and tasteless painting? I don't suppose anything's turned up?"

"I have feelers out. But there's not much to go on. Anything else you can give me would help."

Carson pretended to ponder. "Hm. Yeah. Let's see... well, not really on that front," he glanced at his watch again, trying not to make it look obvious. It wouldn't be long now. "But now that you mention it, there is another matter – closely related. A girl."

"Person of interest?"

"Um-hm. You could say that."

"What's her name?"

"Herron. Kim Herron. You might hear that she disappeared a few months back, but don't believe everything you read on 'missing' posters. I'd like to know where she is."

"And in return?"

"I'm taking Kiki out tonight. Right after work. Big time on the ol' town. Lots of keeping tabs on her."

"Good. Don't let me keep you. I'll see what I can turn up," the shadow started to fade back.

"Uh, yeah," Carson checked his watch again. "By the way, she likes Tic-Tacs, this Herron girl. And... um..." he made a show of thinking. "Coffee. Espresso. Don't know if that will help. Every little bit, right?"

"Sure," Ghost paused. "Are you alright?"

"Me? Oh, yeah, sure. Dope on a rope. Just happy to be working together, happy with our agreement. Say, let's shake on it. Again." Carson stepped forward, hand out. "I really, really, *really,* really appreciate this. Helping Kiki tremendously. You don't know how much. Can we shake? Just to say thanks."

The Ghost hesitated. Then, as before, the short, unassuming, balding man in the tattered long coat stepped forward. Their hands met.

Behind Carson, the door to the store swung wide. Carson relaxed. It was about time.

"Alright, Charity, the answer man is..." Leet froze, the note Carson had asked Dex to tape to the front door crumpled in his fist. He stared at the two conspirators. His eyes flared wide then narrowed sharply. "Oho. What have we here?"

Carson smothered a grin. He couldn't have planned it any better. "Just concluding a little business."

Beside him, Ghost flinched, jerking his hand back as if it had been caught in the cookie jar. He shuffled a step toward the shadows, edgy, but mastered himself with an effort and stood his ground.

Leet marched down the steps into the alley and straight up to the other man. He peered directly into his eyes. "What kind of *business*?"

"Information. Not the kind you find in the Yellow Pages," Carson said pointedly. Leet stalked around the older man, sizing him up and making no attempt to hide his oozing disapproval. For his part, Ghost remained calm, his gray eyes flicking about at his shoes, at the rain-spattered brick walls, the dumpster... and surreptitiously measuring every inch of Leet as well.

"From the looks of it, it's the kind of information you can't find on the Internet either," Leet sneered. "Or any other kind of technology."

"It's the kind you find by pounding the pavement. Takes a long time. It's inefficient. Outdated. Slow."

Ghost's eyes stopped roving. They settled on Leet's. "Sometimes slower is better."

"It's still slower."

"But more reliable. Leg work is worth it."

"Brain work beats leg work."

"Depends on the brain."

Leet's look turned acidic. He drew a breath, but Carson stepped in. "Well, nice to see you two hitting it off, but I've got a shift to get back to, and I'm sure we all have better things to do than get wet," he shot an apologetic look at Ghost. "It makes some people cranky."

Ghost flicked his eyes at Carson then back at Leet. With a slight nod and no further word, he was gone.

Leet, however, was going nowhere. "So," he fumed. "This is the guy?! This little... trenchcoat-in-the-alley, slower-is-better, spy novel reject?! What's he digging up for you? Hunh?! The Curio Shop? Is that it?! The painting? This... this... Herring lady?"

"Herron."

"You want intel?! I'll get you intel! I'll get you intel like you never had intel! 'Depends on the brain...!' Oh, I'll show you a brain, Columbo! You want to see a brain...?!" Leet stomped off, trailing obscenities, his face darker and stormier than the sky.

Carson waited a moment, whistling happily. When he was sure Leet had made his exit, he ducked back into the store.

Dex was at the front counter, looking angry. "That little squid told me to move. I don't think he realizes what I could do to him with just this finger," Dex held up a fat pinky.

"Give the guy a break. He just got schooled," Carson retrieved his Freezie and fished around the bottom of the cup with his straw, sucking up dregs. "Mmm... that's good. That, my friend, is a satisfying taste." He smacked his lips. "Yummy."

Dex cocked his head and regarded his friend. "You played the squid. And your other snitch."

"Some day you'll make a great detective," Carson winked at him. "And 'played' is such a negative term. I look at it as motivation. Leet was slacking. I gave him a reason to be invested."

"You gave him a reason to be pissed off."

"Like I said... 'motivation'."

"And this 'Ghost' dude... how'd he take it?"

"He seemed motivated too. One way or another, I'm expecting big results."

"If they don't find out you're using 'em."

Carson laughed. "Yeah. We'll see."

Dex frowned at him. "You been hanging out too much with the corporates." Then, he shrugged. "But that's your mess."

"Oh, hey... you gonna be home tomorrow? I need to drop by for a sec."

Dex eyed him shrewdly. "Why? You wanna motivate me too?"

"Can't tell," Carson made his eyebrows dance. "It's a secret. Big day tomorrow, lots cooking."

Dex shrugged again. "Sure, I guess. And, uh... speakin' of

secrets," he hesitated, glancing around the store. It was empty. He shifted his big feet, suddenly and uncharacteristically nervous. "Listen, uh... I got one too. Been bustin' to tell somebody," Dex glanced around again. He was fiddling with his handcuffs now. Jangling filled the store.

Carson waited. And waited. And waited. "Not getting any younger..."

Dex cleared his throat. "Right. Well, you see... I, uh... I got me a date."

"By Grabthar's Hammer! The Big Man is on the move! And since the only women you're on speaking terms with are Kiki, Sister Becky and Parson's daughter, my money is on Delilah." Carson whistled as the thought sunk in. "Parsons. Yipes. Kind of a good news-bad news thing there."

Dex snorted. "What's he gonna do, arrest me?" he adopted a dismissive air, but it was not as confident as it should have been.

"Yes. Yes, I believe he will."

Dex looked slightly unsettled. He opened his mouth, closed it. A few moments later, he was paying for a box of Twinkies. When he clocked out at the end of his shift, he still hadn't said a word.

That night, Carson could hardly sleep and woke up early. He had, as he'd told Dex, a busy day and was spoiling to start. It was early afternoon when he stopped by Dex's apartment. Trotting down the cracked walk that spanned a brown, withered lawn, he pressed the door bell on Dex's ground floor apartment. There was some thumping and rustling that sounded like a large man struggling out of bed. The door jerked open.

"Morning, sunshine!" Carson greeted him with a clap on the shoulder.

"Afternoon to some. And don't touch me before 5pm."

"Fair enough. I'd hate to *drive* you crazy. 'Cuz, you know, *driving* is something I could do. On my own. Now." Carson dangled a set of keys from a Captain America keychain.

"Are those...?" Dex squinted through the screen door. "Did you...?!" He swore heartily. "Brotha's got a ride! Let's see it!" He barged out the door, tugging a threadbare robe around himself.

Carson beat him to the curb by a hair. "Behold," he announced, with a magnanimous sweep of his arm. "Wheels!"

There, pulled up crookedly to the curb, was a small, late-model pickup truck of unclear age and color. It looked like it had once been blue.

"I do see wheels. But the rest is rust and dents. You say there's a car nearby?"

"It needs a little paint. C'mon!" Carson jumped in with childlike enthusiasm. He reached across and tugged on the passenger door handle. It wouldn't open. "Hold on..." he lifted his leg and gave the door a hearty kick. With an angry creak, it banged open. Carson was already prattling. "You said to get my own ride. And while I'm sure it was an insult, it was also great advice. I figured, why not?! After all, night manager, right?! Just picked her up this morning!"

Dex made no move to enter. He just stood on the curb looking dubious. "How many miles?"

"Not sure, actually. The... mileage thingy... um..."

"Odometer."

"Yeah, that. It doesn't exactly *work*."

Dex squinted through the windows, eying a thick orange carpet that coated the dash. "What's with the shag?"

"Previous owner. I dunno. Maybe they liked to take their shoes off when they drove."

"And put 'em on the dash?"

"Or in the bed," Carson jerked a thumb over his shoulder. Dex peered into the back which was also coated with orange carpet. "I like it. Gives my ride a homey feel."

"Ride?! That ain't no 'ride', Bro... it's a magic carpet."

"Magic Carpet it is, then," Carson rubbed a hand affectionately across the furry dash. "What do you say – want to fly it around?"

Dex stepped back and folded his giant arms. "No. No, I do not. I got shoes bigger than that, and they *still* hurt my feet."

"Aw, c'mon. Think of it as a challenge..."

It took some doing to both convince Dex and to wedge him into the passenger seat. After a quick tour around the block, they returned. When the guard had pried himself out again, Carson noted with more than a small degree of satisfaction that he was rubbing his lower back.

"It's small. I'll give it that."

"Small but magical. By the way, I'll drive."

"Where?"

"Anywhere. I just wanted to say it."

"Whatever saves me gas money," Dex gave a great stretch of his back, straining his robe alarmingly. "This was your big secret, hunh?"

"One of them," Carson winked several times, alternating eyes.

"Got one more to go. If you think this one is big... tallyho!" He hit the gas, and the truck stuttered, shuddered and nearly died. It gave a great lurch forward then stopped, the engine settling into a nervous, irregular thrum. Carson waved as he drove off into traffic, narrowly avoiding an oncoming SUV.

Making his way through busy afternoon streets, he had just crossed into Belfry's bustling commercial district when his phone rang. He answered without thinking. "Carson here. I'm driving!"

"Hello, Carson," came an almost familiar voice. "It's Professor Looney from Las Calamas Community College."

"Oh, right! Kiki's prof. What a coincidence, I was just on my way to see... yikes!" Horns blared as Carson, distracted, drifted into the oncoming lane. "Hold it a sec!" Juggling the phone, he jerked the little truck awkwardly into a parking lot where it sputtered, lurched and died. "Wow. Not as easy as it looks. Sorry about that."

"Uh..." the professor sounded cautious. "Is this a bad time?"

"Almost. But we can all walk away. What's on your mind?"

"Your cat, actually. I got a few more results back I wanted to share."

"My... oh! Right! My cat. Yes, I remember now my cat. Fuzzy. Fluffy. Or whatever."

"Yes," Professor Looney didn't seem to notice Carson's fumbling or, if he did, seemed not to care. He sounded excited. "As I said before, I was intrigued by some of the initial test results. Although, 'intrigued' probably isn't the right word. More like freaked out."

Carson checked his watch, wishing the man would get to the point. "Uh-huh. Cool. And?"

"I found something. Something... well, frankly, I'm not sure what it is."

"Mm-hm." Carson tapped the dash impatiently. The carpet was scratchy. "Say, Professor, I'm kind of in a hurry. Could you..."

"Oh, of course. What I really wanted to know was... look, I know how silly this is going to sound, so I'll just throw it out there. Um... did your cat ever have a... well... a transplant?"

"Pardon?"

"A transplant. As in organ transplant," the professor's voice sounded cautious. "Kidney, maybe?"

"I... I'm pretty sure that's a no. I mean, I loved Flinky and all, but not that much."

"You're sure?"

"I'm pretty sure I would have noticed."

"Mm."

There was a short pause. Gradually, it started to lengthen. Carson fidgeted, checked his watch again. He could tell he would have to play along if he was ever to get on the road again. "Why do you ask?"

"Well, it's the strangest thing," Looney pounced on the question. Papers rustled, and Carson could picture him poring eagerly over scientific looking notes. "Probably a lab mistake or something, it happens. But anyway, I ran some tests on the blood sample you left me, and I found trace elements of Imuran. It's a drug that's commonly used for preventing organ rejection during transplants. So, I thought maybe..."

"Nope, sorry. No replacement parts as far as I know. Maybe an extra or two," he amended, "but that doesn't matter anymore. Listen, I should tell you; I got a new cat. I'm moving on. I think it's best if we all do."

"Oh," Looney's voice sounded disappointed. "I see. That's too bad. You see, there were a couple of other things that..."

"Well, I'd love to chat, doc, but Fuzzy 2 is out of cream, and I really should go. Thanks for poking around! Teach hard! Yay science!" Carson hung up.

After a few tries, he got the truck started, ground it into first and steered into traffic, eager to make up for lost time. Before long, he was nosing the Magic Carpet into the curb in front of a quaint, comfortably antiquated storefront. The front tire rubbed with a painful squeal as he came to a halt, but it was smoother than last time, Carson noted happily. Above him hung a faded sign depicting a man in coveralls with his arm around a computer monitor wearing bright red lipstick. Underneath it read: "Lucky Earl's Electronics Boutique".

A familiar figure in a red stocking cap was just stepping out the front door, arms full of bulky electronics. Her face looked tired.

Carson tapped his horn, and Kiki started, almost dropping her load. She glanced about for a moment. Then her eyes settled on Carson. And the truck. She frowned. "What is that?"

"That, little lady..." Carson brushed his hand back and forth luxuriously on the orange dashboard. "...is freedom! Also known as the Magic Carpet. I was gonna go with wall to wall, but the sales guy said all the cool kids were just doing the dash. And the bed."

Kiki stared a moment. Her arms sagged under the weight of the load, but one corner of her mouth quirked up valiantly into a smile.

"Well... as long as the cool kids are doing it."

"Oh, here, let me help," Carson opened his door, forgot his belt was fastened, wrestled with it for a moment and then popped out. Together, he and Kiki stowed the equipment inside a distressed delivery van bearing Lucky Earl's logo.

Kiki leaned back, pressing her palms to her lower back. She winced. "Thanks. So. What brings you to Earl's? Looking for something?"

Carson hesitated. Now that he was standing next to her, right there on the sidewalk, things suddenly seemed a lot more real. His stomach gave a gush. "Well, it's a beautiful day," he indicated the gray, sullen sky. "And I happen to have a reason to celebrate," he indicated the truck which was clicking and ticking loudly beside them. A pool of fluid was beginning to collect under the engine. "Now that I've got two seats, I thought I'd pop over and see if you wanted to fill one of them."

"I'm sorry?"

"Dinner. Tonight. You and me. What do you say?"

"I've got class."

"We'll go after."

"I've got homework."

"I'll help you study."

"Carson... dinner...?" her voice trailed off helplessly.

"Right! You got it! So, where do I pick you up, school or home? I could swing by your place around nine..."

"My place... no!" Kiki stiffened. "I mean... look," she calmed with an effort, showing him her palms. "I'm just really... busy... right now. I've got a lot of things on my plate."

"I realize that – and food should be one of them. I'm not blind, lady. I can see you haven't been taking care of yourself. I want to do something about that."

"You sound like my brother again."

"Yeah - I wanna do something about that too."

She stopped.

"I want to take you on a date."

Carson's heart hammered, face red, palms slick. Blue eyes flicked up and met his for the briefest of moments. Then, they flicked away. A sudden, cool breeze blew over them.

Kiki turned her face into it and closed her eyes. She breathed deeply. When she opened them again, they were pointed at the sidewalk. "It would never work."

She turned without another word and disappeared into the store. She didn't look back.

Carson stood still on the sidewalk. The breeze came again, stirring his hair, rustling his hoodie, washing over him. He stayed that way for some time, feeling like he should run but strangely unable to move his legs. Just letting the wind play across his cool, pale cheeks.

It was, he realized vaguely, a lot colder than he had thought.

CHAPTER SEVEN

Whispers

A car flashed past, headlights scattering shadows. The wind of its passing was a momentary refreshment for Carson's sweating face. He ducked across the street, passed through the glow of a street lamp and back into shadow, head down and hoodie up. He didn't mind the quick whiff of exhaust. He'd been in the city - the inner city - too long for that to bother him.

Carson took a few quick boxing jabs to loosen his shoulders. He glanced at his watch. His time was good. Another night time jogger waved from across the street. Carson waved back, smiling to himself. Always in his past when people would ask if he was a runner, his standard reply had been, *"Only when something's chasing me."* Now that he *had* been chased by somethings, he found that running was a lot more meaningful. Practice never hurt.

It was good think time, too, and he had plenty to think about these days. The runs had started a month or two ago since beach volleyball had closed up for the season. He had felt the strange and newly acquired urge to be *doing*. It wasn't enough anymore to sit around and take life at his old, casual, day-at-a-time pace. Ever since he had awakened to the possibility of *purpose* after their encounter with Vanessa, things had changed.

It was still new. Nothing had seemed to motivate him like this before: high school graduation, his parents moving away, the job at the 24/7. Nothing. Not until this year. Now everything seemed different: new job, new ride, new motivation, new skills, new friends, new feelings...

A jolt went through him as his foot went off the curb. His mind had drifted to memories of his date fail with Kiki, and he'd gotten distracted. It wasn't the first time. It had been a few days, but the encounter still made him feel sick. He sighed. There was *good* new... and then there was that.

Carson turned onto his home street. The back door light from Granny's shone through the dark, and he pointed himself toward it and kicked up his speed, suddenly angry with himself. He didn't know why he'd even said anything to Kiki, didn't really know why he'd gone there that day or what he'd been thinking. He hadn't been, probably. It was just the euphoria of beating Deth, the promotion, everything going his way. The life high had gotten tangled with feelings of friendship. He was just mixed up. That was all.

Carson slowed, pulling up in front of Granny's. He knocked back his hood and trotted along the side of the house, the narrow patch of grass spongy and wet. He shook his head and allowed himself a rueful smile as he stepped into the pool of yellow light illuminating the small, tidy patch of concrete that was the back patio. Kiki had been right. It wouldn't work. There was nothing *to* work. She had saved them both from a lot of uncomfortable moments. It was like she said - he was like a brother to her. And she was like a sister to him. Definitely. He nodded firmly to himself.

Definitely.

Unless...

What if she only said that because...

He caught his thoughts slipping again. "Oh no you don't!" he muttered fiercely at them.

"Sorry," the whisper came practically in his ear.

Carson jumped nearly a foot. "WHAT THE BLUE BINKIES?!?" He whirled, heart pounding.

"I'm sorry, Carson," the whisper came again as a blob of dark shifted, separating itself from the garbage can shadows beside the detached garage. "I didn't mean to startle you." The edges of wire-rimmed spectacles winked under a cap's brim.

"Ghost?!" Carson peered hard and was just able to pick out the familiar, shabby outline. He forced himself to ease down, willing both his fists and his sphincter to unclench. "Cats n' crackers, man, you shouldn't do that to someone with an elevated heart rate!"

"I'm sorry," Ghost repeated. "I thought you saw me. You said..."

"Yeah," Carson interrupted, now even angrier at himself. "I... no, I was just... um... forget it. You're here. Hey...!" suddenly the significance of it hit him. "You're *here!* At my place. Why are you at my place?!"

"Routines can be dangerous. It was time to change ours. Apologies. Old habits die hard."

Carson wondered what habits those might be, but let the comment slide. "It's okay – forget about it," he did his best to brush it off. "Hope I didn't keep you waiting."

"No. Your runs usually finish about this time."

"Hold up... did you say..."

"Apologies again. Information is... was... my business," Ghost's whisper drifted away into the rustle of the night breeze. There was a significant silence from the shadows.

After a moment, Carson took it as his cue to move on. "So, what brings you to Dudley Manor?"

"I found something on your painting."

Carson's heart, which had finally settled down, gave another jolt. "Hot potato! Did you find it?!"

"No. But I found one like it. Several actually. I'm guessing it's the same artist, though I can't confirm it. The style and composition are very distinctive. And the circumstances suggest a connection as well - the police confiscated these works during a recent murder investigation. I'm guessing the reason you're interested is because of something equally sinister."

"Recent murder..." a tickle of instinct ran up Carson's spine. "It wasn't in the industrial district, was it? An abandoned meat packing plant?"

"I believe that's correct," pages flipped in a notebook. "The House of Beef. You know it?"

"Know it?" Carson felt goosebumps. "Yeah. I know it." Vanessa's paintings had come from the Curio Shop. Sister Becky had been right - the two *were* connected – big time. Just like Fujikacorp. "Okay, so..." he gathered his spinning thoughts. "You said you couldn't confirm they're by the same artist? Why not?"

"No access. The portraits are still in the police evidence lockup."

"Nuts," Carson frowned, tugging his chin beard. He fell silent, lost in his own musings.

Ghost let a few beats go by then quietly cleared his throat. "How is Kiki?"

"Kiki?!" Carson's stomach squished again as all of his tangled feelings suddenly returned to squeeze it. "Oh, great. Just peachy. Sisterly almost."

"Good. Carson..." there was hesitation in Ghost's whisper, and a moment later, the shadowy form took a cautious step forward. "I wanted to say... thank you. For watching out for her. You have no idea what it means to me."

Carson said nothing. He tried a smile, but it felt thin and forced.

Ghost took another step forward, this time coming almost into the pool of yellow light. His face loomed from the shadows, lined and care-worn, soft and hard all at once, like a caring father with much hard work and too much worry. Gray eyes regarded him carefully. "My name is Joe."

"Uh... okay," Carson wasn't sure why, but the name dropped with weight. This was something important, he realized with a flash, and not only to Ghost. This was something big. This was trust. "Yeah, right. Absolutely. Joe. Um... Joe," he said it again, as if repeating it was his part of accepting the offer. "Joe it is."

A faded smile slipped over Ghost's features, and he drifted back into the shadows and was swallowed by them. "Let's keep it between us, alright? Names can be powerful things."

"Mum's the word."

"Stay close to Kiki."

"Um... yeah. I'll work on that one."

Then, Carson was alone, feeling the clamminess of the sweat cooling on his skin and the hollowness of his final words. He turned to the back door, fishing for his key, wondering why life was so complicated.

After a good night's sleep and a solid day of mini-marting, Carson felt better. Steady holiday traffic, cheerful customers and a solid diet of Christmas tunes boosted his mood. Until *Blue Christmas* came on. Then, he switched off the radio. He was stocking the breakfast cereal, watching the clock tick off the final thirty minutes of his shift, when his phone rang. He answered around a half-finished candy cane.

It was Leet. "So... that painting. It's got a picture of a dude in a hood, right? And a chick on an altar... sacrifice and stuff, right? Just confirming. Lotta hits already, just wanna make sure I'm on the trail of the *right* one."

Carson listened smugly. He could hear the desperation in Leet's voice – it was sweeter than the candy cane. The man had nothing. "Yup yup. Hood, chick, altar. Sounds like you're close. Are you close?"

"Close?!" Leet blew a raspberry. "Closer than fungus! Closer than Christmas! Closer than that object in your rear view mirror! Watch out! Now, uh... the artist... you don't happen to know..."

Carson's heart swelled. "'Fraid not, pally. But I'm dying to know. Can't *wait* 'til you dig it up for me. Hope this isn't digging into your game time too much. How is *Skull Crushing Warbots?* You still busting heads?"

"Yeah. Busting heads. You got it. That's totally me. Hey, did I tell you? I found out some other stuff... scary stuff. Been digging around in general for ya. Weird. The kind you guys are into, if you know what I mean. The kind 'leg work' doesn't always turn up... like some psycho robberies. Bizarre snatch-n-grabs, a whole rash of 'em. Totally cray cray, like 'why would anyone ever steal *that*?' you know? Lab equipment. Doctor stuff. Hospitals, medical supply... even museums! Like that Fujikacorp deal, the last one I helped you with, remember?!"

"I wouldn't put too much stock in it," Carson was sure it was connected but equally sure it no longer mattered. He pictured the raging inferno of Dr. Deth's lab, where much of the equipment Leet was describing was now probably piles of melted slag.

"But... but I'm sure it's hot!" Leet sounded almost whiny. "For positive, there was another one just yesterday! A veterinary clinic! They took..."

"It's unrelated."

"But...!"

"Drop it."

Silence.

Carson could practically see the pout. He pictured the little man huddled in the glow of his computer screen in his dorm room, surrounded by weeks-old empty Yoo-Hoo bottles and his collection of action figures, superhero posters and other geeky clutter. Just like the first time Carson had met him, only sadder. He smirked. Leet had been so cocky then, so puffed up, Kiki's self-proclaimed "criminal contact"...

Carson sat up.

Criminal contact.

Maybe there was a way he could still use Leet. "Hey, dude... remember last time we did this, you said you had... how should I say this... friends?"

"Friends?! Oh yeah! I've got friends! Lots of friends! Why, you want a party or something? No sweat! I could round up a couple... no, a dozen... maybe twenty... it's Christmas break but I could knock on some doors..."

"Let me rephrase," Carson sucked loudly on his candy cane. "I mean *friends*."

There was a beat.

"You mean *criminal* friends."

"I didn't say that."

"Oh baby! Bam! You bet; I got criminal friends! As criminal as you want, man. *Way* criminal. *Totally* pimped out crazy crimi..."

"Yeah, yeah, they're criminal; I get it. So listen, I already got a tip on the painting. Something solid."

"A tip?" Leet's tone was strangled. "Already?"

"Turns out it's not a one and only. There's more in town, only it's not where someone could easily get their hands on it."

"Like where?"

"A police lock up."

Silence.

"That's interesting."

"I thought so, too."

"Friends could help with that. The right ones."

"Yes," Carson sucked thoughtfully on the nub of his candy cane. It was down to the last tasty bit. "They could be helpful. And another thing," he added, struck by inspiration again or perhaps sheer power mad sadism. "When Joe has info, he comes to *me*. Routines are dangerous. Drop the phone calls, and let's play things face to face from now on."

"Joe?" Leet's voice was suddenly soft.

"I mean 'Ghost'. Look, forget it. Just come see me when you've got intel from now on. Copy?"

"Oh, sure. Yeah, you bet. Totally copy. Face to face. Roger

Wilco."

Carson hung up. His conscience was trying to poke him about letting Joe's name slip, but he squashed it. It was just a first name. Not to mention an insanely common first name. What damage could Leet possibly do with it? Crunching through the last of his candy cane, Carson stretched grandly and glanced up at the clock. Quitting time. A great day made even greater. With everyone else suddenly doing his investigating for him, he realized he now had something quite unexpected – free time.

The door gave its warbly, sickly chime as the night shifter sauntered in. Right on time.

"Evening, Carson."

"Hey, Adam!" Carson liked Adam. He was sharp as a tack, normal as white bread, calm, friendly and into gaming – all the qualities about Leet he liked with none of the defects. "How's Diane?"

"Still gorgeous. Still brilliant. Still my wife. Still unavailable."

He was also pleasantly sarcastic. Carson grinned. "Never hurts to ask. I keep hoping she'll dump you over your gaming obsession."

"Never gonna happen," Adam shook his head. "I switched to board games. Board games make you look smart. Chicks dig smart." He tapped his glasses and winked.

"Figures. I'm still into video games."

"Video games make you look immature."

"Hey, some chicks dig immature."

"True. But only when they're selling you video games," Adam traded places with Carson behind the counter.

"Well, at least that explains the size of my collection."

"And your relationship status," Adam smiled good-naturedly, punching his code into the Omni-Biz 7520. He failed to see Carson wince at his comment.

"Welcome back, Adam DiGleria," the Omni-Biz purred in a decidedly feminine voice. *"Let's have a GREAT shift."*

"I see Kinkade uploaded the new voice module," Adam shivered. "Creepy."

Carson sighed. "I don't know... right now she sounds kinda nice. Do you think she's into video games?"

"Let's just say, I think you two would be a great fit. Plus, she's always got money, you can put her in a closet whenever you want and she comes with an instruction manual. How many guys can say that about their gal?"

"Man. What I wouldn't give for an instruction manual."

Adam quirked an eyebrow, sensing something in Carson's heartfelt reply. "You okay, buddy?"

"Me? Oh, yeah. Heck yeah. Bulletproof. Hey," Carson grabbed his coat. "How late is Games A-Plenty open?"

"Nine, I think."

"They have any chicks working there?"

Adam scratched his thin beard, thinking. "Yes. Last time I was in."

"Good," Carson fished his keys out. "Think I'll go find one to sell me *Skull Crushing Warbots of Doom...* "

It was barely an hour later when Carson was heading out of the game store, swinging a bag and humming. He had a full evening planned and his head was already so full of images of giant robots and futuristic machines of mayhem that he hardly noticed the gaunt figure leaning against his truck until he reached for the door handle.

"Whoa...!" Carson jerked his hand back, and the bag slipped out of it, sending the game box sliding across the damp sidewalk.

The figure took a step forward. It was a man, lean and knotted, with black, weathered skin and a perpetual scowl etched into a face that looked more like a block of old wood. The whites of his eyes were an unhealthy yellow, and his nostrils flared like a bull's. Carson's brain also registered that the man was probably three times his age, but that didn't stop him from feeling a surge of panic. There was something about his approach – the set of his shoulders, the swagger in his step, the aura of reckless, undefeatable bravado – as if trapped inside of him was a younger, stronger man who would readily poke any bear he came across. Altogether, he bore an uncanny resemblance to Dex... right down to the hand-me-down army coat.

Carson took a step back, then planted himself, tense and ready. The man said nothing. He just stared, hands clenched at his sides, nostrils still flaring, looking for all the world like he couldn't decide whether to punch Carson in the face or in the gut. As they stood measuring one another, a light, chilling rain began to fall. Carson shivered as it trickled down his back under the collar of his hoodie. The stranger paid it no heed. It rolled off the thin, gray sandpaper of his head as if he were a granite statue.

After a moment, Carson found his voice. "I don't give cash, but I might be persuaded to buy you a sandwich. You hungry?"

"Las' Whitey to acks me that got clean knocked out," the man made a tiny, almost imperceptible twitch. It was not a step forward - but Carson took a step back.

"Okay. Soup maybe."

"Got a message from Joe."

"Ah!" relief flooded Carson. "You must be part of 'us'! Great. Whew! You had me going there. Let's start over," Carson thrust out his hand. "I'm Carson. You are...?"

The other didn't move. "We ain't solid. When we solid, we shake."

Carson retrieved his hand. "Fair enough."

"Joe says he's got a lead – that girl you lookin' fo'. Some place she used ta shack up. Gonna go check it out, didn't know how long it was gonna take, wanted me to get you a message in the meantime. Jus' in case if he found sumpin' for you to come take a look-see at. Wanted you to be ready."

"Right. Look-see. Be ready. Gotcha."

Without further fanfare, the grizzled old bruiser turned away.

"Hey, wait," a sudden concern poked Carson. "He's gonna go check it out? I should probably tell you... this, uh... this girl... she might be just a little, teensy, *tiny* bit, kinda... dangerous."

The dark, weather beaten face glowered at him. "Joe can handle hisself." Yellowed eyes looked Carson up and down, hard, as if looking for a reason to punch him.

The thought made Carson look instinctively at the man's hands. They were large, powerful hands, clenched in large, powerful fists, brutal, knobby and rough, a pair of bone and gristle hammers. The man caught him looking. Again, he made the almost imperceptible twitch toward Carson. Again, Carson took an involuntary step back.

Then, he was off, swaggering away down the street, rain spattering on his gnarled back like sea spray on a breakwater. Carson's tensed shoulders slumped. He retrieved his bag and ducked into the Magic Carpet, quickly starting the engine and pulling away. Anyone who made Dex look warm and fuzzy, he figured, was good to put in your rearview mirror.

* * * * * * *

"You *what*?!" Dex stared at Carson around a half-eaten polish dog. The dog was ungarnished, save for a dollop of relish (which Dex maintained was a vegetable) – no nacho cheese, chili, sour cream or any of his other usual add-ons. It looked sad and lonely in his hand but was evidence of his commitment to the new diet.

"I set up Leet to go after the paintings in the evidence locker," Carson swallowed a bite of his own dog and dabbed at a spot of mustard. "We need to see them, and Leet has criminal contacts who can make it happen. Do the math: if A = B, and B = C, then C = 'someone's gotta break into the police station.'"

"And D = 'now there's a trail connecting us to a felony'," Dex swore and rolled his eyes. "Sounds like two plus two equals trouble." For a moment, he looked as if he might even put down his meal. He settled for taking another large bite.

"I'll take the risk. People are getting hurt, and Parsons isn't doing Jack. Somebody has to step up."

Sister Becky, seated at the counter and snacking quietly on Rudolph's Rockets, pursed her lips thoughtfully. "Mr. Dudley... who?"

"Who what?"

"Who is being hurt?"

"Well... not... I mean, I don't... *know* any of them, but... this painting, the Curio Shop... Vanessa..." he trailed off . "People."

"Eloquently put, dear," she patted his hand. "However, we have no proof of any wrongdoing or risk. As unsettling as I find it to concur with Mr. Jackson, concur I must. Turning Mr. Leet's dubious contacts loose on a thread so thin seems needlessly reckless."

"It may be thin, but right now, it's the only lead we've got," Carson crunched chips and chased them down with a pull on a white Christmas Freezie. He lounged back on his stool, unconcerned by his friends' disapproval. "Besides, aren't you the one who once told me that good causes sometimes require bad decisions? Some old saying about a cow and a lawnmower, I think."

Sister Becky opened her mouth, closed it. "I cannot recall any such addage, Mr. Dudley. Although, I will admit that my zeal, at times, may cause my judgment to become somewhat..." she searched for words.

"Sucky," Dex offered. He stuffed the remainder of his polish dog, somewhere over half, into his mouth.

The creases in Becky's frown deepened. "The Lord has given us a great blessing in the consumption of food, Mr. Jackson. And he has given me a great burden in watching you consume it."

Dex swallowed hard and adopted a pious air. The expression seemed ridiculous on his normally cynical features. "Well, you know what they say in the Good Book: 'There is nothing better for a man under the sun than to eat, drink and be glad.' Ecclesiastes 8:15."

Sister Becky looked as if she might fall off her stool. Her jaw hung slack, and her eyes simply stared. Carson had never seen the scrappy old nun caught so completely off guard. It made him uncomfortable.

"You..." she struggled for words. "Holy Scripture..."

Dex lounged back. "Told you I was getting' me a Bible. Fight fire with fire, I say."

Sister Becky stared a moment longer. Then, she blinked, snapped her mouth shut and squared her shoulders. "Very well, Mr. Jackson, I concede the point. You have obviously researched the matter and found truth in God's Word."

Dex's triumphant grin spread. Then, it slipped. "Hm. Guess I did," he stared into space, pondering whether it was, indeed, he who had scored.

"At any rate, gentlemen," the nun stood smoothly, depositing her tray in the trash. "I must take my leave. There are more pressing matters than breaking and entering to attend to." Her expression took on a worried shadow.

"The Council again?" Carson ventured.

Sister Becky gave a curt nod. "Aye, lad. They have been strangely silent since my ultimatum. I must endeavor to uncover their purpose." She adjusted her hood fretfully and cast an old knit scarf about her neck. It was the only protection she allowed herself against the cold and rain.

"You want a ride?" Carson dangled his car keys. "You haven't yet sampled the magic of the Magic Carpet, and Dex and I were just headed out to do some shooting."

Sister Becky considered briefly, favoring him with a curious, probing gaze. Finally, she gave a single head shake. "I shall decline, Mr. Dudley, though with thanks. I feel that I could benefit from a bit of fresh air." With a nod, she left.

Dex rose, too, hitching up his overloaded equipment belt. "Gonna take one more patrol before we go. Gotta work off that dog. May be nothing better for a man than to eat and drink, but it also don't hurt to know what catches a lady's eye."

Thirty minutes later, they were wedged into the cab of the Magic Carpet, Carson humming happily as he unwrapped a Christmas tree air freshener.

Beside him, Dex cursed and muttered as he worked his legs into a less painful position. The dashboard creaked ominously. "I've dropped ten pounds, but I could lose another hundred, and you still couldn't wedge me into this trashcan in a way that wouldn't make me want to kill you." Dex cursed again and rocked back mightily, shaking the truck. If the seats had still had springs, they would have broken. "Tell me how come you're drivin' again?!"

"Because it's *your* month to go to the chiropractor," Carson looped his air freshener around the rearview mirror and shifted into gear. With a lurch, they pulled out into traffic. "So, how was your date with Delilah?" For a moment, he caught himself hoping it had crashed as badly as his own.

"Glorious," Dex breathed. His countenance melted into a strange combination of euphoria and queasiness. "I really like this girl., but he crushed it. With effort. "So, how come you look like you're going to puke?"

"Same reason."

Carson could see Dex toying with Tia's butterfly necklace. It was usually soothing for the big man, but now it seemed to make him nervous. Carson tried to make his next question nonchalant. "What's her little girl's name?"

"Serena," Dex's tone was careful and controlled.

"Cute. Did she join you?"

"No." The comment did not invite conversation.

"Dex..."

"I don't wanna."

"You'll feel better."

"I hate this!"

"Don't make me get the crowbar..."

Dex whooshed out a huge breath, rubbing sweaty palms on his guard pants. "Okay, okay! It's just..."

"You're scared."

"Damn straight! You know the last time I was scared?!"

"When you heard Hostess was going out of business?"

"I didn't say *mad* - I said *scared*." The guard shook his head vehemently, dreadlocks scraping the window.

Carson arched an eyebrow. "An emotion other than rage. I can see how you must be confused."

"That ain't the worst of it. Now, she wants me to have dinner with the old man."

The truck swerved a little. "Um... *you* at a sit down dinner with Detective Patch Parsons?! I can think of a few other emotions that may be on your horizon."

"To top it off, Delilah told me there's cop tests coming up this Spring - and Parsons is on the board."

"Cripes, man! We gotta call Dr. Phil. This kind of mess is best viewed on national TV."

"It's a mess alright," Dex heaved a huge sigh. "That's why I came down the way I did on this evidence locker thing. We're already on Parsons toilet list. If things go South and he makes a connection..."

"Fear not, my large friend. Everything's gonna work out; you'll see. I give you my personal guarantee that everything will go absolutely according to plan, and there will be beautiful, fulfilling endings for all involved."

Dex eyed him for a moment. Then, he turned to watch the road. "Fine. But I'm going on record that if it doesn't, I will personally kill you."

"Fair enough."

"And by the way," Dex added. "I know you ain't been drivin' long, but this little gauge here..." he indicated the engine temperature light. The needle was wedged up in the red as far as it could go. "...means you're engine is about to explode." As if on cue, the truck gave a jerk and a shake. Something under the hood went *pop!,* and a gout of smoke spewed from underneath it.

"What?! No...!" Carson wrestled the truck to the curb, his face aghast. The engine bucked and gasped, stuttering to a halt as steam and smoke chased each other out of the engine compartment. With a final, shuddering lurch, the truck stopped and died.

"Sassafras!" Carson gave the Christmas tree air freshener a frustrated swat. The rear view mirror fell off.

"Hey, look..." Dex pointed at the mirror where it lay forlornly on the dash. "Carpet broke the fall." He popped his door open and extricated himself with no little difficulty. "We'll take a rain check on shooting. I gotta make me a phone call anyway, and you gotta get acquainted with the first rule of ownin' your own ride."

"What's that?" Carson asked, staring with disbelief at the massive volume of smoke spewing from his stricken truck.

"It's %^&*#@! expensive."

The door slammed shut.

Several days later, as Carson stood huddled in the bus stop shelter, he was still pondering Dex's words. The man was an automotive prophet. It *had* been expensive. Painfully expensive. The worst part, though, was the waiting. It would be weeks at least. He sighed, stuffing his hands deeper into the pockets of his hoodie.

"Hello, Carson."

Carson jumped, as usual, then forced his breathing to slow. "Hey, Joe."

"'Ghost'," came the whisper from the shadows. "Please." The little man's head swiveled, shooting cautious glances up and down the nearly empty street.

"Sorry, forgot that was our little secret. Hey, it's good to see you, though. I may have forgotten to mention it before, but this chick... she might possibly be a little bit of bad news. Be careful around her."

"Understood. KO passed on your warning."

"KO?"

"You met him the other night. He may have introduced himself as Gus."

"Ah. Your buddy. Actually, he didn't introduce himself at all. But he did offer to punch me in the face."

"Apologies. He's had a hard life. But he's a good man. And a friend."

"Everybody should have at least one. Though with his attitude, I'm guessing one is his limit."

"Perhaps," Ghost smiled softly in the dark. "Although, the others are more fond of him than they'll admit."

"Others. You've said that before," Carson's curiosity was suddenly piqued. "Just how many of these 'others' are there?"

"A few," Ghost's tone was more than a little evasive, and he quickly put an end to Carson's line of inquiry. "But that's for later. I found an old address on your person of interest, but it looks like she already cleared out."

"Nertz. Any leads? Personal stuff?"

"We picked up a few clues. May be something there."

"That's a start."

"We'll see where it leads. In the meantime, there's one more small thing."

"Oh?"

"Your most recent operation – the warehouse in Shelly – are you *certain* it was resolved?"

"Yeah," once again, Carson pictured the flames leaping and licking in Deth's lab. "It's resolved."

"You're absolutely sure?"

"Okay, I give up. What's going on?"

Ghost shrugged. "Nothing. Maybe. Whispers. A hunch, perhaps. Word on the street is that someone's been digging through cemeteries, shopping the morgues... nothing definite, but it sounded like it may be connected."

"Thanks, but trust me... that book is closed."

"Understood," the whisper trailed off. A pair of early evening commuters were wandering toward the bus stop, and Ghost edged deeper into darkness.

Carson sensed the meeting was coming to an end and suddenly remembered his plans for reuniting Kiki and Ghost. It could very well be the thing to distract from the awkwardness of the date fail and perhaps put their relationship back on normal footing. If not, it was at least worth a shot. "Say, um... let's do a... um... check-in thing. Sitrep. Soon. Like Thursday night, maybe. Say seven-ish, my place?"

The oncoming couple was a block away. Ghost watched them carefully. He edged another step, a twitch in the shadows. "Are you sure that's wise?"

"I'm really hoping so. Plus, there's something I want to show you. Something long overdue. I think you'll like it."

Ghost was already starting to drift away, the young couple almost within earshot. "Alright. I'll see you at seven."

The bus arrived a few minutes later to take Carson to Granny's. As he climbed on board, he congratulated himself on his newfound talent for nudging people in the right direction. First Leet, now Ghost... it was getting easier every time.

Bouncing through the front door at Granny's, the mouth-watering smell of baking immediately filled Carson's nostrils. His stomach gave a hearty growl. He shucked his jacket and headed for the kitchen. "Cookie robbery!" he hollered. "Give me all your dough...! Oh, hey Sister B. Granny." Carson greeted the two elderly women seated at the cozy little dining table. He was struck once again by the feeling that he had interrupted something. Sister Becky was as placid as ever, but Granny... a shadow of something passed quickly across her face before melting into a smile. The expression looked forced.

Carson stood for a moment, balancing himself against a wave of déjà vu. "Am I...?"

"Interrupting? Not at all, my boy," Granny rose quickly and gave him a peck on the cheek. "Just chatting. Let me go fetch that dough. You look like you mean business," she puttered off to the kitchen.

Carson sank into a seat, staring after her with a thoughtful look. "Why do I get this feeling you and Granny are conspiring? It's not about the Christmas party, is it?" he asked, suddenly hopeful. "You having a change of heart, perhaps?"

Sister Becky clucked. "I am afraid not, dear boy. My mind is set on that matter."

"Okay, then, I give up... why are you here? If I was into nun humor, I would say that you showing up at Granny's is becoming a habit."

She laughed innocently. "Well put, lad! And yes, perhaps it is. Your Grandmother and I have had a... matter... we have been discussing," she stirred her tea casually. "Unfortunately, the details of it are not my place to share. However, today I also bring news about my hearing. The Council has at last broken its silence."

"Shackle and spackle me! Well?! Don't leave me hangin'!"

Sister Becky paused a moment, letting the tension build deliciously. "They have granted my hearing."

"Well butter my biscuits!" Carson gave the table a hearty slap, rattling tea cups. "Props to the Man Upstairs!"

"Indeed, Mr. Dudley," Sister Becky was radiant. "I have been so propping Him."

"When did you find out?!"

"This morning. I must confess, however," her face took on a hint of bemusement. "That I felt like the farmer who planted corn and harvested beets, if you take my meaning."

"Depends. With how I look at beets, that would mean 'disappointed'. I'm guessing you mean 'surprised'."

"Indeed, lad. Completely flabbergasted. Thoroughly perplexed. The matter had stalled so convincingly, in spite of the goosings I administered, that I had all but given up hope. And now..." she shot him a shrewd glance. "The hearing. Almost as if someone interceded on my behalf." Her arched brows asked him the question.

"What, me?" Carson chuckled and dismissed the notion with a wave. "Sorry, sister – if someone interceded, it was God, not me," he felt a tiny, fleeting ruffle of guilt that he *hadn't* acted on her behalf – that the thought hadn't even occurred to him. But it didn't matter. Things had turned out well. "So when's the hearing?"

"Soon – hopefully within the week."

"How do you think it'll go?"

Her eyes took on a gleam that Carson had last seen when she

confronted a horde of walking dead. "Productively, Mr. Dudley. I think it shall go productively. If they thought they had been goosed before, they have no idea what awaits them now."

"Ouch."

"Indeed. Now, what of you?" she shifted gears, fixing him with her business gaze. "How fare your investigations?"

"Not bad. Got a couple irons in the fire." Carson kept his answer deliberately vague. He toyed with one of Granny's doilies, staring nonchalantly into the kitchen.

"Truly, Mr. Dudley? I expected more enthusiasm from you."

Carson smiled. "Just trying to keep you in the realm of plausible deniability. I figure the less you know, the better. Especially now, with the hearing coming up – don't want to monkey wrench it." In truth, Carson realized, it was more than that. Sister Becky had always been his source of confidence, his anchor in new and uncertain waters - until now. Now, she had pulled back. In fact, twice she had been a total no-show. And things had gone just fine. He was starting to realize that maybe he didn't need her as much as he thought.

Sister Becky made a small, non-committal noise, watching him shrewdly with the same queer look she'd been using on him lately. "I am no stranger to risk, Mr. Dudley."

"Thanks Sister B., but really, it's all good. It's nothing I can't handle."

Her eyes became even more shrewd. "Your new informants must be quite resourceful."

"They've got their uses. Especially Ghost and his crew. Apparently, he has a crew. They're a little raw, but they seem to know their stuff."

"Diamonds in the rough."

"More like tire irons in the rough. But compared to Leet... well, frankly, they make him look like a Girl Scout. And I apologize if you got the image in your head of Leet in the uniform like I just got. Yikes. Anyway, if it goes on like this..." Carson shrugged again. "I don't think I'll need him anymore."

"That seems to be a growing trend."

"Sister B.," he faked a pout. "Did you just take a shot at me?"

"I have noticed quite an independent streak in you of late."

"I read *Leadership for Dummies*."

"And precisely what do you feel leadership is?"

Carson considered. "Just figure out *what* you need done, *who* can get it done and *how* you can make them do it. Then, start pushing buttons. Not much to it. It's a lot like our cash register, actually."

"I see." Sister Becky paused, took a sip of tea. Her sharp eyes never left his face. "That was not always your philosophy, Mr. Dudley."

"Guess I've learned a lot."

She took another slow sip of tea, watching him. "Perhaps, Mr. Dudley," she murmured, almost to herself. "Perhaps." She tipped her cup for another sip, found it empty, then placed it gently on the saucer. "And perhaps you still have some things left to learn. I wonder, suddenly, if I am still qualified to teach you?" She stood, her smile pleasant enough but laced with a hint of something else. "You may be correct - perhaps distance is best. You are certainly not the same lad you were those few thin months past when first we met," she extended her hand. "Godspeed in your investigations, Mr. Dudley. I do hope you shall keep me apprised, even if my other responsibilities should keep me from playing a direct hand in them."

Carson shook her hand. There was something in the entire exchange that tugged at his conscience, but he swept such thoughts aside. He *was* different than when they had first met. A lot. Until now he hadn't realized just how much. "No worries, Sister B. I got this."

"So you have said," she gave his hand a final squeeze then turned in a businesslike whirl of robes. "Do be sure to have a word with Roberta if you can spare a moment. I believe she has something to share." With that and a final thin smile, the nun was gone.

The remark struck Carson as odd, but he hardly had time to ponder it. As the front door closed on Sister Becky, the kitchen door opened on Granny Dudley. Granny bustled in with a plate piled high with his favorite treats - greenies, backyard cruncheez and sweet snoodles - and a pitcher of ice cold milk. They made small talk as Carson busily stuffed his face, distracted by the warm, gooey homemades.

Eventually, Granny fell silent, hands folded in her lap. Her happy mouth with its generous laugh lines held for a moment then melted into a small frown. It looked unusual on her. "Carson," she began slowly. "Rebecca has been pressing me to share something with you. Something I've... never told you. Never told anyone. Except for Rebecca." She fell silent again.

For some sudden, inexplicable reason, Carson felt nervous. There was something strange, something unusual in Granny's demeanor. Something serious. He hadn't seen her like this since his grandfather's disappearance, and he had been just a child then, the memories vague and cloudy. The last bite of a cookie sat forgotten in his hand. He waited.

Granny toyed with the hem of her Christmas sweater, searching for words. The cavorting reindeer and jolly Santa face seemed out of place. "I had a Vision once, too," she said at last, her voice soft and purposeful. She looked straight at him, her Dudley-green eyes at once familiar and yet, also, strangely not. "It was about you." Carson felt a shiver at the words. It was like someone else was speaking with his Grandmother's voice. She held his gaze a moment then let hers slip away, wandering along with her thoughts.

"You were young then. So young..." Granny's eyes shone brightly with the memory. She gave a gentle tug on his chin beard. "Just a boy then. So full of life. Such spirit! You broke something every time you came to visit," she beamed at him, no hint of condemnation in her tone. "That day, it was one of Grandpa's airplane models. The P-51 Mustang," she chuckled. "You climbed up on the roof. You wanted it to fly *so* badly." Then, her face clouded as the memories played out. "That was the day Sister Becky first met you."

Carson started. "Sister B.?! Wait... you... but it was just this... when Van..." he struggled to sort through his childhood, searching desperately for an image of a ramrod straight woman-in-black. He could see the model planes. Even the P-51. It had been his favorite. But no nun. "She knew me?"

"She's known you much of your life. Her work kept her out of the country most of the time, but she and I were friends – close friends – all through. She would touch base from time to time, a letter, perhaps, or on rare occasions, a visit. It was during one of these when she met you. John and your mother had dropped you off for a visit. I don't recall why. But I do recall Rebecca's reaction. She was so... curious. You spent the day together. She chased about with you, listening to your stories, asking questions. I love the woman dearly, but Becky has always been somewhat of a mystery to me. Perhaps that's why I have remained so fond of her these many years. She lives the adventures that I can only dream." That thought seemed to draw her back, and she grew sober again.

"Dreams, Carson. That's what I have to tell you about. The ones I had that night. The night Rebecca met you." Granny was fidgeting with her sweater again. "They were dark. Disturbing. So terribly, terribly..." she shuddered with the memory, "...real. You were in danger, Carson. From something. Someone. I never could see his face through the hood, just that he was tall. Dark. A shadow. I knew that he wanted to – that he wanted to hurt you. Or they, rather, for there were other shadows with him. Many of them. I saw things... terrible things... and try as I might, I could do nothing to help. Nothing." Granny's voice faltered.

After a moment, she drew a shuddering breath and looked up bravely. "But there were hands. Others. Hands that reached out to you. Tried to help you, I think. That was never clear. All I could do was shout to them, tell them where to find you... but I don't know if they ever did." She shook her head to clear away the clinging memories. "At any rate, I must have cried out in my sleep. Rebecca woke me, or was there when I awoke. I couldn't shake the dream. It was too real. Too frightening. I must have been a state! She sat up with me for hours, full of questions. She listened. We prayed. And the next day... well, the next day, she said it was more than just a dream. That it was a Vision. She made me write it down." Carson saw her glance into her lap. There on her patterned, flour-dusted apron lay an old, carefully folded piece of paper.

"Not that I needed to, of course. Or wanted to. For the next few months, it was all I could think about. It haunted me. It is a blessing that over the years, the memory of it has faded. But for some reason, it came back to me recently. After your injury. Seeing you in the hospital, hurt and vulnerable. Funny thing... Rebecca recalled the incident, too, even after all these years. She asked me about it recently. If I had my paper still," she touched the paper in her lap. "Funny."

"At any rate," Granny continued with a suddenness that made Carson start. "Rebecca has been urging me to share it with you. After all these years, can you imagine? She thinks it might have some value for you, that it might be good for reflection."

Carson sat still.

Granny leaned toward him and touched his hand. "Listen, dear... I know you've been going through some changes lately. I've seen it. Roberta has seen it. I know life is never easy, and the answers aren't always there, that this probably just sounds like the ramblings of an old woman," she lifted his chin so she could catch his gaze. "But one thing I can tell you with absolute certainty – when Rebecca says that something is important, it is." She gave his cheek a gentle pat then heaved a huge sigh. "So, there, I've done it. Just what she asked. I have shared my Vision," Granny leaned back, smiling. "I only hope it doesn't trouble you."

Carson smiled, too. But he didn't feel it. His head felt strangely numb. He leaned across the table and gave Granny a peck on the forehead. "It won't, Granny. It won't."

A few minutes later, Carson wandered slowly into his basement room. He clicked on a lamp, and there, lying in the center of his bed, was a crumpled wad of paper. He crossed to it, staring down.

It was his Vision.

The last time he had seen it was in the garbage can at Texas Chang's Golden Bull BBQ. After their victory celebration. When he'd thrown it away. He stared for a moment, then turned away. He stepped to his computer, picked up the box for *Skull Crushing Warbots of Doom* and stared at it. He set the box down, turned off the lamp and lay down on his bed, staring up into the unfathomable darkness. He felt suddenly weary. Bone tired.

He didn't go to sleep for a long, long time.

CHAPTER EIGHT

Win Some, Lose Some

Carson kicked a can. It shot away down the rain washed street, skittering past a sidewalk Santa. The fellow ho-ho-ho'ed and rang his bell suggestively over a red kettle, but Carson kept his eyes forward and hurried past. He wasn't in the mood for Christmas cheer. It was Thursday already. D-Day. He'd been trying to get in touch with Kiki to set up the surprise meeting with Ghost – no joy. Carson wasn't sure whether she was avoiding him or whether she was just legitimately busy, but either way, he couldn't wait any longer. It was time to crank things up a notch. He peered up at the relentless gray clouds moodily from under his hoodie, feeling the soft patter on his face. Normally, he liked the rain. Today, it was starting to wear on him.

Rounding the corner, Carson stared down the block at Lucky Eddy's storefront. It didn't make him as uncomfortable as he thought it would. Good sign. He hurried across the street, dodging traffic and puddles. Taking up position under the partial shelter of a store awning, he settled in to wait, trying his hardest not to look or feel like a stalker.

If she wouldn't answer, this was the only way.

It took almost an hour. Numbed by the drone of traffic and the cold, intermittent rain, Carson almost didn't recognize her until she had reached the store.

"Hey!" The shout was startled out of him, and it startled Kiki too.

She paused, hand on the door, eyes narrowed. "Carson?"

"Yeah! Sorry. Didn't mean to spook you," Carson forced a grin, but it slipped as he took in Kiki's appearance. She looked awful. Blond hair hung in damp straggles, and her eyes were shadowed by dark circles. Her backpack was wrapped in a garbage bag, evidently to protect her laptop from the rain, but it gave her a decidedly vagrant feel.

"You look..." Carson started impulsively then stopped himself. "...like you're going to work. So, I'll keep this short." He hurried on. "Just wanted to stop by and ask for a favor. Granny's computer is on the fritz, and I was hoping you could take a look."

She glanced apprehensively at him then at Lucky Earl's, one hand still on the knob. Her guard was up. "Carson, if you..."

"It's a job, Kiki. Just a job. It's you or Leet. Don't make me go there. Please." He tried his grin again.

Kiki's gaze roamed, looking anywhere but his eyes. "Just a job?"

"Yeah. Maybe the kind that pays in corn dogs, but a job."

She still wouldn't meet his eyes, but her answer was a little warmer. "Throw in some mustard?"

"Deal."

"Alright. I'm off at..."

"Can you be there at seven? Um... Granny's night out with the church ladies. I want to surprise her when she gets back."

Kiki shrugged. "Yeah. Okay. So... I gotta go, Carson. Work." She ducked inside the store.

Carson turned away quickly and headed for the nearest bus stop, stomping feeling back into his legs. This was good, he told himself. This was right. It would be just the thing. Reuniting two old friends - even estranged ones – would be a hit. It would give Kiki something else to think about that was for sure. Maybe even something to thank him for. She might, he thought with a spark of hope, even decide to make the Christmas party. With the holiday just a week away, there was still time. Yes. It would definitely be good.

Carson stuffed a hand in his pocket, fiddling for his bus pass, and his fingers found a wad of paper. His Vision. He had put it there yesterday. Carson fingered it for a moment then shoved it deeper into his jeans. From the other pocket, his phone rang, and he grabbed it out, thankful for the distraction.

"Hey, Whitey," Dex's voice was a tiny boom. "By the sound of you suckin' air, I'm guessin' you're still hoofin' it."

"Afraid so. The Magic Carpet is still in the shop."

"Gonna be there long?"

"Depends. What's a head gasket?"

"Expensive. And not hard to spot if it's about to explode. I'm surprised it didn't show up on the inspection."

"Mm."

Dex was silent a moment. "You didn't get an inspection, did you?"

"What's an inspection?"

Dex swore. "You're worse off than I thought."

"Compared to what?"

"Broccoli. I thought it was cute at first, but now it's just sad. Get over yourself. You're getting cocky."

"It's called confidence."

"It's called gettin' taken to the %^&*#@! cleaner 'cuz you didn't do your homework on a broke down sucker-mobile 'cuz you had your head too far up your..."

"Does this call have a point?"

"Just wanted to see if you were up for a workout later. I'll drive."

"Pass. I've got plans." Carson felt satisfaction at turning him down. Sometimes Dex could be such a pain.

"Fine. I suppose you're getting enough exercise now with all that walking..."

Carson hung up. "Jerk," he muttered to no one in particular.

* * * * * * *

"Something to drink?"

Carson stood in Granny's cozy, old-lady dining room. Joe Ghost lurked nearby, wedged into a corner and looking for all the world like he wanted to bolt. There wasn't a single shadow in sight, and he clearly felt it. Painfully. He fidgeted with his hands, glancing about uncomfortably at doilies, giant candy canes and a stack of brightly colored Christmas cards.

"No, thank you."

At the sound of his voice, an animatronic Santa Claus in a cowboy hat lurched to life, belting out a country music rendition of *Holly Jolly Christmas*. Ghost started.

"Maybe, we'd be more comfortable in the living room," Carson gestured then led the way. "You sure no drink? We've got eggnog. Everybody loves eggnog."

They moved into the living room, which was dominated by a large fulsome Christmas tree, its green boughs loaded with ornaments and decorations from countless years of family holidays.

"No, thank you. I'm... not thirsty." Ghost moved for the nearest shadow, parking himself beside the tree and doing his best to disappear inside his own rumpled overcoat.

"Suit yourself," Carson took a long savory slurp from his cup and smacked his lips. "I don't know if there's eggs in it or what exactly 'nog' is, but I can't get enough." He slurped again, leaving a thick yellowish film on his upper lip. "Anything else on the girl, yet?"

"No."

"Great." Carson took another sip of eggnog.

Silence. Awkward silence.

"Carson..."

Bing dong!

The front doorbell sounded. Ghost gave another start and glanced around.

"I'll get it!" Carson hustled for the door, his pulse jumping. He glanced at his watch - just after seven. This was it. Sure enough, Kiki stood outside on the doorstep. "Hey, woman! C'mon in!" He held the door for her, and she slipped inside, looking even more forlorn than before.

"Sorry I'm late," she mumbled. "There was a..." she stopped cold as her eyes met Ghost. Her mouth hung open. Ghost looked, if possible, even more shocked than Kiki.

"Ta-daaaaaaa!" Carson made an elaborate sweep of his arm. "Now, I know this is a bit of a surprise, but I also know that you two are friends. Or were. Or something. Anyway. The way I figure it, you two just need to talk it out. After all," Carson nodded suggestively at the tree. "It's Christmas."

The living room was dominated by an absolute, complete, awful, terrible silence.

Carson gave things a moment. Neither one moved. Not even a twitch. "Okay, maybe things were a little worse than I thought," he started again. "So, let's prime the pump. Joe, why don't you start. Just tell Kiki how you feel about her."

Joe shuffled his feet, looking as if he might throw himself out a window. "I... I don't think this is a good idea..." his eyes probed the floor, his whisper hoarse and faint.

"It's not," Kiki snapped. "It's a stupid idea."

Carson glanced at her, struck by the venom in her voice. "Uh..." he shook his head, tearing his eyes away from the sudden fury that had masked her face. "Uh..." he repeated, unsure of how to continue. It wasn't going at all as he had planned. "Let's just... let's just try to act like adults, shall we? Why don't you two sit and talk, and I'll go get some milk and cookies," he headed for the kitchen. "Unless you want cocoa?"

"I don't want cocoa," the loathing in Kiki's voice stopped him cold. "I don't want *anything* from you." She whirled to face him, her voice a hiss. "I never have! Can't you get that through your thick skull?!"

It was Carson's turn to stare, appalled. Somewhere inside him, a tiny voice was starting to whisper that maybe, just perhaps, this hadn't been the wisest of ideas.

Kiki snapped her gaze back to Ghost, her eyes full of cold blue hate. "And *you*," Ghost cringed like a kicked puppy. "I have *nothing* to say to you. *Nothing!*" She hitched up her bag and turned for the door.

"Wait... hey, you can't...!" Carson took a step towards her.

"The hell I can't!" Kiki whirled, her voice rising.

"Kiki," Ghost's gentle whisper cut through the tension. "I'm sorry it went down like this. It wasn't how I wanted this to go. But we... we love you. We just want to help..."

"*Help*?! You wanna *help* me?!" Kiki rounded, and the look on her face made Carson wish desperately that she would have continued out the door. The muscles of her jaw worked in silent rage, eyes bulging, her hollow cheeks stark and white. "If you wanna *help* me, then get a clue and *leave me the hell alone*!! Both of you! I can take care of myself!!" She raised a clenched fist, words choking in her throat. The wrath of her gaze settled on Carson. "What *is* it with you!?! First..." she floundered, apparently unwilling to put words to what had happened between them. "*That*... and now... *this*?! Why can't you keep out of people's business?! Why can't you keep out of *my* business?!"

"Okay... ouch," Carson drew back, wounded. "Maybe, I overstepped a bit, but let's not get crazy. Let's all just have some cocoa and sort this out," he snatched up a cup from a serving tray and pressed it into her hand.

Kiki's eyes widened more. Her knuckles were white and her hand shook.

"Maybe I should just go," Ghost took a step for the door.

"What?!" Carson's eyes flared. "No, no go! Stay! Talk! C'mon, Joe... say something!" Carson could hear the air raid siren. His carefully laid plans were on the verge of being bombed into oblivion.

Somehow, Ghost found his courage. He paused, cleared his throat. "Kiki, we... I... we... always tried to do right. By you. I know you're mad... I've heard... I'm just worried. Word on the street is... you're not... that you've started again..."

"*NO!*" Kiki shrieked. Carson had thought she was mad before, but now her face shone brighter than the Christmas lights. "*Don't you lecture me*!!! You taught me *everything* I know – don't you *dare* tell me when to use it!!" With a violence that was startling, Kiki hurled her cup into the wall. China smashed and brown splattered.

"Hey! Cup!" Carson blurted.

But Kiki was unstoppable. Obsessed.

She stormed across the room in a cold fury, eyes boring into Ghost. "I *learned* from you, *idolized* you... I *lived* for you!"

"I taught you what you needed to know," Ghost, for his part, met her gaze. Carson didn't know how anyone could. "I was only trying to help."

"I *thought* I *told* you... *I don't need your %^&*#@! help*!!"

They were nose to nose now. The rage in Kiki's face was as stark and glaring as the pain and shame on Ghost's.

"When we found you... after your Dad had... I wanted to..."

"*YOU'RE NOT MY DAD!!!*" Kiki screamed.

"Kiki!" Carson took a step, desperate for the shouting to stop.

"*And YOU...!*" Furious, face contorted, she whirled on him. "*You're not my... ANYTHING*!! *AND YOU NEVER WILL BE!!*" She spun and stormed for the exit.

Carson was totally, completely and utterly aghast. Without thinking, without pausing, without considering, he reached out and took her arm. "Kiki, wait..."

She slapped him.

The stinging violence of it sent shock waves through his brain.

Then, as if to underscore the fact that it was no accident, she slapped him again.

Pictures rattled as the door slammed. Kiki was gone.

Carson didn't move. Couldn't. He simply stood, feeling the awful burn on his cheek. The look of hatred and torment on Kiki's face hurt even worse.

After a moment, he forced his head to turn, staring helplessly into the living room. It was empty. Ghost was gone.

Numbly, Carson stood, oblivious to the slow drip of cocoa running down the wall, grasping for anything that might help explain how things had gone so terribly, terribly wrong.

* * * * * * *

Three days later, although the red hand prints had faded from Carson's face, the memory of them remained. It still stung.

It was another cold, drizzly evening at the 24/7, the night painfully slow and leaving Carson far too much time to think. He sat idly on his stool, chin on fist, doing just that - replaying the scene from Granny's, sifting through every comment, every expression, every word, struggling to suss out just where it had all fallen into the ditch.

Carson rubbed his cheek absently. He tipped back on the stool, musing. The plan had been perfect. It should have worked. Unless...

An uncomfortable thought ruffled him.

Had Kiki been right?

Could it be that he had meddled where he shouldn't have?

Carson snorted. "No way," he muttered, dropping his stool to the floor. It wasn't his fault. It couldn't be. The whole thing was her malfunction, not his. He'd just been trying to help. In fact, if anyone should be angry, it should be *him.* He allowed himself a moment of righteous indignation. Some people. Some people you just couldn't help. He headed for the Freezie machine to drink to the idea and put the whole sorry mess behind him.

Bzzzzz...!

Carson pulled his cell phone from his pocket. "This is Carson Dudley, welcome to the first day of the rest of my life, how can I help you?"

"Carson! Thank heaven."

"Um... Professor Looney? I hope. I hardly recognized your voice. You sound a little... um... is everything okay?"

"Yes, yes, everything's fine," Looney rushed along unconvincingly. "Can you come to the college? I've got something to show you."

"Well, sure, I guess. Maybe tomorrow morn..."

"Not tomorrow. Tonight."

"Tonight?! What's up?"

"It's better if I show you. Hard to explain over the phone."

Carson frowned. The professor's voice sounded odd. "Okay. I'll try. But it'll be late."

"How late?"

"Look, Professor, I'm at work. It's gonna be awhile."

There was a short, calculating silence. "As soon as you can then?"

"You bet, Professor. As soon as I can."

The line went dead. Carson sat back down, his Freezie forgotten. He leaned back on the stool again, wondering at the strain in the Professor's voice and what could possibly be so important at midnight at Las Calamas Community College. A flash of light caught his eye through the front window. Lightning. It was too far away to hear the thunder, but Carson knew instinctively, somehow, that it was getting closer. He frowned at a sudden inexplicable weight in his stomach. There was something in the professor's voice... A glance at his watch showed him it was still several hours until the end of his shift. That wouldn't work.

He rose to head for Kinkade's office, only to look his boss directly in the eye.

Kinkade was standing opposite him on the other side of the counter, tablet in one hand. He was watching Carson, eyes inscrutable behind square lenses. "I couldn't help but overhearing. Trouble?"

"Not sure," Carson played the tape of his conversation with Looney again in his head. "Maybe. Friend of mine. Weird call."

"It's been slow tonight. Why don't you go? I can mind the store."

Carson gaped. He should be getting used to it by now, he knew. "You can mind... you mean, you don't care if I..."

Kinkade displayed a thin-lipped grimace, what Carson had begun to recognize lately as a smile. "Things are slow, and with the weather, they're bound to stay that way. Go. See your friend."

Carson peered at him intently. Kinkade stared back with his usual blank expression. With a mental shrug, Carson smothered his doubts and Sister Becky's vague concerns and reached for his sweatshirt. "Well, if you insist, Mr. Kinkade. Thanks a ton. I really think it's nothing, but... ah, nerts! My truck's on the fritz. And there's no late bus to LC tonight."

"Take my car."

Carson froze. This time, his jaw literally dropped. "Take your... the *Beemer*?!"

Kinkade nodded and produced the keys. He held them out flat in his palm, filling the space between them. They were shiny. "Of course. It's parked out front. I just had it washed."

Carson stared at the keys. "I... I..."

"There you are then," Kinkade pressed them into his hand and steered him toward the door. "Off with you now. Loyalty to friends. *That's* the kind of quality 7 Corporation is looking for."

Minutes later, Carson was nosing the sleek black BMW through light traffic and wondering if too much time staring at a tablet could induce brain damage. He wasn't, however, wondering it too hard. The Beemer was an excellent ride.

Soon he was pulling into visitor parking at Las Calamas Community College, his journey over far too quickly. He stood beside the car a moment, soaking up the sleek black lines, the custom leather interior, the smell of it still on his clothes. It made the thought of picking up – and paying for – the Magic Carpet depressing. With a sigh, he pointed himself toward the Biology building and set off at a trot, barely remembering to *chirp* the car door lock. Another flash of lightning lit the sky, illuminating for a moment the brooding brick buildings and overbearing clouds. After a few seconds, thunder split the sky. He'd been right. Closer.

It was coming fast, too. Carson felt like it was almost on top of him by the time he reached his destination and ducked inside. The door was, strangely enough, unlocked. Once inside, he threw back his hood, spattering dark droplets on the tile floor. He shivered, grateful to be out of the weather. Carson listened for a moment but heard nothing. The whole building was dark and silent. A single light illuminated the stairwell nearby, but otherwise, the place was empty and eerie. He headed for the second floor, eager to be with people.

Carson topped the stairs and faced the long empty hallway that led to the lecture halls. Choked with shadows, its vaulted ceiling lost high overhead, the corridor yawned before him. He could barely make out several recessed doorways set along its sides, like small hungry mouths set inside a much larger, much hungrier one. It felt like a tomb. Rain beat against the floor-to-ceiling, leaded glass window that consumed the entire far wall, masking the rapid beat of his feet on the tiles.

He reached the classroom door and paused. Faint yellow light shone from within. In spite of the professor's invitation, he knocked. "Professor? Hello... Professor Looney?"

No answer.

Carson tried the handle, an ornate iron affair. Like the front door, it was unlatched. He shoved on the door, surprised by its weight. The thing was heavy, made of dark, pitted, polished wood, worn with the years, like the great brooding portal to a castle throne room.

"Professor Looney?"

A flash of lightning illuminated the large chamber, highlighting scattered chairs and the lecture stage. The stage drew his attention, broad wooden tables, clusters of beakers and bottles, grim antique chalkboards covered with spidery sketches and notes. In the center of it all, illuminated for the briefest of instants, was a shadowy silhouette wrapped in a lab coat, hunched over a large, unidentifiable, sheet-covered something. Carson, for the life of him, felt as if he had stepped right onto the set of *Doctor Freakshow's Midnight Horror Jamboree.* Scarcely a second passed when a shuddering, thunderous boom shook the room, as if a bomb had detonated right outside the window. The storm was close now. Right on top of them. The first patters of what would be a very heavy rain began to pelt the windows.

Carson took a breath, willing his heart to stay in his chest, and blinked against the blue-white residuals of the lightning flash. "Hey, Professor! It's me, Carson."

Across the lecture hall, looking small and vulnerable under the towering ceiling and oppressive emptiness, Professor Looney looked up from his work. Yellow light from an antique lamp gleamed off his bald head and made his cheeks look hollow and sunken. "Ah! Carson! Thank goodness! Come. Come quick!" He beckoned urgently, his eyes feverish. "I've found something!"

As he headed down a narrow aisle, Carson's earlier sense of nervousness grew. Without its chattering students and the hum of learning, the place felt too big and too empty and too old. In spite of all that emptiness, he was struck by the sense that he was being watched - like an experiment in a dish, exposed. He had felt that here before. He leapt onto the stage, skipping the steps, bouncy with nerves.

The Professor looked up from a microscope. His face was eager, hungry, almost ghoulish in the long shadows. "It's good to see you, Carson! Thanks for coming – I know this must seem strange, bizarre, even. But believe me, you'll be glad you came! I'll be calling the police, of course, but I wanted to make sure I talked to you first. I've got questions, ones only you can answer, and I'm afraid, once this gets out, they'll take my research and... well... it's just... just unbelievable!" He ruffled through a mess of papers as he talked, selected one and scrawled a note, his movements jerky and agitated.

"Whoa, Prof, just slow down a sec! The police?! Why would you call them? What they hoo-ha-hey is going on?!"

"Your sample, Carson! From your cat. I don't know what this is about - I mean I *really* don't know! - and part of me wishes I'd never even heard of it... but there's... something here. Something important. Something diabolical!" He looked Carson in the eyes. His own were haunted.

"Well," Carson struggled to process. "Uh, yeah. Of course. I mean, you said you found the... what's it called... Regicide... Regulus... Romulan..."

"Regilin!"

"Yeah, that. It's a... what did you say it was... a transplant drug?"

"Yes! But that was just the start," the Professor snatched a worn leather briefcase, jamming papers and notes inside as his words spilled out. "I also told you I thought I'd found something else – something that required further study. That there was more there to discover. Well, I was right! And this is the proof!" he fumbled to remove the slide he'd been studying under the microscope, but his fingers seemed stiff and awkward, unable to work the clips.

"Here, let me," Carson reached for the microscope, fumbled also, then realized his own hands were slick with sweat. His earlier sense of nervousness had spiked and his heart was starting to beat hard again. He wiped his palms on his jeans fiercely, forcing himself to calm down. "Look, Professor, I really don't think you need to worry about any of this. Now that you mention it, I seem to remember Frisky *did* have a transplant... yeah, that's it! I totally remember now," Carson got the slide unlatched and held it out. "There was this weed whacker you see, and she never did have very good depth perception..."

"You don't understand!" The Professor snatched the slide away and placed it carefully in a small black container. Carson could see several others in the briefcase already. "There's more, *much* more! I just verified it again, before you arrived! There's no doubt – some of this tissue is *human*! *Human!* And Carson, that's just the beginning! What I found..."

Lightning flashed again and immediately on its heels thunder boomed and roared, unbelievably loud, swallowing Professor Looney's words like a finch in a hurricane. Carson felt it right through his bones. It rattled Petri dishes and metal instruments up and down the stage, making him feel as if he were inside the world's biggest timpani. He prayed for it to stop.

"...not even from our world!" The Professor's voice rose above the aftershocks. He had been talking non-stop, eyes round and wild inside the dark smudges of sleepless nights and the eerie shadows of the desk lamp. "Don't you *see*?! They're *not*! *They simply can't be*!"

Carson felt the small hairs on the back of his neck rise. With an effort of will, he unclenched his hands and forced his mind away from crazy. Whatever Looney had found, whatever Dr. Deth had been up to, it was moot now. Over. The threat was gone. They'd seen to that. The best bet was to bury it all and not look back.

"Look, Prof," Carson raised his hands placatingly. "Take it easy. Let's just put the brakes on the crazy train here. Whatever you found, I'm sure there's some explanation."

"No, Carson! That's just it! *There is no explanation*! Not for this! You'll see... I'm taking the evidence to the authorities. I've got to. They'll confirm it!" He shook his head feverishly. "I've run every conceivable test, and everything points to..."

Another flash, another unbelievable boom. Carson shielded his eyes and squinted, waiting, praying again for it to stop. When it did, the Professor was still talking, rambling, back to hurriedly cramming papers and samples into his briefcase.

"... human and animal tissue! And then the Regilin – I know what it was used for now! It had to be! It's the only explanation..."

Behind them, somewhere in the dark Stygian depths of the room, Carson's thunder-numbed ears caught a sound. It was faint, mournful, half heard, half imagined.

"*Meeeeoow...*"

"Wait! Professor, did you just hear...?!"

"But it doesn't stop there, Carson – there was something else. Something deeper... something impossible... something... something..." Professor Looney groped for words, his eyes roving wildly.

"*Meeeeoow...*"

"Professor...!"

Looney was oblivious, ranting, words tumbling over words. "...something *undefinable*! You don't get it... *science* can't even explain...!"

"Professor Looney, *shut up!!*"

This time when the lightning went off, the entire wall of windows behind the Professor flashed with the intensity of a thousand searchlights. Carson's eyes clamped involuntarily. It did no good. The white hot flare flashed straight through his eyelids. He could smell the sizzle of electricity. The shuddering, monumental crash of thunder didn't wait, coming almost simultaneously. It was like a freight train through the room and Carson felt as if he were rolling under it.

"*Meeeeoow...!*"

...was the first thing Carson heard when the booming stopped. This time he was sure of it. Desperately sure. In spite of his certainty that Deth was gone, the threat neutralized, the nightmare over – in spite of everything - Carson felt the first, small tickle of fear up his spine. "Okay! Okay, look, I believe you!" Carson put one hand on the Professor's shoulder and another on the briefcase, stopping the mad packing. "We're getting out of here - we'll get someplace not so flippin' freaky and sort this out, okay?! But first, tell me one thing. Please... and I mean *pretty, pretty please with a box of chocolates and a Starbucks gift card...* please tell me you own a cat!"

The Professor stared at Carson, his eyes blank and vacant. "A cat? No. I don't own a cat."

"*Meeeeoow...!*"

Carson felt something brush his leg, and his eyes jerked down.

There, staring up at him with wide, luminous eyes, was a large, hairless cat. Attached to its back, fresh red stitches clearly visible, was a human hand. The fingers stroked his leg.

Carson's stomach gave a lurch. Just as the hand closed on his jeans, he kicked hard out of instinct and revulsion, sending the thing spinning and sliding across the stage with an angry, chopped-off *mewl!*

"Professor... *RUN!!*"

Then, the lightning flashed again and in that heartbeat, over the Professor's shoulder and outside the windows, Carson caught a glimpse of a huge, misshapen bulk swinging toward them like a wrecking ball. The mighty crash of glass and wood burst over them, mingling with the colossal, unearthly chaos of thunder, blending into a single spine-shaking explosion. Something ragged and massive and roaring plowed through tables and equipment and then the Professor like a cannon ball through a sack of sticks. Carson heard bones go and watched Looney's neck snap just as the lamp went out. Something struck him in the chest, and he went over backward, hurtling off the stage.

Crashing into a row of chairs, Carson lost himself momentarily, thrashing desperately through splinters of wood and stabs of pain. He surged to his feet in a world of darkness and madness and the hissing mewling shriek of cats. He hurled himself sideways, away from the thing that had come through the window and the clutching swarm of feline bodies that tangled his feet and clawed and grabbed at his legs. Desperately, he kicked and fought and shouted, banging desks and stumbling over chairs, falling, leaping up, swinging wild, charging blindly.

Suddenly, in the midst of his breathless, heart pounding, full on panic, Carson found himself in the clear, still swinging but momentarily free. He whirled wildly, frantically trying to get his bearings.

Coat racks.

Drinking fountain.

Door.

A dozen feet away. It was close.

As Carson's brain kicked into gear, he dimly realized that something was in his hands. Something he had been swinging, instinctively, gripped tight as if it were his baseball bat. He glanced down, and his heart leaped. The Professor's leather briefcase. Proof.

He launched for the door then slid to a halt as thoughts of Professor Looney brought him up short. He might still be...

From the direction of the stage, a sickening sound burst over him – a pounding, crunching, violent noise, as if someone was taking a sledgehammer to the Christmas goose. Suddenly it stopped, replaced by a low, ominous growl like the thunder in miniature but infinitely more threatening. Wood scraped on wood then crashed as a heavy oak table was hurled effortlessly through the air.

MOVE! his brain screamed. He complied.

Carson's lunge for the door was cut short as something tangled his legs, and he went down amid a swarm of hairless flesh and needle teeth. They tore into his hand, ripped fiercely at his sweatshirt and jeans. The briefcase flew from his grasp and skittered away. Behind him, thudding steps shook the floor and furniture crashed as desks were tossed aside like tinker toys.

Carson thrashed and rolled frantically, galvanized by the sound of approaching destruction. Several handi-cats were torn loose, and in that split-second window, he lunged, driving for where he imagined the briefcase had slid. Mercifully, another flash of lightning split the scene, brilliantly illuminating it. The leather bag was just a few feet away under a desk. Carson felt relief sweep through him and lunged... only to have the way barred by a pack of hissing, spitting felines. Raised claws swiped savagely. The hand on the back of the nearest, this one a woman's Carson noted with detached revulsion, bared its chipped and battered red nails. Carson froze. Then, he did the only thing he could think of:

He barked.

As loud and fierce and desperate as fear and adrenaline could make him.

The cats flinched back.

Without hesitation, Carson shot his hand between them, snatched up the briefcase and swung, scattering the hairless furies with thuds and hisses. Then, he was up and gone, straight for the door, head down, sprinting like a madman. He had just enough presence of mind to catch the edge of the door and fling it shut behind him, and then he was off down the hallway as if it was on fire. As he hit the stairs, something hit the classroom door, going *through* it and slamming off the far wall with a growl that was far enough from human to send goosebumps all over him. Carson took the marble stairs at full tilt, throwing caution to the wind and letting absolute, unhindered panic do the driving. He barely felt the steps, and as he flew into the main hallway on the ground floor, he overshot the exit by a dozen feet, sliding past to a shoe-squeaking stop, arms windmilling.

By the time he rounded, it was too late. A dark mass crashed to the bottom of the stairs behind him with a sound as solid as a wall safe dropped from a second story window. Unlike a safe, it immediately glided forward a few steps, crouching in the deep shadows by the exit. Whatever the thing was, it was fast, powerful and agile - far beyond its obvious bulk. It was also undeniably angry. A violent growl escaped its throat and set Carson's stomach into a flight of butterflies.

This was followed immediately by an electric surge of fear as he realized his position.

The thing was blocking the exit.

Without a second thought, Carson whirled and was off, legs churning, arms pumping, eyes roving frantically for any means of escape. He swept around a corner, down a hallway and smashed through a set of double doors into a library, the shuddering thud of footsteps close on his heels. Another sound – huge, powerful lungs sucking air, like a great iron bellows – told him just how little distance there was between them. The sound put lightning to his heels. Carson flew across the room, vaulting tables, tipping chairs and scattering books into the path of his pursuer, eyes fixed on the glowing green "Exit" sign that lit the darkness ahead. Behind, he heard a guttural grunt and a crash as the whatever-it-was stumbled over a chair he'd toppled. Carson didn't look back. He hit the exit at a full sprint, banged through into another hallway, veered left without checking and met another set of stairs.

"No way...!" Carson slid to a halt, heart sinking. "Up?! Howdy Doody!"

But there was no time to think. Behind him the library doors crashed open, one tearing completely free and smashing into the far wall.

"Up it is!" Willing his burning legs to move, Carson took the stairs three at a time, praising God for his weekly runs and resolving to make them daily runs. The stairway led him back to the second floor but to a different section of the building, this one unfamiliar. Wildly casting about, he spotted a door, prayed and banged into it. It opened. Whipping across the room, he ducked out into another smaller hallway, turned and pounded on, forcing himself to think, trying to map out the building in his mind. Another door, another hall, another door. As he flashed through a cluttered classroom, realization dawned that the last door he'd slammed hadn't crashed open yet, and he slowed his pace to listen, trying to get a bead on his pursuer, nerves jangling and electric.

Somewhere behind him, something banged. It was not the way Carson had come from. His hammering heart gave a great leap of hope. He'd given it the slip.

Ducking into the shadows of an alcove, Carson stopped, breathing hard into his arm to muffle the sound. He could feel his heart slowing. After a moment, he pulled his hoodie over his head and peered cautiously into the hall. Nothing. A door creaked from somewhere to his right, and he jumped. But it wasn't close. Time to move.

He stepped out and drifted down the hallway, scanning for stairs, exit signs, anything. Totally disoriented by his flight, Carson gave up thinking and trusted to luck. His breathing was coming easier now. He turned a corner and found himself facing a long, narrow hallway. At the far end, a welcome sight.

Stairs. Stairs going down.

He just might make it.

Hitching up the briefcase, he took a step.

"*Meeeeoow...*"

"Oh, come *on...!*" Carson froze. At the head of the stairs, a small, four-legged blob of naked flesh detached itself from the shadows and sauntered lazily forward. Then another. And another. Now it was a mob. A flash of lightning lit the scene, sending an eerie shadow of the cats and their casually flexing hands painting the wall behind. The boom of thunder was loud enough to cover their fiendish mewling but not loud enough to mask the sudden thud of heavy feet - from down the hall, just around the corner. Behind him.

He was trapped.

"Ginger S*naaaaaaaps!*" Carson whispered frantically, twisting about for a hiding place, a weapon, anything. His eyes caught a wink of glass in the wall nearby. Fire extinguisher. He considered only a second then moved. Glass smashed as he jerked an elbow into the case. The thudding footsteps stopped, just around the corner, less than ten feet away.

As quietly as he could, Carson levered the fire extinguisher out of its cradle, stepped flat against the wall a foot away from the corner and planted his feet. Quickly, he tested the weight of the cylinder. It was unwieldy but heavy. Solid. Not his baseball bat, not by a long shot, but it would pack a punch. He hoped it was enough. He slowed his breathing and waited.

Rain lashed against a tall ornate window at the end of the hall, a thin stream of light from some distant source passing through it and giving faint illumination to the scene. Carson watched, stifling a gasp as a long, misshapen shadow slanted across the hall. The eerie mewling of the handi-cats was coming closer, but he didn't dare risk a glance behind him. He knew where the greater threat lay. As he stood, feeling the cold sweat trickle down his back, a sudden, desperate idea occurred to him. He glanced again at the window.

Desperate *and* stupid.

Adjusting his grip on the extinguisher, he set his heel against the wall and listened, ears peeled for the telltale scrape or scuff that would warn him that his foe was rounding the corner. But there was nothing. No sound of its approach. Nothing but the hammering of the rain on the glass and the approaching mewl of the cats. He could hear the swish of their tails now, picture their sickening, casual saunter as they approached his hiding place. Carson waited, forcing himself to stand absolutely still.

With a sudden tingle of shock, Carson realized that his assailant was right beside him. What he had thought was merely the darkness of

140

the hallway was actually the darkness of a humanoid form, taller than him by a head and shoulders and close enough to touch. Somehow, it had drifted around the corner on feet more stealthy than humanly possible. Carson caught just a glimpse of pallid flesh - gaunt, shadowed features - stitches. Then, he swung, straight for the face, with all the fury of his full-on panic.

"For the Shire!!"

Bone crunched and metal dented. There was an angry grunt like the snort of a bull. To Carson, it felt like he'd hit a Humvee. Ignoring the jarring numbness in his arm, he swung again, then again, then again, each time rewarded by a grunt as the thing flinched back, giving him precious space. Then, he was ducking past, pelting down the hall toward the window. Without stopping to think, he hurled the fire extinguisher through the glass and followed it with a headlong dive.

Carson had seen bushes on campus and hoped there were some beneath the window. He had been right. He had seen movies where stunt men had fallen from two stories into such bushes and assumed it wouldn't hurt much. He had been wrong. Crashing through sticks and shrubs, he came down mightily on solid earth, only slightly softened by the rain and hard enough to jolt him almost senseless. Fighting to his feet, he was up and staggering away across the lawn in a limping run, immediately aware that his knee was on fire.

Behind him, the ground shuddered as his relentless pursuer followed him out the window. It was still coming.

"Crudlickers!!" Carson fought the urge to look over his shoulder and spurred his aching body to greater speed. He could feel his endurance ebbing. Rain slashed and hammered him, obscuring his vision, blurring everything into a sheet of dark and wet. He couldn't see, didn't know where he was, which way to run. The burning in his knee was incredible.

Suddenly, his legs were clipped out from under him by a terrific impact, and he flew, tumbling, spinning across the sodden grass. He rolled to his elbow in a panic, spotted a hulking shape nearby and almost screamed – then his eyes focused on one of the iron park benches beside the parking lot. He had charged straight into it in the dark. Momentary relief flooded him as he fought his way back to his feet.

His brain clicked.

The parking lot.

"The parking lot!" One hand was already diving for his pocket.

Whirling, Carson set off at a run, desperate hope giving wings to his feet. Dead ahead, he spotted Ross Kinkade's sleek black BMW, sitting alone in the center of the parking lot. He gave a whoop and mashed desperately at the key fob. Blinkers flashed, doors *chirped,* and within seconds, he was inside and listening with a flood of relief as the engine purred smoothly to life. With silent prayers of thanks for Ross Kinkade and German engineering, Carson groped gratefully for the gear shift.

From the darkness of the lawn came a terrific, rending, tearing sound. A dark shape hunched in the shadows then straightened with a powerful twist and a grunt. A darker blob detached and took flight, sailing through the air toward the car. Carson watched dumbly, hand freezing on the stick.

It was the iron park bench.

Galvanized, he slapped the car into reverse and punched the pedal. Tires squealed, smoked and caught. The auto jerked back, throwing Carson's chest into the steering wheel just as the huge bench crashed down in the spot he had just vacated. Pavement cracked. Rivets flew.

Carson kept the pedal down, still accelerating, then jammed the brakes and jerked the wheel, drawing another screech from the tires and spilling a pile of posters over himself from the passenger seat. In the rearview, he could see the hulking shape charging toward him. It was close. Too close. And impossibly fast. Slamming the car into gear, Carson mashed the gas, and the sleek Beemer lunged forward like a panther, fishtailing on the wet pavement then hurtling out onto the street.

Bright headlights, the blare of an air horn, a quick jerk of the wheel and he was past an onrushing semi. Then, Carson was back on the right side of the yellow and putting as much distance between himself and the school as six cylinders and no concern for traffic safety could.

After cooking through a dozen blocks and a few red lights, Carson's panic began to fade and his senses to return. He realized he was awash in paper - the latest marketing blitz from the 24/7. As he spared a hand to shove the stacks aside, the logo on one of the bright, happy posters caught his eye: *Fast service for those on the run!*

With an effort, Carson brought the speedometer back down into double digits. "You ain't kiddin'..."

* * * * * * *

"How's the knee?"

Carson winced as he settled a bag of ice on his injured leg. He glanced at Dex, who stood with his great arms folded, staring down. "It burns - a lot. But I'll live. Which," he added with a grimace, "is more than I can say for Professor Looney. Poor dude." He shook his head. "A lot of people I know die. Is it weird that I'm getting used to it?"

Beside him on the couch, Sister Becky smiled benignly. "Yes, dear. However, you will find it quite practical. In our line of work, it is often that or the Institute of St. Agnes."

"The Institute of St. Agnes?"

"A home for those whose brains have turned to pudding. Now, take your Ibuprofen. It will help with the swelling," she passed him some pills and a glass of water.

Dex waited, tapping his arm impatiently as if the medical attention was an unnecessary delay. "If you're done with all the hand-holdin', let's get to the story. I can't wait to hear this one. Or are we waitin' on Kiki? If so, I'm getting popcorn."

Carson felt his face flush. He bent over his knee, fussing with pillows. "Let's get started. She, uh... she can't make it."

Dex's brows contracted. "Can't make it?! What, she got a date?!"

"I said she's not coming," Carson snapped. He didn't see the point in telling them he hadn't called her. Or that she wouldn't have come anyway. Of that, at least, he was sure. "Now, do you wanna hear the story or not?" Without waiting for an answer, Carson plunged into a rapid retelling of his encounter at the college. When he was finished, Dex let out a grunt.

"Science is a dangerous business," he scratched himself thoughtfully. "Sounds like the Prof turned up something that made him a problem for somebody. And the only somebody that makes sense is Ol' Doc Deth. Could be that he ain't quite as dead as you thought."

Carson shook his head in consternation. "That's all I can think of too. Crepes! How did he do it?!"

"Musta found a way out."

"Or he's supernatural, impervious to fire or has the ability to clone himself. I haven't ruled those out."

"Excellent theories, Mr. Dudley."

"Whatever," Dex cracked his huge knuckles. "What I'm wonderin' about is how he got on our trail?"

"He must have started watching us right after that night. He knew me from the 24/7; that's a cinch. He could've put eyes on us easy with those handi-cats. Or the crats. Probably got wise to the Professor that way. Just followed us right to him. That explains why I always felt creeped out around the college. Deth has probably been watching it for days."

Silence fell as they digested Carson's words.

"We underestimated him," Sister Becky murmured.

"You mean I underestimated him," Carson felt a prickle of resentment at the nun's words - but she was right. He swung his leg off the pillows and hobbled to his nightstand. "I was wrong. I've been doing some thinking. Maybe, I was wrong about more than just that." He snatched up the wrinkled paper containing his Vision. It had been smoothed flat again. "Been going over what dreamy-time Pete told me. I think I goofed part of it," he scanned the page. "Here – this bit. 'Next comes... death. And death, and life, no interruptions.'" His eyes hardly noticed the words. He'd gone over them a hundred times since last night. "When I heard Pete say 'death', I wonder if he meant 'D-e-t-h,' as in 'Doctor' and not 'd-e-a-t-h' as in the opposite of getting up every day and going to work."

Sister Becky stroked her chin thoughtfully. "Next comes Deth, the man, and Deth again, alive when we thought him not. That certainly rings true in the present circumstances. But what of the rest? '...and life, no interruptions'?"

"Don't matter," Dex rumbled. Talk of Carson's Vision always made him fidgety. "It's gotta be Deth. Who else would do that to a cat?"

"That's not all," Carson limped back to the couch and fished through a stack of tabloids. "I turned to the usual sources – same as with Fujikacorp - and did some digging. Figured if Deth was up to something creep-tastic, there was bound to be evidence of it somewhere. Lo and behold, there was," he rifled through pages. "Stolen pets, missing corpses, missing persons... even a few of each with missing *parts*. A couple of big time medical robberies too - lab equipment, chemicals, meds. Then there's this: a guy who claims he saw a two-headed dog chasing his cat. Sound like anyone we know? Though the frog boy... I don't think that's legit," Carson flashed a photo of a youth with the head of a toad.

Sister Becky clucked approvingly. "Excellent detecting, Mr. Dudley. You are developing, how would you say it, 'skills'."

"Thanks," Carson gave a half smile. He didn't bother to tell her that both Ghost and Leet had given him almost exactly the same information, and that he had chosen to ignore it. He knew it was legit now. That was what mattered. "The way I figure it, the best clues we have to whatever is really going on are in here," he patted Professor Looney's worn leather briefcase. It hadn't left his side since last night. "The only problem is, it doesn't make a lick of sense. It's just a bunch of chicken scratch – formulas, notes – plus, a few slides with who-knows-what-kind-of-ick smeared on 'em. I don't know what I'm looking at, much less what it means."

Sister Becky took the briefcase and began to rummage through it.

"Sure would be nice to have a Forensics student 'bout now," Dex frowned, arms still folded. "'Can't make it,'" he snorted derisively.

Carson ignored him. "We gotta be careful who sees it, too. It already got one lab coat killed; I don't need any more on my conscience."

Sister Becky looked up from a sheaf of notes. "What of Detective Parsons? Ms. Masterson spoke of his guest lectures. Certainly, he might have resources sufficient to analyze this?"

Carson made a sour face. "Yeah. Right. Show up on Parson's doorstep with a pile of evidence I took from a crime scene? A crime scene I just *happened* to be at? *Another* crime scene? Another *murder* crime scene?! That would not end well."

Dex nodded quickly, hiding a worried face. "Uh... yup. Second that. Best to keep Parsons outta this. Ain't no good gonna come from dragging him into it."

Carson rolled his eyes inwardly. *No good for your love life,* he thought. Even though Dex was agreeing, the man's obvious bias irked him.

"Your points are well taken, gentlemen," Sister Becky held up a glass slide to the light, squinting at it. "In addition, the obvious supernatural element may place this beyond the reach of scientific discovery."

"Here we go again," Dex threw up his hands.

"What are you smelling, Sister B.? We talking bad science or mad science? You catching a whiff of something funky?"

"More than merely a whiff, Mr. Dudley. We are, as the expression goes, 'awful deep in offal deep'. Consider the normal order of life – the animals abounding on Earth. Their complexity, symmetry and design point quite obviously to a Creator – anyone who looks honestly upon them can hardly draw any other conclusion, unless of course they fear the consequences of having a Creator themselves. In stark contrast, as I am certain you agree, are the products of Mr. Deth's work. These are corrupted perversions, horrific in form and wicked in function, and their very abilities place them outside the realm of Created beings. Outside the realm of traditional science, I would propose. Or irresponsible science. Or even *possible* science. These abominations were spawned, I submit, by an entirely other order of science. As you phrased it..."

"Mad."

Sister Becky nodded approvingly. "Precisely. You theorized moments ago that Mr. Deth had sent his creatures to spy upon us. How would he so instruct them bound by the rules of this world? And how would they report information back to him with the same restrictions? And take for example, this creature... the monstrosity which assaulted you at the college..."

"I'm going with 'Manstruct.' It had stitches. That's not right."

"Indeed. I believe you will agree that this Manstruct exhibited characteristics far beyond the limitations of the Created world. Its strength. Resilience. Speed."

"Um... yeah. I think that's safe to say."

"Then, that leaves only one alternative. As deep as our understanding of science goes, one cannot make *life* out of *unlife,* Mr. Dudley, nor can we enhance that life beyond the earthly limitations by which it is bound. Not without help."

Carson's head was spinning. Sister Becky didn't specify exactly what "help" she was referring to, but he had a fairly good idea of the direction she was headed. He had thought he'd had a handle on it all. But now... his thoughts drifted back to the humanoid mass they had found in the vat at Deth's hideout. He recalled Kiki's dismay – horror even - regarding the blueprints she'd spotted and her refusal to say what they contained.

Then, there was Deth's hat.

Something under it had *moved.* On its own. Twice. How in the world could...

Carson stopped himself. Maybe Becky was right. The possibilities made him shiver. "Professor Looney... just before he died, he said something about... how did he put it..." he remembered back to Looney's fevered rantings.

Not even from our world.

That's what he'd said.

Carson swallowed. "Well, it didn't make sense."

"The only thing that does at this moment, Mr. Dudley, is that your adversary is meddling with powers far beyond the mortal coil. Dark, dangerous and diabolical. And that he knows who you are. And that he has in his employ a brutal and ruthless killer."

"I wanna fight it," Dex flexed his muscles unconsciously.

"It's big, Dex."

"So am I."

Sister Becky sighed loudly. "Yes. Well. Testosterone. At any rate, Mr. Dudley, you must use extreme caution. More observation is called for and much discretion."

"Well," Dex stretched and yawned. "Whatever this ugly is, it's gonna have to wait one more night to get tuned up by the Big Man," he hitched up his overloaded equipment belt. "Gotta cover a shift over at the Super Shop-A-Lot. I'm on 'til five a.m., so if anything comes knockin' before then, you're on your own. Unless you can catch me on a break."

Dex grabbed his coat and moseyed out.

"Is it just me, or should he be taking this more seriously?" Carson pressed back into the couch, his mind full of dark thoughts and worries. His knee was throbbing again.

"I am certain his remarks were spurious, Mr. Dudley. Of course, with the heathen, one can never be totally certain."

""That's a comfort. And speaking of comforts, I couldn't help but notice you said '*you* must use extreme caution.' As in not *you* you but *me* you. As in *you* you won't be helping *me* you."

The nun looked at him, her expression sober. "I need to discuss a matter with you, Mr. Dudley. A matter of some importance." She paused, staring steadily into his eyes. "I have had my hearing."

Carson blinked. "What... your... you mean *the* hearing?! You mean the big... already?! Why didn't you say something?!"

"You have had many burdens of late. I did not wish to add to them. This one was mine to bear, not yours."

"Well..." Carson struggled to feel supportive and not snubbed. Supportive won but barely. "Okay. How did it go? What did they say?"

"In one manner, it went very well. Very well indeed. However, in another manner, it has placed me in a difficult decision. I am faced with a dilemma."

Carson waited.

"I have been offered the chance to renew my work."

"Great jumpin' catfish! No way! That's fabulous... right?" Carson guessed, from the look in her eye, that it wasn't as simple as that.

"Yes. And no. As my Order has been disbanded, I would be

required to operate in a limited capacity at first – a trial basis, as it were. I would also be required to do so under the direct scrutiny of a very specific and select governing body. To put the needle to the rip, Mr. Dudley - I would need to relocate."

"Hm. Um... okay. Where to? LA? San Fran?"

"Naples."

Carson blinked again. "Um... that's, down by... er... far from... is that... east of San Fernando...?"

"It is in Italy, Mr. Dudley. Naples, *Italy*."

Carson had felt snubbed before. Now, he felt punched in the gut. He kept his expression neutral. It wasn't easy. "Tough choice."

"Indeed. And one on which I have already prayed much," Sister Becky fixed her gaze on him.

Carson held it, green eyes on green. She was probing. Testing. His face stayed calm, but inside he was in turmoil. He struggled with his emotions, pushing back against a quick wave of abandonment and disbelief. A spark of righteous anger helped. So what if she left? He had changed, grown; Sister Becky had said so herself. He had wondered before if he even still needed her. Now, he knew.

The expression must have showed on his face. Somehow, that seemed to be just what the nun was waiting for. She broke the gaze and fussed with her skirts. "In the end, however, the proper choice is quite obvious. I must accept the offer. I have a calling to attend to; one I had feared was long dead. I cannot ignore any opportunity to once again give it life. I trust you understand, lad."

"Gal's gotta do what a gal's gotta do. Like you said... it's your calling."

"Quite," she flashed him a prim smile. Then, she rose. "I shall be off at once, of course. There is an old acquaintance of mine in Italy – perhaps you have heard me mention Father Nicholas? I believe he could be of assistance in strengthening my case, and I have arranged a meeting with him in advance of my new assignment. Much to knit and only one candle, as the saying goes." She collected her shawl and, with a bustle of black skirts, was suddenly at the door.

Too suddenly. A wave of uncertainty washed over Carson. "Sister B..."

She stopped, staring back at him. Carson paused. He was on his feet, one hand on the wall for support. His knee throbbed. His thoughts went back to the first time they had met, standing in the 24/7, when she had joined his cause and saved his life.

No, he corrected himself. *Not* the first time they had met.

That had been years before, perhaps in this very room. Granny had told him. Sister Becky had not. Life was suddenly very, very confusing. Carson swallowed what he had intended to say. "Good luck."

The nun gave a curt nod, turned to go, then turned back once more. There was just a hint of melancholy on her weathered face. "My final counsel for you, Mr. Dudley, is this: bumps that hurt the worst teach the best. As far as you have come, dear boy, you have much yet to learn. Some of it comes at a price. Godspeed."

The door closed with a thump behind her.

Carson stood alone in the small room for some time. Finally, with a sigh, he headed for the shower. By the time he'd finished and crawled into bed, he wanted nothing but sleep. His knee was still throbbing, and his body ached everywhere else. The day's events had left him feeling lonely, scraped thin and exhausted. A little oblivion was exactly what he needed.

He was just drifting off to sleep when the phone rang. Carson glanced at the clock. Just past midnight. He groaned and answered it.

"I found out why Kiki wasn't at the meeting," Dex's deep voice rumbled over the line.

"Yeah? Well, good for you. I don't really care."

"You better." There was a pause. "She's in jail."

CHAPTER NINE

Stolen

Carson sat in the foyer of the jail, staring dully at the steady stream of prostitutes, criminals and cops. He had been waiting for over an hour since posting bail for Kiki, and every moment had been a torment - his head whirled, his stomach was in knots, and his knee throbbed. Then, there was the smell. He had long ago given up on trying to get used to it. The one consolation to the whole miserable experience was that Kiki had not been arrested in Patch Parson's precinct. Having to face his nemesis would have been the final crushing blow in a day full of them. It wasn't much, but it was something.

Checking his watch for the hundredth time, Carson hoisted himself out of his seat and limped to the window. He was reassured to see that his truck was still parked at the curb outside. He was not reassured to see that it was still leaking fluids. And still parked in the "15 Minute Parking" zone. In spite of the long wait, he simply hadn't had the energy to move it. At least it hadn't been towed - that was *two* good somethings now. Carson sighed. It was a short list. It wasn't likely to get any longer.

He leaned his head on the cool glass of the window, brooding. He had no idea what he was going to say to Kiki, how she would react to him being here, posting her bail... or even how he was going to afford it. It was a blessing that the Magic Carpet had been fixed and ready for pickup that morning, but the bill was even higher than the quote, and it still made strange noises and leaked. Dex had been right – he had a lot to learn about cars. After that, he'd driven straight to the precinct. And there he had waited. And waited. And waited. He also had a lot to learn about jails.

"You here for Masterson?"

Carson turned, heart in his throat. A grumpy looking sergeant stood by the desk, clipboard in one hand and Kiki in the other. The officer stared at him, but Kiki just stared at the wall. Her stocking cap was absent, hair pale and stringy and exposed. The battered old canvas coat was gone, too, her shoulders poking out of a tank top like a pair of scrawny white chicken wings. Carson had to look twice to make sure it was her.

But it was.

In the police station.

In jail.

"Yeah," he limped over, trying to act like bailing people out of jail was something he did all the time.

The cop shoved a cardboard box at him, not even bothering to address Kiki. "Stuff's in here. Public defender will be in touch... not that it'll help."

Then, he was gone and Carson stood alone with Kiki.

Awkward didn't even begin to describe it.

A painful moment passed. A long, painful, powerfully silent moment. Carson drew a breath to speak. He wasn't sure what he was going to say, but somebody had to start. Kiki, however, saved him the trouble – she snatched the box marched for the exit. Carson hurried after.

He caught up to her on the steps outside, where Kiki was just tugging on her stocking cap. It was askew, but she made no attempt to correct it. Yanking her coat out of the box, she pulled it roughly on and tossed the cardboard.

"Hey," Carson said softly. She didn't respond. "Hey..." he tried again, louder, trotting to keep up. Briefly, he considered grabbing her arm then retracted involuntarily as he recalled the last time he'd touched her. His cheek still burned with the memory. Finally, in frustration, he pushed past and planted himself in her path.

"Stop!"

She stopped. Blue eyes, rimmed with red and haunted by shadows, stuck fast to the pavement. Carson's heart hammered. It was worse than facing Vanessa. Again, words failed him.

Again, Kiki intervened. "I'll pay you back."

In spite of the hurt, the betrayal, the confusion, the questions... it was good to hear her voice. Carson let his breath out. He fished around and, at last, found words. "Look... just get in the truck. I'll take you home."

Kiki didn't move. He could see the lines on her face tighten, the old rigid "no one helps me but me" determination rearing its head again.

Not this time.

"Damn it, Kiki... just get in the truck! You owe me that much!"

Her anger melted into anguish, then pain, then frustration, then guilt... so rapidly Carson had trouble following and couldn't tell which one ended up on top. In the end, though, she gave a tiny, tiny nod. Carson hurried to unlock the door. In a moment, they were driving.

It was miles before she spoke. When she did, her voice was barely audible, little more than a whisper. "How did you know?" She stared out the window at the string of passing cars, eyes as gray and dull as the sky.

"Dex," Carson tried to keep his voice neutral. "One of his security buddies was working the store you robbed." The word sounded awful.

She made no reply.

They rode in silence for another moment. Then, Carson exploded. "That you *robbed!!* Kiki, what were you *thinking*?! Breaking and entering?! This isn't just snatching a candy bar off the rack! This is *real* crime! Serious crime! Bad boys, bad boys... prison... Orange is the New Black kind of crime!" Frustration choked him off. He settled for slapping the steering wheel.

"You don't know how it is," there was an edge to Kiki's voice. The scared, lost little girl was gone, and the street smart survivor had taken her place once again. "Don't talk about what you don't know."

"What I don't know?! What I *don't know?!*" Carson slapped the wheel again. "You're darn tootin' I don't know! And what I don't know is *why*?! Why didn't you come to me? Or Dex? Or Sister B.? You're not alone anymore, Kiki; you've got family! You've got *me*... us... you can come to us; you can..." Carson checked himself. He was shouting. He slowed down, focusing on his breathing. Staring out the window, he realized he had no idea where Kiki lived. "You can tell me where we're going," he finished quietly. "For starters."

"Fisk," Kiki was on auto pilot. She gestured vaguely. "Take a left and keep going."

Carson maneuvered the truck through slow traffic and a steady drizzle, the squeak and scrape of threadbare wipers providing the only sound.

After a few miles, Carson was calmer. He started again. "How long?"

"A couple months," there was no hesitation. The matter-of-fact tone in her voice irked him.

"Months?!" He took another deep breath. "What are we talking here... how much stuff?"

"Enough to get by," she paused. "A girl's gotta eat." It was pure snark.

Carson forced himself not to take the bait, searching back over the last few months in his mind. There had been telltale signs, he realized now. "You stole from school, too, didn't you? Looney's book. That day in the lab."

"Yes. I *borrowed* some things. And yes, I'm aware of how hypocritical 'borrowed' sounds. But I *was* going to return them."

"Did you ever *borrow* from the 24/7?"

For the first time, she looked at him. "How could you even *think* that?!" He felt the hurt in her voice. The tough girl slipped again.

"Up until now, I didn't *think* you could do it at all."

"I *never* took from you! *Never!*" Her savagery stopped him cold. Mentally, Carson took a step back. For whatever reason, he believed her. And that was something. Something he could cling to.

But for Kiki, the damage was done. "Stop – stop the truck!"

Carson obeyed. He pulled into the curb of a long, lonely street. Kiki shouldered the door and dove out.

A wave of guilt washed over Carson. He unbuckled and slid out. "Kiki, wait!"

She stopped, stiff as an iron rod, but didn't turn around. They stood in the shadows of a few squat, industrial looking buildings and a shamble of little apartments not even worthy of being called tenements. Overhead, traffic rumbled by on an overpass. It was a depressing place. Even more depressing was a cluster of cardboard shanties and tattered tents that squatted nearby in the shadows of the overpass. The filthy tent city gave Carson an uncomfortable feeling. Garbage blew about, and rain pattered down from the gray sky, making it even colder and bleaker.

Carson clenched his fists. Kiki had picked a heck of a place to bail. But as mad as he was, he couldn't leave her here. "Look... I'm sorry. I shouldn't have... I shouldn't have said that. Please, just get back in the truck. At least let me take you home."

"You can't."

"Great gobs, woman, why do you have to be so...?!"

"I *am* home."

She broke. Kiki's shoulders caved and she started to cry, great, sobbing racks. In spite of her desperate attempts to stop them, they tore out of her. A look of utter, abject defeat spread across her features. She took a few stumbling steps but not toward a building – toward the underpass. The tent city. She stopped beside a tiny, crude shelter made of cardboard and broken crates. The familiarity of her movements showed Carson it was home. Her home.

It hit him like a punch in the gut.

He followed her, stepping into a world of cast offs, garbage and the smell of human misery, numb, but not with the cold.

Words failed him.

They stood just like that for a few moments, in the cold and the truth. She faced him but didn't look at him. Tears slid down her cheeks, mixing with the rain. After a minute, she swiped at them roughly. When she spoke, her voice was flat and emotionless. "After Fujikacorp... and you... the hospital... well, it was tough. Everything crashed. School was a mess. Getting back in was hard enough academically but financially... impossible. I had debts. Big ones. I took a room with Lucky Earl for a bit, but couldn't even swing that with tuition, books, loans. He offered to let me stay for free, but you know me," she gave a sharp, derisive laugh. "I don't take handouts." Her mouth turned ugly and bitter.

It was all too real. Carson shook his head helplessly. "Kiki... after everything we've been through? I would have... any of us would have... why didn't you just...?"

"Like I said - I don't take handouts. I don't do charity. I do survival. You should know that by now," Kiki wiped fiercely at her tears again, looking disgusted with herself. "I've got nothing, Carson; we've been through it before. No family, no support, no home. School is my one shot. I quit once because of all this monster whacking business, and I won't do it again. Nothing's gonna stop me from finishing. *Nothing.* Not money, not work, not sleeping on the street.

Not even jail. Not even Professor Looney and that stupid Forensics class."

"Yeah," Carson swallowed. "Professor Looney. Forensics. Funny thing..."

"Whatever it is, forget it. I'm not quitting school again, Carson. Period. I'd rather..."

"Live on the street and steal for a living," Carson finished for her. It was a statement, not a quip.

Kiki said nothing. The look in her eyes was answer enough. "It wouldn't be the first time," she muttered, then turned away, dropping her backpack inside the cardboard flap of her shanty.

"Wouldn't be the...? Okay, fine. Let's do this. A couple months ago, back at the Fish n' Ships before the giant zombie squid attacked us..." he hesitated, still startled by the things that came out of his mouth these days. "...you said some things. Or started too. Things about your past. Well... I wanna know. I've been beating around the bush, giving you space, walking on eggshells. I'm tired of it. I care about you, Kiki. You're my friend. You may not know or care or even understand what that means, but I'm calling you out. I wanna know it all. Who *are* you?"

"Who am I?" Kiki's voice was soft, barely audible. She stared hard at the cardboard shack, not seeing it. For a moment, Carson thought she wasn't going to continue. A blush of red crept around her pale cheeks. "Fine. Mom died when I was eight. After that, it was just me and Dad, which was not a good thing. He abused me. Yeah... in that way. I took it until I was twelve. Then, I couldn't anymore. I left. Ran out. Ended up on the street. Not far from here, actually," she gestured, a weak, automatic effort. "I had nowhere else to go."

Carson let it sink in. Things were starting to make sense. Lots of things. "That's where you met Ghost."

Her nod was barely perceptible. "He took me in. Taught me to survive. He and the others... KO, Snitch, Jacket. We were all on the street, everyone for a different reason. But we made it work. We were like... family. Or the closest thing when you're in hell."

"So what happened?"

She darted him a fierce look. "I outgrew them. Okay? I wanted out of there. Out of that life. I woke up one day, and I knew that I was better than them. Better than this," she waved a hand bitterly at what surrounded them. "I walked away and never looked back. That's the difference between them and me... they're gonna die here."

"You said they were family. I don't get it."

"No, you don't!" she snapped, and her expression was now downright venomous. "I'm not like you! I never had a Granny who made me cookies and did my laundry and worried when I stayed out late! My dad didn't love me; he *tortured* me! My mom *died*! She left me to... to *him!*" She faced him full on, face white and stretched. "*That* was my family! That's what family meant to me – torture and death and abandonment! Ghost and all those... bums... they were just as bad! They were no good for me, holding me back, dragging me down, always getting in my way! Just like everyone I've ever known! Just like you..." her voice dropped off, and her eyes fell again. "When you... when you got hurt... I just... I just couldn't... everything got screwed up. School, work, flippin' bills, everything. Every time I get close to someone, things go to crap. That's why when you... when you asked..." she turned away again and stuffed her hands into her coat pockets, miserable but resolute. "I'm better off on my own. Always have been."

Carson felt a pit in his stomach. Her words were like nails in the coffin of their future. Suddenly, he knew how Ghost felt. Suddenly, he was guilty, and lost, and desperate. "Kiki... it's not too late. Don't do this. Don't walk away. I'm sorry. Sorry about your past. Sorry about your family. Sorry I asked you to... to go out with me. But I'm not sorry about one thing – for wanting to help. You're wrong. You *need* people. You can't get through this on your own. None of it. Maybe you hate the idea of family because you just haven't had one yet." She was quiet, face turned down, cloaked in shadows.

Carson stepped closer. "What do you say..." he reached out, hesitantly, gently. "Give me a chance?"

"No." The force of her answer was like another slap. It hurt.

"No?!"

"Carson... I'm not saying I don't *need* your help. I'm saying I don't *want* it. Don't make this harder than it is."

Carson felt a flare of anger now. "*You're* the one making this hard! Stop trying to be a one woman army and just take some frippin' help, would you?!"

Her eyes, at long last, lifted to meet his. Storm clouds gathered there. "I told you... I... don't... *want it!*"

Carson could feel the red rushing to his face. He really really wanted to hit something. "Yeah?! Well, some day, maybe you *will!* And if you keep going like this, maybe when you finally do, maybe I won't be there!"

"Story of my life!" She was shouting, too, fists clenched.

"You better be sure!"

"Screw you!!"

"*Fine!!*"

"*FINE!!!*"

Carson stormed away, threw himself into the Magic Carpet, slammed the door and tore off, tires squealing. The rear view mirror dropped off again and bounced to the floor. He was way past caring. He pounded the dash savagely, a tiny detached part of his brain at last thankful for the carpeting.

"*FINE!!!*" he bellowed again, even though Kiki was blocks away now. It was her call. If that's the way she wanted it, that's the way she'd get it.

As far as he was concerned, they were done.

The drive to Granny's was a blur. Carson realized he was parked in front but didn't know how long he'd been there. He slammed the truck door and limped into the house, intent on reaching the medicine cabinet and a handful of Ibuprofen, so absorbed in his thoughts he didn't see the visitor until he was almost past the living room.

"Hey, Charity."

Carson halted with a start. It was Leet.

"Wanna cookie?" The scrawny hacker held out a plate of Granny's treats then took a big bite of one. He was lounging in Granny's favorite recliner, wearing a *What Are YOU Looking At?!* T-shirt and an expression so smug it made the cat who swallowed the canary look hungry and sad.

Carson struggled to process the scene.

Leet was *here*. In his living room.

Granny sat nearby with a cup of tea, trying very hard to look at ease. "Hello, dear. Your... er... 'friend' stopped by to see you. We've been chatting. He's... so interesting."

"Um, yeah," Carson shook his head to clear it. "So is Fungus Week on the Discovery Channel. Leet... what are you doing here?"

Leet rubbed his large, aristocratic nose, letting crumbs from his treat trickle carelessly into the seat cushions. "It's like you said, Charity: I should be more personable. When I got something to tell you, I should come to you. Remember?" He smirked, stuffing the rest of his cookie into his mouth.

"Yeah," Carson made a mental note to kick himself later. "I

regret... er... remember. Hey Granny, could you give us a sec?"

"Certainly, dear," Granny was halfway to the kitchen before he finished, wearing a huge look of relief. "I'll be in the back yard if you need me."

Carson listened at the kitchen door, making sure she was gone, then rounded on his informant. "Leet, I've had a bad day. Make it quick."

"Sure, sure. Quick is how I do things. After all, you gave the Leet a job to do, remember?"

Carson shot a look toward the kitchen. "Keep your voice down. Yes, I remember. Did you...?"

"The wheels are in motion. I've got some friends as I might have mentioned. Resourceful friends."

"Yeah, you mentioned it," Carson thought back to his talk with Dex and Becky. He found himself suddenly sharing their reservations. Things had seemed so clear back then. Now, the thought of being in bed with Leet's criminal associates made him feel slightly ill. "Look, Leet... I've been considering. I'm not sure this is such a..."

"Whoa there, cowboy, it's too late for considering! You can't stop this train now. It's left the station. My crew has a client and an objective. They're engaged. And they were very interested when they heard your name, too. Apparently, you're picking up a little street cred."

"You used my *name*? Leet, what were you thinking!"

"I was thinking you asked for intel. I was also thinking you rubbed it in my face how good your new source was, and how I needed to show you what *real* results looked like. Which brings me to the other reason for my visit. I did a little digging on the competition. This 'Joe' guy."

Carson's sick feeling got sicker. "You... you dug into Joe?"

"I asked some questions," Leet took a big bite of cookie and chewed luxuriously. "Mmm... delish! Could be better than Yoo-Hoo. Think I could get a to-go bag?"

"No!" Carson snatched the cookie. Then, for good measure, he took the plate, too.

"Hey!"

"Who did you tell, Leet? Who did you go to?!"

"Sources, Charity. I had to go deep, too. This guy is a ghost alright. A totally legit spook. Government connections, intelligence community. Got some skeletons in his closet, too. Some kinda blowup, fallout, betrayal, cloak-and-dagger type stuff or whatever. Some folks still looking for this dude, apparently. People got real interested when I started making inquiries. Shady. Real shady. Not many details yet, but they'll come."

"Drop it, Leet. Leave it alone," Carson felt the room start to spin. He grabbed the little man by the collar.

Leet slapped his hand away. "Cool it, fella! And don't get your panties in a wad," he adjusted his glasses nonchalantly. "You started this boulder rolling with all your trash talking and playing us off against each other – don't think I missed all that. If the boulder crushes you, don't come crying to me. You poke the Leet, you take the heat," he levered himself out of Granny's chair. "And speaking of heat, I'd keep your eyes on the news the next couple days. If things go South with my crew, I'm not sure they'll keep a zipped lip. They're good, but they're also *bad*, if you know what I mean. Might want to keep a bag packed. Joe may not be the only one on the run."

Leet sauntered to the door. "Hey, I just thought of a way you could repay me for all this... tell Granny 'thanks for the cookies.'" He slipped one out of his coat pocket, gave it a big kiss, and was gone.

"Has your friend left, dear?" Granny poked her head out of the kitchen. Carson nodded dumbly.

"Will he ever come back?" she asked with a touch of concern.

"If he does, don't let him in."

Granny looked relieved and bustled out again with a handful of dishes. Carson's phone rang, and he answered it automatically.

"You were supposed to call me, fool. Remember?" Dex was irked.

"Mm."

"What's the story with Kiki? She okay? Did you bail her out? I know you two ain't BFF's right now, but you *did* go see her, didn't you?"

"Yeah. I saw her."

"And?"

"She's out."

Dex was silent a moment, obviously waiting for more news. When none came, he prompted. "How's she doin'?"

"Fine. I guess."

"You *guess*? Whatcha mean, you *guess*? Did you see her? Did you talk to her?!"

"Yeah. Yes. We talked. It was..." Carson faltered. He was suddenly fed up with the whole deal. With Kiki. With Leet. With everyone. "Look, she's the one who chased *me* off! I stuck out the ol' hand of friendship, and she slapped it. Hard. That's her choice! She wants to go this on her own, I say fine. I'm tired of chasing someone who doesn't want to be chased!"

"She made it clear, did she?" Dex's tone was strangely soft.

"Abundantly."

Dex was quiet again. "Man, you *are* a fool."

"What did you say?!"

"I said you're a fool!" Dex snorted. "A big, fat, dumb, %^&*#@! fool... unless you're at work, and then you're a big, fat, dumb Ginger Snappin' fool. Man, I thought I had lady issues. Let me educate you."

Carson was tempted to hang up, but something in Dex's voice kept him on the line. "Fine," he snapped. "Educate me."

"Bottom line: she's *into* you. Anyone can see that. 'Cept you, of course. Time to pull your head out and face facts. When you croaked – or almost croaked – or whatever – when you got all zombified... man, you shoulda seen her. I mean, I was upset and all, but that little lady – she went straight up *ballistic*. Nutso. I'm talkin' full-on Institute of St. Angus, or wherever Attila said they sent the nutjobs."

"You're screwy. Kiki doesn't..."

"Shut up, fool!" Dex's bark hurt Carson's ear. "I ain't done educatin'! You wanna know what's wrong with her?! *You!* She got too close to you, and it wigged her out! She opened up, got vulnerable, got attached and all that. And that's the one thing that scares the %^&*#@! out of her. Gettin' attached."

It was Carson's turn to be silent.

"Here me now, Dud - if there's one person in the world who knows what it's like to be scared of getting close, it's this fat black man right here. Brother, I been there," Dex sighed, a lonely sound. "I been doing a lotta thinkin' lately. 'Bout me and Shari – the ex. Been doing some growing up. Most of our problems... hell, I spent the last couple years blamin' her. But it was really me."

The silence was mutual now. Neither one said a word. Carson didn't know what to think, what to feel. It was surreal. Or maybe it was just real.

After a full minute, Dex broke the silence. "I probably sound like a girl, don't I?"

"Yeah. You do."

Dex chuckled. "It happens. It's this thing with Dee. Delilah." He stopped, and Carson could sense he was pondering something. Something important. "Dud," Dex rushed on suddenly. "I'm backin' off."

"From Delilah? But I thought..."

"No, man. Not from Dee." Another sigh. "From the team. From the monster whackers."

Carson sat down.

"Like I said, I been doing a lot of thinkin'. I'm getting close to this girl. She means a lot to me. I don't know what we got, Brother, but I know I can't risk losing it. And that's exactly what would happen if Parsons got even the tiniest whiff of what we were cookin' up. We got Leet's yahoos breaking into police HQ, a dead college prof, a mad scientist building critters like they was tinker toys, and who knows what else hittin' the fan. Parsons already hates us. Me in particular. I just can't risk it."

More silence.

"You still there?"

Carson forced himself to talk. "Yeah. Just... processing. How about her daughter? The little girl. You okay with that?"

"Serena?" When Dex spoke, he had a peculiar tone in his voice. "She held my hand, Dud. After all this time... I can't describe what that's like."

Carson made a fist. Then, he relaxed it, forcing himself to breathe. He tried to keep his voice light. "But doesn't she have a dog?"

"I still hate the dog," Dex's reply held a hint of relief. He chuckled then grew sober again. "My head just ain't in the game, Dud. I ain't had this in a long time. A lifetime. And it feels good. I don't wanna ruin it just yet."

"I understand."

"You and Attila... you got this, right?"

"Er... yeah. Sister Becky and me," Carson shifted in his chair. He considered telling Dex that the nun was leaving, but didn't. "We got it."

"Good. Give Kiki some time. She'll get back up. Plus, I've seen her pissed off - you may want to keep her like that. Don't tell nobody, but when she's in a state, she kicks more %^&*#@! than I do. You won't even miss me."

"Sure. Hey, I got work. I'll talk to you later. Keep in touch."

Carson hung up abruptly. He was exhausted, achy, miserable and had just been dumped by his best friend. He had a lot to think about. He pushed himself out of the chair and limped for the front door, already fishing out his keys.

Granny poked her head in again, a mixing bowl in hand. "Off to work, dear?"

"Not tonight. I'm just going to talk to an old friend."

A short time later, Carson pulled up in front of a tiny, smart looking bakery decorated with donuts in superhero capes. The sign read *Deep Fat Flyer,* and there was another underneath that declared *Grand Opening!*

Carson clambered slowly out of the truck and hobbled up to the building. He looked it over, nodding in approval. Then, he turned to the foundation and smiled a thin smile. "Hello, Pete."

He stood in silence a long while, letting the soft rain soak into his hair. He registered the cold, but didn't budge. Didn't care. Right now, he didn't care about anything.

"It suits him."

Carson was so engrossed in his emptiness that, for once, the whispered words didn't cause him to jump. He turned his head toward the dim form that lurked in the mouth of a nearby alley. "Pete always did have a sweet tooth. I think it may have been his only one." Rain filled the silence. "Didn't think I'd ever see you again. After Kiki."

"I wasn't sure you would either."

"Look... I'm sorry. It wasn't my place."

"Agreed," the answer was soft but stern. "You really botched it, Carson. You got cocky, lost touch with the situation. You tried to control something you couldn't, and it blew up. Badly. It cost you."

Carson stared at the spot where Pete's remains were ensconced, buried under tons of concrete. Surprisingly, he didn't feel much at Ghost's rebuke. He didn't feel much at all. Perhaps, there just wasn't anywhere further to sink. Regardless, he knew one thing with sudden, absolute clarity: he was a jerk. Ghost was right.

"Guilty as charged. I've been a noodge. An absolute, grade A, certified, top flight, world-record-holding noodge. I lied. I manipulated. I used people. My own friends. I was so cocky and self-deluded, I didn't even see when they were train-wrecking. I suck."

"I think that about covers it," Ghost's whisper was matter-of-fact. "But you meant well. That counts. Don't be too hard on yourself, Carson. You're a good man. You're just not the man you think you are."

"Copy that," Carson muttered. "And while I was figuring that out, I pretty much destroyed every relationship that mattered. I screwed up. Royally. I pushed everybody away. I'm alone. And without my friends... I don't know what I'll do."

Surprisingly, he heard a soft noise from the shadows, and it took him a moment to identify it - laughter. It was the first time he had ever heard Ghost laugh. It was a melancholy, self-deprecating laugh.

"Son... I did my best work after my worst disasters. You can, too. We had a saying where I used to work: 'when your op falls apart, don't try to pick up the pieces - start a new op.'" Ghost stepped forward, hovering just outside the edge of shadow. He stared evenly at Carson. "Start a new op."

In spite of everything, Carson felt a smile spread across his face. "A saying, eh?" It made him miss Sister Becky all the more. "You ever spend time in a convent?"

"I don't follow."

"You just remind me of someone I know. Or at least knew. You have a lot in common."

"I'll take that as a compliment. But enough of that. We have business to discuss."

"Yup – lot in common. Shoot."

"Let me be blunt, Carson – you were wrong," there was an edge to his voice that Carson had never heard before. "I told you that something was going on in Las Calamas. Something terrible. I know you think it's finished, that it ended in that warehouse fire, but you're wrong. The intelligence – you just can't ignore it. There are strange things happening, things that can't easily be explained: thefts, experiments, sightings, disappearances. And Carson..." his voice got even harder. "It's not just cats and dogs anymore. Some of my folk – street folk – are missing."

"Doesn't that... happen? From time to time?" Carson thought back to Kiki, standing quiet and cold by her shanty. He shivered.

"Of course. But there's missing and there's *missing*. Trust me, Carson. They're gone. Whatever is happening is just picking up steam. That painting and the girl you're tracking – they can wait. I don't come out of the shadows often. I haven't in a long time. But this I can't ignore. There are lives at stake. And you may think they're only street people..."

"A life is a life," Carson was surprised by his own passion. "It doesn't matter where they live."

"Then, we're in agreement," there was conviction in Ghost's voice. "I do intelligence, Carson. You do action. Right now, you're the only one. You're up."

"On it. It may be just me, but I'm on it."

"We'll help where we can. Call on us. And don't give up on your friends. Not even Kiki. They may surprise you."

"They've done that plenty. But since I'm assuming you mean in the *good* way, I'll take your advice."

With his customary aura of mystery, Ghost was gone, and Carson was standing alone in the rain. He shivered, suddenly aware of the cold and the wet.

"Thanks, Pete," he smiled wanly at the foundation of the donut shop. "I owe you another one." As he turned away, Carson felt a poke in his brain. Something he should have remembered...

"Sassafras!" Carson slapped his forehead.

Leet.

He whirled, but Joe was gone. Carson slapped himself again. He had meant to come clean about letting Joe's name slip, but it was too late. He made a mental note for next time. Ghost deserved to know.

Back in the Magic Carpet, Carson switched on the heater and sat quietly, pondering his next move. Ghost's words simmered in his head, settling, focusing him. He was up. His town was in trouble. Again. Deth was back in business, no doubt about it. People were going missing. The stakes were raised. Instead of rooting out the problem, Carson had only made it worse. His pride and arrogance had done it, and in addition, they had broken up the team. It had all been his fault. All of it.

Suddenly, and with a flash of shocking clarity, Carson knew exactly what he had to do. It was time to get back on track.

He would start with Kiki.

Throwing the truck in gear, he turned the wheel toward the outskirts of town. Dex had made his case about her, but Carson had been too brain dead, to world weary, too self-absorbed still to consider it. Now, thanks to Ghost, he was thinking clearly. Maybe for the first time in months. He knew Dex was right about Kiki. Totally and completely. And he knew he felt the same as she did. It was time to admit it.

It took Carson some time to find the right overpass. The night was like pitch, clinging to everything, the moon barred in an ominous prison of clouds. Several street lamps were burned out, and precious little light streamed from the scattered industrial sites, many of which were derelict. Carson cruised slowly down side streets until he spotted a familiar cluster of cardboard houses. There were more in his town than he'd realized.

Pulling up slowly, he parked and killed the engine. He hadn't rehearsed anything. Wasn't going to try. It was time to be perfectly, brutally honest and let the chips fall where they may. Just plain, honest talk. The kind he should have used from the beginning. The thought of it felt good.

He slid out of the truck and stood in a cold puddle, getting his bearings. Locating Kiki's shack in the dim shadows ahead, he took a deep breath then set of purposefully.

Reaching the cardboard flap that marked the door, Carson paused. There was no way to knock. He stood helpless for a moment then heard a rustle inside. He cleared his throat. "Kiki? It's me. We need to talk. For real, this time."

The rustling stopped.

"May I, um... come in?"

Nothing. No sound.

Carson reached out tentatively and tugged the cardboard flap aside. There were shapes in the dark which his eyes struggled to resolve. One leaned nearby, looking vaguely like Kiki. "Hope you're decent, girl, 'cuz I've got something to tell you whether you like it or..."

The figure moved.

Carson's heart lurched. He was wrong. It wasn't Kiki. Not even close.

Lunging from the shadows, taking shape in a blur of motion and animal rage, was a hulking, misshapen figure with tangled hair and a jaw like a cracked brick. It was a figure he had seen before. With a swirl of tattered trench coat and a snort like an angry bull it was on him. Lights exploded in Carson's brain as blows struck, and that was the last he knew.

CHAPTER TEN

Deth Trap

Dex stopped pacing. His eyes latched onto a cupboard through the narrow doorway into his kitchen. He knew what was there.

Emergency Twinkies.

It would only take a moment to cross the cramped, untidy apartment and grab the box. Only a moment until the rich, creamy filling and delectable spongecake filled his mouth, numbing the gnawing, seething frustration and anger...

He shook his dreads, clearing the thought.

Then, it would be gone. And he'd have another. And another. Then, the box would be empty, his gut would be aching, and he would be right back where he was before. Just guiltier. And angrier. And wanting more Twinkies.

Not this time.

Dex cracked a window and let in some cool air. He breathed deeply, letting it fill his lungs. The smell of rain. A hint of exhaust. The fuzzy rumble of chatter in the low rent neighborhood. The air felt good on his bare limbs. He wore only a t-shirt and shorts around the house since he was always warm and liked the feel of the carpet on his big bare feet. He breathed again then snapped the window shut.

That was that then. No Twinkie.

Dex nodded to himself encouragingly, slapping his big biceps. He turned away from the kitchen and resumed his pacing. It was getting easier - little by little, bit by agonizing bit - and although he knew the sugar demons were lurking right inside the cupboard door, waiting to exploit the slightest moment of weakness and drag him back into sugar hell, it wouldn't be this time.

Not today.

There was plenty to give them leverage though. Dex glanced at his phone. No message light. No missed calls. He'd been trying to reach Carson for hours, ever since early morning. He'd called the cell, called Granny, even tried calling the 24/7. There was no answer. No one. Not even Kinkade. It was weird. Very weird. Whatever Carson was up to, he'd better turn up soon. The sugar demons never went far.

For Dex, the strangest part was that he had no idea why he was even worried. He couldn't put his finger on it, but try as he might, he couldn't get rid of it either: something wasn't right. It had haunted him ever since last night, since he'd told Carson he was leaving the team. The conversation played over and over in his mind. Something had been bothering Carson, something heavy, and Dex hadn't asked because, frankly, he hadn't wanted to know. He'd wanted the break up to go smoothly, wanted to get out of the monster whackers as quickly and painlessly as possible.

As selfishly as possible.

Dex cursed and slapped his biceps again, but this time, it was more punishment than encouragement. When he'd gone to bed, he'd told himself that the icky, nasty, guilty feeling would be gone in the morning. It wasn't. In fact, it was even worse, gnawing at his insides with the incessant emptiness of hunger and ulcers.

Something was wrong.

Carson was in trouble, and somehow, Dex knew it. He had started his phone calls first thing and then settled into the long emptiness of waiting and pacing and worrying.

Dex cursed again and then smiled, grimly. That was one thing about Dud. He had a way of making you think about other people. Lately, he may have been a selfish jerk, but he was still Carson. You couldn't be around him for long before you found yourself seeing the good in everyone. Wanting to help. This was new for Dex. Very new. It was also – although he would never admit it - part of the reason for his recent change in attitude.

Optimism. Hope.

They were Carson's qualities, and they were infectious. Dex was closer to Carson than anyone else in his life, and it had changed him. It was the reason things with Dee had even gotten started – and why they weren't ruined. Yet. He owed his friend for that. And Dex always paid his debts.

The only question was...

"Where the *hell* are you?!" Dex rumbled quietly. He cursed again, thumped his fist into a familiar dent in the door jamb and stood like a brooding granite statue.

After a moment, he fished his keys out of a cereal bowl. Enough waiting. It was time for action. Optimism and hope still had to share space with impatience and anger.

A loud, urgent knocking hit his front door.

Without hesitation, Dex threw the deadbolt and yanked it open. Somehow, he knew who it would be.

"Cancel your date!" Carson locked eyes with him, his own slightly unfocused. He clutched a bloody rag to the side of his head and looked as if he'd spent the night outside. "She's gone!"

"Say what?! Who's gone?!"

"Kiki!" Carson brushed past him into the apartment, weaving slightly and looking manic. "Deth grabbed her! Manstruct! I need some water! Do you have a band-aid?!"

Dex caught him and spun him round, peering closely into his eyes. "You're gonna sit. You're coming outta shock. Then, you're gonna start making some sense, and we're gonna get busy as two bushy tailed %^&*#@! beavers getting some answers."

"No time! We gotta..."

"SIT!"

Carson sat.

Minutes later, Dex was dabbing matted blood from the side of Carson's head with a kitchen towel. "Stitches wouldn't hurt," he peered at the wound. "Probably got yourself a honey of a concussion, too. But I'm guessing you won't be dashin' off to the medicenter."

"When pigs fly!"

"Good. Ain't a big fan myself. Waste a lot of time with shots and stuff. Anyways, I got me a fresh bottle of Super Glue," Dex reached for the drawer of the coffee table. "Now here, drink more water. You're dehydrated. And while I glue you up, tell me what the %^&*#@! is going on."

"Kiki's gone – she's been taken," Carson's eyes looked more focused now. "By Deth."

"Tell me something I don't know. Facts, Bro."

Carson nodded. "I went to see her last night. Someone jumped me. No, not some*one*... some*thing*. Same something that came after me at the college, the one that killed Professor Looney. The Manstruct. This time, it got the jump on me, knocked me cold. Probably thought I was dead. Aunt Gretta's garters!" Carson punched the couch savagely. "I'm an *idiot*! I *knew* we had a bullseye on us, and I didn't do *Jack*! I was too busy with my pity party!"

"Is that party startin' over? 'Cuz we ain't got time for it."

Carson snapped his mouth shut.

"Good. Don't matter now, just box it up. What else you got?"

"When I came to this morning, she was gone. I found this," Carson tossed Kiki's red stocking cap onto the table. It was soggy and dirty, and one side showed a splat of darker red with strands of blond hair stuck to it.

Dex picked it up, examining it with a practiced eye. "Blood. But not enough to get excited about. Not exactly proof of life but a good sign. What else?"

"Nothing. After I searched the place, I threw up and headed here."

Dex rocked back, snapping the lid on his glue bottle. "Obvious question here is why? Why take her? What would Deth want with Kiki?"

"I don't know. But you can bet it's bad. Real bad. We gotta find her, Dex. Fast! Before hc does... whatever," Carson surged off the couch, still looking slightly unsteady but spoiling for action. "Look – I know I've been a real jerk lately. And I know what this may do to your chances with Delilah. And the cop test. I have no right to ask..."

"That's right, you don't," Dex rose, towering over him. "And you got no way to stop me, neither. So don't even try."

Carson locked eyes with him. "Thanks, Dex. I owe you one."

"Oh, we're *way* past one - but we'll work that out later. Right now, we gotta get our girl back. So, get your brain in gear. What's our play?"

Carson took a few bouncing steps, tugging on his chin beard. It was as sure a sign as any that he was starting to focus. "We call in the cavalry. All hands on deck. Ghost, Leet, everyone. I can't reach Sister Becky; she's probably out of the country by now, but we still have..."

"Out of the country?! Did I miss a meeting?"

"Sorry. Um, yeah, that probably came as a bit of a shock. I'll fill you in, but right now I've gotta make some calls. Get geared up and meet me at Granny's. ASAP."

"What do I bring?"

"Everything."

* * * * * * *

Carson stabbed his phone, cutting off the very polite nun at St. Timothy's Sacred Heart Cathedral. He'd bothered them enough, and if a half dozen urgent phone calls hadn't prompted them to find Sister Becky, one more wouldn't help. Her phone was already disconnected, her room cleared out, and her cab had left that morning. She was gone, and he knew it. He was just calling because there was nothing else to do.

Carson trotted to the door of his room and peered out the window, up the concrete staircase, scanning the small section of street just visible above. Nothing.

He swung away, pacing back into the room, insides twisting in an agony of impatience. Everything was ready, and now the only thing left was the waiting. He hated the waiting.

Part of him wished it all hadn't been so easy. He had hung the bandana for Ghost, called Granny, called Leet, packed up his monster whacking gear and canceled his shift at the 24/7. Kinkade had seemed almost happy to cover for him, and not only had the man offered to do it *himself*, but to do it *indefinitely*. That kind of behavior had become so common now that Carson had come to expect it. A growing part of him, however, was starting to question Kinkade's motivations. It was just too sudden. Too out of character. Too strange. There was definitely something going on. Carson shoved his phone in a pocket and switched off that line of thinking. He'd have to pursue it later. All that mattered now was getting Kiki back.

Stopping by the bed, Carson gently flexed his injured knee. At least it wasn't hurting as badly. Or maybe he just wasn't feeling it due to the adrenaline and urgency. Or maybe it was the concussion. In truth, he didn't care. Deth had Kiki. Just when he'd figured out what she meant to him, she was gone. It was all his fault.

Carson grimaced and shut off those thoughts too. That kind of thinking didn't help. He grabbed his bat and gave it a few practice swings. What was it Dex had said? *Just box it up.* He took a deep breath. Fine. He forced his brain into a course correction. He was going to find Kiki. He was going to save her. And when he did... his hand tightened on the bat. Deth had a home run coming.

Boots stomped down the stairs, and the door burst open. It was Dex, now in his army jacket with a bulging black bag in each hand. He dropped them with a military *thud*. "Hooah! The Big Man is here. I got my action pants and two bags full of angry! When do we start puttin' holes in something, and where is it at?! If we don't start soon, I'm gonna get emotional."

"And I'm gonna have an aneurism! This waiting is killing me! It's worse than the time the doctor..." Carson's phone buzzed, and he snatched it out. "Give me something!"

The voice on the other end was like the hiss of a coiled snake. "*How dare you!*"

Carson frowned. "Ghost?"

"Do you realize what you've *done*?! You leaked my *name*! People have been asking about me! Dangerous people!" Ghost's voice was still a whisper, but now it had a purpose to it, a cold, practical intensity that went well beyond angry.

"Ghost, look... I'm sorry..."

"*Sorry?!* You're *sorry*?! I told you, Carson. I *warned* you what would happen if you crossed that line! We are done. Through! You can take that bandana and burn it, because I will *never*..."

"Kiki's in trouble."

There was a pause. "What do you need?"

"You."

"We'll be right there."

* * * * * * *

It was a full house. Leet arrived next, followed by Ghost and a handful of sketchy, eccentric street folk who ordinarily would have made Carson want to lock up the silver. Tonight, he was just glad to see them. It only took him a few minutes to outline the situation, starting with the raid on Deth's lab and ending with Kiki's abduction.

As he finished, Ghost started. "What intel do we have?" Every hint of malice and righteous anger was gone. The man was all business.

"Not much. Just this," Carson dropped a worn leather briefcase onto the coffee table. "Professor Looney's notes and research on the handi-cat sample. Got it that night the Manstruct pounded him into paste. The way Frankenberry was chasing after it, I figure it must have something in it that points to Deth."

Ghost emptied the case, spreading its contents out in an orderly, methodical fashion: papers, journals, lab samples. His cronies crowded in, joined by Leet, everyone sifting, poking, analyzing, muttering. Carson drifted away. The Professor's research meant nothing more to him now than before. Even if it did, he could hardly think of anything else besides Kiki. He snatched up his bat, checked his grip and started picturing Deth's head.

After too many agonizing minutes, Ghost sat back. "There's not much to go on here. We might be able to gain some insight into Deth's methods, but as for solid leads, I believe our best bet is these samples. Analyzing them will take time. And equipment."

"Yeah... fer sure... equipment," one of the others, a scrawny, wild-haired fellow in a battered suit jacket, mumbled under his breath, still pawing through the evidence. "Expensive equipment."

"We don't have any of that."

The old brawler Carson had met earlier, the one Ghost had called KO, had been standing silently the whole time, mostly just staring daggers into Dex as if willing him to start something. Now, he snorted. "No kiddin'."

"Leet? Anything?"

Leet stared at the contents of a Petri dish, shaking his head. "Negative. Tech is my thing, not CSI. I'm with Ghost. We need equipment. And someone who knows how to work it."

"Okay," Carson tugged his chin beard. "We need resources, and we need them fast." He thought for a moment. "Would the cops have something?"

There was a general shifting of nervousness in the room.

Ghost squinted at the man in the suit jacket. "Scratch?"

The little man considered. He scratched his head, fast, like a dog after a flea. Then, he did the same to his shoulder. Then, he nodded.

"They would," Ghost translated.

Carson reached for his phone.

"Hey, uh, hold up, Charity," Leet licked nervous lips. "There's a whole lot of criminal in here. Are you *really* gonna call the cops?"

"I'll do whatever it takes."

Everyone looked at Carson. He looked back, eyes flinty. "I'm not hearing a lot of options."

"This is your op," Ghost whispered. "We follow your lead. But if you call the authorities on this, you'll need the proper angle. Tell me what you're thinking."

"Well... it's a long shot, but I've got an in with the PD – a homicide detective. He's not a real team player, but he's a good cop. We could reach out..." Carson shot a glance at Dex. He knew what this would mean.

Dex's face was a stone block. "Why you even askin'?"

"Alright. We can call Parsons in," Carson hesitated, phone in hand. "But Ghost is right – we'll need an angle. And it'll have to be a good one," he started to pace, musing. "Dude said next time I came to him, I'd better have a dead body in my trunk."

Ghost rose. "Leave that to us. We'll need your truck."

Carson didn't hesitate. He dropped the keys into Joe's hand. "I'd ask, but I'm pretty sure I don't wanna know."

"We'll be in touch," Ghost was already on the move, his compatriots in a loose phalanx behind him.

"What about me, Charity?" Leet was at Carson's elbow, the concern on his face making him look old and tired. "There's gotta be something I can do!"

Carson paused, patting his bat thoughtfully. A plan was beginning to form. "As a matter of fact, Leet, there is. Tell me - have you ever kidnapped anyone?"

* * * * * * *

In retrospect, Carson was surprised at how easy it was to snatch Detective Parsons. It was easy to make the plan. It was easy for Leet to hack his calendar and figure out where he would be. It was easy to get the few supplies they needed. At the appointed time, it had even been easy to spring the trap. One second Parsons was walking to his car, the next he was in its trunk. Dex himself stuffed the man in. There were no sirens, no alarms, no complications - just a lot of muffled shouting through the burlap bag.

Carson was also surprised at how little guilt he felt over it. He had briefly considered reasoning with Parsons, but he'd tried that in the past already – twice – and it had gotten him nowhere. Fast. And fast was the keyword. Kiki's life was on the line.

Dex maneuvered the detective's maroon sedan through the evening mist, heading toward the coast. The Las Calamas skyline loomed behind them as they cruised through thinning suburbs toward a distant spillway. The ocean ahead looked cold and storm tossed, white-caps peeping through occasional breaks in the evening mist. Partially obscured by the same clinging fog, the moon overhead was a cloudy white eye tracking their progress.

"Dude's gonna be pissed," Dex remarked without any real emotion. "Leet said he was on his way to Serena's Sunday School Christmas Pageant."

"He'll be late to that party."

Dex grunted.

They drove a few miles in silence. From the trunk came an occasional loud thump.

Dex checked the rear view mirror for any signs of pursuit. There were none. "Think he'll listen?"

"Oh, he'll listen," Carson's tone was as cold as the mist outside. "I guarantee it. Here, this is it."

Dex steered the car onto a rutted access road which led to the spillway. Scrub mountains rose up just beyond the large concrete structure, marking the southern boundary of Las Calamas. Their headlights picked out a parked truck. Carson's truck. Dex pulled in beside it and stopped. Carson was out before the dust settled, bat in hand.

Dex popped the trunk, and Carson dragged Parsons out, standing him on his feet. The man was zip-tied hand and foot and wore a burlap hood. Dex drifted up behind and stood like a statue, his huge arms crossed, the night and fog making him an even grimmer specter than usual.

Carson cut through the zip-ties and yanked off Parson's hood. It took him a moment to focus on Carson's face. Then, his eyes flew wide. His fingers flexed unconsciously. A mumbling, gurgling sound spilled out around the duct tape sealing his mouth. The man was so shocked that he didn't even think to yank it off. Carson reached up and did it for him, leaving it half dangling by one sticky end.

"You... *you*!!" Parsons spluttered. "You *sonofa...*!"

"Shut up," Carson cut him off. He wasn't holding his shotgun, but his voice was loaded. He took a step into Parson's bubble. "Listen. Close. I've tried everything to get you to see what's going on in this town: hints, suggestions, clever explanations. Nothing works. So this time, I'm just giving it to you straight up. Plain and simple. Someone is killing people. He's chopping them up and putting them back together in the worst way possible. I don't know how, and I don't know why, but he's doing it. He's a murderer and a psychopath, and now he's taken my friend. You never listened before, and I knew you wouldn't start now, so, yeah, I kidnapped you. I tossed you in a trunk and hauled you out into the middle of this God-forsaken wasteland so I could do you a favor – so I could help you catch him."

Carson stepped toward the bed of his truck, taking hold of the corner of a tarp that covered it. "I knew you wouldn't believe me unless you saw for yourself. You made that clear last time. You told me you wouldn't listen unless I had a dead body. Well... I still don't have a dead body," he yanked the tarp clear. "But I've got part of one."

There, in the carpeted bed of the Magic Carpet, lay the corpse of a hairless cat with a human hand stitched to its back.

Parsons stared.

It was clear by the look on his face that he had seen many corpses revealed in many ways, but that none of them had been anything like this. Not by a long shot. His critical, thoughtful, brown eyes narrowed, then widened, then narrowed as various streams of thought flowed through his mind. The strip of duct tape still dangled from his cheek, but he didn't seem to notice.

"What... is... that?" Parson's voice was small. He rested one hand absently on the bed of the truck, as if to ground himself.

"A wake up call. This guy is a real sicko, and he's just getting started. You know what happened to Professor Looney at LC3? Delilah's forensics teacher?"

Parsons seemed to come awake. "Dee's professor? How did you...?"

"Not important. But it's the same guy who's behind Tabby High Five here. Listen, Detective - there's some Grade A level one nasty whack going on in your city right now, and you have the chance to stop it," Carson dropped the Professor's briefcase at Parson's feet. It raised a little dust cloud. "This is Looney's research. He was looking into this thing, and that's why he was killed. There's evidence in here - unless I'm really really stupid. If you want to help catch a killer, take this to your CSI boys. If it blows their minds, if they find something, let me have a peek. That's all I ask. If not, come arrest me. You know where I live."

Parsons stared into the truck bed, stared at the briefcase, stared at the fog-shrouded moon. He stared at Dex, who stood silently, arms folded, staring right back. Last, he stared at Carson. Slowly, absently, he reached up and tugged loose the dangling strip of duct tape from his cheek. "Tell me this – why not just arrest you right now? Take you down to the station and sort this out there?"

Carson could hear the indecision in Parson's voice. He knew the detective was by-the-book, a linear thinker and someone who believed in the system. All of that would make accepting this offer almost impossible for him. Carson had long suspected that, buried deep within the man, there was something else that just might tip the scale. He prayed he was right. "Because you're a good cop. You want to save lives, and you want to catch a murderer. If we do this by the book, neither one happens. You know that. It's just too slow. This monster took my friend, and he's going to kill her. Or worse. If you don't help us – *right now* – she dies."

They stared at each other a long moment. Each man took the measure of the other.

Slowly, ever so slowly, Parsons reached down, found the handle of the briefcase, and lifted it. His eyes never left Carson's. "I'm driving my own car."

* * * * * *

Carson was doing his best to wear a track in the basement carpet. Parsons had had the briefcase now for hours. They'd been long ones. Dex stood impassively, filling one corner of the room. His expression hadn't changed, and his arms hadn't uncrossed since they had decided to involve the detective.

Carson felt a stab of remorse for the hundredth time. "I'm sorry, Dex. About Dee... the cop test... about everything."

The big man's face didn't change. He just nodded, once. Carson knew the look by now. Underneath the granite was an ocean of pain. He turned and started pacing again.

After a few minutes, there came a knock on the door. Carson jumped to answer it, admitting Ghost and his cohorts. "You did it!" he congratulated them as they filed past. "Parsons got his body, and he took the hook. Where in the name of Sigmund Freud's dog did you dig that up?!"

Ghost shrugged with a look. "Your mark is trafficking in human and animal parts. That means there are bodies. There are only so many places you can hide bodies."

"I'll take your word for that."

"Any payoff yet?"

Carson shook his head. "Parsons hasn't called. But he hasn't come to arrest us, either." Ghost's cronies shuffled nervously. "We'll just have to wait."

They didn't have to wait long. An hour later, Carson's phone buzzed. He listened intently and spoke only a few words, scribbling notes. "We will. And... thanks." Carson ended the call. He turned to the group, practically bursting with determination. "That was Parsons. CSI found just what we hoped – apparently minds were blown. They couldn't ID all of it, but some of the drugs were linked to recent thefts, some were controlled substances, and all together, it was enough for Parsons to start inquiries. Which he did."

"Tell me he dug up something useful," Dex's expression was still flat, but his eyes were practically begging: *Tell me it was worth it.*

"You bet your Fat Aunt Fanny he did," Carson waved the notepaper triumphantly. "He got a hit. Or two, I should say. They searched Professor Looney's office and found some solid intel. Seems the Professor had been doing a little digging of his own. He'd started tracking the thefts, the disappearances, figuring out what kind of resources Deth would need to keep up his work. Parsons found two addresses in Looney's notes. He doesn't know if he can get warrants for them. But he gave them to me."

"He say anything else?"

"Yeah. He said 'go get your friend.'"

Dex picked up his black bags.

"Two addresses," Ghost held a hand out. "That means two teams. We don't have time to waste, Carson. We'll take one, you take the other."

Carson hesitated. "Uh... right. So... no offense and all, but..." he surveyed the rag tag group of hobos with obvious doubt. "I'm not sure you've still got the chops."

There was an ominous silence.

Ghost's motley, shabby crew shifted slowly, drifting into place behind their leader, all eyes fixed on Carson. Suddenly, they looked a lot less motley. There was a gleam of stainless steel as an assortment of blades, brass knuckles and a pistol or two peeked out of stained clothes. Before anyone could speak, KO turned, took three steps and smashed a fist into the front door, knocking a solid wooden panel clean out.

"Alright then," Carson tore the paper and handed half to Ghost. "Take my truck. There's more of you. We'll take Dex's car."

"Copy that. When we find something, we'll contact you."

Carson watched them file out. The door closed behind them with a thump.

"Most of me hopes we get to Deth first," Dex rumbled. "A tiny bit hopes they do."

"Yeah. The Hobo Hit Squad. Wow. But either way, Deth gets what's coming to him," Carson snatched up his bat. "Now, let's go get our girl back."

He had taken just one step, Dex at his heels, when the door swung open. There, silhouetted in the opening, stood a lean figure swathed in black.

"I apologize for the interruption, Mr. Dudley," Sister Becky announced. "But I was afraid you were considering departing without me yet again."

CHAPTER ELEVEN

Deth's Door

Carson was moving before he could think. He caught the old nun in a tight hug, his sudden unexpected joy beyond restraint. "Sister B!"

Sister Becky's face broke into a smile, and she returned his embrace warmly. A moment later, Carson pulled away, holding her at arm's length, incredulous.

"Sassafras and crabapples! I can't believe it! I just can't believe it!"

Behind him, Dex grunted. "Believe it."

Sister Becky inclined her head. "Mr. Jackson."

"Old Goat."

Despite Dex's gruff affectation, Carson caught the shadow of a smile. He made no attempt to hide his own, grinning ear to ear. "You're here! You got my message!" Carson retrieved the black leather satchel she had dropped when he'd embraced her. It was her war bag, and the heft and clink of it filled him with wild courage.

"I did indeed, Mr. Dudley," Sister Becky slung the satchel from her shoulder with practiced ease. "At the proverbial Eleventh Hour, I might add. I had already boarded my flight and was awaiting takeoff when your message reached me."

"My message! Super! That's... wait... what? You mean the phone?"

"Phone, Mr. Dudley? Why, I should think not. The message was a handwritten note, delivered by a stewardess."

"But I didn't..." he looked at her blankly. "What did it say?"

"That you were in grave need. To come at once," she narrowed her eyes, taking the meaning of his expression. "You did not contact the airport?"

"No. No one knew where you were."

Sister Becky's eyes narrowed even more. "Most interesting," she murmured. Then, louder, "But also quite beside the point." She squared her shoulders. "Judging by your appearance, I have arrived in the nick of time."

"Better late than never," Carson's jubilation melted into a look of grim determination. "Kiki's in trouble. We'll brief you on the way..."

Minutes later, they were packed into the familiar crush of Dex's car and speeding and screeching through the rain washed streets. It was late, traffic was light, and Dex was taking full advantage of both.

"What's our address?" He negotiated a particularly aggressive left turn, clipping a mailbox and sending sparks from his rims.

Carson braced his feet against the side panel but for once offered no complaints. He read off the address Parsons had given him.

Dex grunted. "Shelley District. Again."

"That's why I picked this one. Deth is clever. He's proven that. I'm hoping he had another lab set up around here somewhere, a fallback. I should've checked into it before, should've listened to Ghost and Leet. But no way, not me. Not Captain Cocky! I had to go all Tony Stark!"

Sister Becky turned to him from the passenger seat, although with considerable difficulty. Her face, flickering under a veritable strobe of passing streetlights, was bitter with self-recrimination. "I may be unfamiliar with your Mr. Stark, Mr. Dudley, but if pride was his sin, then I share it as well. I was quick to abandon you for my own foolish wants. I was blinded by my selfishness," she shook her head regretfully. "'Pride goeth before destruction and an haughty spirit before a fall'. I failed you, Mr. Dudley."

Carson snorted fiercely. "Pride?! You wanna talk pride?! Yours was the Geico Gecko - mine was Godzilla! And now Kiki..." he shook his head bitterly. "Destruction and a fall... you said a mouthful there."

"There. Now our confession is done," the nun squeezed his knee firmly. "Let us press on with fresh hearts and cease worrying upon the past, for such thoughts balm no wound. We must now bend our wills upon the present and prepare to do what will serve Ms. Masterson best."

"Bust some heads," Dex rumbled.

"Quite."

"But what if she's already... what if we're...?!"

Sister Becky studied the agony in his face. "We shall pray that is not the case, Mr. Dudley. We shall ask for help, just as we do whenever flood waters arise, and we shall prepare ourselves to accept whatever the Father sends, whether that be a boat to bear us or simply the strength to swim. Now then – I was promised a briefing. Tell me everything you know."

Carson took a deep breath. He nodded, but the look of reckless impatience didn't leave his eyes. The strain of worry was starting to show. Without further ado, he launched into a rapid recap of the last few days.

Carson was just finishing when Dex downshifted and flicked off his lights, cruising into the shadows of a huge Gothic structure. Silence descended on the car as Dex let it roll slowly forward a few feet. The building looked like something out of time and place, a thing from Las Calamas' distant past. The sweeping architecture and brooding, faded elegance of the place gave it a presence that went beyond impressive, elevating it to an aged magnificence, like a gray but mighty king holding high his chin in defiance of the newer, more modern skyline beyond.

That this king had seen better days was apparent the more they looked: faded stonework and crumbling brick gave it a worn, tattered look. Newspapers, empty cups and other clutter blew about its broad base, piling in shadowed corners and clustering in the mammoth brass-and-glass revolving door of its once-grand front entrance.

"Is that the old train station?" Dex squinted, trying to pierce the shadows and the undeniable air of mystery that surrounded the building. "Place was built back in the 20's. Been closed down for years."

"Yeah. And it may have Kiki," Carson rasped. "Let's move," he squeezed out onto the shadowy street and trotted toward the corner of an adjacent building. The others clambered out quickly, hurrying to catch him. Carson peered out, shotgun at the ready, bat tucked in his belt. "Looks clear."

"I don't see anything movin'," Dex scanned the area carefully.

"You wanna..."

But Carson was already gone.

Dex swore and hurried to catch up, Sister Becky close on his heels. "Slow down, fool!" He managed to clamp a hand on Carson's shoulder. "There's plenty of ways we can let the bad guys know we're comin', but walking right up to the front door and ringing the bell ain't my pick!"

Carson scowled and shrugged off his hand. "We don't have time to mess around. If she's here..."

"Then, we'll get her. We just gotta play this proper. Trust me, when it's time to get loud," Dex hitched up one of his large black duffel bags. It clanked authoritatively. "We'll get loud."

"Fine. Just don't slow me down," Carson was moving again. Dex made a frustrated noise and stumped after him. Behind them, Sister Becky clucked with concern but said nothing. They caught Carson at the revolving doors, examining a set of rusty chains.

"Look!" He gestured excitedly. "This chain has been here awhile, but the padlock! It's new!" He lifted his shotgun and pointed it at the lock, ready to fire.

"Whoa!" Dex grabbed the barrel and jerked it upward. "Cease fire, you idjit! I thought we decided ringing the bell was a *bad* idea?!"

"No, *you* decided!" Carson whispered fiercely. "Now, I'm deciding it's the quickest way in! So leggo my Eggo and let me blast this!"

"First of all, *if* anyone is in there, all that'll do is let 'em know we're coming, and second of all, it just might get us killed! And Kiki too... *if* she's even in there! Why not just drive a car through the wall?!"

"If I thought it would get us in quicker, I would!"

"Then, maybe you shoulda drove, sucka! I am *not* turning my car into a battering ram!" Dex dropped his voice to a mutter. "Man... first Kiki, now you. I liked it when I was the scary one."

"Gentlemen," Sister Becky's calm whisper intruded. "If I may interject. I believe what Mr. Jackson is suggesting is that, secured as it is, this door would make neither a convenient nor a clandestine entry. If it is inhabited, this building must certainly have another means of ingress." She bent over, like a bloodhound sniffing spore, pacing about the area near the door. "Observe... scuff marks. Boots, perhaps? Large. And quite heavy," she followed a faint trail to the wall a dozen feet away, stopping in the shadow of a distressed gray dumpster. There, she crouched, her fingers tracing a set of deep gouges in the pavement. "This has been dragged," she murmured, gesturing to the trash bin.

"Frequently. Mr. Jackson, if you please?"

Dex put his shoulder to metal and shoved, grunting. Rusted wheels made an angry, squealing sound that put their teeth on edge. Carson crowded in, peering past. There, in the wall behind the trash container, was a wide opening in the brick.

"Yes!" he hissed. "Way to go, Sister B! Deth's gotta be in there!"

"Deth?" Dex eyed the opening with suspicion. "Yeah, maybe. Or a bunch of hobos. Or a meth lab."

"Only one way to find out..." Carson ducked and pushed toward the hole.

This time Dex was one move ahead of him. He sidestepped quickly, sliding his giant frame between Carson and the wall. "Get a *grip*!"

Carson fixed a fierce gaze on Dex, but the big man glared back with equal determination. After a moment, Carson stepped back, fuming.

Dex eased, but kept his body blocking the entrance. "Now look – I know you're 'bout to go postal. I get it. If it was Dee inside, there wouldn't be a force on the planet could keep me out. But I also know that rushin' in blind and half-cocked wouldn't do her no good," Dex unslung his heavy ruck sack and set it on the ground. "I'm not sayin' this *is* the place, and I'm not sayin' it *ain't*. Either way, I ain't goin' in there without a handful of something that goes *boom*. Or in this case, *fwoosh*. I'm gettin' Shari."

Carson glared. "Shari?! You're calling your ex-wife?!"

"Shush, fool." Dex gave him a withering look and yanked his bag open. "Let the Big Man work." He began to pull out parts.

Sister Becky looked on, seemingly unconcerned with their predicament but carefully watching Dex's newest weapon take shape. After a few moments, he straightened. In his hands was a compact black flamethrower, fully assembled and ready for action.

Sister Becky arched a brow. "Shari?"

"My ex. The Dragon Lady," Dex's answer was matter-of-fact. "She earned it. How about you, Old Goat? What kinda heat you packin'? Could be some heavy hitters in there, and I don't think waving a cross at 'em this time is gonna be real convincing."

"You may be correct, Mr. Jackson. However, I am pleased to report," she plunked her own, much smaller, black bag down beside his. "That the Good Lord has equipped me to deal with dangers both spiritual *and* material." She fished a heavy item out of the bag. It gleamed dully, well oiled and professionally maintained.

"A crowbar?! You're gonna give nuns a bad name."

"I shall take that as a compliment, Mr. Jackson," she declared, settling the crowbar on her shoulder like an old friend.

"Alright," Dex hefted his weapon. "Let's do this," he flashed a look at Carson. "Ready?"

"Steady, go!" Carson pushed past him and dove through the opening.

Dex heaved a heavy sigh. "Here we go again."

They stepped out of the night and into the inky blackness of the unknown. Sister Becky produced a small flashlight, its white beam picking out the ghostly shapes of porcelain toilets and a few broken sinks.

"Yup," Dex grumbled. "This is pretty much where I thought we'd end up."

Ahead, the rapid clatter of Carson's footsteps guided them, echoing hollowly off cracked tile. Emerging from the bathroom, they found themselves in a hallway lined with pillaged metal lockers.

Carson was already at the far end, moving quickly in spite of the darkness. Suddenly, he slowed, jerking up his shotgun to point at the cavernous opening at the end of the hall. A faded, age-worn sign read *TERMINAL*. Cautiously, Dex and Becky stole forward, reaching Carson's side and discovering the reason for his pause. Strange, unsettling noises began to grow around them, an odd, eerie mix of industry and science.

Exchanging a few quick looks, the three stepped through the doorway and into another world. They reconnoitered silently from the cover of a row of ancient benches.

The room before them was vast, its vaulted ceiling supported grandly by a series of flying buttresses. More broken benches were heaped against their bases like piled bones, turning the room's once-casual elegance into a dark and brooding clutter. At the far end of the room, the broad boarding platform had been converted into a makeshift laboratory. Cluttered with scientific and medical equipment of every type and variety, from antique to modern, it looked the spitting image of Dr. Deth's basement lab they had destroyed, complete with arcing blue electricity and stainless steel centrifuges.

With one exception.

Kiki.

Strapped to a heavy table on the center of the platform, naked and exposed, she lay still, her blond hair cascading like a spill of frozen yellow milk. Her body was deathly pale, more than usual, eyes closed and cheeks hollow and shadowed. Massive leather straps held her tight to the table and electrodes were attached to her chest, shoulders, thighs and forehead.

Carson registered the scene. A heartbeat passed. Then, he brought up the King and started up from his crouch, his face a mask.

Dex caught him and pulled him back. "Hold up, Bro," he rumbled softly. "She ain't alone up there!"

Carson flashed an angry look and jerked his arm away. However, he did give the platform another careful glance and, this time, picked out the hunched form of Dr. Deth with his eerie greenish skin and black soulless goggles, fiddling with the controls of a large, antique-looking electrical contraption that was connected by giant copper coils to Kiki's table. As they watched, a handi-cat sauntered from a cabinet and handed the doctor a tool. He took it without looking, making another adjustment as he watched the gauge that currently held his attention.

"Deth..." Carson hissed, his words ugly with hate.

"That, Mr. Dudley, is the proverbial least of our worries. If you would shift your gaze slightly to his right..."

There, in the thick shadows between hulking equipment towers, something stirred. Something huge.

Carson stiffened.

Every few moments, an arc of blue light pulsed, showing the thing's features more plainly, though it was difficult to tell which were blurred by uncertain light and which were blurred by the bizarre science of its creation. Everything about the figure seemed out of proportion and symmetry, close to natural yet missing the mark, unsettling, like some grotesque child's toy assembled from dirty, mismatched, cast-off parts. The chest was barrel shaped yet bulged in odd areas, while huge shoulders supported powerful arms that hung just a bit too long. Lank hair straggled down over a wide forehead and concealed half the face, which was a mercy due to the frank ugliness of it. One bloodshot eye peered out, dull and yet watchful, and the huge anvil-shaped jaw hung open, making the thing look slack-jawed but also hungry and feral. Cracked, dirty fingernails showed through fingerless gloves, and Carson could still remember the clutch of them on his skin. He shivered.

The thing's entire appearance was patchwork, right down to its clothing and skin. Surgical scars crisscrossed its flesh, which, though shrouded in shadow, was clearly not uniform - some patches were pallid, some swarthy, some in between. Thankfully, much of the creature was concealed under a filthy, mud-spattered leather trench coat, also stitched and patched. Overall, it had a powerful though unwholesome look: massive, solid, immovable and unmoving, a dirty, brown, misshapen, mighty something that should not be.

And yet, there it stood.

Carson whispered the words they were all thinking: "The Manstruct."

"And it ain't alone," Dex fingered the trigger of his flamethrower. "Got some crats up there," he nodded his head toward the flying buttresses high above where a cluster of shifting black shapes crawled restlessly across the stone. "I spotted a couple of two-jos skulking around the base of the platform, too. Could be more of them. It's a big room."

"Yeah. We're in it. Awful deep in offal deep," Carson muttered darkly. His eyes were locked on Deth.

"So how you wanna play it?"

"Fast and loose. Forget the critters for now. The Manstruct - that's the one you worry about. He's yours. Sister B., go for Kiki. And Deth..." Carson racked the pump on the King with a hearty *ch-chak*! "He's mine."

"Fine by me. Been waitin' for this."

"We'd better hurry, too. Whatever Deth has planned for Kiki, I don't think we've got much ti..."

ZZZZZZZZZZZZZZZZ!

A crackling, surging, electrical scream tore through the room, accompanied by a flash of hot blue-white light that pulsed the air like lightning. Unlike lightning, it didn't stop. The scorching sound beat on, arcing, sizzling, cracking the air.

Carson stared in shock as Kiki's body jerked, writhed and smoked. Deth's hand still rested on a lever; his face, cold and etched, simply stared as she convulsed in indescribable agony. Hot blue arcs crawled like hideous hungry snakes across her body. Blue light and shadow flicked and danced across Deth's face, but no emotion showed. Just a cold, callous, unfeeling, detached watchfulness.

A second passed.

Then Carson's cry of rage tore through the room, rising above the agonizing sound of electrical current. Deth looked. Dark goggles panned, found, focused on the source of the disturbance. An instant later, every biological construct in the room, two legged, four legged and winged, snapped to attention and turned toward the spot.

To Dex and Becky, it was unnerving and astonishing. Every creature seemed in eerie concert, in tune with Deth's will.

To Carson, it didn't even register. He was moving. Launching toward the platform in a desperate and mindless fury, he drew a bead on Deth.

BOOM!

A two-jo leapt in the path of Carson's shot, yelped and flung sideways. Deth stood rooted, unmoving in spite of the threat. Carson pumped and bellowed and fired again. Again, the two-jo leapt in to take the hit. This time blood spattered, and it didn't rise.

Carson pumped again, face contorted. This time, Deth moved, drifting right and taking partial shelter behind a large bank of dials and controls, still bathed in the flickering blue light of Kiki's torment. Just as Carson squeezed, an avalanche of wings and claws and screeches descended on him from above as a wave of crats swooped in, biting and clawing. Again, his shot deflected, this time in an explosion of black feathers and fur. He gave a wordless shout, throwing up his arms and battering madly with the King.

Seconds late,r the black cloud pulled away to regroup, and Carson broke free, stumbling and slipping over hairy, feathered bodies. He wiped blood from the cuts on his face and whirled desperately, trying to get his bearings, seeking madly for the platform. What he saw instead was a stainless steel centrifuge the size of a washing machine flying straight at him. Behind it, the Manstruct looked on, its body still bent from the effort of the throw.

"DOWN!!"

A huge arm hooked Carson's shoulders and yanked him off his feet. As he slammed into the ground, the missile smashed a hole in the marble floor where he had stood a split second before.

Carson flipped to his back and stared Dex in the face. "What are you doing?!"

"Saving your life, fool!"

Carson shook off his momentary daze and shoved at Dex's huge frame, frantic with panic. "Forget me... Kiki!"

As he fought his way to his feet, savage barks slammed into them. A hulking mastiff charged, this time a three-jo, filling the air with animal noise and flying drool.

Carson jerked the trigger on the King.

Click

Empty.

Desperately reversing his grip, he swung hard just as the thing leapt, smashing it solidly in one of its heads, then rolled aside to avoid a quick bite from another. Still on his back, Dex roared and kicked the beast squarely in the ribs, his heavy boot sending it squeaking and scrabbling across the marble. The floor shook as it smashed into heavy crates.

Then, the floor shook again. Only this time, much, much louder. Dex and Carson looked. The Manstruct straightened from where it had landed after a tremendous leap off the platform. One bloodshot eye peered through a greasy tangle of hair, fixed hard on the two intruders. It began to run, an unstoppable juggernaut, steel toed boots thudding on the floor. The lights shook.

Carson and Dex scrambled to their feet, Carson fumbling shells from his pocket and thumbing them into the King, his eyes on the thundering onrush of the Manstruct. Behind it, he could see the tortured form of Kiki, still in the grip of the scorching, unceasing, soul wrenching *ZZZZZZZZZZZZZ!* With a wordless battle cry, he lowered his head and prepared to charge.

But a huge hand stopped him.

"No!" Dex yanked him roughly back. "Only God can save her now!"

"Wha...?!"

Dex nodded savagely toward the far side of the room. Just past the base of a flying buttress, Carson caught a blur of black robes. Sister Becky. She was rushing the platform.

"If they spot her..." Dex didn't need to finish his sentence. They were Sister Becky's only chance. And Kiki's. He dragged the pair of . 45 automatics from his belt. The flamethrower was gone, tossed aside as he'd rescued Carson. "Dogs or crats?!"

Carson froze, his eyes taking in the scene in a split-second. The Manstruct thundered on, seconds from impact. Overhead, the roiling cloud of crats had re-gathered and was preparing to swoop. A roaring bark warned them that the three-jo had recovered and was gathering its legs for a spring.

"Crats!"

Dex stepped up beside him. "Ready?"

"Steady!"

"Go!"

They whirled. Dex fired point blank, letting the Wonder Twins loose as the beastly hound hurled itself at them. Bullets tore into its heavy carriage, knocking it around in mid-air like an oversized, freakish, three-headed rag doll. At the same moment, the cloud of crats broke and dove. Carson fired straight up into the swarm. He got off three quick shots, sending puffs of feathers and fur exploding and temporarily dispersing the swarm. Then, he whirled like a cat to meet the charge of the onrushing Manstruct, still with a second to spare.

Or so he thought.

Quick, brutal hands smacked the King away as the great grim juggernaut kept straight on, shouldering into Carson like a runaway rhino. Carson took the impact full on. He crashed down in a poof of dust and splinters among a row of old benches over a dozen feet away.

The Manstruct thudded a few more steps, then stopped and whirled, hunting Dex. It wasn't hard to find him. Dex stood, feet wide, stance loose and ready, the deadly barrel of one of the Wonder Twins pointing straight at the creature.

"Dex!" Carson gasped, dragging himself painfully up over splintered wood. "Flame... flame... throw...!"

"Won't need it," Dex grated. "Only wish I had time to slap you around a little, Ginger Snap," Dex shook his head. "But our girl's in a pickle. This one's for Kiki."

He fired.

The booming shot slammed the Manstruct straight in the chest. It grunted and rocked back. Then, it took a step toward Dex.

Dex gaped.

He looked down at his pistol, looked back at the misshapen bulk that was now thudding toward him at a loping run. He fired again, his aim a little less certain, smacking the creature in the shoulder. This time it didn't even grunt. A third shot flared just as it reached him, one long arm sweeping up to knock the weapon aside, the other driving a great gnarled fist straight into Dex's chest with all the power of a falling anvil. Carson felt the crunch from across the room.

Amazingly, through some superhuman effort, the big man kept his feet, although he stumbled backwards several steps, and one of his pistols clattered to the marble. The second came up in a wide swing, smashing into the creature's massive, misshapen jaw, then back again for a vicious crossing strike.

The Manstruct didn't move.

With a growl, it swatted Dex's hand like a bear would a fish, sending the second Twin arcing far away onto the platform. With a roar of mingled rage and pain, Dex lifted a massive boot and jammed it straight into the creature's belly.

This time, the Manstruct did move.

Dex stepped in to follow up, folded slightly over his injured chest but seething with savagery. Blow after blow he drove into the thing's hideous face, big knuckles leaving dents and drawing spatters of thick, dark blood. The creature, however, was far from done. With a growl more animal than human, it struck back, battering Dex's body and head with fearsome power and a precision that belied its brutish exterior.

Carson, on his feet now and weaving unsteadily toward them, stared in shock at the raw savagery of the two combatants. It was like watching a pair of prize bulls ram and butt and spike with no care of self, just a total surrender to violence and carnage. Carson had seen Dex fight. He'd seen him fight for his life. But he'd never seen him truly cut loose. As he stood toe to toe with the creature, the big man unleashed every ounce of power, rage and training he possessed. It was terrifying.

In the end, however, against the cold, relentless, inhuman power of the Manstruct, not even Dex could last.

Faster than was comforting, the fury of Dex's assault slowed, while the creature took every shot and answered without hesitation. At last, after deflecting a punch, Dex's counter came a hair too slow. The Manstruct slapped his fist aside, reared back and drove its massive forehead straight down into Dex's face. The crack was like a split coconut.

Dex's legs wobbled.

If the scene hadn't made Carson almost physically ill, it would have seemed comical. The big man teetered, struggled to right himself, took three stumbling steps and crashed down like a felled oak. Without pause, the Manstruct stepped to his side and started stomping. Great boots drove down like pistons into Dex's undefended body. Things crunched.

Carson launched forward, gritting his teeth against a wave of dizziness and pain. If he didn't get to Dex, his friend was dead. Setting his jaw, he drew the bat from his belt and charged.

His first shot took the Manstruct behind the ear, followed by three more lightning blows to the side of the head and neck, all of which got the thing's attention. A long arm shot out, quick as a python, seizing Carson by the neck. Effortlessly, it raised him from his feet and into the air. The thing glared at him through cold, bloodshot eyes and a veil of greasy hair, ignoring the feeble battering of Carson's bat against its skull.

Carson kicked and twisted, clutching at the hand of steel that was slowly crushing his windpipe. He now had a fine closeup of the thing, and as his brain began to reel, he honed in with a sick and helpless fascination. A rip in the shoulder of the trench coat exposed bulging muscles, snaking veins and a disturbing network of surgical scars. Part of Carson's brain registered two portions of two separate tattoos, connected by a seam of stitches. He shuddered, gasping for breath, kicking at the heavy torso. All it did was hurt his feet.

The vise grip squeezed harder.

The room began to spin and close in. From the edges of his vision, darkness crept slowly in. Carson was falling... falling...

Then, he really was falling.

The echoes of a mighty, metallic crash rang through the cotton filling his ears as he slowly registered the hard cold marble beneath him. Something tinkled and pattered over his body. Glass. His injured knee was screaming again, but he was glad for it – it meant he was alive. He shifted and rolled, struggling to move...

Then, he was seized and lifted into the air once more.

His eyes jerked open, and he started to kick then stopped as relief flooded him. It was Dex.

The big man stood him on his feet. "Up and... at 'em, Bro... this ain't... over..."

Over Dex's shoulder, as the room once more drew into focus, Carson caught sight of the Manstruct lying prone among the remains of the broken centrifuge that Dex had smashed over its head. Momentary joy turned to dismay as the thing jerked, cast off the wreckage with a growl and surged to its feet.

"How's that... flamethrower... sound now?!"

Dex could only nod weakly, wiping blood from his battered face.

With a barrel-chested growl, the Manstruct charged.

* * * * * * *

Moments earlier, Sister Becky had found herself facing her own peril. Taking advantage of the chaos, she had reached the platform undetected and mounted quickly up the side steps, intent on freeing

Kiki with all possible haste. Her only obstacle now was Deth, still standing beside the table where his victim writhed and jerked in the deadly grip of the blue arcs. The fiend seemed oblivious to all else in the room. He simply stared, eerily unfazed by the battle raging behind him. More importantly, Sister Becky noted, he seemed oblivious to her. She hefted her crowbar, picturing the exact spot on the bald head where she would strike.

Unfortunately, Deth was not alone.

As the nun closed within a few meters, a snarling, bristling mass of fur and muscle leapt onto the platform. Bared teeth and savage growls barred her way. Deth swiveled his head, slowly, strangely, like a mantis. His eyes unsearchable behind the goggles, Deth simply stared. Flickers of electricity danced across his stark face.

Then, he turned back to his dials and gauges.

The hideous two-jo cut loose with a savage bark and snapped the air. Saliva from twin jowls splattered the front of Sister Becky's robes. She hitched up her grip on the crowbar, eyes slits. Beyond the beast, agonizingly close, Kiki's naked form danced and bucked. The large black switch that Deth had used to activate the current sat close by his right hand, agonizingly close. Urgency and a cold rage surged through Sister Becky. She breathed a prayer. The heavy crowbar drew back, and she forced herself to focus, judging distance. She breathed deeply, murmured another prayer and hurled the crowbar with all of her might.

It sailed straight over the two-jo and struck the switch full on.

As Sister Becky had hoped, the impact flipped the lever neatly to the off position. Exceeding her expectations, it also snapped the metal off right at the base. The switch was useless.

Instantly, the harsh buzz of current ceased. Somewhere, turbines whined a long, receding hum. Kiki's thrashing, jerking body stilled.

Deth stared. If his face had been capable of emotion at all, it would have, at this moment, most certainly displayed some.

Not bound by similar limitations, Sister Becky smiled a cold grin.

The victory, however, was short lived. Deth turned his stark features toward Sister Becky, and as he did so, the pair of dog heads followed in perfect unison. Throaty growling rose from the beast's shared chest, threatening a painful, toothy revenge.

Sister Becky, feeling suddenly vulnerable, glanced first at her empty, weaponless hands and then heavenward.

"Now, Lord," she breathed. "Would be an ideal moment for a miracle."

A nickel-plated .45 suddenly dropped from the sky into her palms.
"That will do," she muttered.
The two-jo leaped. Jerking the weapon up, Sister Becky fired.

* * * * * * *

"Move!" Dex roared, shoving Carson clear and lurching forward
to take the Manstruct's charge head on. The impact shook a battered
chandelier overhead, making the few remaining crystals dance and
jingle. Incredibly, Dex kept his feet.

Sent sprawling, Carson slid to a halt, scrabbling to his hands and
knees in time to see the Manstruct slam a flurry of hammerlike blows
into Dex's head. The guard reeled, slipped in blood, dropped to one
knee, his head sagging. The fight had taken its toll at last. Dex was
spent.

Then, the impossible happened.

The Manstruct seized Dex's massive frame and, like a butcher with
a side of beef, hoisted him bodily over its head. Muscles bulging, veins
popping, jaw set like an iron vise, the fearsome brute stood with Dex
held suspended, incredibly, in the air above it.

They stood poised that way for one terrible moment.

Without a sound, the Manstruct slammed Dex's body down.

There was an awful, awful, sickening *crack!* Dex didn't move.
The creature's bloodshot eyes rolled slowly to Carson.

It was then, as he sat sick and hollow and hopeless, that Carson
finally registered one tiny fact that had been struggling to push its way
in: the scorching sizzle of electricity was gone. The fearsome current
that had held Kiki captive in torment had been shut off.

Sister Becky had done it.

Hope surged through him, and he followed it, forcing himself to
move. He tore his eyes from the horrifying image of Dex's crumpled
body, and they lit almost instantly on a familiar object – his shotgun. It
lay in the clear hardly a dozen feet away. Carson lunged, dove, sliding
on the marble, and seconds later, his fingers closed on the comforting
shape of the stock. Rolling to his back, he jammed a shell into the
breech and fired, point blank, just as the Manstruct reached down for
him.

With enough presence of mind to recall Dex's ineffective shots,

Carson set his sights lower – and was rewarded. The blast struck the monster in the shin, knocking its leg out from under it. With a startled grunt, it staggered sideways. Carson scrambled backwards, slammed more shells into the King, then followed up with another shot to the same leg, then another to the face. The brute roared a bear's roar of pain and lurched back. Carson felt another surge of hope. Perhaps it wasn't invulnerable after all. He reached eagerly for more shells.

Then, from within the darkness of the Manstruct's tattered trench coat, something shot out and lashed toward Carson.

Something long and green.

The appendage slapped at Carson's shotgun, sending it spinning away across the chamber, before slithering back under the coat like a high tension retractable cord.

Carson froze, momentarily unable to accept or process what had just happened.

With a growl, the Manstruct took a step toward him and swung a backhand. The blow sent Carson flying, spinning, crashing down across a stack of benches. He rolled off, struck something metal, shook his head to clear it and staggered to his feet as the Manstruct arrived. It struck him a grazing blow as he twisted aside, but he hardly felt it. He ducked under another, took a shot in the back as he dove under an arm, then vaulted gracelessly over benches, catching a foot and sprawling flat.

Struggling through pain and panic, Carson surged to his feet. Behind him, wood creaked and smashed as the Manstruct tossed aside all obstacles in its relentless pursuit.

Carson ignored it all, eyes roving desperately, searching. They had one chance. Just one.

But it would only work if Dex was alive.

His eyes lit on the motionless form of the guard. He breathed a wordless prayer and hurled himself forward, collapsing at his side.

"Dex! *Dex!!*" Carson shook him, frantic.

To his immense relief, the big man groaned and twitched. Carson shook again, and this time Dex shuddered, rolling to his side. His sweat-streaked face a mask of agony, he reached for his left leg. Carson saw blood and a spike of white. His stomach lurched.

"Dude... your leg!"

"Got... another one... help me... onto it!"

"Better idea! Get to those benches!"

"Which...?!"

"Now!"

Carson rolled clear, just as thudding steps announced the Manstruct's arrival. He found his feet, dodged, twisted and took another glancing punch to the face that made lights dance in his head. Somehow, he kept his balance. Somehow, he kept moving. Pitching over an old brass turnstile, he rolled clumsily to his feet again and was moving, circling right, drawing the Manstruct away.

The monster gave chase, hampered less by its injured leg as its rage grew. Carson barely kept out of reach as he dodged madly across the floor, pulling up every self defense tip Dex had drilled into his brain over the past months of training. He moved frantically but always with subtle purpose. Always with direction. Finally, with a last twisting lunge, he ducked under monstrous hands, dove forward and slid to a halt inside a U-shaped stack of benches. It was the same stack he had been thrown into moments ago. He had gone in a circle.

Carson sucked in great gasps of air, his strength almost gone, backing up carefully until he felt wood poke his back. The monster slowed, crouching just at the mouth of the U, arms spread wide to stop any escape. Carson was trapped. There was no way out. He only hoped Dex had had enough time.

For a moment, they stood, staring, predator and prey. Carson took stock, waited another heartbeat, breathing, drawing out the moment as long as he could. A final, fierce flicker in the creature's bloodshot eyes told him his time was up. The Manstruct was about to charge. It was now or never.

"You like... grabbing girls..." Carson gasped, wiping at the sweat and blood on his face. "I got... one... for you. Her name... is Shari!" Carson hurled himself to the ground and yanked his hoodie over his head.

Nothing happened.

The Manstruct gave a low growl.

"I said, 'Her name is *Shari!!!'*"

Still nothing. Carson peeked out from under his hoodie. The monster was just feet away, arms reaching, eyes savage.

"Shari, Shari, Shari!!! For the frippin' love of Pete, Dex, NOW!!!"

The stack of benches on the right suddenly toppled back with a crash. Dex stood revealed, slumped against a flying buttress, blood streaming from his wounded leg. In his hands, he clutched the flamethrower. "Here she comes, Brother... a hunka hunka burnin'

195

love!!"

FWOOSH!

With a rush of heat, a dragon's tongue of flame billowed out and engulfed the Manstruct. It staggered sideways, arms waving, body jerking, strangely and eerily silent.

Dex poured on burst after burst, shouting: "*That's* for Kiki! And *that's* for my %^&*#@! leg! And *that's* for my %^&*#@! guns! And *that's* for messing up my %^&*#@! love life!!! And *that's* for...!"

Carson didn't wait to hear what else it was for. He was already moving. Every thought was now bent on Kiki. Knowing she had been kidnapped had given him the focus to find her. Seeing her a prisoner of that horrible table had given him the strength to fight for her. But now... now that it was over... there was a sudden feeling in the pit of his stomach, an impossible, aching, hollowness of dread. He feared what he would know next. And what he might have to do for her.

It only took Carson a heartbeat to reach the platform. It felt like an eternity. He arrived at a scene so surreal and unbelievable that everything dropped into slow motion: Sister Becky crouching on top of Kiki, black robes draped across her limp body like a shroud, pumping compressions down steadily into her chest, pausing to pinch nose and chin and force deep breaths into her mouth.

CPR.

It was what you did when people were dying.

Or already dead.

Carson registered but couldn't process. His brain went numb. He noted, distantly but with sharp clarity, Sister Becky's ashen, tortured face, the deathly pallor on Kiki's sunken cheeks, the awful blue of her lips. Sound seemed to recede into a hollow, empty void as the world pressed close around him. Stiffly, Carson clambered up onto the platform. He stared at Sister Becky's back, unable to look at Kiki, watching the nun work mechanically. Sister Becky stopped to check for a pulse. When she started again, there was less determination on her face and more gray. Carson turned away, feeling sick.

He stared straight into the face of Dr. Deth.

Only that much was visible, framed in the dark rectangle of a doorway at the rear of the platform. Black goggles held Carson's gaze for a moment, implacable, unreadable, unburdened with emotion. Then, they faded backwards into the shadows and were gone.

Carson's hand tightened on his bat. A cold, cruel, dark rage flared inside him. Time started moving again and so did Carson. He stepped toward the doorway.

"Dud!" Dex slumped heavily against the edge of the platform. "Where you goin'?!"

"Crazy."

There were more words from behind him, shouting, but Carson didn't hear them. He didn't bother to look back at Sister Becky, still working over Kiki's motionless form. He knew it was useless. He knew it was too late.

And he knew who to blame.

"Not this time, you *ginger FLIPPIN' snap! BATTER UP!!!*"

Carson charged through the doorway.

And into a nightmare.

He wasn't sure what he had expected, and in his state, he didn't care. He was beyond caring for anything or anyone except punishing the man who had brought this unbearable grief upon him. Images flashed by in the dark. A shadowed hall with living walls. Twisted, bizarre growths, shapes and crawling things draped from ceiling and creeping across floors. Pools and drips of fluids, sticky and sickly-stinky sweet. And parts. Everywhere, parts.

Ahead, a blob of light flicked on, pink and cold. Carson ran for it, ignoring a flood of revulsion and the way his sneakers squished and his socks filled with liquid. He plunged headlong into a small room and came up short, gasping and shaking.

Deth was there.

He stood by a strange contraption: an oval frame as tall as a man, carved from obsidian and notched with glyphs. Wires and organic tubes crawled from its base to a strange, dark metal box. Stretched across the frame, sinister and translucent and pulsing with an unearthly energy, was a moist black membrane. A faint vibration filled the air, setting Carson's teeth on edge.

Deth paused, one black-gloved hand on a queer old-fashioned dial, one foot poised on the threshold of the obsidian frame, as if he were preparing to step through. Goggles stared at Carson, black pits. The scene was unreal, unearthly. For a moment, shock and horror balanced Carson's rage. He hesitated.

Then, something snatched his attention, and his eyes slipped up to the surgical cap snug on Deth's head. Underneath it, something moved. A sudden jumping poke against the fabric. As he stared, it moved again, this time a slow drag.

With an explosion of revulsion and rage, Carson leapt and swung, straight for that spot. The bat took Deth on the side of the skull, and Carson heard something crack and something squish. Then, Deth was falling backwards, his body passing through the membrane, sucked through, disappearing. There was a crackle of power, a flash of black light and a pressure in Carson's ears.

Then, all was silent. He stood, bat raised and ready, staring through the obsidian ring at the other side of the room.

An empty room.

The membrane was gone. Deth was gone.

Slowly, his bat came down.

Rage and adrenaline drained away. As they did, he remembered Kiki. The chamber, the device, the horror. Whirling, Carson ran.

By the time he reached the platform, the scene had changed. All of the frantic action and chaos were gone. He was met only with stillness and silence. Sister Becky stood beside Kiki's body, now covered in her outer robe. As Carson watched, the nun's aged hand slowly, gently, drew Kiki's lids down over staring eyes. She turned to Carson, her face full of pity, and grief, and tears.

"Oh, Mr. Dudley... my dear, dear lad..."

Carson's bat clattered to the floor. Then, his legs gave out, and he followed it. Sister Becky descended on him, wrapping him in her arms as he sobbed.

For some time, Dex stood near watching, his own broad face numb with shock and sorrow. Abruptly, he wiped fiercely at his eyes and straightened. "Uh-uh," he muttered. "Not yet. I got to kill me somethin'." He turned from the despair of the platform and limped out into the room, leaning on a crude crutch he had fashioned. A feline hiss drew his gaze. A handi-cat, spitting and arching, turned its hateful green eyes on him from an open doorway.

"You'll do," Dex flicked a switch on Shari. The pilot light kicked on with a wicked hiss of its own. "Heeeere kitty kitty..."

The cat ducked away into the opening, and Dex set off after it at an unsteady lurch. Silence descended on the station, save for the sterile hum of Deth's machines and Carson's slowly ebbing sobs.

Until Dex's voice boomed out, muffled but full of urgency. "Hey! Get over here! Ginger SNAPS!" In his shock, Dex, for once, neglected to curse. "You ain't gonna *believe* this!"

Carson lifted his head. He frowned, catching Sister Becky's gaze. There was something in Dex's voice...

Without a word, they ran for the doorway, Carson with his bat in hand. They slid to a halt outside a long narrow room. Like Deth's operating platform, it was crowded with medical and scientific equipment, some new and shiny, some straight from the set of a Bela Lugosi film. Long tables held queer tools and implements, jars of dark, viscous liquids with half-glimpsed organic masses. Worse than all of that, though, and unlike the platform, was the feeling of the place. It was something indescribable, something undefinable, something that made the little hairs on the back of everyone's neck rise. The place felt... Carson struggled to place it, but the best he could come up with was *wrong*. Like the hallway he had chased Deth down. In spite of his grief and emptiness, he shivered.

"Dex?" Carson could see the big man standing near the center of the room - just standing, shoulders slack, staring at something. Carson couldn't see past him. "Dude... what is it?"

Dex could only point.

Carson stepped to his side. He froze.

Before them stood several tall, cylindrical tanks, filled with murky green. A few were empty, while others contained partially formed shapes, definitely organic and disturbingly humanoid.

In the center one was Kiki.

She floated peacefully, naked and pale, eyes closed, blond hair floating in a halo around her head. The tank was unmarked. A quiet hum from an unseen source filled the silence.

For a moment, no one spoke.

No one moved.

No one could.

"Uh... should... uh..." Dex's voice sounded small. "Should we..." he indicated a grimy keypad on the face of the tank.

Carson lifted his bat and bashed the keypad - bashed and bashed and bashed until it broke free in a tangle of wires and sparks. A hatch popped loose, and a jet of water sprayed out around the seal. Carson threw his bat down and attacked the door, digging at the edges with his bare hands, prying with his fingers and tearing at the glass. The door came loose and swung open, thick fluid spilling out in a gush onto the floor, soaking his legs and front and filling the place with a foul chemical stench. He ignored it, plunging his hands into the flow to catch Kiki's body as it washed out.

Carefully, slipping in the wet, wrestling the awkward limp body, Carson half carried, half dragged her free. Dex took her legs as they carried her clear, his crutch and pain forgotten. Gently, they lowered her to the floor. Something dark and fleshy was clamped over her mouth, but Carson ripped it off, then yanked off his hoodie and covered her thin, fragile body.

Sister Becky knelt quickly by Kiki's side, nimble fingers seeking a pulse.

"Is she...?" Carson's voice was hoarse, uncertain.

The nun shook her head, brow furrowed. "That is unclear. I cannot..."

With a sudden spasm and a spurt of yuck, Kiki's body came to life. She rolled to her side, retching fluid, body jerking with vicious coughs, sucking air in between. It lasted for a minute. When she was finished, she collapsed back into Carson's lap and lay still. Her eyes never opened.

Carson, completely and utterly stunned, just held her. He couldn't believe it, didn't understand it, never had hoped for or even imagined it. But here it was. Kiki was in his arms. Alive.

"How did..." Dex licked his split lips, looking slightly dizzy. "Is that really...? What about...?" His eyes wandered to the outer room, where he could just glimpse one leg of the body on the platform. Kiki's body. Lifeless. Cold. "I don't..." his voice trailed off. "*Ginger Snaps.*"

Sister Becky stared at the new Kiki, her eyes troubled. "Quite, Mr. Jackson. Quite. Perhaps there exists some clue here that will assist us in determining..."

"No," Carson's voice cracked like a whip. "We wipe this place off the map." He gave the room an ugly look, eyes full of tears but empty of pity. "Burn it to the ground. Everything. Then, we get Kiki out of here."

"'Kiki'?! Bro, you really think that's..."

Carson shot him a look. It was the same one he had given Deth.

"Uh... right," Dex nodded. "We get Kiki out of here."

"Mr. Dudley," Sister Becky ventured. "Are you certain it is wise to..."

"Torch it," Carson stood, lifting Kiki. She made a weak, whimpering sound then buried her head in his shoulder. "This place is hell. Ashes are too good for it."

Dex shot a concerned glance at Sister Becky, who returned it ounce for ounce. After a moment, she lifted her hands helplessly.

Dex shrugged. "Shari always did like a barbecue."

As flames licked up behind him, Carson made his slow, steady way toward the exit. His wounds ached, his knee throbbed, and the body was heavy in his arms.

Heavy and warm.

That, in itself, was a comfort. That meant it was real. And for now, real was enough.

CHAPTER TWELVE

Christmas

"You're... we're... closing the store? Tonight?!"

"We are. It is Christmas Eve," Kinkade blinked at him. "And I believe you have a function to attend."

Carson eyed his boss shrewdly. "Yup." He couldn't think of anything else to say. All of the generosity and kindness was finally starting to unnerve him.

Kinkade held his gaze innocently for a moment then turned back to his tablet. "I shall expect you back in the store the day after tomorrow, of course, rested and ready for post-holiday protocols. We're on target for year end inventory, as discussed."

"You got it. Wait..." Carson's jaw dropped. "Day *after*...?! We're closing on *Christmas* also? *Two* days?!" His hand stopped on the way to his face where it strayed often to gently scratch around numerous cuts and abrasions, especially the stitches in his forehead. They were healing nicely but had the itch that came with.

This time, Kinkade didn't even look up. "It's Christmas," he repeated, as if that explained everything.

Carson, now thoroughly flummoxed, stared at Ross Kinkade as the man worked his tablet, casting an occasional eye over the hot dog warmer. Kinkade hadn't said a word about Carson's face, much less the three days of work he'd missed during the events revolving around Kiki's rescue. Unscheduled days. Unexcused days. Unexplained days. He hadn't even asked to hear Carson's carefully prepared excuse. He had simply greeted him when he returned and filled him in on a new rotation cycle for bread.

Carson made no effort to disguise his dismay, just stared openly at Kinkade as if the man had suddenly donned a leprechaun outfit and started dancing around the room tossing out gold coins. Before, it had been weird, Kinkade's disinterest. Now, it was just plain creepy.

"By the way," Kinkade didn't look up from the tablet as he spoke. "I have decided to make it official. Your Manager-In-Training status was scheduled to last through first quarter next year, but I see no reason to wait. You've been progressing adequately. I have submitted the necessary paperwork to 7 Corporation Headquarters. As of January 1, you will be the official Night Manager of Franchise Unit #417, Belfry. Congratulations."

That was the last straw.

"No."

Kinkade, for once, stopped tapping. "I beg your pardon?"

Carson stood his ground, staring his boss straight in the face. "I said, 'No'... as in 'no way', as in, 'I am the *worst* employee *ever* and you just handed me the keys to the store. As in 'I should be getting a pink slip at the least and probably a good solid kick in the crotch at the most, and instead, you're *putting me in charge?*!" He waved his hands about incredulously. "I am sorry, Mr. Kinkade, but I'm calling shenanigans. Shenanigans!! I'm saying 'no', and you don't get a 'yes' out of me until I get some sense out of you! *What in the name of Gabriel's big brass trumpet is going on*?!"

Kinkade blinked. "If you're referring to your employment history..."

"Yes!! I am referring to my employment history!"

"7 Corporation accepts the fact that every employee has his quirks."

"Quirks?!" Carson barked derisively and rolled his eyes. "*Quirks*?! Let's rattle off a list of my 'quirks,' shall we?! For starters, I *attacked* you, Mr. Kinkade – I smashed your tablet into a thousand pieces! Then, I let the store get destroyed. DE-STROY-ED! I spent the first three weeks as manager-in-training for Franchise Unit #417 in the hospital... flat on my back... *and you paid me*! My friends use the store as a clubhouse, I conduct personal business on the job, and I frequently disappear without notice, apology or rational explanation. To top it all off, I just plain fall off the map, during the busiest time of the year, for three days, with no excuse, and show up looking like I've been wearing a bag of sociopathic squirrels over my head! And what do I get for it?! A reprimand? A demotion? A pink slip?! No! Oh, no... *I get to drive the boss's car and a promotion!*" Carson appealed helplessly to the empty store, exasperated, arms still waving. "I... am... the... *worst... employee... ever*!! What in the hoo-ha-hey is going on?!"

Kinkade stared at him. His expression, as usual, was expressionless. "I admire your honesty, Carson. As I have stated before, *that* is the type of employee 7 Corporation is looking for..."

"No! No it is NOT! *No one* looks for that type of employee! Not even the Nazis! No! Uh-uh! No way! I'm not buying it," Carson shook his head vehemently. "Not this time. Not after everything I've been through," he planted himself, arms folded. Pride may have been his downfall in the past weeks, but it had sprung from a budding sense of confidence. Of determination. He had learned better when and how to stick to his guns, and this was one of those times. "I've worked here long enough and seen enough to know one thing: there's more going on here than I know. So, let me tell you one thing for durn sure: now... I want to know."

Kinkade was still staring at him. Only this time... Carson felt goosebumps race each other up his neck. This time, for the first time, it felt like Kinkade was actually *seeing* him. There was something different in those brown eyes. Something keen. Penetrating. The faintest trace of a smile, the same ghost that Carson had been sensing during recent weeks, traced the corners of thin lips.

When Kinkade spoke, he used a tone Carson had only heard once before - when he had visited him in the hospital after the encounter at Fujikacorp. It was soft. Quiet. Potent. And full of something more than words. "7 Corporation is a peculiar company, Carson. Most peculiar. Our interests occasionally stray from what you might call 'traditional' corporate concerns. Interests, we believe, that you share. That is why my superiors have afforded you special latitude in your work. Hear me very carefully when I say that they've had their eye on you – and they are starting to believe that you are *indeed* the type of person they're looking for. In fact, some believe that, if you are given time and opportunity, you might become a very valuable member of our organization. It is our hope that this recent string of concessions will show 7 Corporation's commitment to you. It is also our hope that they will allow you the time to pursue your... other interests... and decide if they are, as we suspect, in line with our own."

Carson felt his heart beating rapidly. He desperately wanted to say something but feared that if he did, Kinkade might stop talking. He kept his mouth clamped shut.

"As for your friends frequenting the store... 7 Corporation also understands the importance of friendships and how they can help define us. Help bring out our best qualities. Since we put a high price on qualities, we could hardly intervene. Except, of course, when those friends attempt to leave town."

There was a very loaded pause. As Kinkade's words sunk in, Carson's heart skipped a beat. Again, he felt like he should speak. This time he simply had no words.

"Now then," Kinkade turned away, heading for his coat. "Let's call it a night, shall we? I have an engagement of my own to attend, and I'm sure your friends are waiting. If you still wish to know more about 7 Corporation, you would do well to consider our motto," he gestured to the plaque hanging in the shadows above the employee lockers. "Mottos are an excellent source of insight into a company's culture. Lock up, will you? I'll get the lights." Kinkade hit the switch then pulled the chain on the OPEN sign. It flickered and went out. "Oh, and Carson," his voice floated mysteriously out of the shadows. "Merry Christmas."

The door chime warbled softly in his wake. Carson stared after him for a moment then up at the bronze plaque hanging hauntingly over the lockers.

"*Eternus Vigilo,*" he read softly and for the countless time. After a moment, he scratched his chin beard. He dug out his phone, tapped the Internet and did a quick translation of the Latin. He stared at the screen, waiting for results. "Hmph," he scratched his beard again. "'Always watching.' Just like last fifty times. Stupid..." then he looked below at the alternative translation buried in fine print. He had missed it before.

Ever vigilant.

Carson stood silently, lost in thought.

He was still pondering when he pulled in at Granny's a half hour later. Warm lights and noise floated out through the windows. Good noise. The noise of Christmas. More specifically, a Christmas party. Carson let his pondering fade and his breath out. It was party time. He needed it.

As he strolled to the front door, Carson reflected happily on how the Christmas party had come together. In spite of all odds, in the face of everything, his cherished function had gone from DOA to full-on yuletide jam in nothing flat. After her rescue from Deth's hideout, they had taken Kiki straight to the hospital. She was released in a matter of hours with a clean bill of health. Patch Parsons had, officially and miraculously, buried the incident without naming names. After all that, a party had seemed only natural. Carson hadn't pushed it. It had just happened. Everyone was coming. Dex even offered to bring punch.

Carson stepped through the front door. Christmas lights and warmth and hearty greetings flooded over him. Before he knew it, he was holding a mug of eggnog and a fresh cookie, and Granny was bustling off to the kitchen for more of both.

As the others dispersed, Leet hovered at his elbow. "You better eat that quick, Charity," he stared at the gooey morsel in Carson's hand like a hawk at a mouse. "To paraphrase the man: I've got a fever... and the only cure is sweet snoodles."

Carson sank his teeth into the cookie, still warm and soft from the oven. They just kept sinking. He sighed and chewed, watching the envious, almost heartbroken look on Leet's face.

The little man licked his lips. "I'm not kidding. I really think I have a fever. A legit addiction. These cookies are like Yoo-Hoo that you put in the oven. Only better. By the way, nice stitches," Leet indicated the line of thread on Carson's forehead. "Frankenstein's got nothing on you."

"I'm aware of the irony." Carson stuffed the rest of the cookie into his mouth. "Tell me something I don't know."

"Okay. How 'bout this..." Something in Leet's voice caught Carson's attention. It was casual but soft. "Essen Wurmhardt."

Carson frowned. "Should I know that name?"

"Nope. But you should probably write it down," Leet glanced around cautiously. "Once you break into the evidence room at Cop HQ, you usually don't get a second visit."

"Oh!" Carson quickly lowered his voice. "Oh. Right. The uh... you mean that's..."

"Mr. I-Like-to-Paint-Weirdos-Sacrificing-Virgins. Yeah. The artist who made all those creep-tastic works of 'art'," Leet made finger quotes around the word. "My boys did their thing. Just like I said. They're good."

"Cripes. Um... so I guess you're saying it's too late to pull the plug on that whole 'robbery' thing?"

"Too late?!" Leet's eyes bugged. "I'll say! Stick a fork in this one, Charity – it's done. I told you before, you don't dangle a carrot for these guys and then yank it away. The deed is complete, like it or not. Oh, and you might owe them a favor now, too. That's how these things work. And it won't be Yoo-Hoo they'll be wanting. It'll most likely be something illegal. Or immoral. Or both."

"Great." It suddenly felt a lot less like Christmas.

"You're welcome. Now, since we're on the topic, just remember where you got this info. Remember who delivered," Leet glanced pointedly across the room. Ghost hovered in a corner, conversing quietly with Sister Becky. He looked thoroughly uncomfortable. "I don't like him," Leet muttered, staring daggers. "Or trust him. Next time shady intel is on your Christmas list, you come to me. That scruffy spook is not an asset; he's a liability. Just how much of a liability is what I intend to find out, too. He's got dirty laundry plenty, and I'm gonna dig into that big government hamper until I find..."

"Leet," Carson cut him short, pinning him with a steady, level gaze. "Drop it." He spoke quietly and clearly.

The little man looked up sharply, startled, a crude retort already forming. Something, however, stopped him. "Or else what?"

Carson nodded toward the kitchen where Granny had just stepped out with a fresh plate of cookies. Steam still rose from them. "Your fever loses its cure."

Leet glanced over, licking his lips. "Curse you, Charity. Okay, I'll drop it. Dang! But if that dry old fart tries to cut in on my turf again, there's gonna be trouble," ferret eyes strayed hungrily to the platter of cookies. "Merry Christmas. Dang! I gotta go," Leet drifted away, heading straight for Granny.

Carson's smile was grim. He had learned a few good lessons after all. And whatever future entanglements Leet's associates might bring, it was pointless to worry about them now. There were closer, more urgent matters at hand. Squaring his shoulders, Carson headed for Ghost.

When he arrived, Sister Becky had just excused herself. They were alone. "Look..." Carson caught gray eyes. Ghost stood quietly, expressionless. Carson couldn't tell whether he was very angry or very calm. He took a deep breath. "I was wrong. You were right. I screwed up, I got cocky, I lost my way. Totally and completely. I was only looking out for number one, and it blew up in my face. I put you at risk, along with pretty much everyone else I know and care about. I really screwed up a lot of people and a lot of things. I wouldn't blame you if you never worked with me again. So, I'm here to let you know that I won't be playing the Kiki card anymore. Or any cards. I won't be asking for any more favors. I don't deserve them."

Ghost watched him closely in the silence that followed, searching his face. "Apology accepted." He proffered a hand.

Carson shook it, feeling weight lift. "Wow! That was a lot easier than I thought it would be."

"Imagine how easy it would have been if you hadn't completely cocked things up in the first place."

"Yeah, okay, that's more like what I thought it would be."

Ghost's grin was barely perceptible. "As for working together... let's just see what the future brings. I'm not going anywhere, no matter who's asking questions. I don't have a lot left to lose. Just Kiki."

"About that," Kiki stood in front of them.

It took Carson a moment to adjust to her, as usual. Light from the Christmas tree gleamed from the rosy skin of her cheeks, sparkled in her blue eyes. She wore no stocking cap, just a baby-blue hoodie. Maybe that was what put him off. No hat. She was still smart, still quiet, still Kiki. But since they had rescued her from Deth, it had always taken him a moment to process her.

"I'm sorry to interrupt," she said softly. "But I needed to tell you something, and it couldn't wait." She was looking at Ghost. He stared back, looking as if he might bolt. After a moment, he nodded.

"I'm glad you're here." She smiled.

Ghost stood staring. After a moment, he ducked his head. When he looked back, his eyes were moist. He nodded again.

"Yo!" A voice boomed. "It's your turn, girl! You can't just walk out on Trivial Pursuit! It ain't that kinda trivial!"

Kiki rolled her eyes and sighed. "Apologies, fellas. Some people can't wait to lose," she slipped away with a wave. They watched her for a moment as she settled in next to Dex on the couch.

"You know... sometimes the best gift is getting to keep what we already have," Carson grinned. "Merry Christmas, Ghost."

Ghost said nothing, just stared at Kiki as she listened to Dex read a question. She was laughing. After a moment, he stirred himself. With a final nod at Carson, he turned up his collar and started toward the door. He had the look of a man who had everything he needed. "I've got to go. Take care of her."

"Hey, um..." Carson stopped him. "Does she seem... well... okay... to you?"

Ghost glanced back at him, gray eyes unreadable. "Yes." His answer was fast and final.

Carson shrugged. "Yeah. I agree. Of course. Totally. Just... just wondered if you..."

"Some things are too precious to question, Carson," Ghost stole a glance at Kiki, peering at her from under the brim of his hat. "When you need me... you know what to do."

After Ghost left, Carson wandered into the living room and watched Dex receive a vicious trivia beating. He was finally given a respite when Granny summoned Kiki to the kitchen.

"You think she knows I'm letting her win?" Dex kicked back on the couch, propping his casted leg on the coffee table. Scrawled signatures and well wishes decorated the long white cocoon that ran almost up to his hip.

"I don't see how. When I think 'sweet talk', I think 'Dexter Jackson'."

"Yup. If 'kick-%^&*#@!' wasn't my middle name, it would be that."

"Like honey in my ears."

"Speaking of sweet talk, how'd you get outta work? Didn't think you were gonna make it 'til late."

"I'm not quite sure. One minute the store was open, the next it was closed."

"Closed?! Last time that happened, it took a zombie attack."

"This time, all it took was Kinkade."

Dex grunted his surprise. "We talking about *Ross* Kinkade, right? Brown suit, super kung-fu tablet tapping action, big ol' stick stuck up his..."

"That's the one."

"He say why?"

"Sure did. His reason - and I quote - 'It's Christmas.'"

Dex whistled. "Maybe it ain't a stick – maybe it's a candy cane."

"Either way, I'm not complaining."

"I hear that. After all, Christmas is when miracles happen, right? I mean, look at me! I'm at a ginger snappin' Christmas party!"

"And you said 'ginger-snappin'."

"%^&*#@! straight. It's a whole new me!"

Carson chose not to reply.

"You know somethin'?" Dex gazed at the Christmas tree, his fingers toying absently with the butterfly necklace that seemed to never be far from reach. "I think I could get back into this. It was Tia's favorite time of year, Brother. She loved it, my little baby butterfly," his smile was fond and sad. "We did it up right, too. Tree, presents, lights all over the place. I even wore the Santa thing."

"I'm trying *real* hard to picture that in my mind."

Dex sighed. "Me too, man. Me too."

"Here's to miracles," Carson lifted his glass. They toasted. The kitchen door swung open, and Granny emerged with a fresh plate of treats.

"Oh, baby," Dex levered himself off the couch, a hungry look in his eyes. "Let's get on them goodies before the little weirdo sees 'em," he directed himself toward the snack table with hardly a limp. "I don't know what your Granny puts in them things, but the Big Man is *hooked!*"

Carson trailed along. "It's her mystery ingredient. She says it's 'love'. Personally, I think it's triple the listed amount of butter and sugar."

"I'm fine with 'love'. Love won't screw up my diet."

"Right on. Hey, speaking of mysteries... there's something I want to run by you. It's been bugging me for awhile now, and since the action's all done I've finally had time to think it through. I've got a theory, and I could use your opinion."

"Uh huh," Dex muttered disinterestedly, browsing the stacks of baked goods.

"It's Sister Becky. I think she's got a guardian angel."

Dex snorted. "You want my opinion on that?! Okay... sure, she's got a guardian angel," his voice dripped with sarcasm. "Just like I got me a Fairy Grandmother."

"Godmother."

"Same diff."

"I'm just thinking back to the phone call that got the council moving, convinced them to finally give her a hearing – someone went out of their way to make sure she got a fair shake. Must have been a pretty forceful someone to move that bunch of old curmudgeons."

"Mm-hm," Dex was staring innocently at a large Christmas cookie, as if absorbed with the frosted snowman on it.

"Sounds like a guardian angel to me, don't you think?" Carson stood at his elbow, watching him closely.

"Mm."

"I mean, not a lot of people would be close enough to the situation to help. Just me, and... oh... a couple of others."

"Guess we'll never know," Dex avoided his eyes, dropping the cookie on his plate and quickly adding several more.

"Unless we have Kiki pull phone records."

"Uh-huh. Well, hey, if you think it's worth it," the big man turned away and headed back for his spot on the couch. "But if you wanna know who could *really* use a guardian angel," he continued, quickly changing the subject. "It's me. You know that dinner Dee set up with me and Pops?"

"Oh man... you didn't..."

"I sure did. I figured, what the hey, might as well just go and let the chips fall where they may. I'm too crazy about this girl to throw it all away."

"I hate to ask, but... how did it go?"

"Like a root canal. Ol' Parsons, he didn't even let me in the house. Just took one look and slammed the door in my face," a whimsical smile drifted across Dex's features. "It was almost worth it, you know. The look in his eyes when he opened that door..." The smile faded. "Almost." Dex heaved a huge sigh, stared at the cookie in his hand and set it back on his plate. "She was already gone, Dud. As soon as you showed up on my doorstep that day, I knew it."

Carson didn't know what to say. So he said nothing.

After a moment, and quite unexpectedly, Dex lit up. "But here's the darnedest part. You know that cop test? The one I been breakin' my back for? Guess who's got a seat at the table?!"

"Waaaa?! No way! You?! Even after Parsons..." Carson waved his hand in a shooing motion. "And with..." he waved again at Dex's cast. "Not to mention..." he waved a third time to indicate the general events of recent days. "Holy cow! First, you in a Santa suit and now this?! The whole world has stopped making sense."

"I know, it beats all, don't it? But it's official. Got my letter just this morning. Christmas miracle, that's what that is."

"But... how?!"

"I have *no* idea," Dex said with feeling. "But I'll take it. Who knows? Maybe Parsons figured I wasn't good enough to take out his daughter, but I was bad enough to take out Deth."

"Unlikely. Parsons has a one track mind, and it always tracks against us. I'll take his recent aberrant behavior as another of your Christmas miracles, but I wouldn't count on it continuing. And I don't see him vouching for any of us, not without a serious nudge. He doesn't know you the way I do. I mean, anyone with his own flamethrower is the kind of bad I want to be on the good side of. And I'll drink to that," Carson toasted his own cup and took a healthy swig.

"You know what? You're right," Dex's jaw set suddenly, impulsively. "So here's another thing - I ain't givin' up on Dee. I'll just have to show Daddy Parsons that I'm good enough for both. And if that girl's got any of her daddy in her, I won't be going it alone. Count on it."

"I'll drink to that, too." They toasted.

"A most happy Christmas, gentlemen!" Carson felt an affectionate squeeze on his arm. He greeted Sister Becky warmly as Dex mumbled something about more eggnog and limped away.

"What particular bee has found its way under Mr. Jackson's bonnet, pray tell?" Sister Becky frowned after him.

"He's just getting used to his wings."

"Wings, Mr. Dudley?"

"Long story. Speaking of stories, I haven't had a chance to ask, and honestly, I can't wait until Christmas morning to unwrap this particular gift, so I'm shaking it hard: are you back for good or not?!"

"I always trusted that I would grow wiser with age, Mr. Dudley," the nun tucked hands primly into sleeves. "That is one of many assumptions among the wreckage of which I am now standing. In regard to my hastiness to depart Las Calamas, I see now that I should have threaded that particular needle before starting to sew, as the saying goes."

"Still shaking the gift," Carson mimed the action, listening hard. "Can't quuiiiiiite make out the sound..."

"I will be staying. Indefinitely. I may be stubborn, but I am no fool. I was blinded my own selfishness, and the Good Lord has revealed that to me quite plainly. It is both humbling and invigorating to know that He still has much to teach me." She clucked at her own foibles. "My place, lad, is here with you and the others. Of that I, at last, have no doubt. There are enough wolves in this wood without seeking them elsewhere. Perhaps even more than we know. If our Father wants me here until we have hunted them down, then here is where I shall remain and hunt is what I shall do, as long as strength remains. On that, you have my hand, Mr. Dudley," she thrust out slim, strong fingers.

Carson shook them gratefully. "Yee-freakin'-haw! Just what I wanted! Merry Christmas to me and a big ol' fat hallelujah; you can throw away the gift receipt, I won't be needing it!"

"It does this old heart good to see the young rejoice."

"I'm rejoicing, lady! This is just as good as Dex getting into the cop test. Though not as weird. You heard about it, right? Busted leg, burning down the crime scene, putting the moves on Parson's daughter – and *still* he gets in. Man, I just can't figure it."

Silence.

"Sister B.?"

"Yes, dear. I heard you."

Carson glanced at her. She was staring innocently at a nativity scene, absorbed with the detail of the wise men.

"That's pretty weird, don't you think? It's not like Parsons to cut us a break."

"Mm-hm."

Carson narrowed his eyes. "You know, now that I think about it, I guess someone could have nudged him. Called Parsons and twisted his arm, I mean. No, no... better yet," he angled so he could study Sister Becky's face. "Maybe, someone even went over his head – right to the top. Some influential citizen, for example. Someone respectable, who could put in a good word. Vouch for Dex."

"Mm."

"Almost as if he had a Fairy Grandmother."

"Godmother."

"Same diff."

"I suppose we shall never know," Sister Becky avoided his eyes, carefully adjusting one of the ceramic sheep that was slightly out of place.

"Unless we have Kiki pull phone records."

"Well, yes. Certainly, my lad. If you believe the effort is warranted," she turned away and fetched herself a glass of eggnog. "However, if you would like to know what I find of a great deal more interest," she continued, quickly changing the subject. "Is the information you reported about Mr. Deth's disappearance and the monstrous nature of his inner chambers. Most informative and most distressing. I chide myself that I failed to recognize the signs," Sister Becky pursed her lips. "He had the unmistakable taint of ODB about him, but I was too distracted to detect it."

"ODB?"

"*Other Dimensional Beings,* dear. Mythological creatures of great evil from the Beyond. Primitive cultures worshiped them as gods, offered blood sacrifices, disfigured themselves in exchange for powers. Monstrous abominations they were. Tentacles. All of them, tentacles everywhere. Their tales can be traced even through Scripture. My Order sees through their charade, however. They are undoubtedly Infernals - demonic forces masking their true identity to hide their intentions."

"Infernals... like Ashihitokage? The Warlord of Death's master?"

"Precisely."

The thought gave Carson pause. "Kiki said that thing threatened you. Or at least she thought so. Could this Deth guy... this ODB connection... could it be related?"

Sister Becky's age-lined face became a study in concentration. "Perhaps, Mr. Dudley. Perhaps. Although in regards to Ashihitokage," her voice dropped to a thoughtful murmur. "I have long suspected that *particular* Infernal had something else on its mind. Something else entirely..." she fell silent, her thoughts clearly elsewhere.

"Sister B.?"

"Ah! Nothing dear, nothing to trouble you. Merely musings. At any rate, that cow has now wandered into another pasture, has it not? Much like our Mr. Deth. Now we are left to surmise and presume based on our recollections, and that we shall do with gusto. For myself, I believe the two are indeed related, though not perhaps in the manner in which you suspect. The common element here, quite clearly, is the Curio Shop. I believe..."

"... it was defending itself." Carson finished her sentence. He held his breath. The thought had been growing inside him for some time, but he had not yet dared to voice it.

The nun nodded. "Quite."

"Somehow, it summoned Deth. Just like it attracted Fujika and led him to awaken the Warlord of Death."

"As it drew our vampiress as well, I believe. There is a connection, is there not? The paintings we saw in Ms. Vanessa's boudoir? I believe you discovered that they originated from the Curio Shop."

"They did. And I've discovered something else about 'em too."

Sister Becky caught the eager look in his eye. "You have news, lad? Speak it!"

"Just a name: 'Essen Wurmhardt'. He's the dude who painted

them."

"You are certain?! Essen Wurmhardt," she repeated the name, trying it out. "Most intriguing. Most intriguing indeed," Sister Becky's mouth turned up into a thin, hungry smile.

"Yeah. I got the same feeling. I don't know how or why, but that painting I saw in my Vision, the one with Captain Cultist and the Virgin Sacrifice – it's real. I saw it in the Curio Shop the night we busted in, just as solid and touchable as Granny's cookies. Same exact painting. If Pete showed it to me, it must be important. This Wurmhardt wacko painted it, painted all of 'em. That puts him smack dab in the center of this hot little mess. I don't know why, but I'm sure of it. What's more, I'm pretty sure now that my panic attack that night wasn't just me, and it wasn't a bad burrito. It was malice. It was the Shop. Pure and simple. It was pushing back, trying to scare me off. I aim to find out why."

"A mystery worth solving, Mr. Dudley. As I said, there is still much work to be done!"

"No kidding. We still don't know who or where this Herron chick is, what finally happened to zombie Josh when he got to Pittsville, and now Deth is unaccounted for – though, at the very least, he's got one of the world's biggest headaches."

"One most well deserved."

"True that. Hm," Carson tugged his chin beard. "In spite of how satisfying that is, it does make me realize one thing: for cleaning up this town, we sure seem to leave a lot of loose ends."

"If it is one thing I have learned about this business, Mr. Dudley, it is that loose ends are its natural byproduct. You must accept them but not dwell upon them. 'To break clean with troubles, break a trouble clean,' as the saying goes."

"I hear you. Some troubles are just harder to break." Carson found his eyes wandering to Kiki. "Sister Becky... does Kiki seem... I mean, have you noticed... like, anything..."

"Come to the point, lad. Stammering makes you seem simple-minded."

"Different."

Sister Becky studied his face carefully, then glanced across the room to where Kiki stood chatting with Granny. "She has undergone a tremendous trauma. Pain of that magnitude changes people."

"That's not the kind of 'different' I'm talking about. And it's not an answer," Carson stuffed his hands in his jeans' pockets, suddenly moody. "After we pulled her out of that tank..." he shook his head. "I was just so happy to see her. To know she was alive. But now, I just can't help thinking about the *other* Kiki. The one on the table. The one that..." he couldn't finish the sentence. "What if...?"

"Do it."

"Say wha'?"

"Speak to her, lad," Sister Becky eyed him shrewdly. "You have been avoiding it all evening. No, even longer - since the day of the rescue. Those doubts of yours will not disappear by keeping them to yourself. They will only grow there in the dark."

Carson swallowed. Sister Becky was right. He knew it. "Now?"

"Can you think of a better time?"

Carson sighed. With a nod, he set off wordlessly toward Kiki. He reached her just as Granny was heading for the kitchen to reload.

Kiki smiled up at him. "Just the guy I wanted to talk to. But first... cookie? Granny said these are your faves."

Carson took one off the tray. "Thanks. Actually, I, uh... I wanted to talk to you, too."

"Oh?"

Carson hesitated. Words formed, then faded. He hedged. "Yeah. I've got something for you," he fumbled in his back pocket for a wadded plastic bag. "I, uh, just saw this and thought of you. Sorry it's not wrapped, but I didn't know if you'd... you know, accept it. Charity and all that. But this is a gift, so I hope you do. Well, anyway. Merry Christmas." He handed over the bag.

Kiki dug into it carefully and drew out a bright red stocking cap. Blue eyes smiled up into his. "It's perfect. Thanks, Carson."

"Yeah. Sure," relief flooded through him. "Don't mention it. I know your other one... well, I know you needed one," he felt his face flush and decided to quit while he was ahead. "So, uh... you... you said you wanted to talk to me?"

"I did. I do. See, I've been piecing together what happened that night. Most of it's a blur, unfortunately. Or fortunately," Kiki's smile thinned. "Anyway, one of the things I do remember is the last time we talked. As I recall, it was a little... heated."

"Heated, yes. Little, no."

"Yeah. Figured. So, here's the deal. I've been looking at things a little differently lately. I guess recent events have given me, well, a new perspective. I've been thinking about that conversation. I said a lot of things that night. Most of them I regret. I wish I could take them back, but I know that's impossible, so I want to do the next best thing.

Carson... I'm sorry. Will you forgive me?"

Carson's cookie dropped onto the plate. He stared into Kiki's blue eyes, so earnest, so intent.

"I forgive you."

"Whew! Load off!" Carson could tell by the look on her face that she meant it. "So, now that's out of the way, I have to ask you something else," Kiki paused, weighing thoughts. "I know you came back to my shack that night - you were the one who found out I was taken; Dex told me. I have to know, Carson... why? After our fight, all that nastiness... why did you come back?"

Carson stared down into her face. It had bothered him for awhile now, the changes he saw there. It was so frank, so open, so fresh and healthy that it seemed foreign. His mind whirled, dragging him back through the tangled, thorny, briar of memories of the past week. Back to that night.

He did indeed remember why he'd gone back.

He looked away, at the tree, the old-fashioned bulb lights, the old timey decorations he remembered with affection from his youth. It struck him how different he was now. How much he had changed. How much of that had been just in the last few months. He had discovered purpose. And determination. He had failed, and succeeded, and risen from the proverbial dead. He had a crew, a signature weapon, his own ride, a career. He felt like a super from one of his favorite flicks. A hero. Something he realized that, deep down, he had always yearned for. Something every kid did.

And he would give it all away for this girl.

Every last bit of it. He had gone there that night to tell her that.

And now... he saw her again, still and cold on the table. Dead. Yet here she was, standing before him, full of life and warmth.

"Carson?"

"Uh huh. Yeah, the reason I came back..." he met her eyes again. They searched his, unreadable, mysterious, waiting. "I was... I was going to say..." he hesitated. "I was going to say sorry too. I was a jerk."

"Oh," Kiki sank back on her heels. Carson couldn't tell if she was relieved or disappointed. "Looks like it's sorries all around then," blue eyes flicked to the floor momentarily, then back up to his face. Her smile was small and hopeful. "Friends?"

"Always," Carson gave her his lopsided grin.

Kiki started to turn away then stopped. She put her hand on his arm, squeezing gently but in earnest. "Carson... I know you have doubts about that night. Doubts about me. About what happened. I just want to say, don't worry. Everything's okay. *I'm* okay," she smiled up at him. "I feel like a brand new person." With a final squeeze, she was gone.

"Well?" Sister Becky appeared almost instantly at his elbow.

Carson stared after Kiki, rubbing the spot on his arm that was still warm from her touch.

Her touch.

She had touched him.

"She, uh... she feels like a brand new person. Apparently. Sassafras..." he shook his head. "I *really* wish she hadn't said that."

"I know your doubts, Mr. Dudley. But people make up parts of us," Sister Becky's voice was quiet but penetrating. "And we parts of them. Interconnected. Inseparable. If you had *truly* lost one of those parts, do you not think you would be aware?"

"Honestly?" Carson struggled with his thoughts then shrugged helplessly. He had no answer to give.

Sister Becky nodded her understanding. She paused a moment. When she spoke, her voice was wistful. "Father Nicholas."

"I beg your... who?"

"Father Nicholas," she repeated, sighing around the name. "An old compatriot of mine. Also in the trade. Italian, but only in the best ways. Heart of a lion, faith of a saint, steadfast, strong. We worked together for a time, when we were young and adventurous. We stood shoulder to shoulder against the worst evils in the world."

"Saving souls, eh?"

"More like cracking skulls. It was glorious," Sister Becky's eyes sparkled. "But after a time, we came to realize that our connection was becoming more than professional, our feelings deeper than friendship. We also realized this would cause entanglements and danger, not only to our lives but also our conscience. We were held together by our mission... and also kept apart by it. And so we said goodbye."

"That sucks."

"Indeed. However, Mr. Dudley... such was the depth of our connection that, if something were to happen to him, even to this very day and in spite of time and distance, I believe I would be aware." She turned deep, soulful eyes on him. "So I ask you, dear boy – would *you* be aware?"

He paused, searching. "Maybe. I don't know," it was Carson's turn to sigh. "It hurts."

"That is what it is to be a part of someone - painful at times, beautiful at others, but all in accordance with our Father's plan. We could not survive otherwise. Indeed, we would be fools to try. What value death, and life, without those we hold dear?"

Carson watched Kiki from across the room. She had rejoined her game with Dex and was laughing freely now, head cast back and sides shaking. Slowly, almost unconsciously, she pulled her red stocking cap on.

Carson was suddenly struck by Sister Becky's last comment, and it triggered a recollection of his Vision. Of Pete's words.

Next comes... death. And death, and life, no interruptions.

Or maybe he'd had it wrong this whole time.

Next comes... Deth. And Deth, and life, no interruptions.

No interruptions.

A slow smile spread across Carson's face. "Thanks, Sister B." He hugged her.

Sister Becky laughed, the silver tinkle she used on rare occasions when her joy overcame her decorum. "You are entirely welcome, Mr. Dudley! Now come, let us rejoin the others. Christmas has come alive for me once again, and we have much to celebrate, in addition to the birth of our Savior. I am most intrigued by this 'White Elephant' ceremony, and I do not wish to miss it."

"Go get started. I'll be right there."

Carson watched Sister Becky rejoin their friends. She was right. They had plenty to celebrate, and he was tired of thinking and ready to do just that. But before he did, before he took his brain entirely out of monster-whacking mode, and for everyone's sake, he had a resolution to make.

The Curio Shop.

Whatever it was, wherever it came from, the place was playing hard ball. Well, that was a game two could play. Carson flicked his eyes heavenward and made his silent promise to God that he would never, ever let the Shop hurt Kiki – or anyone else – again. Not if he could help it.

He let the names of villains and victims play through his mind: Vanessa. Darren Carey. Kimberly Herron. Stinky Pete. Ichiro Fujika. Josh Decker. Professor Looney. Dr. Julius Deth.

And now... Essen Wurmhardt.

He may have loose ends, but now he also had a fresh thread. He intended to tug on it until something unraveled.

With the matter settled, Carson set his brooding aside. Slipping his smile back on, he headed for the party. Sister Becky was right. The Curio Shop could wait. It was Christmas, after all, and all the parts he cared about most were right here in this room.

For tonight, that was all that mattered.

About the Author

Chris Weedin was born in 1970 and grew up with a healthy dislike for horror. But somewhere along the line, his life was forever changed by a strange supernatural event... and now he absolutely loves the stuff! He has worked as an associate pastor, furniture deliveryman, security guard, professional tutor, youth minister, computer system admin and school safety director and holds both a Bachelor's Degree in History and a black belt in Tae Kwon Do. He is the creator and developer of *Horror Rules, the Simply Horrible Roleplaying Game,* author of the *Graveyard Shift* series and owner of Crucifiction Games. He spends his time speaking, writing, running, churching and playing (and creating) alternative boardgames. He lives in Selah, WA with his lovely wife and two lovely and obedient children, all three of whom are almost never scary.

Parts is over... but fear not!
Carson and the Gang will return in Book 4:

Sister Becky's ancient foe, a lost love, the truth about Kinkade and 7 Corporation, everyone leaves Las Calamas and (gasp!)...
SOMEONE DIES!